D1326079

Sinners and Shadows

Sinners and Shadows

CATRIN COLLIER

ORION

First published in Great Britain in 2004 by Orion
an imprint of the Orion Publishing Group Ltd.

A CIP catalogue record for this book is available
from the British Library.

ISBNs 0 75286 698 2 (hardback) 0 75286 699 0 (trade paperback)

Typeset at The Spartan Press Ltd,
Lymington, Hants

Printed in Great Britain by Clays Ltd, St Ives plc

The Orion Publishing Group Ltd
Orion House
5 Upper Saint Martin's Lane
London, WC2H 9EA

www.orionbooks.co.uk

For the best 'big brother' I could have hoped for, my cousin David John Williams. With love and gratitude that I may not have fully expressed at the time, for giving me my first puff of a cigarette at five, teaching me to throw my rubbish over the cinema balcony in the 'Workies' on to the hapless children below, smuggling me into cinemas under his coat so I could see X-rated Dracula films before I reached my teens, showing me what happens when you pull the communication cord on a train and fighting all my primary-school battles for me.

You added so much magic to my childhood by allowing me, a mere girl, six years your junior, to tag on to your 'gang'.

Acknowledgements

I would like to thank everyone who helped me research this book and so generously gave of their time and expertise.

All the dedicated staff of Rhondda Cynon Taff's exceptional library service, especially Mrs Lindsay Morris for her ongoing help and support. Hywel Matthews and Catherine Morgan, the archivists at Pontypridd, and Nick Kelland, the archivist at Treorchy library.

The staff of Pontypridd Museum, Brian Davies, David Gwyer and Ann Cleary, for allowing me to dip into their extensive collection of old photographs and for doing such a wonderful job of preserving the history of Pontypridd.

Deirdre Beddoe for her meticulously documented accounts of women's lives in Wales during the last century.

The people of Tonypandy and the Rhondda, the friendliest, most hospitable people on earth, who are always prepared to talk to and listen to a stranger.

My husband John and our children Ralph, Ross, Sophie, Nick, and my parents Glyn and Gerda for their love, support and the time they gave me to write this book.

Margaret Bloomfield for her friendship and help in so many ways.

My agent, Ken Griffiths, for his friendship, inspiring imagination and sales technique. Absolutely everyone at Orion, especially my editor Yvette Goulden for her encouragement and constructive criticism, Rachel Leyshon my eagle-eyed copy-editor, Emma Noble my miracle-working publicist, Juliet Ewers, Sara O'Keeffe, Jenny Page, Dean Mitchell and all the editorial, sales and marketing teams.

And all the booksellers and readers who make writing such a privileged occupation.

And while I wish to acknowledge all the assistance I received, I wish to state that any errors in *Sinners and Shadows* are entirely mine.

Catrin Collier

Note

Again, I have taken the liberty of putting my fictional characters in events which actually occurred, occasionally with historical figures.

Broncho Bill toured with 'Buffalo Bill' (William Frederick Cody) in his Wild West Exhibition in both the United States and Europe before setting up his own 'Wild West Exhibition' and following in his ex-employer's footsteps.

Broncho Bill's two ring circus which afforded seating for 10,000 spectators visited Pontypridd in 1914. After setting up camp in the Malsters' field he opened his exhibition (neither he, nor Buffalo Bill ever referred to their spectacles as 'shows') on Wednesday 2 April 1914. The event was well documented in the issues of the *Pontypridd Observer* preceding and following the grand opening.

Ynysangharad House and the estate were bought by public subscription and donations from Miners' Union Funds in the early 1920s. The land was laid out as a public park and named the Ynysangharad Memorial Park as a tribute to all the men from the area who lost their lives in the First World War.

The munitions factory at Pembrey where Rhian, Julia, Bronwen, Jinny and Meriel worked was a 'Controlled Establishment' (government-controlled for the duration and privately owned). The conditions of work there were generally agreed to be appalling and there is in existence a heartbreaking photograph of the funeral procession of two women who were killed in an explosion there, Mildred Owen aged eighteen and Dorothy Watson aged nineteen. Their funeral took place in Swansea and was described in the *South Wales Daily Post* of the 4 August 1917.

The names of the munitionettes who were killed in the factories of South Wales during the Great War can occasionally be found on war memorials of the period in recognition of the fact that they too laid down their lives for their country.

Note

Again, I have taken the liberty of putting my fictional characters in events which actually occurred, occasionally with historical figures.

Broncho Bill toured with 'Buffalo Bill' (William Frederick Cody) in his Wild West Exhibition in both the United States and Europe before setting up his own 'Wild West Exhibition' and following in his ex-employer's footsteps.

Broncho Bill's two ring circus which afforded seating for 10,000 spectators visited Pontypridd in 1914. After setting up camp in the Malsters' field he opened his exhibition (neither he, nor Buffalo Bill ever referred to their spectacles as 'shows') on Wednesday 2 April 1914. The event was well documented in the issues of the *Pontypridd Observer* preceding and following the grand opening.

Ynysangharad House and the estate were bought by public subscription and donations from Miners' Union Funds in the early 1920s. The land was laid out as a public park and named the Ynysangharad Memorial Park as a tribute to all the men from the area who lost their lives in the First World War.

The munitions factory at Pembrey where Rhian, Julia, Bronwen, Jinny and Meriel worked was a 'Controlled Establishment' (government-controlled for the duration and privately owned). The conditions of work there were generally agreed to be appalling and there is in existence a heartbreaking photograph of the funeral procession of two women who were killed in an explosion there, Mildred Owen aged eighteen and Dorothy Watson aged nineteen. Their funeral took place in Swansea and was described in the *South Wales Daily Post* of the 4 August 1917.

The names of the munitionettes who were killed in the factories of South Wales during the Great War can occasionally be found on war memorials of the period in recognition of the fact that they too laid down their lives for their country.

Chapter 1

RHIAN JONES STACKED the last piece of breakfast china from the table on to her tray, left the dining room and sedately crossed the oak-panelled hall of Llan House. The moment the door to the narrow servants' staircase closed behind her, she charged as fast as she could down the stone staircase and into the basement kitchen.

'Gwilym James opened their doors at half past seven this morning, it's almost half past eight and it will take you twenty minutes to walk to Dunraven Street.' The housekeeper, Mrs Williams, glanced up from the tradesmen's account books that she had spread out on the table.

'It's not my fault I'm behind this morning, Mrs Williams.' Rhian dumped the tray next to the Belfast sink where the ten-year-old kitchen maid, Mair, was washing dishes.

'I know,' Mrs Williams murmured sympathetically.

'Some people will have camped out all night to get the best bargains. There'll be nothing left worth having by the time you get there,' Meriel the cook predicted gloomily from the stove where she was making stock from a chicken carcass.

'Miss Julia reminded the mistress three times over breakfast that she had run out of perfume and wanted me to pick up a bottle of Zenobia Violets from Thomas the chemist's this morning. But the mistress still insisted on having a third cup of tea and a fourth slice of toast.' Rhian pulled the hairpins that secured her maid's cap from her blonde curls.

'The way madam eats, I think her family must have starved her before she married the master. Have you noticed how much weight she's put on these last six months?' Meriel, who wasn't

1

exactly a lightweight herself, dropped a bundle of bay leaves into the stock, moved the pan on to a smaller hob and set the lid on it.

'We have,' Mrs Williams endorsed dryly. 'Here's the grocery order for Rodney's, Rhian, and mind you tell Mrs Rodney that we don't want any of her substitutes this week. When I say I want Lifebuoy soap, I mean Lifebuoy not Sunlight, and the same goes for biscuits. If she hasn't any Huntley and Palmer's Bath Olivers, we'll go to a shop that has. Understand?' She handed Rhian the list.

'Yes, Mrs Williams.' Rhian untied her apron and lifted it over her head, before taking her cloak down from the pegs on the back of the door.

'This really is only fit for the rag bag, Rhian.' Meriel inspected the hem of the serge cloak Rhian had bought when she had started work in Llan House four years before. She had bleached out the dye along with mud stains and it was more rusty than black in places.

'Which is why Rhian is on her way to the sale.' Mrs Williams looked out of the window. 'I wouldn't wear your hat, Rhian. It will get ruined. It's hailing and sleeting out there. Take my umbrella.'

'Thanks, Mrs Williams.' Rhian threw her cloak around her shoulders.

'The family will all be out until tea-time and I'll give Bronwen a hand with the bedrooms when I've finished totalling these figures, so you can take as long as you like but mind you buy quality. It's easy to get carried away by low prices, but remember, even in the sales, you only get what you pay for. And don't forget to pick up Miss Julia's things in the chemist's,' Mrs Williams warned.

'You have the list safe?' Meriel checked when Rhian went to the back door.

'Yes.' Rhian lifted it from her uniform pocket to show her before buttoning it back in.

'And your money?' Mrs Williams asked.

'In my purse in my mitten.'

'Then off with you, girl.'

Rhian dived out of the door. A gust of wind caught it, slamming it behind her. Frozen raindrops stung her face and snarled her blonde curls, which were prone to tangling at the best of times. Realizing that Mrs Williams's umbrella would blow inside out the second she tried to put it up, she gripped it and the front of her hood with one hand, held the edges of her cloak together with the other, put her head down and ran as fast as she could, while trying not to imagine hordes of shoppers bearing down on the sale rack of winter coats in Gwilym James.

The department store was the largest and most expensive in Tonypandy and it sold only high-quality goods. A ladies' slim-cut, black cashmere coat had been the centre highlight of the window display of winter fashions since last September. Coveted by every fashion-conscious woman and girl in the town, at seven guineas it was priced out of the reach of all but the wealthiest people.

Rhian earned her keep, plus washing, uniform and twelve pounds a year in Llan House. But when it came to buying clothes, her wages didn't go far. The week before Christmas the price tickets on the goods in the window display had been slashed to encourage interest ahead of the traditional first of January sale. The coat had been reduced from seven to two guineas and it had seemed almost within her grasp – until she had run late that morning.

Miss Julia and Mrs Williams had done what they could to help her get away early because they both knew that if she asked permission from the new mistress, who had married Mr Larch only two months before, it would be withheld. But even they couldn't arrange for her to get out of serving the family breakfast.

She crossed her fingers, and – not exactly prayed because she felt that it would be sinful to pray for something material – wished that just one black cashmere coat would be left in her size.

Her heart sank when she reached the main street. The pavement outside Gwilym James was so crammed with shoppers it was impossible to work out who was trying to get in and who was trying to get out of the store. Bracing herself, she joined the scrum, parrying inadvertent blows from elbows and knees as she fought her way inside. Buffeted first one way, then another by the crowd, she paused to take her bearings. The lingerie counter was surrounded by a five-deep circle of women pawing through the discounted underwear, the ones in the outer ring grabbing at anything and everything that they could reach.

She spotted the discounted racks of coats but a horde of women at the knitwear counter blocked her path and the store manager, Joey Evans, was attempting to calm a situation that was threatening to turn ugly.

'Please, ladies, there are plenty of bargains for everyone.' He pitched his voice above the hubbub while smiling at two elderly women who had locked their fingers into the same grey cardigan. 'Mrs Jones, looking beautiful as ever on this cold and miserable morning.' He clasped the fist she had raised to her rival, Mrs Hopkins, and kissed the back of her hand.

'Save the charm for girls young and stupid enough to believe it, Joey Evans. I saw this first.' Mrs Jones snatched the cardigan from Mrs Hopkins but Joey intervened and held it fast.

'Wouldn't you prefer it in your favourite navy, Mrs Jones?' He signalled over her head to the supervisor. 'Miss Robertson, send one of the boys to the stockroom to get this cardigan in navy in a –' he ran a practised eye over Mrs Jones's ample figure – 'forty-four-inch chest.'

'We weren't going to put the navy out until tomorrow, Mr Evans,' she replied frostily.

'We can make an exception for a special customer like Mrs Jones, Miss Robertson.' His smile broadened but it failed to reach his eyes.

'Mr Evans . . . Mr Evans . . .'

Rhian ducked behind a display of mannequins in the hope of escaping Joey's attention. She knew him and his family well, because her closest friend, Sali, was married to his eldest brother, Lloyd. But then every girl in Tonypandy knew Joey Evans, and not just because he was the manager of Gwilym James.

Twenty-two years old, six-foot tall, with black curly hair and dark eyes that he had inherited from his Spanish mother, he looked more gypsy than Welsh. But he wasn't just handsome. He oozed charm, and it was his charisma, coupled with his ability to make friends in every strata of Rhondda society, that had won him promotion to the position of store manager at such a young age.

However, his penchant for flirting with women – young, old, single or married – made her uneasy. She'd never known quite how to respond to compliments too lavish to be sincere.

Turning her back on Joey and his adoring audience of assistants and shoppers, she continued to fight her way towards the coat racks. There were plenty of grey, brown, blue and red woollen coats, but she had set her heart on the black cashmere. She could scarcely believe her eyes when she saw it on the rail. She lifted it close and ran her fingers over the cloth.

Just as she'd hoped from the sheen, it was the same quality as the mistress's and Miss Julia's Sunday coats. She retreated to a comparatively empty space close to the back wall of the store.

'It's no use to you.'

She looked up. Joey Evans was behind her. 'Why not?' Assuming he was teasing her, she tried not to allow her irritation to show.

'It's a forty-four inch bust, it will drown you.'

'I can take it in.' She pulled off her cloak, bundled it over her arm and slipped on the coat.

'There's no way you can take this in.' He gripped the empty shoulders. 'You could put a gorilla in there with you and still have room to spare.'

She glanced down at her feet. At five feet six inches she wasn't short, but the coat was dragging on the floor. 'Do you have it in any other sizes?'

'We did, but they were the first to go. Twenty people started queuing before we closed yesterday, and given the weather they had to put up with overnight, you can hardly blame them for grabbing the best bargains this morning.' He looked her up and down then took a plain black woollen coat from the rack. 'This looks more your size. Thirty-four-inch chest, fifty-five-inch length?'

She shook her head. 'No thank you.'

'No thank you, I don't like the coat? Or no thank you, it's not my size? Or no thank you, I've set my heart on the cashmere?'

'I know I shouldn't have set my heart on the cashmere, but I have.' Reluctant to let it go, she continued to hold on to it.

'Tonia!' Joey shouted to an assistant who was carrying an armful of scarves out of the stockroom.

'Coming, *Mr* Evans, *sir*.' Tonia smiled at Rhian. 'Come down from Llan House to pick up a bargain?'

'I had hoped to find one.' Rhian returned Tonia's smile. She was the same age as her, and they knew one another well. Tonia's mother, Connie, owned Rodney's, the grocers that supplied Llan House.

'Tonia, do me a favour. After you've dumped those scarves, go into the office and ask Sam to telephone the Pontypridd and Cardiff stores and check if they've any of the ladies' cashmere coats in a thirty-four chest left on sale. If they have, tell them to set one aside for me.'

'I will, *Mr* Evans, *sir*.'

'And less of your cheek, Miss George,' Joey reprimanded, not entirely humorously. Tonia was his cousin. Unhappy working for her mother in Rodney's, she had begged him to give her a job in the store. When he had finally capitulated, he had assumed – wrongly as it turned out – that she'd assume a professional distance and not presume on family connections.

'Yes, Mr Evans.' Subdued, Tonia dumped the scarves on the knitwear counter and headed for the manager's office.

'I always take a break about now, and given what I've had to put up with this morning,' Joey looked at the crowds and raised his eyebrows, 'I think I've earned my tea and cakes ten times over. How about we go next door?'

'I have to put an order into Rodney's and pick up some things from Thomas the chemist's.'

'You can spare ten minutes.' He closed his hand around her elbow and steered her towards the door. Hemmed in by customers frantically searching for bargains, she had little choice but to comply.

The peace of the teashop was blissful after the noisy, teeming chaos of the store. Too late for tradesmen's breakfasts and too early for shoppers' 'elevenses', they had the place to themselves apart from the waitress and a retired school teacher, who was reading the *Glamorgan Gazette* over a pot of tea.

'Table for two, please, Ruby, there's a love.' Joey winked at the waitress and she blushed to the roots of her grey hair.

'How about your favourite, Mr Evans?' She showed them to a corner table that couldn't be seen from the window. It was cleanly laid with a fresh linen cloth and napkins.

'A pot of tea and a plate of cream cakes for two. That is all right, isn't it?' Joey flashed Rhian a smile.

'Tea would be fine, thank you. But I'm not hungry.'

'You don't have to be to enjoy the cakes here. They're little slices of heaven, baked by Ruby's sister, who has the touch of an angel.' He kissed the tips of his fingers and waved them in the air.

'You have the gift of the gab, Mr Evans, and no mistake.' Ruby scribbled down their order and left for the counter.

Joey shook out Rhian's napkin and laid it with a flourish over her lap. 'I've been meaning to talk to you for some time.' He sat opposite her and placed his hand close to hers on the table.

Rhian withdrew her hands on to her lap. 'What about?'

'I think it's time we got to know one another better.'

'Why?' she enquired warily.

'My brother is married to your best friend. That makes us practically family. And it's occurred to me that I know absolutely nothing about you.'

'There isn't much to know,' she countered. 'And my being Sali's friend and you being Lloyd's brother doesn't make us related.'

'You're their children's aunt and I'm their uncle.'

'You're a real one, I'm honorary.'

He changed the subject abruptly. 'When's your next day off?'

'Why do you want to know?' She wasn't sure why she was asking, when she'd already guessed the answer.

'Because I'm going to take you out. I know you haven't much chance of getting Sunday off and that's my only free day but—'

'I have no chance. It's the family's favourite day for entertaining and between their lunch and tea parties, and church for them and chapel for us servants, it's the busiest day of the week.' She was glad of an excuse to turn down his invitation, but she couldn't understand why her heart was thundering loud enough for the waitress and their fellow customer to hear.

7

'There's always the evenings. The shop only opens late on a Thursday, Friday and Saturday.'

'Thursday is my day off.' She glanced at him, only to look away when she saw him staring intently at her.

'Can't you change it?'

'No.'

'I'm entitled to one and a half days off a week, not that I always take the half day,' he continued. 'But I can arrange for the assistant manager to cover for me next Thursday afternoon. The store doesn't get busy until eight o'clock in the evening. We can go down to Pontypridd late morning, have lunch in the City Restaurant and catch a film in the Park Hall. They open every afternoon at three. I'll take you back to Llan House by half past six and still be in time to oversee the rush. And then, unfortunately, it's bedlam until we close at ten. And to think that I used to love Pandy Parade when I worked underground. It's a different story now.'

Thursday was the traditional pay night for the miners when, flush with the men's wages, families embarked on their weekly shop. And, as practically the entire population of Tonypandy turned out, it had become known as 'Pandy Parade'.

'I've made arrangements for next Thursday.'

'You're going to see Sali.'

'How do you know?' she asked suspiciously.

'Because I pay the children toffees to spy for me and they've told me that you always visit them on Thursday afternoons.'

'I do other things as well.' She suddenly realized that outside of Llan House, Sali's family, chapel and her rare shopping trips, she had no life.

'I'm sure that you haven't made a single appointment next Thursday afternoon that can't be rearranged or cancelled,' he dismissed. 'I'll pick you up at Llan House after I've opened the store. Ten o'clock suit you?'

'No, I meant it when I said I've made arrangements. I really do need to get a winter coat—'

'Which, now that I know your size, I promise to organize for you,' he interrupted.

'I need to do some other shopping.'

'Then we'll meet at the railway station and get the half past ten train.'

'You don't understand the meaning of "no" do you?' she demanded irritably.

'Not when you say it, because I know you don't really mean it. Admit it – you can't wait to go out with me.' He beamed at her.

'That is nonsense.'

'Is it?'

'Why don't you ask one of your other girls to go out with you?' She wanted him to know that she was aware of his reputation.

'Because I'm asking you,' he persisted.

'I'm not looking for a young man.'

'I'm glad to hear it. Because you've just found one.'

She was glad when the waitress interrupted them with the tea and cakes.

'I've put two of all your favourites on the plate, Mr Evans. I know how you love our cream puffs and custard slices.'

'You also know the way to a man's heart, Ruby. These look delicious. Cream puff?' He picked up one with his fork and spoon and held it over the plate Ruby had set in front of Rhian.

'I really haven't time.' She rose to her feet.

'It's raining cats, dogs and elephants out there. You can't go anywhere until it eases, so you may as well sit down, drink your tea and eat your cake.'

'You always this bossy?'

He continued to gaze unabashed into her eyes. 'Only with difficult women.'

She sat down and looked down at the cake on her plate. 'This is enormous.' She picked up her knife and fork and poked at it.

'You always visit Sali on your day off, don't you?'

'I thought the children were your spies?'

He ignored the gibe. 'As she's the ladies' fashion buyer for all three Gwilym James stores, I'm surprised you didn't ask her to set aside a coat for you.'

'Every time I ask Sali to get me something from Gwilym James, she insists on giving it to me as a present.'

'And you're an independent lady who doesn't like to receive presents?'

'I love getting presents on Christmas and birthdays,' she qualified.

He quartered his cream puff. 'So, what did Sali buy you for Christmas this year?'

'A beautiful cream silk and lace evening dress.'

'With a lace over-tunic and lace trimming at the neck and hem?'

'Yes.' She found it distinctly odd to be discussing clothes with a man.

'I know the one, it's stunning. I'll have to take you somewhere where you can show it off.'

'I won't go out with you.'

'How much do you want to bet you'll change your mind?'

She poured extra milk into her tea to cool it, finished her cake, delved into her mitten for her purse and extracted three pennies. 'That's one for the tea and two for the cake. Now, I really must go.'

'The tea and cake are on me.'

'I don't accept refreshments from men.'

'That sounds like one of the maxims Mrs Williams gives to the female staff in Llan House.'

'I've heard her talking about you.'

'And knowing her, saying nothing good.' He left his chair and pushed the pennies back towards her. 'You can pay next time.'

'There won't be a next time.'

'There will be,' he countered confidently. 'I'll wait for you outside the station from a quarter past ten on Thursday. I'll let you know if I've tracked down a coat then.'

'I won't be there.'

'Yes, you will, if only to find out about the coat.' He stared at her shabby cloak. 'I wish you'd let me know just how much you were in need of a new one before the sale started.'

The following week had never dragged so much for Rhian. The more she tried to put all thoughts of Joey Evans from her mind, the more she found herself dwelling on his invitation to spend part of her day off with him. His image – handsome, smiling – rose unbidden at the oddest moments, especially when she was carrying out dreary tasks, like dusting, polishing or cleaning the silver.

She didn't dare tell Mrs Williams that he had asked her out. The housekeeper disapproved of the maids having boyfriends and it had taken a couple of years to work out that her attitude wasn't down to an aversion to men, but annoyance at having to look for replacement staff whenever a servant left to marry.

Mrs Williams gave Bronwen's sweetheart of two years, shy, hardworking collier, Ianto Miles, a hard time whenever he walked Bronwen back to Llan House after her day off. But she felt that the housekeeper's condemnation of poor Ianto would be nothing compared to the contempt that she would show Joey Evans, should he venture to the back door of Llan House.

She normally looked forward to Thursday mornings, because she could lie in beyond her usual rising time of five o'clock. But for once she was awake before Mrs Williams tapped the door of the attic room she shared with Bronwen. She lay back on her pillow and watched Bronwen strike a match, light a candle and leave their bed.

'Water's frozen again.' Bronwen held the japanned metal jug upside down over the enamel basin.

'Do me a favour?' Rhian's breath misted in the ice-cold air.

'Bring up a jug of warm water for you when I come back after laying and lighting the fires?' Bronwen guessed.

'You're an angel.' Rhian's nose stiffened from cold and she buried it back beneath the blankets. She carried out a swift mental check of her winter wardrobe, which didn't take long. A dark-blue knitted suit, a plain black woollen dress she kept for church, a grey skirt and sweater. It would have to be the blue suit with the grey sweater.

Ignoring Bronwen's return and the sound of her washing and dressing in the khaki overalls they wore to do the rough work first thing in the morning, she drifted back to sleep. When she next opened her eyes, Bronwen was changing into her grey housemaid's dress, starched white cap and apron.

'It's seven o'clock. I've brought warm water up for you.'

'Thank you.' Rhian sat up in the bed and shivered.

'So, I'm dying to know: are you going to meet Joey Evans at the station this morning, or not?' Bronwen brushed out her hair and twisted it into a knot she secured with hairpins.

'Probably,' Rhian conceded, 'but only to see if he's found me a coat.'

'I don't blame you. He is *very* good-looking.' Bronwen pushed in the last hairpin and reached for her maid's cap.

'You're so besotted with Ianto, I'm surprised you noticed.'

'Being besotted with Ianto doesn't stop me from looking around at what else is on offer.'

'Joey Evans is on offer to any girl who'll go out with him,' Rhian pronounced, hoping Bronwen knew more gossip about him than she'd told her.

'Did I ever mention that he went out with my sister Ruby?'

'No. Which one is Ruby?' Bronwen had five sisters and Rhian hadn't met them often enough to sort one from the other.

'She's two years older than me. You must have seen her in chapel. She's the only one of us who doesn't have brown hair and brown eyes. My father still jokes she's the milkman's daughter.'

'Is she the pretty one with dark hair and blue eyes?'

'Depends on what you call pretty. She has my gran's Irish looks,' Bronwen said dismissively. 'Anyway, she only went out with Joey a few times but that didn't stop her from mooning over him for months afterwards. She even went to the library and took out a book of Lord Byron's poetry because it had a colour plate of a portrait of him in the front. She tore it out. Luckily for her the librarian didn't notice.'

'Why Lord Byron?' Rhian asked, mystified.

'Because Joey Evans is the spitting image of him. If you don't believe me, look at the collected works of Lord Byron the next time you dust the library. It has the same picture inside as the one Ruby stole.'

'What happened between him and your sister?' Rhian tried to sound casual.

'He brought her home one Saturday night after taking her to the Empire Theatre, thanked her for a nice evening, kissed her goodnight, and the next day she saw him walking out with Anwen Stephens. She got no sympathy from any of us. As my mother said at the time, "More fool her for going out with a Don Juan in the first place." ' Bronwen squinted into the tiny scrap of brown-spotted mirror that was all the new mistress would allow in the attic on the grounds that the old cracked cheval mirror encouraged vanity. 'Well, that's me done and ready to lay the breakfast table. The washstand is all yours.'

'Thanks.' Trembling in anticipation of the cold, Rhian gingerly stepped out of bed on to the wooden floorboards.

'You going down to do Miss Julia's hair before breakfast?'

'Don't I always?' Rhian rinsed out the tin basin with cold water and tipped it into the slop bucket, before filling it with the jug of warm that Bronwen had brought up.

'Yes, but I still think it's a bit much of her to expect you to dress her hair on your day off.'

'I don't mind, Miss Julia's good to me.' Rhian unbuttoned her nightdress, pulled it down to her waist and soaped her flannel.

'That's the mistress shouting, I hope it's at the master and not for me.' Bronwen slipped on her apron and tied the strings as she ran down the stairs.

Rhian washed and dried herself before sprinkling lavender-scented talcum powder and cologne over her skin. She opened the chest at the foot of the bed where she kept her underclothes and stared down at the neat pile of winter-weight woollen vests, bust-shapers and drawers. Her summer-weight, embroidered and lace-trimmed Nairnsook underclothes were so much prettier. But then who would see them, or know she was wearing them?

Deciding that she would, she went for the pretty set and began to dress.

Rhian set her candle on the window ledge of the first-floor landing on the back staircase and knocked on the door that connected the servants' quarters with the family's at the front of the house. When there was no reply she opened the door and blinked against the glare of the electric lights Mr Larch had recently installed in the 'upstairs' rooms. The passage was deserted, but Mrs Larch's rebuff, cold and clear, echoed from behind her dressing-room door.

'I'm dressing, Edward. I'll see you at breakfast.'

Rhian waited until she heard the master's bedroom door close before blowing out the candle, and walking along the corridor to the opposite end of the landing. She tapped softly and it was flung wide. Julia Larch, her master's 27-year-old daughter, grabbed her hand and pulled her inside her room.

'You look pretty. I love that suit on you and your hair is perfect.'

'Thank you, Miss Julia.' Rhian slipped off her cloak.

All the staff liked Miss Julia. She was kind, considerate and had a quiet, diffident manner that prompted even Meriel, who was more easily riled than most cooks (and there wasn't one who had the reputation of being easy-going in the Rhondda), to work harder whenever she asked her do anything. But none of the servants was closer to her, or adored her more than Rhian.

Rhian had come to Llan House shortly after her fifteenth birthday. When Julia had discovered that she was bright, intelligent and had received virtually no schooling she offered to lend her books. Julia's passion for history, art, archaeology, geography and romance had become Rhian's, and although they both observed the social mores of mistress and maid in public, they had grown close enough to adopt a familiarity in private that was rare between a servant and a member of her employer's family.

'You going anywhere special today, Miss Julia?' Rhian picked up a silver-backed hairbrush from the dressing table.

Julia made a face. 'Shopping in Pontypridd with my stepmother. She thinks there's a better class of people there than in Tony-pandy.' She sat on her stool and deliberately turned away from the mirror.

Julia had no illusions about her appearance. At five feet ten inches she towered above every girl she knew, and most men. Thin, angular, with straight red hair, hazel eyes, large hands and feet, and a face so long that the girls at her school had nicknamed her Dobbin, she'd never considered herself even passably attract-ive. But the little self-esteem her mother had nurtured throughout her childhood had been completely eroded by her stepmother, Mabel, who never missed an opportunity to make a disparaging remark about her plain looks and lack of grace and personality. The remarks hurt more than Julia would have admitted to anyone, even her adored father, whom she had never entirely forgiven for marrying a shrewish, avaricious and snobbish woman less than three months after her beloved mother's death.

'I wish I had hair as thick and straight as yours. It never tangles or frizzes, just stays put when you pin it.' Rhian brushed it out, caught the end and twisted it into a neat knot on the crown of Julia's head.

'You wouldn't like the colour.' Julia picked up her hairpin box.

'I think it's lovely.'

'I don't. I'd give anything to have blonde curls and big blue eyes like you.'

'And be a maid?' When Julia didn't answer, she added, 'Mrs Williams says we always want what we can't have. Pass me a pin, please.'

'Have you decided whether or not to meet Mr Evans today?' Rhian and Julia had no secrets from one another and Rhian had told her about Joey's offer to get her a coat and his invitation to spend the afternoon with him.

'I still haven't mind up my mind.'

'You only have a couple of hours left.'

'I know.'

'I'm dreading tonight. Mrs Larch has invited thirty people for a New Year supper.' Ignoring the fact that Julia was two years younger than her, Mabel Larch had demanded that both her stepchildren address her as 'mother' with the result that Julia and her brother Gerald avoided calling her anything to her face and 'Mrs Larch' when they had to resort to naming her.

'With thirty people coming, there's bound to be someone nice you can talk to,' Rhian reassured.

'Is there?' Julia enquired sceptically. 'I scanned the guest list. I scarcely know any of them. And,' she wrinkled her nose, 'I doubt my father and brother do either.'

'You never know, one of them might be an explorer or

archaeologist who can't wait to tell you about his latest find.' The authors who had fired Rhian's imagination the most were Rider Haggard and Kipling.

'Can you see Mrs Larch inviting an explorer into her drawing room? She'd be terrified that he'd bring a pet lion cub or wear muddy boots.'

'Real explorers would do both.' Rhian looked at Julia and they burst into giggles.

'It would be wonderful if an Alan Quartermain did walk into our drawing room tonight, but even if by some miracle he did, he wouldn't want to talk to me.' Julia fingered the gold locket around her neck that held a photograph of her mother.

'Why wouldn't he?' Rhian slipped the last pin into the knot. She leaned forward, studied Julia's reflection in the mirror and teased a light fringe out on to her forehead.

'Because I'm dull and boring.'

Rhian suspected that Julia was repeating something Mrs Larch had said. But she wasn't in a position to criticize her mistress. 'You read so many books and you know so much about art and music, you could never be boring, Miss Julia. There, your hair is all done.'

'Could it be you don't find me boring because you're a good listener, Rhian?' Julia left the stool.

'No, because I've learned a lot from you, and, while I think of it, thank you for lending me *Kim*.'

'Have you finished it?'

'Not yet, because Bronwen won't let me use up a week's attic candle ration in a night. Do you want it back?'

'Not until you finish it. And if you're short of candles, sneak some from the storeroom.'

'The mistress inspects the attic.'

'If you've a spare half hour, come in here, switch on the electric light, empty the top drawer of my dressing table on to the bed and if she finds you, tell her I ordered to you to tidy my room.' Julia gave Rhian a rare smile that lit up her face and added sparkle to her eyes. 'Since Mother died, you're the only person I can talk to about books. Father likes reading, but between work and his other commitments he never has time. And all Gerald wants to do is ride his bike and sneak whisky from the cabinet in my father's study.' Julia plucked nervously at her gown. It was black, like all her clothes. Despite her father's remarriage she had refused to stop wearing mourning for her mother.

'I have to go down and eat breakfast before Bronwen starts serving it upstairs.' Rhian gathered her cloak and bag from the chair.

'And I have to go down and check that Mrs Williams has everything in hand. The slightest thing out of place seems to upset Mrs Larch.'

Neither of them doubted that the housekeeper would have everything under control, but whether Mrs Williams's arrangements would be to Mrs Larch's satisfaction was another thing. Julia opened the door and they stepped out on to the landing. Edward Larch was leaving his bedroom. He stopped and looked at both of them.

Embarrassed to be seen in the family quarters out of uniform, Rhian bobbed a curtsy. 'Sorry, sir.'

'It's Rhian's day off, Father,' Julia reminded him.

Edward loved Julia dearly but every time he saw her he couldn't help wondering how he, and petite, delicate Amelia, with her fair hair and gentle grey eyes, had produced such a daughter. He and his son, Gerald, were tall, slim, fair-haired and blue-eyed, like his Scottish father. But if they owed their looks to some raping, pillaging Norseman, Julia had reached even further back, to a time when flame-haired, raw-boned, uncouth Scottish clansmen had ruled the Glens. She would have made a striking peasant. A cart-horse of a woman, sought as a wife for her strength and capability for hard work. Certainly, she would have looked more at home in a primitive croft than a drawing room. Whereas Rhian . . .

'Father?'

Edward realized then that he was staring at the maid. 'Sorry, I was miles away,' he lied. It was the first time in months he had seen the girl out of uniform and he was amazed that he'd never noticed her resemblance to his late wife before. Freed from her uniform cap, her blonde curls were the exact same shade as the lock of hair secreted in the back of his wallet. Her eyes were just as blue – and worryingly disturbing. 'Enjoy your day off, Rhian,' he snapped, more abrupt than he'd intended.

'I will, sir.' Glad to be gone, Rhian put her head down and walked to the end of the passage. Just as she closed the door to the servants' staircase she heard Mrs Larch shout.

'Edward, what is that girl doing in the family quarters, out of uniform?'

Chapter 2

JOEY SET HIS grey felt trilby on his head and checked his reflection in the mirror he had hung behind his office door. Pleased with what he saw, he smiled. Since his fifteenth birthday, his good looks, coupled with his well-knit, six-foot frame and open easy manner, had attracted women. The problem was he no longer wanted to attract women in general, just one in particular. And, to his frustration, she was proving difficult to impress.

He tilted his hat at a rakish angle, buttoned his overcoat, picked up his leather gloves and looked around for the parcel he had asked Miss Robertson to deliver to his office. The carrier bag bearing the Gwilym James logo was beneath his desk. He opened it and checked the contents.

'It was delivered from the Cardiff store this morning, Mr Evans. One ladies' cashmere coat in a fifty-five-inch length and thirty-four-inch chest; that was the size you wanted?' Like the Cheshire Cat in Alice in Wonderland, Miss Robertson materialized in the open doorway without sound or warning.

Sensing her disapproval, Joey reminded himself, as he did at least half a dozen times every working day, that as store manager, he was the supervisor's superior. 'It is, Miss Robertson. You arranged to put it on my account?' He gave her his most charming smile but it died, wasted on his lips.

'Yes, Mr Evans. Two guineas, less the employees' twenty per cent discount.' Tall, skeletal, hook-nosed, with more wrinkles than a withered winter apple and dressed in the store uniform of black dress, shoes and stockings, Thora Robertson bore an uncanny resemblance to the illustrations of witches in his childhood copy of

Grimm's fairy tales. He suspected that the transfer his sister-in-law, Sali, had arranged from the Pontypridd store to Tonypandy owed as much to the woman's brittle manner as her efficiency.

She'd told him on her first day that she found it difficult to take orders from a boy his age and the store had only been open a week when he'd overheard one of her assistants complain that 'Sob Rob' (Miss Robertson's nickname because she made so many girls cry) ruled ladies' fashion with an iron fist in an iron glove.

He removed his watch from his waistcoat and opened it. It was a quarter to ten, half an hour before he was due to meet Rhian at the station, a five-minute walk away – that's if she turned up, and he wasn't at all certain she would. But he had no intention of spending the interim with Thora Robertson.

'Thank you for arranging for the coat to be brought here, Miss Robertson.' He'd intended the remark as a dismissal but she continued to hover in the doorway. 'Is there anything else you wish to discuss?'

'There is, Mr Evans.' She cleared her throat. 'I hope you don't think that I am talking out of turn, but you know what gossips the girls are.'

'I trust you to put a stop to their idle talk, Miss Robertson.' As she was blocking the doorway, he set down the carrier bag, thrust his hands into his pockets and leaned against his desk.

'It's rule number eight, Mr Evans. Staff are only allowed to buy goods for their immediate family, especially sale goods, which are in high demand by our regular customers.'

'If you are referring to the coat, I bought it for my sister-in-law, Miss Robertson,' Joey lied glibly.

'But Mrs Evans works for the company.'

'I have two sisters-in-law, Miss Robertson. My eldest brother's wife, Mrs Sali Evans, does indeed work for the company. But I thought that my other brother, Victor's wife, Mrs Megan Evans, would appreciate a present after her confinement.'

Thora Robertson's cheeks flamed crimson at his reference to pregnancy. 'Please accept my apologies for raising the matter, Mr Evans.'

'Who did you think I bought the coat for, Miss Robertson?' he challenged.'

'I didn't know . . .' Her voice trailed off in embarrassment.

He turned to the window in his office that overlooked the shop floor. Tonia was standing behind the ladies' underwear counter and he recalled asking her to relay a message about the coat to his assistant manager, Sam. She had seen him with Rhian, guessed that the coat had been for her and no doubt told the entire staff that he was buying a coat for Rhian Jones.

The displays, glass-fronted drawers and cupboards in Tonia's section were immaculate. Her hair was neatly combed, her black dress and white lace collar prim and businesslike. She was the embodiment of the highly-trained, efficient Gwilym James assistant, yet less than two weeks after she'd begun to work in the store, he was sorry he'd allowed her to talk him into taking her on. And not just because she was overly familiar with him during working hours.

The four-year age gap between them had led him to treat Tonia in much the same way Lloyd and Victor did; as an immature and occasionally annoying little sister. If they were closer than most cousins, it was simply because they lived in the same town and their respective families always celebrated birthdays, Christmas and Easter together. But since her first day in the store, Tonia had volunteered for every errand that brought her near his office, used every pretext to dog him and deliberately hung back when the store closed because his path to his father's house took him past her mother's shop.

Her crush on him was embarrassing and exasperating in equal measure. But the one thing he couldn't understand after being subjected to her increasingly blatant flirting was the request she'd made for a transfer to the Pontypridd store soon after she'd started work. She'd informed Miss Robertson that she wanted to leave Tonypandy because too many people knew her in the town and came in to talk to her without any intention of buying anything.

It was an excellent excuse – if excuse it was – because the supervisor was continually shooing Tonia's old school friends away from her counter. But he couldn't help suspecting that another reason lay behind Tonia's application. However, if there was one, he couldn't fathom it.

He would have gladly sent her to Timbuktu if it meant she'd leave him alone. Unfortunately, there wasn't a vacancy in the Pontypridd store, and one wasn't expected to arise for another month. He only hoped he could survive her irritating adoration until then.

Miss Robertson saw him staring at Tonia and realized she had been transparent in her reference to 'gossip'. 'Now you have acquainted me with the facts, Mr Evans, I will put an end to the girls' rumour-mongering.'

'See that you do, Miss Robertson.' Joey retrieved the bag. 'Is there anything else?'

'No, Mr Evans.'

'I will return at seven o'clock. In the meantime, should any problems arise, consult Mr Carter.'

Miss Robertson looked disapprovingly down her hooked nose. 'Yes, Mr Evans.'

Joey tipped his hat and walked past her. Thora Robertson's hostility towards his assistant manager, Samuel Carter, was another source of annoyance. At twenty-five, Sam was three years older than him, but unfortunately not as assertive, and Miss Robertson continually belittled him in an attempt to undermine his authority. It didn't help that Sam, like the girls in her department, was terrified of her, and diffident and reluctant to give her orders.

Joey waved to Sam, who was overseeing the transfer of the last of the sales stock from the warehouse on to the shop floor, and quickened his step. For the next few hours Sam, Thora Robertson and Gwilym James would just have to get on without him as best they could. And, with any luck, every Thursday in future, because if that was the only day Rhian was free, he intended to spend as much of it with her as he possibly could.

He slowed his pace when he left the store and stopped to greet friends and neighbours as he strolled down Dunraven Street, but it was still only ten o'clock when he reached the station. Entering the nearest confectioner's, he braved the hostility of an old girlfriend who served there and splashed out on a half-pound, shilling box of Rowntree's assorted chocolates.

Between the chocolates, train fare, lunch in the City Restaurant and the film in the Park Hall he had promised Rhian, it was going to be an expensive day. But it would be money well spent if he succeeded in convincing her that he was serious about wanting to court her. He was behind the door, packing the chocolates into the carrier bag that held the coat, when Rhian walked in. She went to the counter without seeing him.

'Two penny bars of Fry's five boys chocolate, please.'

He tapped her on the shoulder. 'You don't have to get those. I've bought us a box.'

Rhian blushed when she saw the young female assistant staring at her. 'They're for Sali's children.'

'We'll call in on her together.' Joey dug his hand into his pocket again and pulled out two shillings. 'I'll have a tin of Mackintosh's toffees as well, please, Sara.'

'You two courting?' Sara enquired bluntly.

'Since when has courting been a criminal offence?' Joey answered, avoiding her question.

'Since you took it up,' Sara retorted. 'I'd be careful if I were you, miss. Think again before going out with this one. He had a girl for every day of the week and two for Sundays, even when we were in the babies' class in school.'

'We were three years old, Sara,' Joey protested.

'That didn't stop you calling on me, or my dad from sending you packing. Everyone could see what you were like, even then.' There was an edge to her flippant tone and Rhian had a feeling that Sara wasn't just talking about when she and Joey had been three years old.

Joey dropped the toffees alongside the chocolates in his bag, opened the door and held it for Rhian. 'Bye, Sara.'

'Bye, Joey. Enjoy the chocolates, miss.'

Joey offered Rhian his arm as they walked up the street.

'No, thank you,' she refused primly.

'It's pointless trying to pretend that you're not with me. Now that Sara has seen us together, it'll be all over Tonypandy in an hour that we're courting strong.'

'But we're not!' she exclaimed indignantly.

'If we're not, why did you meet me?'

'Because you promised to try to find me a coat,' she blurted thoughtlessly.

'Mercenary little thing, aren't you? Will you shoot me if I tell you that I failed?'

Stung by his use of the word 'mercenary' and struggling to hide her disappointment, she said, 'Thank you for trying,' as graciously as she could.

'The very least I can do for such a gushing display of disappointed gratitude is to buy you lunch.'

'No, thank you. I really do have to look in the shops for a coat.'

'And afterwards, we'll visit Sali and the children,' he continued as if she hadn't spoken.

'I would prefer to call on them alone.'

'Because if we call on them together, Sali will think that we're courting?' he asked.

'Yes.'

'Let her.' He thrust his free hand into his overcoat pocket as they approached the ticket booth and pushed two silver threepenny joeys through the window. 'Two returns to Pontypridd, please, Tom.'

Rhian waited until he had pocketed the tickets and they had walked on to the platform before opening her handbag. She lifted out her purse and extracted three pennies. 'I will pay for my own train fare.'

'I invited you out.'

'And I refused to go with you.'

'You're here,' he pointed out maddeningly. 'And we made plans to have lunch and visit the Park Hall.'

'You made plans, I didn't.'

'You wouldn't disappoint me, would you? Not now we've come this far together.' He smiled and looked into her eyes again and her heart seemed to move up into her throat, choking her.

When she finally found her voice she mumbled, 'I don't want to give you the wrong impression.'

'So far, the only impression you've given me is that you're inordinately fond of the word "no".'

'If we do lunch together and go to the Park Hall, it will be as friends. The sort of outing I would make with one of the girls I work with in Llan House.'

'That's the only way you will go out with me?' he asked keenly.

'Yes,' she retorted firmly.

'Then that's the way it will have to be.' He took her three pennies and pushed them into his pocket. 'But you will allow me to try to make it more?'

'Not today.'

'Next week?' he suggested optimistically.

A signal clunked lower down the track. A whistle blew and a train chugged slowly and noisily towards them, belching out smut-laden steam.

Rhian remembered Bronwen's story about her sister, and imagined the devastation Ruby must have felt at losing a boyfriend she had been fond of. And it would be so easy to become fond of Joey – if she allowed him to get close to her. 'Not ever,' she said decisively.

Ignoring the other diners in the City Restaurant, Joey pushed his dessert bowl aside, leaned across the table towards Rhian and continued relating his life history.

'. . . So, when the colliery management refused to give my father, Lloyd, Victor and me our jobs back after the strike because Dad and Lloyd were strike leaders and union officials, we thought we'd have to leave the valleys. None of us had ever considered working anywhere other than the pit. Even now, Lloyd considers himself lucky because he succeeded in finding a management job with another mining company.'

'But you are happy working in Gwilym James?' she asked.

'Only since they made me manager of the Tonypandy store,' he replied half seriously. 'But when Sali first suggested I apply for a trainee manager's position I thought she was mad.' He leaned back from the table as the waitress arrived to clear their plates. Both he and Rhian had opted for the three-course, ninepenny lunchtime special: brown soup followed by pork chops, swede, mashed potatoes, apple sauce, and gravy; and for dessert, jam roly-poly and vanilla custard. The portions were liberal enough to satisfy the hungriest navvy, and he had only managed to eat a quarter of his jam roly-poly. But Rhian had given up halfway through her dinner and barely touched her dessert.

'Anything wrong with this, miss?' The waitress poked at Rhian's roly-poly with her spoon.

'Nothing, thank you. I'm just not used to eating like this in the middle of the day,' Rhian apologized.

'Tea or coffee? Both are served as part of the special.'

'Tea, please,' Rhian answered.

'Me too, please.' Joey leaned towards Rhian again as soon as the waitress left. 'In answer to your question, yes, I am happy working in Gwilym James. Very happy. I never saw myself wearing a suit to work every day, or managing a store, but I have always liked people.'

Trying not to sound as if she were carping, she murmured, 'Especially women people.'

Trusting that honesty would prove the best policy, Joey confessed, 'I took Sara to the Empire Theatre once. When I invited her to come out with me again, she refused. I never asked her again.'

'The show was that bad?'

'The show was fine.' He had the grace to look ashamed. 'In fact it was so good I took her best friend to see it later in the same week. Both of them were furious when they found out.'

'They had every right to be angry.'

'I was only seventeen. I've done a lot of growing up during the last five years.'

'And now you only go out with one girl at a time?' she smiled.

'I've spent so much time building up trade in the store during the last two years I've hardly gone out with any girls.' He fell serious. 'I really am looking for someone special. Someone I can spend the rest of my life with.' He reached out, intending to cover

26

her hand with his, but she pushed her chair back from the table and moved her hands out of his reach, just as she'd done in the teashop in Tonypandy.

'How many girls have you said that to?' She was growing warier of him by the minute. Already, she was beginning to understand why so many women liked him. He was easy company, and he was confiding his thoughts as if she were the only person in the world he could talk to.

'None,' he answered, 'and not just lately – ever.'

'Do you expect me to believe you?'

'It's the truth, but knowing what the gossips say about me, no. And before you tell me again that this is an outing based on friendship, let me explain. I love my family to bits, but there have been times when I've hated being the youngest. Lloyd is nine years older than me; Victor, six. They were allowed to do everything that mattered years before me. Go to school, leave school, wear long trousers, stay up late, work, take out girls – and that's with-out bringing drinking and pubs into the equation. But I've never been as jealous of either of them as I have been since they married. Victor and Megan are so wrapped in one another and their farm I sometimes wonder if the rest of the world exists for them. And I only have to see the way Sali looks at Lloyd to turn green with envy. Not that I want Sali to look at me in that way,' he clarified hastily. 'But I do hope that one day I can be part of a marriage as strong as theirs.'

'They are happy together.' Rhian didn't dare tell him that she too envied Sali and Lloyd's close relationship. Or how much she dreamed of being a part of a family like theirs.

'Have you ever noticed the way Lloyd and Sali finish one an-other's sentences, or exchange glances as if they know exactly what the other is thinking? Or listened while they talk to their children?' Joey watched the waitress set their tea, sugar and milk on the table.

Rhian was amazed to think that a man could feel the same way as her about marriage. But her past was very different to Joey's and she'd never entirely put it behind her. Orphaned at eight, her early memories of her father's drunken rages and the beatings he'd given her mother still had the power to bring tears to her eyes. 'There's nothing worse than a bad marriage,' she pronounced bitterly.

'And nothing better than a good one.' Joey handed her the sugar bowl. 'I'm not just talking about my brothers and their wives. My parents were very happy together until my mother died a few years ago. In some ways I don't think my father ever recovered from losing her.'

'You've been lucky in your family.' She could only imagine what it would have been like to grow up in a houseful of people who cared about one another. She hadn't even known what it was like to have a friend until she had met Sali.

'But as I said, Lloyd and Victor have been luckier still and, like school, long trousers and being allowed into pubs, I hope my turn will come.' He gazed intently into her eyes. 'I know what people think of me, I know how they talk and I know I've been no angel in the past. But can't you see this could be different? That's why I'm trying to tell you that I want more than simply a good time with you, Rhian.'

Her heart turned somersaults. Joey was offering to make all her dreams of a husband and a family of her own come true. But she also felt that it was ridiculous of him to talk like this on their first outing. It was one thing to be envious of his brothers' domestic bliss, quite another to insist that his intentions towards her were serious when he only really knew her as an acquaintance. It was as though he was prepared to consider any eligible, presentable woman as a possible wife. And flattering though it was to be considered presentable by Joey Evans, she was too cautious to entrust her feelings and happiness to what would probably turn out to be another of his passing fancies.

'And if all I want at the moment is a good time?' She deliberately kept her voice light.

'So long as the good times are with me, fine.' He pulled his wallet from his inside pocket and winked at the waitress to gain her attention. Flustered, the girl dropped her notepad and pencil.

Rhian smiled and shook her head. 'You're incorrigible.'

'In what way?' he asked in surprise.

'One minute you sit there and tell me that you want one special person in your life, the next you flirt with the waitress.'

'I wasn't flirting with her.'

She counted out tenpence from her purse. 'You winked at her and in a woman's eyes that's flirting, especially when the wink is accompanied by the smile you just gave her. When she brings the bill she'll be expecting an invitation out.'

'Don't be silly, I'm with you.'

The waitress set the bill beside Joey's empty cup. 'Can I get you anything else, sir?' she purred seductively.

'No, thank you. My brother and I have finished,' Rhian answered before Joey had a chance to speak.

Joey took Rhian's tenpence and handed the girl two shillings. She covered his fingers with hers and he was forced to tug his hand away to free them.

'I'll bring your change in a moment, sir.'

'See what I mean?' Rhian lifted her eyebrows. 'Another wink and she'll do a lot more than hold your hand.'

'It's just banter. It goes on all the time between men and women.'

'In my experience only when you're involved.'

'All right, I solemnly promise that I'll never wink or flirt with a woman from this moment on.'

She burst out laughing.

'Now what's funny?' he demanded touchily.

'You. I doubt that you could stop making eyes at women, even if you tried. Every time I've been in your company you've flirted with someone. It makes no difference whether they're young or old, married or single, and you're not even aware that you're doing it.'

'It means nothing, surely you can see that.' He sat back with his arms folded, forcing the waitress to drop his sixpence change on to the tablecloth. He took it after she left and pushed her tuppence tip under his cup.

'You might think it means nothing, but what about your legions of ex-girlfriends?' Rhian tugged on her gloves.

'Legions! I admit I've sown a few wild oats—'

'And none wilder than today. You're lucky you were talking to me. Another girl might have dragged you halfway to the altar by now. You can't just wake up one morning, decide to marry and look around for a wife. Haven't you heard the expression "marry in haste repent at leisure"?'

'I didn't have to look around for a wife, as you put it. I made up my mind months ago that you were the girl for me. It's taken me this long to get you to agree to come out with me.'

'What time does the Park Hall open?' She left her chair.

'Three o'clock.'

She glanced at the clock on the wall. 'It's not even one yet, and we've already walked twice around the town.'

'We could go to Ynysangharad House. Sali will be home. She's not returning to work until the end of Harry's holidays and he has to go back to boarding school.' His eyes were dark, probing, and she sensed him daring her to take up his invitation and announce to his family that they were going out together.

'Fine, we'll visit Sali and the children – as friends.'

He offered her his arm. 'Let's go.'

'POW!' Harry stuffed a matchstick into a toy cannon and fired it. The missile hit a lead soldier in the middle of the row Joey had set up in front of the small fort Victor had made. The figure wavered, hitting the ones either side. When it finally toppled, the entire row followed suit. 'All your officers are killed, Uncle Joey.' Harry triumphantly scooped up Joey's 'dead' men and piled them behind him. 'Now your troops have no one to order them about you'll lose the war.'

'No, I won't, because my sergeants will take over, and everyone knows it's the sergeants who are really in charge of every army.' Joey moved two battered figures forward to replace his officers. One was missing an arm, the other a leg, and it took a little care to balance them.

The door opened and Sali's housekeeper, Mari Williams, wheeled a loaded trolley alongside the sofa where Sali was sitting with Rhian and her three-year-old daughter, Bella.

'Thank you, Mari. Go to Auntie Rhian until I've poured the tea, poppet.' Sali handed Bella her picture book and the little girl climbed on Rhian's lap, settling down contentedly.

'Is there chocolate cake, Mari?' Harry pushed another matchstick into his cannon.

'Only for polite boys, who look at Mari when they speak to her and say please and thank you,' Sali reprimanded.

'If I look up, Uncle Joey will kill all my men.'

'I call a truce until after tea.' Joey rose from the hearthrug in time to see Mari nod from him to Rhian and give Sali a questioning look. 'Yes, Mari, Rhian and I arrived together.'

'Does my sister know that you are spending your day off with this one, Rhian?' Mari pointed at Joey.

'I have no doubt that Llan House's Mrs Williams will have heard that we left Tonypandy on the same train this morning by now.' Joey perched on the arm of the sofa next to Rhian and Bella.

'We're not spending the day together, Mari,' Rhian explained. 'We're spending it here. I happened to mention that I was going to visit Sali and Joey decided to tag along.'

'Just so long as that is all it is,' Mari pronounced disapprovingly. 'Given his reputation, you shouldn't need telling what he's like.'

'I am here and I'm not deaf, Mari.' Before Joey could say another word in his defence the front door closed.

Harry leapt to his feet and ran out into the hall. 'It's Daddy, Bella,' he shouted back excitedly. 'Daddy, you'll never guess who's here.'

'Auntie Rhian.' Lloyd carried Harry back into the drawing room on his shoulders.

'And Uncle Joey.'

'So I see.' Lloyd swung Harry down. 'Hello, sweetheart.' He kissed Sali's lips and Rhian's cheek. 'Joey,' he acknowledged his brother. 'I didn't think you could take a Thursday afternoon off.'

'I can now I have the store running like clockwork. Four sugars in my tea, please, Sali. And I'd love one of the scones with raspberry jam and clotted cream, Mari.'

'You're worse than Master Harry and he has the excuse of being eight years old,' she grumbled. 'As I keep telling him, no cakes, jam or cream until he's eaten at least two sandwiches and as you're twice his size, in your case that'll be four. Ham, chicken or tongue?'

'Chicken, please, Mari. They look delicious.'

'And you can stop flattering me. Cook made them and I'm too long in the tooth to be taken in like one of your Tonypandy floozies.'

'What's a Tonypandy floozy when it's at home?' Joey laughed.

'A kind of cake,' Lloyd broke in, with a significant look at Harry and Bella who were apt to pick up every word.

Sali busied herself with pouring the tea. Fond as she was of Joey, she couldn't help feeling that a courtship between him and Rhian might prove disastrous. The only question was, for which one of them?

'You're not returning to the store again today, Joey?' Lloyd sat in an armchair next to the hearth.

'Even clockwork needs checking every couple of hours. I told Sam and the ubiquitous Miss Robertson that I'd be back at seven o'clock before the rush. Thank you, Mari.' He took the plate of sandwiches she gave him.

'Why is Miss Robertson ubiquitous?' Harry set his plate down next to his soldiers.

'Because it's impossible to run away from her,' Joey answered.

'Why do you want to run away from her when she works in your shop, Uncle Joey?'

'It's not my shop, Harry, I only manage it.'

'And your Uncle Joey was joking, Harry. How about I drive you and Rhian back to Tonypandy?' Lloyd avoided Sali's eye because he knew she'd guess he'd only made the offer out of concern for Rhian.

'I'm sorry, Mr Lloyd.' It had taken two years of living in the same house for Mari to stop addressing Lloyd as 'Mr Evans'. Although he'd asked her to call him Lloyd, 'Mr Lloyd' was as familiar as the housekeeper was prepared to get. 'Robert told me to tell you that the car is out of service again. The mechanic at the garage has promised to call round first thing in the morning to look at it.'

'That car spends more time out of commission than working,' Lloyd complained.

'We could ask Robert to harness the carriage.' Sali placed four of Lloyd's favourite ham and cress sandwiches on to a plate and handed them to him.

'Please, Mam, can I go too?' Harry begged. He loved riding in the car but he loved the horses more.

'Me too,' Bella lisped.

'Why not?' Sali agreed. 'It may take us longer to get there but there'll still be time to call on Granddad after we've left Joey at the store. And Rhian can visit him with us.'

'That's a good idea.' Curious to see how Joey would react to his and Sali's manoeuvring, Lloyd glanced at his brother.

'But Uncle Joey and I have to finish our game first.' Harry wiped his fingers on his napkin and dived behind his men.

'That must be some game you two are playing if it's made you forget chocolate cake, Harry.' Lloyd helped Bella climb on to his lap.

'What time do you have to be in tonight, Rhian?' Sali asked.

'Ten o'clock as usual.'

'I wish I could go home with you.' Joey took the matchstick Harry handed him and loaded it into his own miniature cannon.

'Even the store manager is entitled to a half-day off a week besides Sunday.' Sali leaned forward and wiped crumbs from Bella's mouth in her own napkin.

'I couldn't take Pandy Parade night off, especially at sale time; it's the busiest of the week. Do me a favour, Rhian?' Joey fired the cannon and knocked over two of Harry's cavalry. 'Put another two of those chicken sandwiches on to my plate for me. War is a hungry business.'

'What do you think you're doing?' Lloyd asked his brother after Mari had cleared away the tea things and Rhian and Sali had taken the children upstairs.

'Clearing up Harry's toys.' Joey lifted the forts and boxes of soldiers on to a side table, ready to be carried to the nursery.

'Don't be clever with me. You know what I'm talking about.'

'Rhian?' Joey sat in the chair opposite Lloyd's.

'She's a nice girl.'

'I wouldn't have asked her out for the afternoon if she wasn't.'

'You know what you're like,' Lloyd said impatiently.

'I know what I *was* like. I've changed. I want to settle down.'

Before Lloyd had time to digest what Joey had said, Sali joined them. She picked up her handbag from the sofa. 'I needed my hairbrush but even if I hadn't, I would have found an excuse to come back. In case you don't know, Joey, Rhian had nothing but grief, misery and tragedy in her life before she went to Llan House. From what I've been told, her father was a violent bully, her mother incapable of protecting her, and I know her brother treated her worse than an unpaid slave and skivvy after they died when she was eight. He was kinder to his dogs than to her and when he wasn't beating them, he kept them chained up on minimum rations in his yard. She didn't so much as hear a kind word until she met me. So, I'm warning you now, you hurt her and I'll never speak to you again.' Without waiting for Joey to reply, she left, closing the door behind her.

Lloyd glanced at his brother. 'That, in a nutshell is the gist of what I was about to say to you, Joey.'

Chapter 3

RHIAN RAN HER fingers over the silk blouse Sali had lifted out of her wardrobe. 'It's lovely, but I couldn't possibly accept it unless you allow me to pay for it.'

'Pay for my cast-offs? I wouldn't hear of it.' Sali held it in front of her. 'Just look at how much weight I've put on. It will be a long time before I can get into this again.'

'Two months,' Rhian suggested.

'I doubt it will stretch over my bust after the baby is born, and it has a back fastening, so it would be useless for nursing.'

'And when you finish nursing the baby?'

'It will be out of fashion. Besides, Lloyd and I have no intention of stopping at three.'

'You want more children?' Rhian asked in surprise.

'I'll let you know after this one is born, but I wouldn't mind four, or even five.'

Rhian took the blouse from Sali. It was high-necked and light cream with a frill of lace around the collar. She turned it around and saw a price tag fixed to the top button. 'It cost a guinea and you've never even worn it!'

'I grew too fat before I had a chance.'

Rhian imagined it teamed with her cream linen summer skirt or the blue winter suit she was wearing. It would look perfect, as she suspected Sali well knew. 'If you're sure . . .'

'You'd be doing me a favour. I have a rule never to buy anything new until I've cleared something old from my wardrobe. If I didn't stick to it, we'd have to buy another half a dozen bedroom suites to accommodate my clothes. You have no idea what a temptation it is to work in Gwilym James. Every time I buy in a new line I want to keep most of it for myself.' Sali folded the blouse into a paper bag, 'About Joey?' she began hesitantly.

'I met him at Tonypandy station. We had lunch in the City Restaurant, and we were going to see the moving pictures in the Park Hall but came here instead. Thank you for this.' Rhian took the bag from Sali. Seeing that she was still worried, she added, 'You really don't need to worry about me and Joey because we are just friends.'

'Really?' Sali didn't look convinced.

'Really,' Rhian reiterated. 'I made it clear to Joey before we got on the train this morning that this outing wasn't going to be any different to the outings I make with the girls. We each paid our own way and all we've done is talk.'

'And what did Joey say when you told him that going out with him was no different to going out with the girls?' Sali probed.

'He said it was fine by him.' Rhian kept Joey's full answer to herself.

'That doesn't sound like the Joey Evans I know.' Sali took a woollen shawl from a drawer. 'If we're going to get Joey back to the shop by seven we ought to make a move.'

'We could just as easily take the train.'

'If you do, it won't give Lloyd an excuse to call on his father. Although Joey lives at home he works such long hours Lloyd can't help worrying. His father hasn't been strong since he lost his leg in the train crash.'

'But he is all right, isn't he?' Mr Evans's gruff manner had terrified Rhian when she'd first met him, but it hadn't taken her long to realize that beneath the brusque crust was a kind heart.

'I think so,' Sali answered cautiously. 'He visits Victor and Megan at the farm a couple of times a week and sometimes stays over with them. We'd love to have him here more often, but,' she gave an apologetic shrug, 'he hates being surrounded by servants and although Lloyd and I would like to live more simply, the trustees of Harry's estate prefer him to live in the house that he will inherit. My solicitor, Mr Richards, said that if we shut up the house, it would probably cost more to get it back in good condition by the time Harry comes of age than it would to pay the running costs, which are offset by the produce from the farms that come with the estate. And by living here, Lloyd and I can deal with any small problems as they arise rather than wait until the next trustees meeting.'

'It is a lovely house.' Rhian looked around. The bedroom suite was Victorian, too ornate to appeal to modern taste, but there was no denying the craftsmanship that had gone into carving the mahogany four-poster bed, matching wardrobes, dressing table, washstand and desk. Two chairs upholstered in blue velvet stood either side of a sofa table in front of a huge window that overlooked the gardens. A Persian rug covered most of the floor and white silk drapes on the bed and windows and a white silk bedcover lightened the impact of the furniture. 'I used to think Llan House was big until I visited here.'

'It is big, but it's also beginning to feel like home. It's amazing how much space children take up,' Sali patted her 'bump', 'even before they're born. Just when I thought that I could clear some room in the nursery by putting away Bella's baby things they're needed for this one.'

'You are lucky.'

'With Lloyd and the children?' Sali smiled. 'I know. But I'm also lucky with the house. I always liked visiting my aunt when I was a child, and I feel close to her here. It was so generous of her to leave everything she owned to Harry.'

'I have a small present for you. That's if you want it.' Rhian opened her bag.

'You shouldn't have,' Sali protested. 'Not after that lovely vase you gave us for Christmas, not to mention the doll you bought for Bella and the drawing materials for Harry.'

'It's small and it didn't cost me anything. Mr Larch always takes photographs of all the staff on New Year's Eve. This year he gave each of us three copies as presents.' She handed Sali a cardboard folder.

'This is beautiful.' Sali studied the photograph. 'You're wearing the dress I gave you for Christmas.'

'He said we could put on our best clothes.'

37

'I have to get a silver frame for this. You look stunning. Your face, your hair . . .'

'Mr Larch says that I'm one of those people who photograph well. I must be, because I don't believe for one minute that I look like that.'

'The camera never lies. This is exactly what you look like. I have to show this to Lloyd.' Before Rhian could stop her, Sali swept from the room and down the stairs.

Joey leaned against the newel post at the foot of the stairs, watching Lloyd, Sali and Mari mill around the hall as they dressed the children in their outdoor clothes.

'So can I have a photograph?' he whispered to Rhian when she stepped back from the mirror after pinning on her hat.

'No.'

'That's not fair. You have three,' he complained.

'Two after giving Sali one. Besides, you know what people would think if I gave you a photograph of myself.'

'No, tell me?' He gazed at her through teasing eyes.

'They'd think we were boy and girlfriend.'

'That's exactly what you told me we were this morning.'

'Not that kind of boy and girlfriend.'

'There's different sorts?' he questioned, feigning innocence.

'You know there are,' she answered, refusing to be irritated by him.

'I'd keep it safe on the chest of drawers next to my bed. No one would see it except me. And I'd kiss it every night to remind myself that the original would never grant me that favour.'

Rhian was glad when the elderly butler, Mr Jenkins, opened the porch door at the sound of carriage wheels crunching over gravel.

'It's Robert, Miss Sali,' he announced.

'Rhian?' Joey called softly, when Sali, Lloyd and the children went to the front door.

'The answer's no.'

'All right, I understand that you're not prepared to part with a photograph but you're not going back to Llan House wearing that old cloak, are you?'

She glanced down. Her cloak looked shabbier than ever in the elegant surroundings of Ynysangharad House. 'I did intend to go shopping this afternoon. Somehow I never got around to it.'

'A fairy godfather went for you.' He held up the carrier bag he had brought from Tonypandy.

Curious, she looked inside. 'Oh, Joey!'

'The ladies top-of-the-range cashmere.' He pulled it out as if he were a conjurer producing a rabbit from a top hat. 'And in your size, I believe, madam.'

'You told me you couldn't get one,' she said accusingly.

'I lied. I had it sent up from the Cardiff store.'

'I have to pay you for it.'

'It's a present.'

'There is no way that I am accepting an expensive present, let alone clothes from you,' she said heatedly.

'I'd swap it for a photograph.'

'The answer's no!'

' "*A lady may only accept a token gift from a gentleman,*" ' he recited in a high-pitched voice that was a fair imitation of Mrs Larch's. ' "*An embroidered handkerchief, an unostentatious box of sweets or chocolates or a very small bottle of cologne. She may never, never accept anything expensive, especially clothing and expect to,*" ' he reduced his voice to a whisper, ' "*remain a lady.*" '

'You read the lady's manual?' She laughed at the idea of Joey reading a guide to etiquette.

'How else would I know how to behave around a real lady?'

'And you've met Mrs Larch?'

'She deigned to come into the store once, although she wasted no time in letting us know that it wasn't up to the standards of the stores she usually patronized.' He shook out the coat. 'Try it on.'

'Not until I pay for it.'

'I won't pay for it until the end of the month when the purchases I've made against my personal account are due, so why should you pay me sooner?'

She gazed longingly at the coat that she had coveted for so many months. 'I won't try it on until you take the two guineas.'

'If you absolutely insist on paying, it's two guineas less twenty per cent discount, which is,' Joey looked to the ceiling for a few seconds, 'one pound thirteen shillings and fourpence halfpenny, rounded down to the nearest halfpence.'

'That was quick.'

'I'm not just a handsome face, although that's all most girls see.' He lifted her cloak from her shoulders and held out the coat. She slipped her arms into the sleeves and fastened the buttons.

'You two ever coming?' Lloyd shouted impatiently. He glanced back at them. 'Nice coat, Rhian.'

'The girl has taste,' Joey agreed.

'Sali and the children are waiting.'

'One second and we'll be with you, Lloyd.' Joey stuffed Rhian's cloak into the bag. 'I forgot all about the toffees I bought for the children. See what a bad influence you are on me.' He set the tin on the hallstand.

'I'll pay you the two guineas for this or nothing at all.' Rhian gazed at herself in the hall mirror. The coat looked even better on her than she hoped it would. The fashionable slim cut flattered her trim figure and the sheen on the cloth gleamed in the electric light of the hall.

'Then I'll take nothing at all.' Joey crossed the hall and handed the butler the bag. 'Mr Jenkins, would you be kind enough to pass this on to someone who can use it.'

'Yes, Mr Evans.'

'Goodnight, Mr Jenkins.' Rhian caught up with Joey.

'Goodnight, Miss Rhian.' He gave her a rare and rusty smile.

'I'll still pay you the two guineas,' Rhian hissed as Joey helped her up the iron steps into the carriage.

'You will pay me exactly what I paid for the coat, and one more thing,' he whispered in her ear as she took his arm. 'Ask your Mrs Williams if you can change your day off with one of the other girls. And preferably not for a Friday or Saturday. A Tuesday or Wednesday would suit me perfectly.'

Bronwen bustled into the kitchen. 'More tea, toast and butter please, Cook.' She turned to Rhian. 'They've almost finished their porridge so you can take up the haddock but be warned, the mistress is in a worse mood than usual.'

'We don't need telling.' Meriel picked up the fish slice and began lifting the smoked haddock fillets from the milky stock she'd used to simmer them. 'I heard her shouting at the master when I went out to the *ty bach* half an hour ago. And the way she was yelling, I wouldn't be surprised if they were stuffing cotton wool into their ears at the top end of the valley.'

'I can understand the master marrying a woman half his age three months after the mistress passed on. After all, he's a man,' Bronwen declared, as if his sex was excuse enough. 'But what I can't understand is why the new mistress married him if she had no intention of sleeping in his bed.'

'You have no business discussing the master and mistress, Bronwen,' Mrs Williams reproved. 'Mr and Mrs Larch pay our wages, the least we can do is respect their privacy.'

'We're only talking among ourselves, and we all know what's going on.' Meriel eased a second haddock into the tureen. 'There's no way we wouldn't, given the way Mrs Larch screams blue murder whenever the master knocks her bedroom door. And when she starts on Miss Julia, Master Gerald or us, I think she's training to take a job as a caller on Ponty market.'

'Tea, toast and clear the porridge bowls before Rhian gets up there with the fish.' Mrs Williams filled Bronwen's tray and sent her out.

Rhian watched Meriel arrange the sixth and last fillet of smoked haddock in the tureen. She covered it with a lid, placed it on her tray and walked up the stairs. Bronwen was leaving the dining room with the empty bowls. She rolled her eyes heavenwards as she passed. Rhian knocked on the dining room door and opened it.

Silence, cold and glacial, had settled over the Larches' breakfast table, chilling the atmosphere and freezing out conversation. Rhian couldn't help but contrast the strained atmosphere with the friendly one the late mistress had fostered at family meals.

'At last!' Mabel Larch exclaimed. 'I thought we'd be here waiting at lunch-time.'

41

'Sorry, ma'am.' Rhian eased the tray on to one arm, lifted the lid of the tureen with the other and handed the mistress the fish slice and fork. Mabel helped herself to the largest fillet.

Julia gave Rhian a smile of commiseration when she carried the tureen to her chair. Julia took a small fillet. Edward Larch set aside the copy of *The Times* he had been reading and picked up the fish slice. The fillet broke as he tried to lift it, Rhian leaned forward in the hope of catching the broken piece on her tray but the tureen slipped and fell upside down on the carpet.

'You stupid girl!' Mabel Larch flew out of her chair and slapped Rhian soundly across the face with her right hand, which was holding a knife.

Shocked, momentarily stunned, Rhian stared at her mistress for a moment. As blood began to flow down her cheek, pain set in and she gulped back a sob. Dropping her tray on top of the tureen, she fled from the room across the hall and down the stairs barely aware of the master's shouts behind her.

'You're lucky you didn't lose your eye.' Mrs Williams pressed a tea towel soaked in cold water over the side of Rhian's face.

'Old witch! Hitting us! For two pins I'd back my bags and clear off right now,' said Meriel.

'I hope not after the time you've been here, Cook.' Edward Larch knocked the open door. 'May I come in?'

'This is your house, sir,' Mrs Williams said coldly.

'And the kitchen is your and Cook's preserve, Mrs Williams.' He studied Rhian with real concern. 'How are you?'

'As you see, sir.' Mrs Williams lifted the towel to reveal Rhian's bloodshot eye and bruised cheekbone.

'I have come to apologize for my wife's behaviour. She wasn't feeling well this morning.'

'If you don't mind me saying so, sir, that's a pathetic excuse,' Mrs Williams observed, anger overcoming her usual reserve with the master.

'I know I have no right to ask, but I was hoping that we could keep the knowledge of this incident within the house.' Edward looked to the housekeeper. When she remained silent, he added, 'I have no doubt that Mrs Larch will apologize to Rhian herself later in the day.'

'I will bring the matter up with Mrs Larch in Rhian's presence, sir,' Mrs Williams said firmly. 'I cannot have my staff treated in this fashion and I would prefer not to leave any of them alone with her in future.'

'You run the household as you see fit,' Edward conceded, in the hope of preventing any of them from walking out. 'Take the day off and rest, Rhian. You will let me know how she is this evening, Mrs Williams?'

'I will, sir.'

'I could tell my friends that I walked into a door,' Rhian suggested, hating the thought of anyone leaving Larch House because of what had happened to her.

'I would be grateful, Rhian,' Edward said quickly. 'My wife has retired to her room, Mrs Williams. I will tell her to expect you later on this morning.'

'You have finished breakfast, sir?' the housekeeper enquired pointedly.

'We have, Mrs Williams, thank you.'

'Then Bronwen and I will clear the table.' Mrs Williams signalled to Bronwen, who picked up two trays and handed one to the housekeeper. They followed the master up the stairs and into the hall where Gerald and Julia were dressing in their overcoats.

'Where are you going?' Edward asked.

'I promised Simon Rowan that I'd help him build a station for his model train set before term starts and I have to go back to school.' His stepmother's display of temper had embarrassed Gerald and he couldn't look his father in the eye.

Julia buttoned on her gloves. 'I promised Mrs Rowan that I would call into the vicarage some time to discuss the Sunday School arrangements for Easter. I know it's months away, but she likes to plan ahead.'

'Will you be in for lunch?' Edward glanced through the open dining room door. Mrs Williams had picked up the tureen, which was miraculously undamaged, and was heaping the fish back into it. If the carpet was stained, he couldn't see it.

'We thought we'd go on from the vicarage to Pontypridd, Father. Gerald wants to see *David Copperfield* in the Park Cinema and I'd like to treat him and Simon.'

'In that case, enjoy yourselves.' As it was obvious that neither of his children wanted to remain in the house with Mabel, Edward took a sovereign from his pocket and handed it to his son. 'You can treat your sister and Simon to lunch in the Park Hotel on me, Gerald.'

'Thank you, Father.'

'I'll see you at dinner. Mrs Williams, there's no point in laying the lunch table just for the mistress. Perhaps you could send a tray up to her room?'

'I will, sir.'

Edward waited until Julia and Gerald left the house, before climbing the stairs.

'If that is you, Edward, I am changing,' Mabel called out, when he knocked her bedroom door.

Edward turned the knob. The door held fast. He set his knee beneath the lock and pushed with all his strength. The doorframe splintered at his third attempt. Brushing shards of wood from his trousers, he walked in. Mabel leapt to her feet from the chaise longue, where she had been lying, reading a copy of *Woman's Weekly*. She tugged the neck of the robe she had changed into, high around her throat and tightened the belt.

'How dare you break in on me when I am resting in the privacy of my room!'

He pushed the door behind him. 'How dare you assault the staff in *my* house!'

'The girl was clumsy—'

'The girl was serving me and it was an accident.'

'What is the point of me working hard to refurbish your house when the servants ruin my new carpets?'

'Mrs Williams was cleaning the carpet when I left and it didn't look ruined to me.'

'It wouldn't. Men never see dirt, even when it's staring them in the face. I am mistress of this house—'

44

'You won't be mistress of anything if you slap any of the staff like that again, Mabel. You weren't even aware that you were holding a knife. You could have killed Rhian.'

'Rubbish!' The chill expression in his eyes unnerved her. 'You will be late for the office.'

'I think it more important that I deal with this situation. I told Mrs Williams you are unwell, and I have asked the servants not to mention what happened outside of this house.'

'Really, Edward, so much fuss for a slap the girl deserved.'

'Mrs Williams told me that she won't allow any of the maids to remain alone in a room with you.'

'And you agreed? You'd take her side—'

'This is not a question of sides but common decency. Did you ever hit any of your maids at your father's vicarage?' he demanded sternly. He'd regretted marrying Mabel on their wedding night, but it was only now that he was beginning to understand just what an act she'd put on when they'd met, and how little he really knew her.

'Father says they need to be chastized, like children.'

'Not in this house. Do I make myself clear? *Do I?*' he reiterated.

'You would allow that girl to go unpunished?'

'I have never punished anyone for an accident and I'm not about to start now. Stay here until Mrs Williams comes up. When she does, you will apologize not only to Rhian but also to her.'

'I will do no such thing,' she retorted warmly.

'Then you will leave this house.' He spoke quietly but there was no mistaking his resolve.

'As your wife I am entitled to your respect.'

'Respect has to be earned, Mabel, and you have done nothing whatsoever to earn it from the servants, the children, or,' he paused for the import of his words to sink in, 'me. Frankly, even before your appalling behaviour this morning, I was sorry I met you, let alone married you. Now, I can only wonder at my insanity in ever allowing you near me.'

'You promise you will tell us all about the show when you get back, Rhian?' Bronwen pleaded.

'I promise. But I don't doubt that it will be the same show that you and Cook saw last Thursday afternoon,' Rhian answered.

'If it's any different, I'll get Ianto to take me again this Thursday. He's on mornings in the pit this week. But then I might do that anyway. He hasn't seen it and it will give me an excuse to go again; it was really good.'

Rhian went to the window. It was a Tuesday morning in early April, over three months since she had spent her first day off with Joey. The sun was shining, the few clouds in the sky wispy and white, but the trees that bordered the garden were dipping and swaying alarmingly in the wind.

'If you're checking the weather, Rhian, I can tell you now, it's bitter out there.' Mrs Williams waved to the milkman, closed the kitchen door and dropped his account book into the dresser drawer where she kept the tradesmen's records. 'Williams the milk was just saying it's a north wind that's blowing, making it colder out there than it was last month.'

'But it looks as though it's going to be dry.' Rhian refused to let the temperature spoil the day ahead that she and Joey had planned.

'It does,' Mrs Williams agreed. 'But it's also going to be freezing in the Malsters' Field in Pontypridd. So don't go thinking that you can dress for spring. That blouse is far too thin.'

'Not with this jacket, Mrs Williams.' Rhian slipped the cardigan of her knitted suit over the cream blouse Sali had given her.

'I suppose not, provided you wear your winter coat and muffler on top.'

'I intend to, Mrs Williams.'

'You going to call in on Mrs Evans?'

'We are.' Rhian smiled.

Mrs Williams thrust a package at her. 'Something small I made for the new arrival, I only hope it still fits her. I never knit a stitch until after the birth for fear of tempting fate and the way the mistress has been lately it's taken me two weeks to finish it.'

'Whatever it is, I'm sure Sali and baby Edyth will love it.' Rhian smiled.

'I wish I was going to Broncho Bill's Great Wild West Exhibition,' Mair sighed enviously.

'Isn't your mam taking you tomorrow?' Mrs Williams poured herself and Mair second cups of tea.

'She is, but it won't be like going today. Just think, real-life Cowboys and Indians, in Ponty, like in the pictures.'

'Not like in the pictures, Mair, because they are real. You wait until you see the Indians, Rhian, and the attack on the Deadwood Coach, and there's an Indian girl who's the best woman shot in the West—'

'Let the poor girl see them for herself, Cook,' Mrs Williams admonished.

Rhian wrapped a white mohair muffler around her throat and pulled on the beret and gloves she'd knitted to match it.

'You did a good job on that accessory set, Rhian. You couldn't have bought better in any shop in Cardiff.' Mrs Williams sniffed loudly and Rhian sensed she was about to make one of her disparaging remarks about Joey. 'I suppose you're going with—'

'Joey Evans, Mrs Williams, yes.' Rhian unclipped her handbag and slipped the package the housekeeper had given her into it.

'Well, I give him this much, if he has been out with any other girls since he's been walking out with you, he's kept them well hidden these last thirteen weeks. But that's not to say they don't exist, mind.'

'We are just friends, Mrs Williams.'

'So you keep saying.'

Rhian went cold at the thought of Joey paying court to another girl. She saw the housekeeper watching her, and repeated, 'We really are just friends, Mrs Williams.'

'You may think so, my girl, but I don't believe for one minute that friendship is all that boy has on his mind. Has he ever talked to you about his intentions?'

'Friends don't have intentions. They go out together and have a good time.'

'Speak of the devil and he appears.' Mrs Williams shouted, 'Come in,' at the door.

Joey removed his trilby and smiled. 'Good morning, Mrs Williams, Bronwen, Meriel, Mair.'

47

'Is it a good morning, Joey Evans? I hadn't noticed,' Mrs Williams replied flatly.

'It's beautiful, Mrs Williams. Cold, crisp and clear.'

'Never mind the weather, just you take good care of Rhian.' The housekeeper picked a thread of lint from Rhian's coat. 'You'll be in by ten.'

'I'll have her safely back by then, Mrs Williams.'

'See that you do. Have a good time, Rhian, and make sure he behaves himself.' The housekeeper closed the door behind them.

'Rhian's so lucky.' Mair gave another of her theatrical sighs. 'Beautiful clothes, a handsome boyfriend who looks like a matinée idol—'

'The first lesson every young girl should learn is "handsome is as handsome does,"' Mrs Williams interrupted briskly. 'And Joey Evans has a long way to go before he'll convince me that he's changed his wandering ways. Now if we're going to get the upstairs breakfast served on time, we have to get our skates on. Mair, clear this table; Bronwen, lay the table in the breakfast room. I'll check the menu with Cook and set up the trays.'

'I think Mrs Williams is actually beginning to like me.' Joey took Rhian's hand and nestled it in the crook of his arm as they walked down the drive of Llan House.

'I don't know how you can say that. She's downright rude to you.'

'It's not what she says; it's the way she says it. I can tell that underneath it all, she's fond of me.' He pulled two tickets from his inside pocket and waved them under her nose. 'The best seats, undercover . . .'

'Bronwen said all the seats are undercover. They've put up the most enormous marquee that seats ten thousand people.'

'Some seats are more undercover than others,' he continued unabashed. 'The most expensive have the best view of both rings. And *these* are the most expensive and comfortable. The man at the box office promised me that we'd get cushions.'

'I hope we also get space. Bronwen said the tent was packed so full when she went with Meriel they had difficulty drawing breath.'

'I'm surprised anyone can draw breath around Cook, given the size of her. She probably swallows all the available oxygen for miles around.'

'That is cruel. She can't help her size.'

'She doesn't overeat?' Joey asked in surprise.

'No more than the rest of us.' Furious with Joey, Rhian wasn't prepared to let the matter drop. 'Looks aren't everything, Joey. You might be handsome but as Mrs Williams says—'

'Handsome is as handsome does,' he chanted in a bored tone. 'I wish I had a penny for every time she has said that about me. And I can't help the way I look any more than Cook can.'

'No, but—'

'What?' He stopped walking and stood in front of her.

'You could try to be nicer.' As always, whenever he looked her directly in the eye, she became flustered.

'I thought I was always nice to you,' he said softly.

'Well, you're not,' she countered.

'Tell me how I can be nicer?'

'By walking me to the station in time to buy chocolates for the children, and catch the early train so we can visit Sali before the show.'

'We said we'd have lunch with Sali, not breakfast.' Despite his protest he stepped back and offered her his arm again.

'I'd like to spend some time with Bella and Edyth.'

'The doting aunt.'

'And why not?' she retorted in indignation.

'I spoke as the doting uncle. What is the matter with you? I thought we'd planned the perfect day out and you're spitting pins and needles.'

'Nothing's the matter with me,' she retorted unconvincingly.

'Mrs Williams been having a go at you about me again?'

'No more than usual.'

'Perhaps she'll leave off after today.'

She didn't ask him to explain his remark because she guessed what he meant. But she had absolutely no idea how she would react when he brought the subject up again.

*

49

Rhian refused Joey's offer to hire a cab when they arrived in Pontypridd and insisted on walking to Ynysangharad House. When they left the top end of Taff Street, she stepped off Victoria Bridge, which carried traffic over the River Taff, and climbed the steep steps of the Old Bridge alongside it. A crowd of small boys in ragged clothes were leaning precariously over the edge of the stone parapet, trying to see the animals tethered at the back of the enormous marquee that almost filled the Malsters' Field.

'. . . My granddad saw Buffalo Bill's show in Cardiff when he was young and he said they had real buffaloes. They were 'normous.' One of the urchins sketched an outline in the air to indicate just how enormous a buffalo was.

'I doubt there are any buffaloes in Broncho Bill's show.' Joey pulled the boy back from the edge before he plunged into the river fifty feet below. 'If there were, the *Observer* would have printed pictures of them. And they only mentioned horses.'

'I know there aren't any,' one boy smaller and thinner than the rest said authoritatively. 'But there is a band, Prairie Bob's Great Cowboy Band. They're real cowboys, with guns and hats and everything. I saw them and heard them play.' He held out his hand. 'Give us sixpence, mister, and I'll show you a place where you can crawl under the tent and see the show for free.'

Joey looked at Rhian. 'What do you say? Shall we crawl under the tent and see the show for free?'

'Most certainly not. You'll be sorry if a policeman catches you. You'll get half a dozen strokes of the birch,' she lectured the boy.

'Thanks for the offer, son, but it would spoil the lady's dress. But here you go.' Joey opened the tin of toffees he had bought for Bella and Harry and handed each of the boys a sweet.

'You do realize that you've just rewarded criminal behaviour,' Rhian informed him when they reached the other side of the river.

'My brothers and I did a lot worse than sneak under a circus tent to see a show for free when we were kids.'

'Lloyd and Victor criminals? I don't believe it.'

'Thank you. From that comment I take it that you think I'm capable of worse than them. But believe you me, my brothers weren't always the upright citizens they are now. Shall we walk up to the house alongside the canal? I know it's cold but the primroses might be out and we can pick a bunch for Sali if they are.'

'All right.' She tried to sound casual. The canal walk to the house was longer, prettier – and more secluded than the main drive.

He took her hand when they left Bridge Street. 'It's times like this I realize just how little fresh air there is in Tonypandy, especially in the store, and most especially between the perfume and shoe and luggage departments. Between the smell of leather and the scents of violet, gardenia and attar of roses it's a wonder I can breathe.'

'Perhaps you should move the departments further apart.'

'That, madam, would make for too much work.' He dropped her hand, picked up a stone and tossed it into the narrow canal.

'If everyone did that, there'd soon be no canal for the barges to float on.'

'One stone – and it's probably already sunk deep into the mud.'

'It's one stone more than was there a minute ago,' she said with mock gravity. 'If the canal fills up, everyone will know who to blame.'

He picked up another stone and pressed it into her hand. 'Go on, try it. It's fun. I promise not to tell if you don't.'

'You just want to make me as guilty as you are.'

'Of course.'

'I refuse.' She dropped the stone on to the path.

'Have you ever thought how one tiny instant can change your whole life?'

'Like throwing one small stone?'

He brushed his gloves together to rid them of the dirt he'd picked up, opened his coat and took a small box from his inside pocket. She looked from the box into his face and froze. She sensed what he was about to say and she was terrified. All she wanted was for things to remain as they were, but she knew that nothing she could say would stop him. Not now. But that didn't prevent her from trying.

'Please, don't, Joey!' She didn't hear herself speak and she knew her plea had remained unspoken.

'You changed my life that day we escaped the sales and went into the tea shop. I knew I loved you before then, but that morning I realized that I didn't want to live without you. I hope you'll accept this, even though it's everything a lady should reject,' he warned with mock gravity. 'It's too valuable to be a token. And it's not something that you can use and discard like perfume, sweets, chocolates or a handkerchief.' He opened the box and she stared, mesmerized by the ring nestling on its bed of worn black velvet.

'I know it's old-fashioned but it was my mother's. And that's why I hope you'd like and wear it.'

'I couldn't possibly accept a family heirloom from you. What would your father and brothers say?' She gasped, finally finding her voice.

'My father gave it to me, just as he gave Lloyd my mother's wedding band for Sali and her engagement ring to Victor for Megan. This was my mother's regard ring. He bought it for her when they started courting. Apparently they were all the rage thirty odd years ago and they were called regard rings because the stones spell out the word "regard".' He pointed to the gems set in a simple gold band. 'Ruby, emerald, garnet, amethyst, another ruby and finally a small but real diamond. Most of my father's friends gave their girlfriends paste rings set with glass, but he said that he knew my mother was the only girl for him from the moment he set eyes on her, so he bought her the real thing. She deserved it, and,' he dropped the mocking note from his voice, 'so do you.'

'It's beautiful, Joey.'

'It's not an engagement ring, but I thought you'd prefer to choose your own. I also hoped you'd like this one enough to wear it as well. Do you like it?'

She nodded dumbly.

'And a lady could accept it and remain a lady, provided she agreed to marry the man who gave to her.'

'You're really asking me to marry you!' Unwilling to believe what was happening, beset by a bewildering mix of emotions she turned aside.

'If you won't, I've been wasting my time for the last three months and more.' He then did something he hadn't done in all the days they had spent together. He wrapped his arms around her and kissed her.

The trees, the bank, the water swirled in a kaleidoscope of brilliant, sun-drenched spring colours, Dizzy and faint, she clung to him as the scent of his cologne filled her nostrils and the warmth of his body percolated to hers even though the thick layers of clothing they were wearing.

'You will marry me?' He drew his head back from hers and looked down at her.

Her voice rasped with suppressed emotion but there was no mistaking the finality of her reply. 'No, Joey, I'm sorry, but I can't.'

Chapter 4

'MRS LARCH, MISS Larch, I have personally supervised the loading of your purchases into your carriage.' Geraint Watkin Jones, the assistant manager of the Pontypridd branch of Gwilym James, breezed past the doorman and escorted the two ladies into Market Square where their coachman, Harris, was waiting.

'Thank you, Mr Watkin Jones.' Julia gave him a tentative smile.

'Come along, Julia, I've booked a table for lunch in the Park Hotel, and we've no time to spare if we are to meet your father in time for the exhibition this afternoon.' Mabel Larch climbed the steps the coachman had unfolded and entered the carriage.

Julia took the hand her stepmother had spurned and allowed Geraint to help her inside.

'Hope to see you again, and very soon, Mrs Larch. Miss Larch. It was a pleasure, as always, to wait on you.' Geraint watched the coachman fold the iron steps and close the door. The Larches' carriage rounded the corner into Taff Street and he turned back to the store.

Having been brought up to expect to lead a gentleman's life with an income sufficient to indulge his whims as well as cater for his needs, he detested having to work. But his uncle, who had also been his guardian, had gambled away the fortune his father had left him before he had been old enough to take possession of it.

He hated having to take orders from the store manager, Mr Horton. He hated seeing his sister, Sali – Mrs Sali Evans, since she had married a common collier for all that she called him an engineer – greet staff, customers and suppliers as if she actually enjoyed debasing herself by serving those born beneath her. But

54

above all, he hated having to bow, scrape and be pleasant to people who wouldn't have dared approach his father's front door, and would have been diffident about knocking on the tradesman's entrance at the back.

'Taking the air, Mr Watkin Jones?' Mr Horton joined him.

'I saw Mrs and Miss Larch into their carriage,' Geraint prevaricated.

'Didn't they leave some time ago?'

'As they are valued customers, I took the time to exchange a few pleasantries with them, Mr Horton.'

'You exchanged pleasantries with the new Mrs Larch?' Mr Horton enquired suspiciously. It was common knowledge that Mrs Larch regarded people in trade so far beneath her; he doubted that she had exchanged a pleasantry with a shop assistant in her life. 'May I remind you that your time is Gwilym James's time, Mr Watkin Jones. They are short-staffed in household linens. Perhaps you'd be good enough to assist the supervisor in bringing down more stock.'

Geraint gave the only answer he could before returning to the store but the words almost choked him. 'Yes, Mr Horton.'

Joey strode along the canal bank ahead of Rhian. When the strain of the silence that had fallen between them and the effort of trying to keep up with him became too much, she halted.

'If you don't want to spend the rest of the day with me, I'll understand,' she shouted at his back.

He turned a stony face to hers. 'Are you refusing to marry me because of my reputation?'

'Partly,' she answered honestly.

'And the other part?'

'Because when you're in this mood, I don't want to know you.'

'Surely you don't expect me to take your refusal to marry me with a smile on my face after we've been walking out together for three months?'

'We went out together as friends,' she protested.

'You said we were friends, Rhian, not me.'

'What was I supposed to think when you've never even tried to kiss me before now?' Emotionally and physically drained, wishing she could take back her thoughtless remark; she leaned against an ivy-clad oak for support.

'So, you wanted me to kiss you?' He rested his hand above her head.

She looked up into his eyes, dark and enigmatic in the muted green light beneath the trees.

'Did you want me to try and kiss you?' he reiterated softly.

'We were just friends,' she repeated hollowly.

'I had hoped we could be a whole lot more.' When she refused to meet his gaze, he stepped back, took off his hat and ran his fingers through his thick black curls. 'Obviously you didn't feel the same way.'

'I never thought about it,' she lied.

'And that's it? You don't like my past and it's "thanks for the good times, Joey, and goodbye?"'

'Don't put words into my mouth.'

'You wouldn't think any the worse of me if I'd sneaked around with girls behind everyone's back, because you wouldn't have known about them,' he said defensively.

'You tried sneaking round with the married ones but the gossips found you out.' Rhian couldn't resist reminding him of the rumours that credited him with destroying several marriages, including his neighbour's and the local schoolmaster's.

'The damned gossips have never left me alone. Sometimes I wonder who they would have talked about if I'd never been born.' He paced to the canal and stared into its murky waters before turning back to her. 'For what it's worth, I never made love to a woman who didn't want me to, and if some of them happened to be married, all I can say is they couldn't have had much of a marriage if they wanted to spend time with me.'

'That doesn't make what you did right,' she reproached.

'No, it doesn't, but it took two of us to break the rules and I'm the only one on trial here.'

'You're not on trial.'

'No, I'm not,' he concurred bitterly. 'You've convicted and sentenced me without even bothering to listen to my side of the story.'

'It's not just the gossip, Joey. Listen to yourself, there's no reasoning with you when you're in this mood.'

'Is it any wonder I'm angry? The old wives in Tonypandy credit me with seducing half the women in the Rhondda. Not to mention all the barmaids and every chorus girl who has ever danced in the Empire, and you choose to believe them. Stupid, narrow-minded gossips have led such sheltered lives they've no idea how impossible it is to seduce an unwilling woman.'

'You've tried?' Her pathetic attempt to lighten the atmosphere fell flat.

He looked her in the eye again. 'You were the most difficult of all. But I fooled myself that I'd succeeded.'

'It's been wonderful going out with you. I've had some really good times.' Her intended compliment sounded patronizing.

'And that's all I was to you, the provider of a good time on your day off?'

'I know gossips exaggerate, Joey, but you have to admit you've been wild. And as we only see one another once a week, I wasn't sure that I was the only girl you were walking out with.'

'I told you that I wanted our relationship to be special—'

'Yes, you did. The first afternoon we spent together. How was I to know that you were serious?'

'Dear God, you thought I was joking!' He stared up at the sky. 'You want to know something? Right this minute I'm sorry that I ever looked at another woman before I fell in love with you, but I can't turn the clock back.' He took the ring box from his pocket and held it out to her. 'You won't reconsider?'

'Not now, Joey.'

'Perhaps sometime in the future?' He clutched at the possibility.

'Maybe . . . I don't know.' She knew that even if she made an effort to ignore the gossip and jokes about Joey's past, she wouldn't forget how angry the girl in the sweetshop, Sara, had been with him. Or the warning she'd given her about going out with him. And in the last few months Joey had been forced to introduce her to dozens of 'Saras'.

And there was the way that the girls who worked in Gwilym James flocked around him every time he walked on to the shop floor. She couldn't help feeling that he revelled in their adoration. And she knew that she would find it difficult, if not downright impossible, to live with a husband who constantly sought and needed the attention of other women.

'You've made up your mind, haven't you?' he broke in on her thoughts. 'Nothing that I say or do will make the slightest difference.'

'Please, Joey, don't let this spoil our day.'

'My day's already spoilt,' he retorted acidly. 'But what the hell? Sali's expecting us for lunch. And, as I already have the tickets, we may as well go to the exhibition. It's good of you to give a condemned man the pleasure of your company for a last good time.'

Tonia George glanced surreptitiously at her reflection in the mirror behind the display of ladies' hats. Her 'uniform' of plain black ankle-length wool skirt, crisply starched white cotton blouse and black bow tie was immaculate. Her shoes gleamed with polish, her stocking seams were straight and her hair was neatly tied back with a bow that matched her tie. She had been working in the hat department of Gwilym James's Pontypridd store since the middle of February. She had preferred it to Tonypandy from the outset. And not only because her supervisor, Miss Adams, was less strict than Miss Robertson.

She glanced up, ostensibly looking out for customers while secretly studying Geraint Watkin Jones. He too was perfectly turned out in a grey pinstripe suite, stiff white starched high collar and broad knotted grey silk tie. When he stopped to speak to Mr Hughes, who was putting the final touches to a display of mannequins in tennis clothes, she listened intently. Mr Watkin Jones's voice was too low for her to hear what he was saying but not too low to make out his beautifully modulated tones.

'Mr Watkin Jones is a real gentleman, isn't he?' Miss Adams whispered.

Tonia realized that she had been too obvious in her admiration. 'He is.'

'Did you know that he had a fortune and a big house? His uncle lost the lot before he was old enough to inherit. And now he has to work for a living. It's such a pity.'

'Why is it a pity that he has to work for a living?' their junior, Belinda asked. 'We do.'

'We weren't brought up to expect better, Belinda. And juniors never speak unless they are asked a direct question.' Miss Adams handed her a duster. 'Polish that mirror.'

Tonia sneaked another look at the assistant manager. His features were clean-cut, his eyes and hair a deep rich brown. As Miss Adams had said, he looked a real gentleman, and although there was no difference between the cut of his suit and Mr Hughes's, it was obvious that Geraint belonged to a superior class. The only wonder was that she could have ever believed herself in love with Joey, when there were men like Geraint Watkin Jones around. But then, she had never met anyone quite like him before.

Miss Howard from ladies' fashions commandeered Miss Adams and Belinda to ferry hats to a private fitting room for a bridal party who were co-ordinating their outfits, leaving her with an elderly lady who insisted on trying on every black hat they had in stock.

When the lady moved on after an hour without making a single purchase Tonia could have screamed. She had observed the Gwilym James' rule of replacing every hat in its allotted display position as soon as it had been rejected. But the lady's companion hadn't. And while she'd been trying to please her customer, the irritating woman had repositioned most of the hats, ruining the entire display.

'Miss George?' Geraint handed her a hat that had fallen behind a chair.

'Thank you, Mr Watkin Jones.'

'I will be needing help this afternoon with the stocktaking. I hope you don't mind me asking Miss Adams if you can be spared.'

'Not at all, Mr Watkin Jones.'

'I am glad to hear it.' He walked on but glanced back after he'd taken a few paces. Lowering his eyelid, he gave her an unmistakeable, if inappropriate to Gwilym James, wink.

Her spirits soared. But then she knew exactly what that wink meant.

*

'What's the matter with Joey?' Sali asked Rhian, after he left for the stables with Harry, who was home for the Easter holidays, and Mari had carried Bella and Edyth off to the nursery for their afternoon naps.

'We had a few words before we came here.' Rhian followed Sali into her bedroom.

'Judging by the look on your faces, they weren't good ones. Here, sit on the stool and I'll brush out your hair for you,' Sali offered.

Rhian opened her handbag, found her hairbrush and comb and handed them to Sali.

'Anything Lloyd or I can do to help?' Sali asked.

Rhian bit her lip thoughtfully. She needed advice from someone and if any other man had asked her to marry him she would have gone straight to Sali. But Joey was Lloyd's brother . . . 'Promise you won't tell anyone, not even Lloyd,' she begged.

'Not if you don't want me to.' Sali crossed her fingers in the hope that Rhian wasn't about to confide a secret she'd find impossible to keep from her husband.

'Joey asked me to marry him.'

'And you said no.'

'It was so sudden, so unexpected.' Even as Rhian came out with the excuses, she felt they were ludicrous when she considered that she had spent every minute of her free time with Joey since January.

'You never thought that he might be falling in love with you?'

'No . . . yes . . . But there's his reputation . . .'

'Which I thought might have put off any sensible girl from walking as far as the corner shop with him. But given the number of girlfriends he's had, it didn't deter them – or you.' Sali spoke quietly in an attempt to soften the sting.

'I like Joey, he's fun to be with and, as I said the first time we came here together, we agreed to go out together as friends.'

'You might have thought you were friends, I'm sure Joey never did.'

'So he told me this morning,' Rhian said sadly.

'So what happens now? Given the way he behaved at lunch I hardly think you can go to Broncho Bill's Wild West Exhibition and have a good time.' Sali removed the last pin from Rhian's hair and allowed her curls to fall to her waist.

'We can go to the exhibition but a good time is out,' Rhian agreed.

'I wouldn't like to say which one of you looks the most miserable.' Sali began to brush Rhian's hair from the bottom up, gently teasing out the tangles. 'I've suspected for months that he loves you.'

'Why didn't you say something?' Rhian picked up the hairpins she'd dropped on Sali's tray and made a neat row that she pushed between her fingers.

'Would you have listened, or repeated that you were just friends?'

'Probably repeated that we were just friends,' Rhian conceded miserably.

'I know Joey. He wouldn't have asked you to marry him if he didn't love you. The question is: do you love him?' Sali twisted a strand of hair into a neat curl that she pinned at the nape of Rhian's neck.

Rhian hesitated before answering. Joey might be Sali's brother-in-law, but Sali knew his faults as well, if not better, than most of the women he'd gone out with. 'Joey's had so many girlfriends. You have no idea what's it's like being the latest in a long line. No matter where we go, a shop, a café, a hotel, Tonypandy, Pontypridd or Cardiff, it makes no difference; there's always at least one girl who knows him and from the snide remarks, better than she should.'

'But you knew it would be like that that before you agreed to go out with him.'

'Yes, but—'

'You're not sure that you can forgive him his past?'

'Life's so unfair for women.' Rhian waited until Sali had finished pinning up her hair before turning on the stool and looking up at her. 'On the one hand there's poor Jinny—'

'Who is poor Jinny?' Sali interrupted.

'One of Bronwen's sisters – the girl I share with in Llan House. She was a maid at the vicarage. She went out with the same boy for over a year, but the moment he found out that she was having his baby he cleared off. Her mistress threw her out, her father refused to allow her to come home, so she had no choice but to go to the workhouse. If she's lucky they'll find her a job after the baby's born but she'll have to leave it in the orphanage and no man will ever look at her the same way again. Overnight she's gone from being a "good" girl to a "bad" one. Yet boys like Joey can sleep with as many women as they like and no one thinks any the worse of them.'

'I do,' Sali countered firmly. 'And the same goes for Joey's father and brothers. Until he started going out with you they were always lecturing him about his behaviour.'

'But it didn't do any good.'

'It didn't until January. But you were the one who said "boys like Joey". Fair or not, generally people don't think any the less of a boy for sowing his wild oats, which is why most of them behave so badly. I'm not making excuses for Joey. He's behaved worse than most and he's certainly been talked about more than any other boy in Tonypandy. If a girl tried to do a fraction of the things he's done, she'd be ostracized from decent society and sent to the workhouse for moral re-education.'

'My point exactly.'

'I agree with you, dual standards are unacceptable. It's appalling that girls are treated differently from boys when it comes to courting, marriage and a million and one other things, like education and jobs. That's why I've joined the suffragettes. But I'm not optimistic enough to think that the world is going to change overnight.'

'You've joined the suffragettes?'

'Yes, and we'll have a long talk about it some other time.' It was the last thing Sali wanted to discuss at that moment. 'You knew about Joey's past before you went out with him. Why should it bother you now?'

'Because it's now that he's asked me to marry him.'

'And you're worried that if you do, he'll carry on the way he did when he was single?' she asked perceptively.

'Yes.' Rhian left the stool and went to the window that overlooked the rose garden. The bushes were in leaf but the wind was giving them such a battering she wondered if they'd survive long enough to flower. 'You don't have to answer this if you don't want to, but did Lloyd have lots of girlfriends before you married him?'

'He was twenty-eight,' Sali reminded her. 'And I was hardly a virgin after having Harry. Lloyd forgave me my past and I forgave him his. No – forgave is not the right word,' she corrected. 'Lloyd made me see that what happened before we married wasn't relevant to our life together.'

'The women Lloyd walked out with. Do you know who they are?'

'If you mean Lloyd's lovers,' Sali said bluntly, 'yes. But when Lloyd and I fell in love he told them it was over. I never think about them and I am certain that he doesn't. But then Lloyd and I trust one another implicitly. If you don't mind me saying so, it's obvious that you don't trust Joey.'

'I'd like to.'

'Have you tried telling him how you feel?'

'Yes.' Rhian left the window and walked back to the dressing table.

'But Joey Evans's infamous and irrational temper got in the way.'

Rhian would have liked to agree with Sali but she felt that it would somehow be disloyal to Joey.

'Try to talk to him again,' Sali counselled.

'But that would make me sound like a nagging wife before we even marry.' She picked up her hairbrush and returned it to her bag.

'That sounds to me like you're seriously considering his offer. And a wife should be able to talk about anything to her husband, even at the risk of being called a nag.' Sali glanced at the bedside clock. 'If you're ready, we'll go and find Joey. Harry's probably dragged him off to the stables to see the colt that was born the day before yesterday. He spends so much time down there with Robert, I suspect we're going to have trouble getting him back to school when the summer term starts.'

'Perhaps Harry could come with us to the show—'

'Absolutely not,' Sali said. 'For a start you haven't a ticket for him and he's seen it twice already. Lloyd and I took him and Bella, and then my solicitor, Mr Richards, turned up with tickets for himself and Harry. He insisted a client had given them to him but I think he bought them because he wanted to see the show and used Harry as an excuse.'

'You can't blame him. I've heard that it's very good.' Rhian checked her hair in the mirror.

'It is, but as it doesn't start for another hour, I suggest that you and Joey walk very slowly from here to the Malsters' Field.'

'It's a ten-minute walk.'

'It will take you the other fifty to sort out your differences.'

'You think I should marry him, don't you?'

'Oh no,' Sali smiled, 'you don't put that one on me. Whether or not you should marry Joey, or any man come to that, is entirely your decision.'

'But you would like me to marry him,' Rhian persisted.

Sali kissed Rhian's cheek then opened the door. 'I am blissfully happy with Lloyd and the children but that doesn't mean I think marriage suits everyone. I have no idea if it will suit you, or Joey. All I want is for both of you to be happy. And the only advice I can give you is to think very carefully before you agree to marry him, or anyone.'

'Julia, have you heard a single word I've said?' Mabel Larch demanded imperiously.

Julia looked up from her Palestine Soup. 'You were telling me that you wished you'd bought the green silk evening gown as well as the blue velvet.'

'The cut was perfect.' Mabel crumbled her bread roll into small pieces.

'You did say that you disliked the colour,' Julia ventured.

'I could have had it dyed. I really don't know why you bothered to come shopping with me, you're no company and you've bought hardly anything.'

Julia refrained from reminding Mabel that she'd only joined her at her insistence, and then in the hope that it would put her step-mother in a less aggressive mood, and consequently make her father's life a little easier. 'I purchased everything I needed.'

'A few sets of exceedingly ugly underwear,' Mabel said. 'You should have bought some evening wear. You can't keep wearing that figured black velvet. It's positively drab, not to mention years out of date.'

'The necks on all the gowns my size were too low.' Acutely aware of her lack of cleavage, Julia only wore high collars.

'They were classic styles. I simply don't understand why you persist in covering yourself neck to toe like a nun. And in mourning! You're not getting any younger. The way you carry on, you'll be living with me and your father when you are in your dotage. No one likes an old maid, and that's what you will be in another year or two. Sometimes, when I look at the way you dress and behave I wonder if you are there already.'

Aware that her stepmother wanted both her and her brother out of the house, and wishing to avoid an argument on the subject, Julia refrained from biting back.

'It's a woman's duty to dress well, and it's not as if you haven't the money. Just look at what you're wearing now. That black drains what little colour you have and there's more shape to a collier's cloth cap than that hat you're wearing. You never put on as much as a dab of perfume . . .'

Julia recalled the pressure Mr Watkin Jones had exerted on her fingers when he had helped her into the carriage, the warmth of his smile when he stood watching them drive away and his final words: *Hope to see you again, and very soon, Mrs Larch. Miss Larch. It was a pleasure, as always, to wait on you.*

'. . . Of course, he's heard that you've inherited an absolute fortune from your mother.'

'Who?' Confused, Julia looked across at her stepmother.

'Mr Geraint Watkin Jones. You don't think he is that attentive to all the customers, do you? He knows you're wealthy and practically on the shelf. And he's astute enough to realize that a girl with your looks hasn't been overwhelmed with suitors.'

'No one with a brain in their head could think that.' Julia didn't quite succeed in keeping the bitterness from her voice.

'Mr Watkin Jones may as well pin an advertisement on his back: "Rich wife wanted for gentleman who has fallen on hard times." Mrs Hadley was only telling me last week in the Ladies' Circle that she had to ask her husband to speak to him after he started bothering her daughter, Elizabeth.'

'Elizabeth Hadley has a tongue in her head. Couldn't she tell Mr Watkin Jones to stop bothering her, herself?'

The irony was lost on Mabel. 'Geraint Watkin Jones ignored the Hadleys when he had Danygraig House and his fortune. Yet, six months ago, when Elizabeth Hadley celebrated her twenty-first birthday and it was all round the town that she'd inherited her grandfather's farm and coach-building business, Mr Watkin Jones became exceedingly attentive. He changed pews in St Catherine's so he could sit behind her in church. He wrote his name against every one of the waltzes on Elizabeth's dance card at the Christmas Charity Ball. He even had the gall to invite her to the moving pictures, and when Mr Hadley told him that he wouldn't allow his daughter to step out with a young man she wasn't acquainted with, Mr Watkin Jones invited the entire Hadley family to dine with him and his mother in the annex of Ynysangharad House. Everyone knows that before she died, his mother hadn't left her bed in years, and his sister and her family lived entirely separate from them, so it effectively meant that he'd be their host. I ask you, a shop assistant, inviting the Hadleys to dine.'

'But he does live in Ynysangharad House,' Julia said in Geraint's defence.

'Not for much longer, according to Mrs Hadley. His sister and the trustees of her son's estate are anxious to shut up the wing that he and his mother occupied. I can't say I'm surprised. It's obvious that they were living on his sister's or rather nephew's charity and now the mother's gone, there's no earthly reason why he should continue to reside there. Lodgings are good enough for a shop assistant. Mrs Hadley said that the family has gone to the dogs since their uncle lost their money. The eldest girl married to that miner—'

'Mr Evans is an engineer and he does business with Father.'

'Unfortunately business dictates that your father has to deal with all sorts of unsuitable people.'

'Father's solicitors' practice makes most of its money from colliery business.' Julia suppressed the temptation to remind her stepmother that colliery business had paid for the gowns she had just purchased.

'Your father has made many sacrifices for you and your brother. And I think it's high time you both contributed more to the household expenses now that you have taken possession of your mother's fortune—'

Julia stopped listening as her stepmother continued to expound arguments that had become all too familiar. She hadn't needed Mabel's warning about Geraint Watkin Jones's intentions, any more than she'd needed to hear her disparaging judgement on her appearance.

She wondered if it would it be so terrible to have a husband who'd only married her for her money? At least he would have cause to be grateful to her. Geraint Watkin Jones was tall, good-looking and had been brought up as a gentleman, even if he had come down in the world. The fortune she had inherited on her mother's death, which Mabel so bitterly resented, would enable them to buy a decent house anywhere they chose and fund a comfortable lifestyle. They could have carriages, servants, fine furniture and clothes, and possibly even a social life that included real friends.

Closing her ears to Mabel's prattling, she imagined herself walking into a ballroom with her arm resting on Geraint's, sitting next to him in a theatre box, travelling to a seaside resort in the summer – and lying next to him in bed. She knew about her father's problems with Mabel. Everyone in the house did, because there was no escaping their increasingly ugly rows. Could sharing a bed with a man possibly be as awful as Mabel said?

If that was the case, why had her mother never complained? And what about all the other married women she was acquainted with who seemed to be happy? People like Sali Evans, who was always laughing and smiling whenever she appeared with her husband at the town's social and charitable events.

She couldn't help pitying her father, even if it was his own fault that he was tied to Mabel. But then he, like her, had found himself marooned in a terrible emotional wasteland after her mother's death. They had been too crushed to reach out to one another for comfort, because each had been deeply enmeshed in their own selfish grief. She suspected that he had turned to Mabel because he had been unbearably lonely, and the one thing she understood only too well was the desperation of absolute loneliness.

Geraint Watkin Jones was kind and attentive, even if he was only after her money, and Mabel was reason enough for her to leave her father's house. She was of age and able to dictate her own destiny. The only problem was how could she see more of Geraint without exciting Mabel's suspicions? Because if Mabel discovered what she was up to, she would take great delight in telling her father that his only daughter had developed an interest in an 'unsuitable' man.

She knew her father would realize that Geraint was only after her money, and that would lead to even more arguments in the house, between them, as well as between him and Mabel. If she pretended to shop, Mabel would accompany her, and Geraint Watkin Jones would never dare to invite her anywhere while they remained within Mabel's earshot. It was up to her. She would have to wait for an opportunity – or make one. And when it came, swallow her pride and risk incurring her stepmother's wrath by inviting Mr Watkin Jones to spend time with her.

As Sali had predicted, they found Harry and Joey in the stables with Robert, Ynysangharad House's groom-cum-chauffeur. Harry was perched on Joey's shoulders and all three were gazing into the stall where the new foal was tottering around his mother on unsteady legs.

'Come and see Toffee, Auntie Rhian,' Harry shouted when he spotted her in the doorway with his mother.

'That's a strange name for a horse.' Rhian glanced sideways at Joey as she stood alongside them.

'Dad said I could name him and ride him as soon he's old

enough to be broken in. I called him Toffee because of his colour,' Harry explained.

'The exact same shade as the toffee Mari makes from Golden Syrup.' Sali stood the other side of Joey and her son. 'I think you're more enamoured with the foal than you are with your new sister, young man.'

'All Edyth does is eat, sleep, cry and fill her nappies,' Harry said with the frankness of a child.

'So did you at her age,' Sali laughed. 'But you grew up to be more interesting.'

'I'm going to get myself a six-gun like Broncho Bill, and race Toffee round the fields, lassoing the other horses and ponies and chasing off the Indians.'

'Not that there are many Indians in Pontypridd,' Sali said practically. 'I think two visits to the Wild West Exhibition was one too many for you, Harry.'

'Do you want to stroke Toffee again before I go to clean the car, Master Harry?' Robert asked.

'Yes, please, Robert.'

Joey continued to stand, taciturn and self-contained, after he lifted Harry from his shoulders.

'Time you two were on your way if you want to get a good seat at the exhibition,' Sali hinted.

'I have booked the best seats,' Joey snapped.

'So did Lloyd, but they aren't numbered and there are six rows in the section. The one nearest to the ring gets filled first because it has the best view.' Sali leaned over the half-door and watched the foal nuzzle Harry's hand.

'He already knows you, Master Harry.' Robert freshened the water bucket and set it beside the mare.

'Thanks to your tutoring, Robert,' Sali said gratefully.

Feeling as though Sali couldn't wait to get rid of him and Rhian, Joey buttoned his coat, pulled his gloves from his pocket and put them on. 'Do you have to go back into the house?' he asked Rhian.

'No? You?'

'No,' he answered emphatically.

'Why don't you come back here for tea after the exhibition?'

Sali invited, aware that Joey was annoyed with her for suggesting they leave.

'I have to call into the Pontypridd store.' Joey adjusted his hat.

'It's your day off.'

'We're missing an order of men's boots. They may have been delivered to Market Square by mistake.'

'Surely you could have sorted that by telephone.' Sali held out her hand to Harry when Robert opened the stable door.

'If I sort things personally, I know they're done. Thank you for the lunch, Sali. Say goodbye to Mari for me. See you soon, Harry.' Joey pretended to shadow-box Harry but even that was a half-hearted gesture. 'Bye, Robert.'

'Thank you for lunch and the talk.' Rhian kissed Sali's cheek. 'See you soon.' Drawing strength from Sali's look of sympathy, she shook Harry's hand and said goodbye to Robert before following Joey down the drive.

'If you don't want to sit next to me at the exhibition, you don't have to,' Joey snarled when she drew alongside him.

'That would be childish.' Braving rejection, she took his arm. 'I talked to Sali.'

'About us?' He gave her a withering look.

'I needed advice. I don't have anyone else to turn to except Mrs Williams. And we both know what she thinks of you.'

'And Sali's view of me is so different to your Mrs Williams's?' he said acidly.

'Sali loves you like a brother and you know it.'

'I bet her love didn't extend to recommending that you accept my proposal.' Shaking her hand from his arm, he adjusted his muffler.

'She suggested that I try talking to you, but I can see it's useless while you remain in this mood. And the longer you do, the more convinced I'll be that I've made the right decision.' She finally allowed her own anger to surface. 'You're behaving like a small boy who's throwing a tantrum because he can't have all the sweets in the shop.'

'I have a right to be upset.'

'With me, but not with Sali, Harry, Bella and Mari. You were unbearable at lunch.'

He spotted a bench set in a shrubbery on the edge of the croquet lawn. 'If you're determined to carry on punishing me, we can spare ten minutes for you to have a real go.'

'I am not punishing you,' she said crossly, walking across to the bench with him. 'Just because I didn't go all dewy-eyed and gasp, "Oh yes, please, Joey," when you asked me to marry you—'

Without warning, he pulled her into the shelter of the trees and silenced her by kissing her a second time. When he released her he looked down into her eyes. 'Why are you so angry with me?'

'Because you are angry with me.'

'Just answer me one question. Could you love me?'

'I already do,' she confessed.

'Then forgive me and marry me,' he pressed.

'Sali said it's best not to forgive but rather forget what happened before you marry someone.'

'Sali's right. I told you, Rhian, I wish I didn't have a past—'

She held a gloved finger over his lips. 'It's not the past that concerns me, Joey, it's the future. Can't you understand that?'

He slipped his fingers beneath her chin and lifted her face to his. 'I solemnly promise you, Rhian, that if you marry me, I will never do anything to hurt you.'

'Never?' she whispered, wanting to believe him.

'Never,' he reiterated soberly. He slipped the glove from her left hand and took the ring from the box. 'You'll take this?'

She looked into his eyes, saw the love mirrored in them and gave him the answer he had been waiting for. 'Yes.'

Chapter 5

CONSCIOUS ONLY OF the ring on her finger and Joey sitting beside her, the exhibition passed in a haze for Rhian. The colour, the cries of the Cowboys, Cowgirls and Indians, the thundering of the horses' hooves, the smell of horseflesh and cordite when the guns were fired, made little impression. She was aware of the spectacle, but she couldn't entirely dispel the sensation that she was watching it from a distance or even on screen in the Park Hall.

She gripped Joey's hand, gasped along with the rest of the audience when they watched the Indian attack on the Deadwood stagecoach, saw Broncho Busters lasso horses and crack their whips. But even the 'Ride for Life' where a Cowboy and Indian raced their horses against one another in a re-enactment of an actual event when the loser lost not only his horse, but also his life, failed to rouse her.

All she could think about was the man sitting beside her and their future − together. She imagined their wedding: a small, special occasion with all of his family and Mrs Williams, Miss Julia and the maids at Llan House present. She pictured the dress she'd wear: white, elegant, bridal but not too bridal to wear to a party or dance afterwards. She'd carry flowers − something simple, lilies perhaps − and Bella would be her bridesmaid in a new frock in her favourite pink.

And afterwards she and Joey would honeymoon, hopefully by the sea, which she'd never seen, in a rented cottage. Spending long days and moonlit nights walking on beaches, eating romantic meals in cafés and then a train journey back to Tonypandy and . . . her blood ran cold as her imagination painted a picture of their daily life.

Joey going to work, not like most men in the Rhondda, dressed in moleskin trousers, flat cap and miners' boots, but a tailored suit with a waistcoat, white collar, shirt and tie. Coming home as clean as he went out, and in between . . . She recalled the pretty young girls who worked in the Tonypandy store. Would she turn into a suspicious, nagging, jealous wife? Would Joey really change his wandering ways?

'Can I get you something to eat or drink? There's tea, orange juice, buns, biscuits and sweets,' Joey asked when an intermission was announced so the arena could be prepared for the 'back-woodsmen's log chariot race'.

'Not after that lunch we had at Sali's.'

'You ate about as much of that as I did,' he reminded. 'And it's not that warm. How about I get us two hot teas and a packet of biscuits?'

'If you like.' Already she didn't want to let him out of her sight.

'I won't be long.'

She felt ridiculously bereft when Joey left her side to join the queue outside the refreshment kiosk. Then a piercing voice she recognized rang down from the seats behind her.

'Really, Edward, you told me that you had reserved the best seats and here we are, sitting in the same section and only one row away from our parlour maid.'

Rhian glanced behind her and saw Mr and Mrs Larch, Miss Julia, Master Gerald and his friend from the vicarage. Miss Julia mouthed a silent apology but she turned back quickly. It was too late to hide from the mistress but she didn't want to fuel Mrs Larch's indignation by staring.

'Two teas and two buns, they'd run out of biscuits by the time I got to the head of the queue.' Joey handed Rhian a cup and saucer. 'Mrs Larch, Miss Larch, Mr Larch, boys.' He acknowledged Edward and his family.

'Mr Evans, Rhian. Wonderful show, isn't it?' Edward answered.

'Yes, it is, Mr Larch.' Setting the buns and his tea on his seat, Joey lifted his hat to the Larch ladies.

Taking courage from Joey, Rhian turned to her employers and said a shy 'hello'. Mrs Larch ignored her but Julia gave her a broad conspiratorial smile. She had just lent her James Fenimore Cooper's *The Last of the Mohicans* and the exhibition couldn't have been more perfect to conjure up the atmosphere of the Wild West.

Joey took his seat. 'Enjoying the exhibition?'

'It's wonderful.'

He lowered his voice. 'I heard what Mrs Larch said.'

'I am her parlour maid—'

'And you have every right to sit in the seats we paid for,' he said warmly.

'Sometimes you sound just like Lloyd and your father.'

'I might not be a fully paid-up member of the Communist party like them, but I believe just as fervently in the doctrine of liberty, fraternity, equality and workers' rights.' That time he didn't bother to soften his voice and Mabel Larch exhaled sharply behind them. The band struck up a march and the brass instruments drowned out all chance of further conversation.

Broncho Bill moved into the centre of the ring, the horses drew the log chariots into a circle ranged along the outer edge. Broncho Bill fired his gun, the horses reared, Joey squeezed her hand under cover of her coat and the race began.

'Mr Larch seems a nice man.' Joey acknowledged Rhian's employer and his family again when they joined the crowd streaming away from the marquee.

'He is kind and thoughtful, his first wife was too.'

'You've not said much about his second.' He took her hand and guided her through the mass of people. 'In fact, you never say much about life in Llan House, apart from the doings of Mrs Williams and the other maids.'

'Servants should never talk about their employers outside or inside the house.'

'That sounds like one of Mrs Williams's maxims.'

'You're beginning to recognize them.'

'But if what the second Mrs Larch said about not wanting to sit close to one of her maids is an indication as to what she's like—'

'It is, and I'll say no more on the subject,' she interrupted. She had been terrified of Mrs Larch ever since she'd slapped her, and she didn't want to discuss her with Joey for fear she'd let something slip. He and Sali had questioned her long and hard about the bruises on her face and she'd never been entirely sure that they'd believed her story about colliding with Bronwen in a doorway. The mistress had a hot temper, but Joey's was worse, and there was no saying what he'd do if he discovered that Mrs Larch had harmed her. She looked around. 'We're walking into town?'

'I told you I have to call into the store. I'll only be a few minutes. You don't mind, do you?'

'Of course not.'

'I thought we'd accept Sali's invitation to tea, that way we can talk about our engagement on the way back when we won't be surrounded by people. And we can also break the news to Sali and Lloyd when he comes home from work.'

'I'm wearing your ring so there's nothing more to talk about.'

'Given the trouble I had in getting you to accept it, there's lots to talk about. Like where and when we are going to get married, where we are going to honeymoon, where we are going to live. What kind of furniture and china we are going to buy—'

'We've months to settle all that,' she broke in quickly.

'Months! I'd like to get married before the summer.'

'Joey, let's not talk about this now,' she urged as a tall, fat man pushed his elbow into her face.

'I don't think I've ever seen Ponty so full.' He sidestepped past the man only to find himself in the centre of a crowd of giggling girls.

By walking in the road instead of the pavement, they finally managed to push their way through Bridge Street and Taff Street into Market Square.

'I'll have a look around ladies' fashions while you search for your boots.' Rhian smiled at the doorman who ushered them into the store.

'There's an excellent bridalwear department.' He bent his head to hers and she pushed him away.

'Not in public.'

'That's another thing we have to discuss,' he whispered. 'The list is growing longer by the minute'

'Mr Evans.'

'Miss Gulliford, beautiful as ever.' He took the middle-aged supervisor's hand, lifted it to his lips and kissed it. 'Is Mr Horton in his office?'

Rhian watched him flirt with Miss Gulliford before walking away. Joey was right; they did have a lot to discuss. And she suspected that he wasn't going to like some of the things she was going to say.

'Mr Watkin Jones is stocktaking, Mr Evans. He should be able to help you locate the boots, that's if they were delivered here by mistake.' Mr Horton reached for the bell on his desk. 'Can I offer you a cup of tea before you go upstairs?'

'No, thank you, Mr Horton. As I said, this is my day off and I've promised to visit my brother.'

'Well, as you trained here, you should know your way to the stockrooms.'

'I haven't forgotten my way around, Mr Horton.' Glad to be dismissed from the strait-laced, excessively formal manager's presence so easily, Joey left the office and strode down the corridor to the lifts. He pressed the button and the liftboy opened the cage doors.

'Stockroom, please.'

'Yes, Mr Evans.'

'You're Geoff Matthews's brother, aren't you?' Joey asked, seeing a resemblance between the red-headed boy and a stockroom assistant who worked for him in Tonypandy.

'Yes, sir. Anything going in Tonypandy, sir?' the boy asked as the lift travelled upwards.

'You're not happy here?' Joey braced himself when the lift juddered to a halt.

'Not happy working on the lift, sir. I've been on it now for six months, and I hardly see daylight during working hours.'

'So what do you want to do?'

'Work on menswear.'

'You mean you want the suit that comes with an assistant's job.' Joey knew that no boy past the age of fourteen liked wearing the pageboy outfit of the lift operator. 'Have you talked to Mr Horton about how you feel?'

'Me, talk to Mr Horton, sir? No,' the boy gasped.

'Mr Watkin Jones then.'

'I can't talk to the managers, sir.'

'You're talking to me,' Joey reminded.

'Our Geoff said he can talk to you about anything, sir. That's why I asked if there was anything going in Tonypandy.'

Joey suppressed a smile. His management style had raised a few eyebrows amongst the trustees of Harry's estate when he had first taken over the Tonypandy store. But when the sales figures of Gwilym James in Tonypandy had risen beyond even their expectations, they'd ceased questioning his decisions. 'You'll never get on if you won't talk to the managers here, boy. Tell you what, I'll mention it to Miss Gulliford, she can bring the matter up with Mr Horton for you.'

'You won't have a word on my behalf with him, would you, sir?' The boy opened the lift doors.

'I manage the Tonypandy store, not this one, but I will talk to Miss Gulliford, and I suggest you do the same.'

'I'll try, sir.' The boy climbed back into the lift and closed the cage doors.

Joey walked down the corridor that housed the stockrooms. Every door was marked with the name of a department. He stopped outside 'footwear' and turned the doorknob. It seemed stiff but he tried again and it burst open. Only then did he realize that the door had been locked.

Geraint Watkin Jones was kneeling between the splayed legs of a dark-haired girl, his trousers and underpants down around his ankles; her drawers lay, discarded, at their feet.

Embarrassed, but not as mortified as Tonia and Geraint appeared to be, Joey muttered, 'Sorry, I was looking for some boots,' before closing the door.

A few seconds later Geraint emerged into the corridor, red-faced and blustering. 'We were stocktaking.'

'You do know that Tonia is my cousin,' Joey informed him frigidly.

'It's not what it looks like. We're engaged.'

'Funny, her mother never said a word to me about it the last time I saw her.' Joey crossed his arms and confronted Geraint head on.

'We haven't told her yet.'

'Could that be because Tonia's only eighteen and you know Connie wouldn't give you permission to marry?'

'We need time—'

'You might be Sali's brother, but you're lower than a bloody worm, Geraint,' Joey hissed, losing his temper. 'You don't give a fig about Tonia; you're after her mother's money and business. And by taking down Tonia's drawers you hope to get her pregnant so Connie will have to let you marry her.'

'That is a foul thing to say, Joey, especially after the number of girls' drawers you've taken down.' Eyes blazing, Tonia wrenched open the stockroom door and joined them. 'I love Geraint and he loves me.'

'He's using you!' Joey countered. 'This is your penniless spend-thrift father and mother all over again.'

Tonia lifted her hand and slapped Joey across the face.

'Hit me if you like.' Joey rubbed his face but made no effort to retaliate. 'It won't change anything. And let's see how strong this great love of yours is after I've told Geraint who owns Rodney's Provisions.'

'What do you mean?' Geraint said.

'Connie's father was so worried that her husband would gamble away his business and life savings that he left everything to Lloyd. .

And, knowing my brother, if you do force Tonia to marry you, he'll see that you don't get a single penny of Connie's money, or a share of her business.'

'Is this true?' Geraint demanded of Tonia.

'What if it is?' Tonia dismissed carelessly. 'It doesn't matter. We love one another. You said we'd elope. That we'd marry in Scotland. Tell Joey that you're arranging everything.'

'I am, but we have to be practical, Tonia.'

'Practical. You sound like my mother. We're in love . . . we . . .'

Tonia looked from Geraint to Joey. In one blinding instant she saw him through Joey's eyes. Joey opened his arms. But she held back, standing firm and upright as tears poured down her cheeks. 'I hate you, Joey Evans. Hate you! As long as I live I'll never forgive you for this.'

'I'm sorry, Tonia.' He glared at Sali's brother. 'I'll see you again, Geraint, and when I do it will be a pleasure – for me.' Forgetting all about the boots, he walked away.

Tonia ran after him. 'Promise, Joey, you won't tell anyone what you saw. Promise! You have to promise!' Her voice rose hysterically. She rested her hand on his shoulder. 'Promise!'

'I promise, Tonia.' Knowing that if he looked at Geraint again he'd hit him, he didn't turn around.

He heard Tonia run back down the corridor. The stockroom door slammed shut. He heard Geraint knocking at it and calling Tonia's name, but he didn't look back. Devastated by the thought of how Geraint had hurt the girl he'd regarded as his little sister, he stood in front of the lift cage and pressed the button.

'Did something happen in the store?' Rhian asked. She and Joey had walked back through the town and were heading over the bridge towards Ynysangharad House.

'What makes you ask?' he answered warily.

'You've a face like thunder and you've hardly said a word since we left.'

Already regretting his promise to Tonia, because the last thing he wanted was to begin his engagement to Rhian by lying to her,

Joey decided a half-truth was better than an outright evasion. 'I had an argument with Geraint Watkin Jones.' He squeezed her hand lightly. 'I'm sorry, I'm a fool to let it upset me and spoil what's left of our day.'

Rhian returned the pressure of his fingers. Having suffered from Geraint's arrogance herself, she was aware of the hostility between Sali's brother and Lloyd's family and respected Joey's decision not to burden her with the details.

'So,' Joey determinedly pushed the scene in the stockroom into the 'to be thought of later' compartment of his mind, 'what do you say to a June wedding?'

'That would be lovely. It will give us over a year to plan everything.'

'A year! No, no, no, that won't do at all. I was talking about this June.'

'But it's April already.'

'Father Kelly will only need three weeks to call the banns so we could make it May.' He chose to deliberately misunderstand her.

'Joey, I've only just agreed to marry you.'

'You need time to get used to the idea?' He stopped to open one of the high gates to the drive.

'Frankly, yes.' She walked through and waited for him to close it.

'I'd be happy to walk up the aisle with you tomorrow.'

She took his arm again. 'Then you want Father Kelly to marry us in your Catholic Church?'

'Not if you want to marry me in your Methodist Chapel,' he answered easily.

'I'd like to know more about your religion.' Her brother had insisted that she attend chapel with him twice every Sunday until she had run away and left him. Since then she had attended the chapel in Tonypandy with Mrs Williams and the rest of the staff of Llan House, but it was more from habit than any strong religious feelings or commitment on her part.

'Surely you don't want to convert?' Joey was alarmed at the

80

thought of the time it would take Father Kelly to instruct her, time which would undoubtedly delay their wedding.

'I don't know enough about Catholicism to answer that.'

'If you ask Father Kelly to tell you about the Catholic Church, you'll convert,' he predicted dryly. 'Please, don't feel that you have to. Megan hasn't, and neither has Sali, but then Lloyd's a Communist and atheist like my father so he wouldn't want her to. There's a nice enough service for mixed couples, we'll go for that one.'

'What on earth are mixed couples?'

'Mixed religion, but where we marry isn't important. How soon is. Down the pit or in a register office, anywhere, it makes no difference to me, so long as we can live and,' his dark eyes glowed mischievously, 'start loving together.'

Rhian thought of Bronwen's oldest sister Pearl and all the girls she knew who'd left service to rush down the register office because they already had a baby on the way. She couldn't bear the thought of Mrs Williams, or anyone else who knew her, believing that was why she and Joey were marrying. 'I would like to wait a few months before we set the date.'

'There's no reason for us to wait,' he said impatiently. 'I'm earning a good salary. We can move in with my father. And if you don't want to live with him, we'll take one of the other houses he owns as soon as one becomes vacant. Tenants are always coming and going.'

'I'd love to live with your father.'

'Good, because I'd rather not leave him on his own. Although Betty Morgan might prove a problem,' he mused. 'She's used to keeping house for us and needs the money we pay her. But I understand that you won't want another woman interfering in your kitchen—'

'Joey, if you allow me to get a word in edgewise, can I say that before you make too many plans, I would like to enjoy our engagement.'

'Enjoy it by all means but don't make a meal of it.' They had reached a part of the drive that couldn't be seen from Bridge Street or the house, and he took advantage of the seclusion to draw her under the oaks that lined the carriageway.

He brushed his lips lightly, gently, over hers. Slowly, tentatively, she began to relax and finally respond to his touch. He slipped the buttons on her coat. Pushing aside her muffler, he slid his hand inside her cardigan and cupped her breast. His fingers burned, searing her skin through the thin silk of her blouse and bust-shaper. She tried and failed to quell the uneasy thought that his skill at lovemaking had been honed during his relationships with so many other women.

'No!' She pushed him aside.

'Rhian, we're engaged.'

'Engaged to be married.' She buttoned her cardigan and coat. 'And there'll be no more of that until after the wedding.'

He took a deep breath to steady himself. 'That's fine by me provided you set the date right now.'

'Not before September.'

'But that's six months away.'

'Exactly.'

'I . . .' He fell silent as she stared at him.

'Can't wait that long?' she finished for him.

'Not without a damned good reason.'

'There's no need to swear.'

'Sorry,' he apologized. 'Not that I'm complaining, but you have a lot to learn about men.'

'We have a lot to learn about one another.' She held up her hand to silence him when he tried to interrupt. 'And before you say anything, I realize that we've been acquainted for five years and spent some time together the last three months—'

'Not some time, your every free moment,' he corrected.

'All right, all my free time, but I'm terrified of making a mistake that I'll spend a lifetime regretting.'

'You're that unsure about marrying me?'

'I just need—'

'Time to convince yourself that you're making the right decision?' he mocked.

'I'm wearing your mother's ring.'

'And you've said that you love me.'

'I wouldn't have taken the ring if I didn't.'

'And you know how much I love you, so how can we possibly be making a mistake?' he said seriously.

'I need time to get to know you properly.'

'Fat chance of that when you only get one day off a week. If we marry right away we'll have all the time in the world to get to know one another, starting with the honeymoon.' He gave her his most winsome smile.

'I'd still prefer to wait. And, if you don't mind, I'd rather not tell anyone we're engaged for a while.'

'That I won't agree to. I'm so happy I could shout the news from the rooftops. Besides,' he entwined his gloved fingers in hers, and pulled her towards him, 'I can see the ring even through your glove.'

'Then perhaps I shouldn't wear it just yet.' She removed her glove, slipped the ring from her finger and tried to hand it back to him.

He released her hand and thrust his arms behind his back. 'Now you've taken it, you can't give it back. Rules of engagement.'

'I thought rules of engagement only applied to battles, not this kind of engagement.'

'And how many times have you been engaged before?'

'None.' She looked up at him. 'You?'

He realized she was in earnest. 'This is the first and it will be the only time.' He took the ring from her, slipped it back on to her finger and buttoned on her glove.

'You do know that I won't forgive you if you walk out with another girl?'

'Yes,' he answered solemnly.

'And you're sure that you're ready to forsake all others.'

'I made you a promise, Rhian, I won't break it.' He grabbed her hand. 'Come on, let's tell Sali, and Lloyd if he's home, that they're about to acquire another sister-in-law.'

*

Lloyd's car was parked at the front of Ynysangharad House, the door was open and Lloyd, Sali, Harry and Bella were in the hall putting on their hats and coats. Baby Edyth lay wrapped in a shawl in her pram.

'We saw you walking up the drive, Uncle Joey.' Harry was hopping from one foot to the other, clearly anxious to be gone.

'If you're going out just to avoid giving us tea, we promise not to eat much.' Joey smiled at Rhian when she picked up the baby, who was awake and making grizzling noises.

'Dad telephoned from the White Hart an hour ago.' Lloyd tied Bella's muffler around her neck. 'He and Betty Morgan are moving in with Victor and Megan for a couple of weeks.'

'Megan's had the baby?' Rhian broke in eagerly.

'At two o'clock this afternoon. Harry, calm down, or go and run around the car for two minutes until we're all ready to leave.' Sali took a bunch of freshly-cut daffodils and tulips from the hall-stand.

'Boy or girl?' Joey beamed.

'We waited so you could visit them with us and see for your-selves.' Lloyd checked his pockets for his keys.

'I can't wait that long to find out if we poor boys have even more females in the family to contend with.' Joey intercepted Harry who was racing back inside and swung him up on to his shoulders.

'It's boys, Uncle Joey.'

'You are going to have to learn how to keep secrets if you want a quiet life, Harry,' Lloyd teased his stepson.

'Boys?' Joey looked from Lloyd to Sali.

'Twins,' Sali confirmed, 'and from what the midwife told Dad, Megan was surprised but Victor's in shock.'

Betty Morgan carried a teacup down the farmhouse's narrow staircase and nodded to Sali and Rhian who were hovering in the passage.

'Go on up. She's looking forward to seeing you both.'

'Is she all right?' Sali asked in concern.

'Tired, but better than Victor, who's been in a daze since Billy and I got here. But then I saw to it that Megan had a good rest after the birth. Perhaps I should have put Victor to bed as well.'

Rhian crept up the old wooden staircase behind Sali. The door to Victor and Megan's bedroom was open. Megan was sitting up in the massive oak bed that had been left behind by the previous owner of the farm, a baby cradled in each arm.

'You clever girl.' Sali set the flowers she had arranged in a vase on the dressing table before kissing her.

'They are absolutely gorgeous, Megan.' Rhian gazed down at the two tiny, pink-faced babies.

'Aren't they just?' Megan turned from one to the other. She untied the strings on the babies' bonnets and pulled them off. 'Victor's pleased. But I can't say I am; look, they both have my red hair.'

'May I?' Sali held out her hands.

'Take one each,' Megan offered.

'Did you have any idea that you were having twins?' Rhian sat in a rocking chair at the side of the bed before taking one of the babies from Megan.

'Not until after the first one arrived. This is the eldest.' She retied the ribbons on the cap of the baby Rhian was cuddling. 'Victor wants to call him Jack.'

'And this one?' Sali looked down at the baby in her arms.

'Victor wants to name him Tom. Not Thomas, but Tom.' Megan stretched out her arms. 'It's nice to hand them over to someone else for five minutes.'

'Good plain names.' Sali pushed her finger into the baby's minute palm.

'I would have liked to have called them William and Victor but Victor said they would be given nicknames if we used his and his father's names and he couldn't bear the thought of Little Billy, or Young Vic. And he wanted something ordinary because he's never forgiven his father for allowing his mother to call him Sebastian.'

'I didn't know Victor's name was Sebastian.' Rhian glanced up from the baby, who appeared to be squinting up at her through half-closed eyes.

'His middle name,' Megan divulged, 'and he hates it. I'm trying to persuade him to call the boys Jack William Evans and Tom Victor Evans, but I'm not having much success. He says one name is more than enough for any man.'

'He's probably right,' Sali agreed philosophically. 'After all, how often do any of us use our middle names?'

'Well, Jack, what do you think of the name your father wants to give you?' Rhian watched the baby yawn.

'All three of you must be exhausted,' Sali said.

'I am tired,' Megan conceded. 'But according to the midwife, I had an easy time. The pains didn't start until ten o'clock this morning. Victor sent the boy to get the midwife, she arrived at eleven o'clock, Jack was born at two and Tom half an hour later.'

'You may have had a quick time, but I doubt it was easy, whatever the midwife said. Take a tip from an experienced mother,' Sali advised. 'Don't get up for a full ten days. It's bad enough trying to look after a baby, a toddler and Harry when he's home. I can't imagine what it will be like to care for two babies who'll want feeding, changing and nursing at the same time.'

'Victor and I have already decided that they are going to be perfectly behaved.' Megan slid down in the bed.

'Deciding and being are two different things. Is there anything I can do to help?' Sali asked.

'I don't think so. Mrs Morgan seems to have everything in hand in the house. It's good of her and Victor's dad to move in with us. They said they don't mind staying as long as they are needed. Spring is a busy time. But Dad is a real help around the farm. Come in?' Megan called at a knock on the door.

Carrying the baby, Sali opened it. Lloyd, Victor and Joey stood in the doorway with Harry and Bella.

'Hello, Megan.' Joey smiled at her, then looked at the baby Sali was holding. 'One of my nephews, I presume?'

'The youngest, Tom,' Victor said proudly after pulling back the shawl to check.

Joey glanced from the baby to the one Rhian was holding. 'All babies look the same to me but these two are mirror images. How can you tell them apart?'

'That's easy; Jack has a smaller nose and a fatter face.' Victor walked past Sali and sat beside Megan on the bed. 'Want to come and look at your cousins, Harry, Bella?' He held out his hand to the children who were hanging back.

'You'll have to teach them to play soldiers with us as soon as they're old enough, Harry.' Joey turned to Rhian. 'If you want to be back at Llan House by ten, it's time we left.'

'I'll get my coat.' She kissed the baby and, after a final cuddle, reluctantly handed him over to Lloyd.

'When are you having the next two, Megan?' Joey asked.

'We've done our bit to carry the Evans name into the next generation. It's your turn,' Megan answered. 'And in case you thought no one had noticed, I spotted your new ring, Rhian. Congratulations, although if you don't mind me saying so, I think Joey's getting a better wife than he'll be a husband.'

'Thank you, Megan. It's good to know that my sister-in-law thinks so well of me.' Joey made a face at her.

'You two could have said something,' Lloyd remonstrated.

'You could have noticed.' Joey shook the hand Lloyd offered him. 'I finally convinced Rhian that we should get engaged this afternoon and I don't mind telling you, it's the hardest day's work that I've ever done.'

Sali shook her head at Bella who was trying to climb on to Megan's high bed. 'I think we're wearing Auntie Megan out.' She tucked the baby she was holding into the crib beside the bed. 'You'll have to make another one of these, Victor.'

'I intend to, but the babies are so small they fit in nicely together.'

'They won't be small for long,' Lloyd warned.

'Take care of your family, Victor. I'll be up again before we go to say goodnight.' Sali blew a kiss to Megan and ushered the children from the room.

'I can drive you and Rhian to Llan House, Joey.' Lloyd handed the other baby to Victor.

'Thank you, but we'd prefer to walk.' Joey peered at the baby Sali had set down in the crib then at the one Victor was holding.

Megan laughed at the puzzled expression on his face. 'If you keep looking, the difference between them will become obvious.'

Joey continued to glance from one to the other. 'Not to me, it won't.'

'When's the happy day?' Megan asked Rhian.

'When these two can walk up the aisle as pageboys,' Rhian replied.

'As I have no intention of waiting that long, they'll have to be carried. Can we call in on Rhian's day off next week?' Joey asked.

'There'll be trouble if you don't.' Megan gripped Rhian's hand when she bent to kiss her goodbye. 'I am so glad that you are going to be my second sister-in-law.'

'So am I. You sure about next week? We don't want to make work for you.'

'You won't, Rhian.' Betty Morgan pushed past the men, carrying a tray of soup and bread. 'I've made some *cawl* for you, Megan. You need to get your strength back and when you get it, keep it. The rest of you,' she glowered at Joey and Lloyd, 'out of here so mother and babies can get some peace and quiet. And that goes for you too, Victor. Give the poor girl a moment to herself.'

'We're going. Night, Megan.' Joey kissed Megan's cheek but although he, Rhian, and Lloyd went to the door, Victor didn't attempt to move from the bed.

'Your poor father is watching his supper get cold downstairs while he waits for you to join him,' Betty scolded.

'I'm staying,' Victor said flatly.

'You want him to?' Betty asked Megan.

'Most definitely,' Megan answered.

'In that case you can, but no tiring your wife or your sons.' Betty set down the tray and bustled out of the room.

'You'll call in again?' Megan held out her hand to Lloyd.

'Tomorrow, but just for ten minutes.' He glanced in Betty Morgan's direction. 'Rest.'

'As if I could do anything else with Betty and Victor bullying me.'

'It really is no trouble to give you and Rhian a lift, Joey,' Lloyd offered again as they went down the stairs. 'That way you can stay for supper.'

'No thanks. We'll enjoy the walk and Rhian has supper waiting for her in Llan House.'

'You're going back to an empty house,' Lloyd reminded his brother.

'With a well-stocked pantry, and I'm not one of those men who don't know how to boil an egg or butter a slice of bread.'

'Mrs Hopkins across the road said she'd keep the fire in for you and do whatever needs to be done around the house, including your washing.' Billy Evans joined them in the passageway.

'There won't be much, I know how to look after myself,' Joey assured him.

Sali hugged Rhian. 'Let me know as soon as you set the date. I'll help in any way I can and, if you can bear to be parted from Joey for an hour next Tuesday, I'll arrange for you to see some wedding dresses in the store.' She glanced slyly at Joey. 'Pontypridd might be better. The manager in Tonypandy's quite nosy and it's bad luck for the groom to see the dress before the ceremony.'

'Sali told me that congratulations are in order.' Billy Evans smiled at Rhian before kissing her. 'I must say my sons were all born under lucky stars. I couldn't have wished for three nicer or prettier daughters-in-law. We'll organize an engagement party for you as soon as Betty and I leave here.'

'It will be a wedding celebration by then.' Joey held out Rhian's coat and helped her on with it.

'No, it won't,' Rhian contradicted.

'Joey's a fortunate man. I only hope you know what you're taking on with him, Rhian.'

'I do, Mr Evans.' Rhian gave Joey a sideways glance. 'It's not going to be easy to keep him in line but I'll try.'

'Did anyone else detect a cautious note when Rhian accepted our congratulations?' Lloyd gave a last wave before closing the kitchen door.

His father sat at the table. 'Given our Joey's past exploits, any girl would be an idiot to be anything but cautious with him.'

'If anyone can keep him on the straight and narrow, it's Rhian.' Sali picked up the ladle and moved behind the tureen. 'Pass me the bowls, Harry, and I'll dish out supper.'

Chapter 6

THE WIND HAD dropped and thousands of tiny stars shone down from a cold and startlingly clear night sky.

'So, when will you marry me?' Joey asked seriously after he and Rhian left the lights of the farmhouse behind them and headed down the mountain track towards the ribbons of street lamps that criss-crossed Tonypandy.

'I told you, not before September.'

'I can't persuade you to bring the date forward?'

'No.'

'August,' he suggested. 'That's only four weeks sooner but it doesn't seem as far away as September. And don't say you'll think about it.'

'If I agree to August, will you promise not to nag me to move it closer still?'

'If I have to,' he conceded reluctantly.

'It's only five months away. And there's so much to be done. I'll need to save to buy a dress and a bottom drawer—'

'No, you won't, because I've all the savings we'll need and if we move in with my father the house is already furnished, so we won't have to buy a single thing.'

'I'd at least like to get our own china and bedding. And, as I won't be wearing a uniform every day, I'll need more clothes. A trousseau! Don't brides have a trousseau?'

'They do. I'll buy you one as a wedding present.'

'No, you won't.'

'Don't argue with me. This has been a magical evening, one that I'll want to remember all my life.' He took her in his arms and kissed her. 'I have a beautiful fiancée, a wedding to plan and two new nephews.'

'To teach how to be naughty like you have done Harry.'

'Children don't need to be taught how to be naughty. They come that way naturally. And, after seeing those two and Edyth, Harry and Bella today, I hope we have babies. Lots of them and soon.'

'Not too soon, I hope, and not two at a time.' They reached the town and she checked her watch under the light of a lamp. 'We need to hurry.'

'Your fault for dawdling.'

'Yours for kissing me.'

'Race you up the hill.' He gave her a head start.

They were both breathless when they reached the back door of Llan House. Joey opened his arms and Rhian practically fell into them.

'How am I going to survive without you and your kisses until next Tuesday?' he whispered, when he finally summoned the will-power to tear his lips from hers.

'If I'm sent on any errands I'll call in the store.'

'I'll save up all my tea and lunch breaks on the off-chance, so we can sneak half an hour together.' He almost added 'in the stockroom' then he remembered the scene he'd witnessed in Pontypridd.

The door opened and a shaft of harsh yellow light fell on them.

'Joey Evans!'

'I recognize that voice.' He turned to face the housekeeper. 'Mrs Williams.' He lifted his hat, then pulled off Rhian's glove. 'Before you get that carpet-beater you keep threatening to thrash me with, please note, Rhian's wearing my mother's ring and we've set the date for the first of August.'

'I didn't agree to the first of August,' Rhian remonstrated.

'You didn't disagree either and I just happen to know that the first is a Saturday. A good, traditional day to marry.'

'How do you know?'

'I checked the calendar in Megan and Victor's kitchen.' He looked to the housekeeper. 'Don't tell me you're too speechless to wish us luck, Mrs Williams.'

'I'll wish Rhian luck, Joey Evans. She'll need it; you won't, because you've already had more of that commodity than any one man is entitled to in a lifetime. But what can I say? If the girl is fool enough to marry you, nothing I can say will stop her. But you're not just getting a girl who looks and behaves like an angel; you're also getting yourself a first-class cook and housekeeper. Of all the girls I've trained over the years, she's the best.'

'And that, Mrs Williams, is why I asked her to become my wife.' Joey gave Rhian one last kiss on the cheek.

'So much has happened today, I almost forgot.' Rhian opened her handbag and handed Joey an envelope.

'What is it?'

'My engagement present to you. Don't open it until you get home.'

Joey smiled cheekily at the housekeeper, lifted his hat a second time and walked back down the drive.

'But you promised you'd tell us about Broncho Bill's Wild West Exhibition, Rhian,' Mair whined plaintively.

'Rhian has more important things to think and talk about than the exhibition, Mair. And, as you're going to see it for yourself with your mam, you can tell us all about it at the supper table tomorrow night.' Mrs Williams collected the plates, cups and saucers from the table, effectively putting an end to the meal. 'Come on girl, up to bed.'

'If you two want to go up, I'll help Mrs Williams with the supper dishes,' Rhian said to Bronwen and Cook.

'Thanks. Here, you can have my apron to cover your suit.' Bronwen untied hers and handed it over.

'Rhian, you're a pal.' Yawning, Cook followed Bronwen and Mair up the back staircase.

Mrs Williams stacked the dishes on the wooden draining board next to the Belfast sink.

'You haven't said much other than "congratulations",' Rhian ventured, anxious for Mrs Williams's blessing. She was the one woman she respected more than anyone else outside of Sali and Miss Julia.

'You're marrying into a good family that's growing at quite a pace. Here we are only into April and there are three new little ones.' Mrs Williams filled two enamel bowls with water from the brass boiler set in the range and carried them to the sink before refilling the boiler.

'Victor and Megan looked so proud – and happy.'

'Poor Megan Evans has every right to be proud. It must be jolly hard work bringing twins into the world. But I must say I've never quite understood why a man is congratulated when he becomes a father. His part is easy.' The housekeeper tossed a handful of soda crystals into the water and plunged in the cleanest plates. 'Do you want another cup of cocoa before going to bed?'

'Yes, please.' Rhian was still hoping that the housekeeper would pass an opinion on her engagement.

'I'll join you, so boil enough milk for two cups. It's been quite a day for you, hasn't it? Going to the exhibition, getting engaged, seeing newborn twins.'

'It was a lovely day.' Rhian unhooked a tea towel from the rack and lifted the first plate from the rinsing bowl.

'But you're still not sure you've done the right thing in getting engaged to Joey Evans?'

'What makes you say that?' Rhian set the plate she'd dried on the dresser.

'Because you're waiting for me to pass judgement on your choice.'

'Joey promised me faithfully that he'd never so much as look at another woman again.'

'Did he now?'

'You don't believe him?' Rhian stacked the dishes on the dresser and watched the housekeeper's face carefully.

'Whether *I* do or don't, doesn't matter. What does matter is that you believe him and he fulfils his promise. There, that's the last dish.' Mrs Williams smiled. 'There's no need to look so serious; this should be the happiest time of your life. And, for what it's worth, I do believe that since January you've changed Mr Joseph Evans for the better. Not that there was a lot wrong with him before, other than his wandering eye when it came to girls who were no better than they should be. As I've already said, he has a lovely family. And a steady, well-paid job. You'll want for nothing. But then, with you for a wife, neither will he.'

'Sali and everyone else in Joey's family were so happy when we told them tonight.' The milk began to boil; Rhian lifted the pan from the hob and poured it over the paste of cocoa powder and cold milk she'd mixed.

'And so they should be.' Mrs Williams left the dishwater in the bowls, rinsed the dishcloth out in cold, running water, wrung it out and set it on the tap to dry. She pulled a chair from under the table and sat down. 'Do you want to inform the master that you're engaged, or do you want me to tell him for you?'

'Does he have to know so soon?' Rhian sat next to the house-keeper.

'Yes, but for my sake not his. Mair is willing enough but she's young. I wouldn't like to take on another girl who needs training. Your replacement will have to be experienced and capable. Of course, it goes without saying that whoever she is, she won't be as good as you.'

'But I won't be leaving for five months.'

'The best staff go from the Labour Exchange within hours, and it wouldn't hurt to take someone on sooner so you could show them the ropes for a month or so. Although the master may not want to pay double wages for that long. I'll talk it over with him tomorrow.' She took Rhian's hand and admired the ring. 'Very pretty, I had one just like it when I was your age.'

'A regard ring,' Rhian said in surprise.

'You know what it is.'

'Joey told me.'

'I may be old and fat now, but I've had my moments.' Mrs Williams looked back into a world she'd never mentioned to Rhian before. 'Strange, at the time I believed I couldn't live without my sweetheart. Now, I've forgotten what he looked like.'

'What happened?' Rhian asked.

'We quarrelled. I can't even remember over what. He went away and I never saw him again.'

'I'm sorry.'

'I'm not.' Mrs Williams lifted her feet on to the fender to warm them. 'He was a sailor. Probably with a wife in every port. And he was a drinker. If I had married him I would have led a miserable and poor existence. As it is, I've a comfortable home here and enough savings to see me through until God calls me.' She patted Rhian's hand. 'Put that ring somewhere safe while you're working, we don't want the mistress accusing you of scratching any of her precious furniture.'

'I will.' Rhian finished her cocoa.

'I'll see to the cups. You go on up to bed. And sweet dreams.' Mrs Williams's eyes twinkled. 'Your Joey may be a bit of a handful, but he is very good-looking. Some girls would give their eye-teeth and a full head of hair for a husband who's half as handsome. One more thing, wait until morning to give Miss Julia your news. And don't give me that innocent look; I know you two are as thick as thieves, even if no one else in the house does.'

Joey turned the key that was kept in his father's front door, whether anyone was in the house or not. He switched on the electric light that had been installed in the downstairs of the house, walked down the passage and opened the kitchen door.

'Tonia!' Startled, he stepped back as his cousin rose from the easy chair next to the hearth. 'What are you doing here at this time of night?' He looked around. 'Is your mother with you?'

'No.'

'Don't tell me that you've been sitting here alone waiting for me?'

'I have to see you.'

'I want you out of here now.' Gripping her by the shoulders, he propelled her out of the kitchen.

'No one knows I'm here. My mother thinks I went to bed early but I sneaked down the back staircase while she and Annie were listening to the gramophone.'

'I hate to disappoint you, but at least half, if not all the women in the street know you're here. They've so little to do; they've been watching my comings and goings for years.'

'I came in the back way, so no one would see me.'

'That's even worse. All of the kitchen and most of the bedroom windows on this side of the street overlook our back garden.' He opened the door.

'Let me at least get my coat,' she said crossly.

'You have thirty seconds.' He stood on the doorstep while she walked back down the passage.

'I have to talk to you.' She lifted her coat from the rack.

'About what I saw this afternoon? I told you I wouldn't tell anyone, and I won't.'

'Joey, Tonia, bit late to be visiting, isn't it?' Mrs Hopkins pushed past them and entered the house.

'There's no need for you to come in, Mrs Hopkins,' Joey protested. 'I've just this minute returned from Victor's. I'll see to whatever needs doing.'

Mrs Hopkins looked suspiciously from Joey to Tonia. 'You seem to have your hands too full to see to anything beside your cousin at the moment, Joey.'

'Tonia came up with a message from her mother. Megan has had twin boys. They're calling them Jack and Tom. I've just been up to see them.' Feeling unaccountably guilty, Joey was conscious that he was talking too quickly and saying more than necessary.

'I heard she'd had twins. Both of you went to see her and the babies?' Mrs Hopkins blatantly fished for information.

'Just me, Mrs Hopkins,' Joey answered uneasily.

'I see. Well, it's late. If you're sure about the fire, Joey—'

'I am, Mrs Hopkins.' Joey held the front door open. 'I'll see to it as soon as I've walked Tonia home.'

'I can see myself home.' Tonia flounced out on to the pavement.

'You've caused trouble enough for one day,' Joey muttered too low for Mrs Hopkins to hear. He jammed his hat back on his head and joined her. 'Goodnight, Mrs Hopkins,' he called when she crossed the road.

'Goodnight, Joey, Tonia.'

Joey was aware that Mrs Hopkins was standing on her doorstep watching their backs as they walked down the street.

'I only—'

'Not another word, Tonia,' Joey snapped. 'The last thing I need is any gossip about you and me. I asked Rhian to marry me today.'

'And she said yes?'

'I managed to persuade her.' He found it difficult to ignore her sneering tone. 'And if Mrs Hopkins, or anyone else, tells her that they saw us alone together in our house, I'll expect you to tell Rhian exactly why you thought it necessary to visit me at this hour of the night.'

'You promised you wouldn't tell anyone about this afternoon.'

'That was before Mrs Hopkins saw us together.'

'I wanted you to know that it's over between Geraint and me.'

'Which one of you ended it?'

'Does it matter?'

'It does if he used and dropped you.'

'All of a sudden you're concerned about me?' she said sulkily.

'You're my cousin. That makes you family and I want to know if I have to beat him up.'

'Don't put yourself to any trouble on my account, Joey Evans.' She ran off up the street and around to the back of the shop, leaving him angrier than ever with her – but most of all with Geraint Watkin Jones.

Joey returned home, took off his jacket, rolled up his sleeves, banked down the fire for the night and filled the coalscuttle. Restless, he almost wished there was more work to keep him busy. But there was nothing else to be done because Betty had been keeping the house even more immaculate than usual in expectation of the imminent arrival of Megan's baby. He brewed a pot of tea, and it was only when he lifted a cup and saucer from the dresser that he realized he was spending a night alone for the first time in his life.

He poured his tea and sat at the table. The stillness and emptiness closed in on him, and his thoughts drifted back to his childhood. He saw his mother sitting in 'her' chair next to the hearth, mending the family's shirts and trousers and smiling down at him while he played with his toys on the hearthrug. His father and Lloyd reading to him when he'd still been small enough to climb on to their laps, not fairy tales, but whole chunks of *Das Kapital*. His mother remonstrating with him and his brothers when they had burst in after school, and later the colliery, scavenging through her tins for cakes and biscuits because they could never wait more than a minute for their tea. Both his parents presiding over the table at meal times, trying to keep him, Lloyd and Victor in check as they teased one another.

The terrible time when ill-health and weakness had forced his mother to take to her bed and the meals he, his father and brothers had placed on trays and carried into the front parlour where his father had set up her bed. Meals they had carried out again untouched. The awful, strained atmosphere of his mother's funeral tea. And afterwards the rapid succession of housekeepers that his father had employed and fired before Sali had come to the house and eventually married Lloyd. And the future . . .

He tried to imagine himself sitting in his father's chair opposite Rhian twenty years from now, children lined up on the chairs between them.

He shuddered. He was not only tempting fate but wishing his father if not dead, then certainly elsewhere and there was no way that he could ever fill his shoes. He finished his tea, dumped the tealeaves in the pigswill bin, rinsed his cup and saucer in cold water and picked up his jacket ready to go to bed.

He heard the crackle of paper and remembered the envelope Rhian had given him. He removed it from his inside pocket, opened it and withdrew a copy of the photograph he had begged her to give him the first day they had spent together. He smiled, realizing that he hadn't been the only one who thought it was time to move their relationship out of friendship and on to a more intimate footing.

Rhian looked beautiful, but also unattainable. He had the strangest feeling that he was looking at one of the picture postcards that could be bought in any newsagent's or stationer's of royalty or film stars. He had never loved anything or anyone as much as he loved her. But whether it was nervousness generated by Tonia's visit or Rhian's uneasiness about his past, he had the strangest pre—monition that she might never be entirely his.

*

The night after Tonia's visit proved a sleepless one. The days that followed were even worse. Every time someone knocked at his office door, fear crawled over Joey's skin, drying his mouth and generating a sour, sick feeling in the pit of his stomach as he steeled himself for another confrontation – with Tonia, or Connie if she'd discovered that her daughter had called on him late at night.

The one he dreaded most was Rhian. If Mrs Hopkins told anyone what she'd seen, he didn't doubt that the news would reach Mrs Williams. And given the housekeeper's fondness for Rhian and contempt for him, he suspected that she wouldn't waste any time in passing it on. He hated the thought of Rhian suspecting that he'd broken his promise to her the very day he'd made it.

He wrote to Rhian every night before he went to bed. He thanked her for the photograph, which he'd framed and placed on his bedside cabinet, just as he'd told her he would in January. He told her how much he loved her, how happy he was that she'd agreed to be his wife, and as the week progressed, outlined his thoughts and ideas for their wedding, honeymoon and future. But whenever he tried to broach the subject of Tonia's visit, he found it impossible to explain why he and his cousin were alone together in his house late at night, without breaking his promise to Tonia. And the mere fact of mentioning it without the explanation, made the visit sound as though they'd planned it.

Rhian sent back gentle, loving letters that always began 'My dearest darling Joey' and ended 'all my love now and for ever'. In between she agreed to all the practical suggestions he made for turning his father's rarely used middle parlour into their private sitting room, and organizing a small reception after their wedding in the Catholic Hall because his father's house wouldn't be large enough to accommodate all the friends he'd like to invite.

When she wrote that she couldn't wait to honeymoon in his aunt's farm cottage in Port Eynon on the Gower because she had never seen the sea, he realized that despite what Sali had told him about Rhian's past, he had given very little thought to the kind of life she'd led before she'd begun work in Llan House. He began both to long for and dread her next day off. When Tuesday finally arrived, he rose earlier than usual. After lighting the fire and tidying the house, he dressed in his best suit and set out for Llan House.

Feeling guilty, although he couldn't quantify why, and wanting his relationship with Rhian to begin, as he intended it to continue, in complete honesty, he rehearsed various speeches in his mind as he walked.

There was the ostensibly casual approach: 'Guess what, Rhian? When I got home last Tuesday, Tonia was waiting for me . . . No, I've absolutely no idea why she was there. She ran off before she explained.'

The solemn declaration: 'Tonia came to see me last Tuesday night and Mrs Hopkins saw us together . . . No, of course we weren't doing anything but, well I saw her doing something with someone. I can't say what, or who the person was.'

He could try to be direct: 'Has anyone said anything to you about Tonia and me?' which would undoubtedly make her suspicious and lead her to ask all sorts of questions he couldn't answer, which in turn would make him sound guiltier than ever.

'Talking to yourself now, Joey Evans.'

Mrs Williams's voice shattered his concentration. Obviously he had spoken aloud. But had he said anything incriminating? Adopting what he trusted was an innocent expression, he raised his trilby and managed a 'good morning' when she caught up with him at the gates of Llan House.

'That's the first sign, you know.'

'First sign of what, Mrs Williams?' Joey was too shaken to try to make sense of what she was saying.

'Madness, or so they say.' She handed him a basket loaded with sodden, newspaper-wrapped parcels. 'I've been to the fish-monger's. I always go down at the start of the season to pick out the best of the salmon. If I ask them to send up a couple they always give the boy the small ones no one else wants, and Mr Larch enjoys a thick-cut, broiled cutlet in shrimp sauce.'

'That's tradesmen for you.' Joey automatically repeated the standard Tonypandy housewife's lament. 'How are you, Mrs

Williams, and how is Rhian?' He tried to sound as if he were merely making conversation.

'I'm as fit as flea. Rhian is as crazy as a collier after he's downed twelve pints in the Pandy. If she weren't, she wouldn't have agreed to marry you. But then, there's no accounting for taste. Her head's been in the clouds all week, and it's infectious. All the maids can think about is white lace, satin, orange blossom and wedding marches. I've had to warn all of them twice this week about dusting in the corners of the rooms.' She opened the kitchen door and breezed in. 'Put the basket on the table. Do you want a cup of tea?'

'No, thank you.' Joey did as she ordered before removing his hat. Cook nodded to him as she checked the cabbage Mair was shredding. There was no sign of Rhian or Bronwen.

'Take a seat. I'll tell Rhian you're here.' Mrs Williams disappeared through the door that led to the back staircase. Joey sat in the housekeeper's easy chair at the side of the range and waited in trepidation. It was no use reminding himself that he had nothing to feel guilty about. He simply did. And with nothing else to occupy his mind, he began counting the minute lines off the railway-sized clock that dominated the room.

Rhian knows that Tonia and I were alone in my house and she believes the worse: she does, she doesn't, she does, she doesn't . . .

Rhian secured Julia's hat with a jet-headed hatpin, stood back and surveyed her handiwork.

'It's kind of you to spare the time to do my hair on your day off,' Julia said gratefully. 'I know you can't wait to see your Mr Evans.'

'I can't,' Rhian confessed. 'This last week has felt more like seven years than seven days. Mrs Williams didn't send me into town on a single errand this week.'

'So you couldn't even see him for a few minutes,' Julia sympathized.

'He's written to me every day.'

'It must be wonderful to be in love,' Julia murmured pensively.

'It will happen to you one day, you'll see.' When she managed to set her doubts about Joey's faithfulness from her mind, Rhian was ecstatically happy and wanted everyone to be in the same blissful state.

'People like me don't fall in love.'

'Yes, they do, and you never know, it could be today. You look wonderful, all bubbly and cheerful as if you're going to a party. Are you sure you're only attending a suffrage committee meeting.'

'Promise you won't tell a soul?' Julia was bursting to tell some-one about her plan to invite Geraint Watkin Jones to go to a meeting with her. And Rhian was the obvious choice. The more distant she'd grown from her father and brother, the closer she'd become to the maid.

'Not if it's one of your secrets, Miss Julia,' Rhian assured her.

'I'm going to see someone.'

'A man someone?'

'It's nothing, not yet.' Julia hesitated.

'But it could be,' Rhian broke in eagerly.

'That's my father calling.' Glad of the interruption that she sensed had come just in time to stop her from making a fool of herself, Julia left the stool. There was nothing between her and Geraint Watkin Jones and, given his good looks and her plain ones, there was never likely to be, other than in her dreams. 'I'm taking the carriage to Pontypridd and dropping Father off at his office on the way.' She grabbed Rhian's hand. 'Tell me everything that happens today.'

'I will.' As keen as Julia for the day to start, Rhian forced herself to walk calmly to the end of the corridor to the servants' staircase, then charged up to the attic as fast as she could, to fetch her coat.

'You never consider anyone other than yourself, Julia,' Mabel Larch rebuked her stepdaughter. 'I believe you only volunteered to help Miss Bedford with the correspondence of the Women's Suffrage Society because it would give you an excuse not to attend my coffee morning.'

'I didn't realize the dates clashed when I agreed to the arrangements.' Julia was unable to look either Mabel or her father in the eye.

'It is most unbecoming for an unmarried woman of your age to involve herself in the Suffrage Society. Sensible men abhor feminists and consider them to be laughing stocks.'

'I disagree, Mabel.' Edward folded his copy of *The Times* and tucked it under his arm. 'In fact, I'd go so far as to say that sensible men admire and respect women as intellectual beings and have sympathy with the cause. Some even attend their meetings.'

'But no woman of social consequence in the Rhondda would dream of demeaning herself by attending,' Mabel maintained resolutely. 'Mrs Hodges and Mrs Hadley abhor the Suffrage Society and despair of the way it encourages women to neglect their domestic duties and renounce their femininity in favour of unbecoming masculine pursuits. And both ladies have promised to attend this morning. Think how it will look when you will not be here to greet them, Julia. They will assume that you have no respect for me as your stepmother, or desire to offer them the courtesy that is due to them as our friends and neighbours. They will take your absence as a personal affront.'

'This is your coffee morning, not Julia's, Mabel. Arranged by you to impress people neither I nor Julia wish to become better acquainted with,' Edward interposed.

'Mrs Hodges and Mrs Hadley are highly-respected ladies—'

'Not by me, Mabel.' He shrugged on his overcoat. 'You've ordered the carriage, Julia?'

'Yes, Father.' Julia's hands shook as she buttoned on her gloves. She would never have lied to her stepmother about assisting the headmistress of Pontypridd Intermediate Girls' School with the secretarial duties of the Women's Suffrage Society if her step-mother and the headmistress moved in the same circles. But they didn't. Miss Bedford was a passionate advocacy of feminism and Mabel had no interest in anything or anyone outside of the social circle she was aspiring to penetrate.

Julia tried to console herself with the thought that she hadn't entirely told an untruth. Her offer to help with the correspondence had been accepted and she was meeting Miss Bedford and the other ladies at five o'clock that afternoon.

'I won't need the carriage again until my train gets into Tonypandy station at ten-thirty tonight, Julia, so Harris can wait and bring you home after your suffrage meeting. I will be dining at my club in Cardiff, Mabel.'

'You're never home these days.'

'It is business,' Edward snapped. 'Good morning, Mabel.'

Mabel went to the dining-room window after Edward and Julia left. She watched her husband hand his daughter into the coach.

'May I clear the table now, ma'am?' Mindful of Mrs William's rule that no maid was to remain alone in the same room as the mistress, Bronwen hovered in the hall.

'Yes, Bronwen,' Mabel snapped. She walked to the door. 'Has Mrs Williams returned from the fishmonger's?'

'Yes, ma'am.'

'Tell her that I want to see her in the library immediately. The ladies will be arriving in two hours. You have prepared the drawing room?'

'Yes, ma'am. Mrs Williams ordered it done first thing.'

Mabel crossed the hall and entered the drawing room. Everything was exactly as she'd envisaged it during the planning stage. The Victorian brown varnished paper, oak dado and flowered frieze had been ripped out and replaced by tasteful wallpaper; a most becoming small blue flower pattern on a cream background. She had banished the dark oak furniture her predecessor had chosen, exchanging it for up-to-the-minute pieces that she had picked out from the catalogue of Liberty's in London. Two elegant, beechwood sofas and three chairs, all upholstered in cream velvet, were grouped around the fireplace. The antique bronzes and Staffordshire ornaments Edward's father had bequeathed him had been packed away. In their stead stood a collection of brass candlesticks she had inherited from her maternal grandmother and modern silverware that she had bought for an exorbitant price from the catalogue of a silversmith in Bond Street.

The drapes and tablecloth were cream damask; the oil painting that hung above the fireplace an original her father had given her and Edward as a wedding present. Painted by a Carmarthenshire artist who had once exhibited at the Royal Academy and entitled *Noontide Peace*, it depicted four horses and a dog sleeping in a sun-drenched field.

The room had pleased her – until she had compared it to Mrs Hadley's recently refurbished drawing room. Now, the furniture looked dated. It was, after all, several months old, and Mrs Hadley had opted for a patterned dark-blue chintz. So much more serviceable than plain cream, which showed every mark, including the one Gerald had made when he had dropped a lobster mayonnaise sandwich on to the sofa at Easter tea-time. Probably deliberately just to annoy her.

She loathed boys and, although she would never have admitted it, was a little afraid of them, regarding them as clumsy, sniggering and disrespectful louts. She wished Edward would find somewhere other than Llan House for his son to live during the school holidays. Mrs Hadley sent her sons to France every summer. The entire roomful of ladies had laughed when she had told them about it.

'They can learn the language and do whatever it is boys want to do without disrupting *my* household.'

If only she were on better terms with Edward so she could suggest it to him.

Not wanting to think about how far her relations with her husband had deteriorated, she returned to her critical study of the room. The candlesticks also looked wrong. Brass was not only old-fashioned, it belonged in a farmhouse. But then her grandmother had been a farmer's wife. And the silverware she had lavished so much time in choosing and so much of Edward's money on buying was too shiny, too contemporary and too ostentatious. She imagined Mrs Hadley whispering in Mrs Hodges's ear.

'You can see she comes from farming stock. *So nouveau riche.*'

She ran her finger over the mahogany mantelpiece, hoping to find fault so she could reproach Mrs Williams. But she was disappointed. Her finger left a smudge on the polish and the more she rubbed it, the worse it became.

The room would have looked better if Edward had allowed her

to change the fireplace. She had even picked the one she wanted. A design featuring cherubs in light-cream marble, just like the one in the garden room at the manor house nearest to her father's vicarage. But Edward had not only baulked at the price, he had disliked the style, referring to it as 'overblown and tasteless'.

She sank her head in her hands. All her life she had wanted a husband and a home of her own. But she had never expected to pay the price of loneliness to achieve her goal. Or be so despised by the man she married, once she'd realized it.

Chapter 7

'JOEY, I DIDN'T expect you this early.' Rhian breezed into the kitchen in her knitted suit, carrying her coat and hat. Her smile was infectious, her pleasure at the sight of him so obvious, Joey weakened in relief. He had considered asking Mrs Hopkins not to mention Tonia's visit to anyone, but he suspected that she would take his request as an open invitation to spread gossip. And the one thing he was certain of was that if his neighbour had said anything to anyone, the news would have reached Mrs Williams by now.

'I want to make the most of our time together. Sali's commandeered an hour, remember?' He helped her on with her coat.

'I remember.' She kissed his cheek and Mair giggled self-consciously.

'Quiet, girl!' Mrs Williams scolded.

Rhian pinned on her hat and checked her reflection in the mirror above the sink. 'Bye, everyone.'

'In before ten o'clock, mind, Rhian.' Mrs Williams continued to put the finishing touches to a tray of vases she had filled with white tulips, white being Mrs Larch's preferred colour of the moment. 'Joey, as you are now officially engaged to Rhian, you can walk her to the back door and give her a goodnight kiss. But I'll be watching from the pantry window and if you misbehave in any way or keep her out until one minute past ten—'

'You'll get out your carpet-beater,' he grinned.

'You've got it in one.'

Julia ordered her father's coachman, Harris, to set her down in the yard of Pontypridd railway station and asked him to pick her up outside Miss Bedford's house in Tyfica Road at seven o'clock that evening. She waited until he drove off, before walking briskly down Taff Street. She had spent the last week trying to devise excuses that would allow her to visit Pontypridd – alone – so she could call into Gwilym James and see Geraint Watkin Jones. When her stepmother had set the date for her all-consuming, all-important coffee morning, she had seized the opportunity it offered. But now the moment was actually upon her, she didn't feel anywhere near as brave or determined as she had done in the privacy of her bedroom.

She entered Market Square, faced Gwilym James, squared her shoulders, forced herself to put one foot in front of the other and marched towards the front door as if she were about to go into battle.

'Miss Larch.'

She nodded to the doorman and kept walking. Everything depended on her seeing Geraint Watkin Jones. And if she didn't? If today should prove to be his day off? What then? It might be months before her father's wife organized another coffee morning, especially if it didn't turn out to be the success she hoped for.

'Miss Larch.' Geraint Watkin Jones joined her as she hesitated in the aisle that separated hosiery from lingerie.

'Mr Watkin Jones, can you help me?' she blurted breathlessly. 'I am looking for a birthday present for my father.' Her father's birthday wasn't until September but Geraint Watkin Jones wasn't to know that.

'I am always delighted to help you in any way I can, Miss Larch,' he replied smoothly. 'Have you any particular gift in mind?'

'None.' She looked up into his deep-brown eyes and felt the colour rush to her cheeks. She was big-boned, square and clumsy and had a face like a horse. Would a man as handsome and cul-tured as Geraint Watkin Jones really consider marrying her, even for the fifty thousand pounds her grandfather had left her?

'Perhaps I might suggest a few things. Clothing, or perhaps jewellery? A gift of cuff links or a tiepin is always considered acceptable.'

'Do you have any of the new wristwatches?' Ever since she could remember, her father had worn the pocket gold watch her mother had given him as a wedding present. But wristwatches were becoming more common. Her brother had mentioned that the boys at his school found them more convenient. She wasn't sure her father would appreciate one, but the fashion in wrist-watches was not dependent on the season, so she wouldn't have to explain why she was giving him a lightweight summer shirt in September when the warm weather was ending.

'We have some very fine wristwatches, Miss Larch. If you will come this way, I trust we will be able to accommodate you.' Geraint stood back to allow Julia to precede him to the jewellery counters. He clicked his fingers at the assistant. The young man folded the cloth he'd been using to polish a chain and stood to attention in front of them.

'Would you prefer to see gold or silver wristwatches, Miss Larch?' In one sentence Geraint downgraded the assistant to an errand boy.

'Gold.' She gripped the counter to steady herself. So far her plan was going better than she'd fantasized in her wildest day-dreams. She was basking in the warmth of Geraint's body as he stood next to her, breathing in the heady aroma of his cologne, richer and spicier than her father's. The breath caught in her throat as her imagination ran riot and she pictured herself spending every day of the rest of her life with him.

He took the tray the boy handed him and she noticed that his hands were square and capable, with manicured fingernails. He flicked open half a dozen boxes in turn. 'All gold and, as you see,' he handed her a watch, 'all hallmarked eighteen carat. We do, of course, have nine carat, which some gentlemen prefer as it doesn't mark or show signs of wear so easily. We also have watches with leather straps, which are more suited to an active gentleman.'

Wishing the assistant to the other end of the store, Julia tried to concentrate on the watches but they all looked the same to her. 'I'd prefer eighteen carat.' She recalled that her father's pocket watch was eighteen carat and she didn't want to buy him anything less.

'These are Swiss made.' He lined up the boxes in front of her. 'As you are aware, Miss Larch, Swiss movements are prized for their accuracy and quality.'

'How much is this?' Julia held out the one he had handed her.

'At twenty guineas, that is the most expensive we stock. The price reflects the quality of the gold in the case and strap. And that particular model has an eighteen jewel movement.'

'I'll take it.' She had chosen the watch solely because it was the first one Geraint had handed her.

'An excellent choice, Miss Larch.' Geraint tried to keep his voice on an even and subservient keel as befitting his position. But it wasn't easy. The watch Julia Larch had taken barely five minutes to purchase would cost her more than he earned in six weeks. 'It will be waiting for you at the cashier's desk when you leave. Do you have any other purchases to make?'

Julia opened her handbag when the assistant moved to the other end of the counter to invoice and wrap the watch. 'No, Mr Watkin Jones, I do not. But,' she rummaged past her purse, hairbrush, smelling salts, handkerchief, fountain pen and cologne, too terrified to look up at him in case he rejected her, 'Miss Bedford has asked me to sell tickets for a Women's Suffrage Society meeting to be held on Friday in the YMCA. There will be several eminent speakers and refreshments will be served afterwards.'

'What time is the meeting being held, Miss Larch?'

Her spirits soared. He wouldn't have asked the time if he didn't want to attend, and surely he realized that she had only asked him to buy a ticket because she would be there. 'Seven o'clock, Mr Watkin Jones.'

'Then I am afraid that I will not be able to attend. The store is open until ten o'clock on Thursday, Friday and Saturday evenings.'

Julia stuffed the tickets back into her bag and snapped it shut. 'Of course, how stupid of me.'

'I am embarrassed to confess, Miss Larch, that I know virtually nothing of the Women's Suffrage Society.' Geraint sounded anything but. 'I do, however, have Mondays off. Perhaps you would do me the honour of accompanying me to Cardiff, where I can buy you lunch so you can enlighten me as to the aims of the organization. And afterwards, if you have time, perhaps we could visit a motion picture theatre?'

'I would like that very much indeed, Mr Watkin Jones. Thank you.' Overwhelmed, she found it difficult to restrain her relief – and delight.

'Shall I meet you at twelve o'clock on Cardiff station?' Geraint knew that if he arranged to meet her on Pontypridd station, they would be seen and tongues would wag. His experience with Elizabeth Hadley had taught him that if he were going to succeed in his aim of marrying money, his courting would have to be circumspect and out of the sight of his target's parents.

'I will be there, Mr Watkin Jones.'

'Until then, Miss Larch.' He gave a slight bow, but was careful not to touch her or shake her hand lest anyone notice their familiarity.

'Until then, Mr Watkin Jones.'

He remained at the jewellery counter, watching as she walked to the cashier's desk. Her figure was more suited to a washer-woman or barmaid than a lady of fashion. Her clothes were drab, her complexion even dingier. She was worse than plain, she was ugly, and he wondered why he hadn't thought of Julia Larch before he had approached Elizabeth Hadley.

An unattractive girl was bound to be more appreciative of a man's attentions than a pretty one because the experience would be entirely new to her. Julia was of age, her own mistress, and rumoured to be worth a fortune. He had also seen at first hand the antagonism between her and her stepmother. As a consequence, she would probably be anxious to leave home. All he had to do was discover her exact worth and if it was sufficient for him to live the life of a gentleman, woo and marry her. Then he would be able to leave Gwilym James – for good.

'Mrs Evans told me to tell you that she is waiting in the fitting room, Mr Evans. And on no account are you to accompany your fiancée there.'

'I know when I'm not wanted,' Joey answered the doorman in a resigned voice. 'I'll meet you back here in one hour,' he said to

Rhian. 'If you are going to be any longer, send someone down to tell me that you've been delayed.'

'I will.' Rhian walked up the stairs to the second-floor fitting rooms.

'Is Mr Horton in?' Joey didn't particularly want to see the manager but he felt that as he was in the store he ought to pay his respects.

'Mr Horton is away attending a family funeral, Mr Evans. But Mr Watkin Jones is in the manager's office. Shall I tell him that you want to see him, sir?'

'There's no need for you to trouble yourself, Sam.' Joey forced a smile. 'I'll announce myself.'

Julia crossed Market Square, entered the arcade and walked into the teashop. Oblivious to the women sitting around her, she ordered a plate of cream cakes and a pot of tea. She had made progress. Only a beginning, but an auspicious one. She felt as though she had taken her first step on the path that would lead her to the rest of her life, and hopefully a better and happier one than the one she was living at present.

Joey knocked once on Mr Horton's office door before walking in. Geraint was sitting behind the manager's desk, staring into space.

'*So* sorry to disturb you when you are hard at work.' Joey closed the door behind him.

Geraint's face darkened. 'It is customary to wait outside a door until permission is given to enter.'

'I am a manager; you are an assistant manager.' Without waiting to be invited, Joey sat in the visitor's chair.

'You are not the manager of this store.'

'I hold a senior position to yours in the company.' Joey pulled a silver case from the inside pocket of his coat. He opened it and removed a cigarette without offering it to Geraint.

'A monkey can wear a crown and still remain a monkey,' Geraint said childishly.

Joey flicked the silver lighter Lloyd and Sali had given him for

113

Christmas. 'Tonia told me that you two are finished. Did you walk away from her because of what I told you about Connie's store?'

'What happened was between Antonia and me, and is none of your business.' Geraint moved his chair back and it hit the wall.

'Careful, you're chipping the plaster, and that won't please Mr Horton. You know how particular he is about his office.'

'He allows me to use it in his absence.'

'Really?' Joey raised a sceptical eyebrow. 'And for your information, what happened isn't just between you and Tonia. She is eighteen, three years under age, and six years younger than you. Tell me, if you weren't after Connie's store, why did you set out to seduce her?' Joey's tone was conversational, the expression in his eyes, menacing.

'I didn't,' Geraint blustered, 'I—'

'Before you say another word, I saw exactly what you were doing to my cousin.'

Intimidated by the look in Joey's eyes, Geraint left his chair and backed towards the door, but Joey was quicker than him. He leapt up and hit Geraint soundly on the jaw.

Caught off guard, Geraint flew back and hit his head against the wall. He slid down, slumping in a crumpled and bleeding heap at Joey's feet.

'It's beautiful, Sali, but a gown like this costs the earth. I couldn't possibly afford it.' Rhian gazed at herself in the cheval mirror. She was finding it difficult to believe that the reflection was her and not an illustration of a princess from one of Bella's fairy tale books.

The store's senior dressmaker, Miss Collins, took a pin from one of her juniors and tucked in a fold of white satin at the back of the gown. She concealed it beneath the train that flowed loose from the shoulder seams and swept for a full yard over the ground behind the hem. 'This particular model is two sizes too large for you, madam. But I doubt you'll find another wedding gown that will suit you half as well.'

'It is perfect, Rhian,' Sali concurred.

'It will take twelve weeks to make one to madam's exact measurements. It's the Austrian crystals, Mrs Evans,' Miss Collins apologized to Sali. 'They are a special order and we have to send to Vienna for them.'

'Rhian has plenty of time, Miss Collins. She is not getting married until the first of August.' The gown was the height of fashion but that wasn't why Sali had picked it out. The instant she saw it, she knew that it would highlight Rhian's slim figure and delicate colouring. Slender-cut with a high waist, knee-length lace over-tunic and richly-beaded lace and satin train, it was decorated with pendent bands of sparkling crystals that swung in glittering hoops from the shoulders to the hips.

'Shall I order one made in your measurements, madam?' Miss Collins asked Rhian.

'All you need is a lace veil, crystal tiara, elbow-length lace gloves and satin slippers to transform you into the perfect bride, Rhian. And I don't want to hear a word about money. Your outfit is Lloyd's and my wedding present to you and Joey.'

'I couldn't—'

'You could.'

'My wedding dress is hardly something for Joey,' Rhian demurred.

'The woman inside it will be. But are you sure that you don't want to look at any others? I'd hate to think that I forced this one on you. We have a wide selection of more traditional as well as fashionable gowns.'

Rhian shook her head. 'None of them could possibly make me look as good as this one does.'

'They wouldn't,' Miss Collins concurred.

'Then you'll let me buy it for you?'

Rhian hesitated.

'It would give Lloyd and me such pleasure.'

'Yes, please, but only if you let me buy the accessories,' Rhian conceded.

'I won't because a wedding outfit is a package. Miss Collins, you'll take Rhian's measurements and send for the appropriate accessories?'

'I will, Mrs Evans.' The dressmaker reached for her tape measure.

Sali glanced at her watch. 'As we're running over the hour, I'll tell Joey that you'll be late. You'll come to the house for tea?'

'I'm sorry, we can't. Joey's made an appointment for us to see Father Kelly and we promised to visit Victor and Megan afterwards.'

'We were there yesterday. Give her my love, kiss the twins for me and we'll see you next week.'

'You will, and thank you. I never thought I'd have a wedding dress like this.' Rhian glanced back into the mirror.

Sali opened the door and saw the supervisor from menswear running towards her. She stepped into the corridor and closed the door behind her.

'Mr Paige sent me to get you, Mrs Evans. Mr Watkin Jones has met with an accident in Mr Horton's office.'

'Joey, how could you?' Sali demanded irately after Geraint had been examined by a doctor, packed into a cab and sent back to Ynysangharad House to be cared for by his housekeeper.

'Very easily.' Joey rubbed his fist. His knuckles had already turned the peculiar shade of red that precedes severe bruising.

'I've often felt like hitting Geraint myself, but I've always managed to control myself. Couldn't you?'

'No.' Joey lifted his head and looked her in the eye.

'If Geraint has done something to you—'

'Not to me, but to someone close to me.'

'Rhian?' Sali asked quickly.

He shook his head. 'Please, don't ask me any more questions, Sali. I can't answer them.'

'Why?' she demanded.

'Because I made someone a promise and I won't break it.'

'You do realize that I will ask Geraint about this.'

'He won't give you any more answers than I have.'

'You seem very confident about that.'

'I am,' he declared flatly.

'Geraint's my brother; I have a right to know what he's done.'

'Not when the knowledge will hurt a third . . .' Joey almost said 'and innocent party' but given Tonia's recent behaviour the last thing he could call her was innocent.

'You're fortunate Geraint refused to press charges.'

'He knew what would happen to him if he tried.' Joey left the chair and went to the door. 'And if it ever came out, it wouldn't be just me hitting him.'

'Lloyd, Victor?' Sali looked at him in alarm.

'I've said all I am going to. Do you think Rhian will be ready now?'

'Possibly,' Sali answered non-committaly.

He opened the door. 'Do me a favour, don't mention this to her.'

'I won't, but you can bet your last sixpence that someone has by now. Gossip flies around this store faster than smoke up a chimney.'

'You do know that I would tell you if I could.'

She nodded. It wasn't idle curiosity that had led her to press Joey. The alternative to not knowing why Joey had hit Geraint was imagining all kinds of lurid reasons. And given Geraint's faults, she hated herself for even thinking what some of them might be.

Sali was right, Rhian had heard about the altercation between Joey and Geraint before she'd left the fitting room. And she was as annoyed as Sali at his refusal to tell her any more.

'We have time to lunch in the New Inn,' he offered, in an attempt to change the subject.

'The New Inn is monstrously expensive.'

'A celebratory lunch for our engagement,' he suggested, elated by his momentary success in steering the conversation away from him and Geraint.

'After hearing what you've just done, I'm hardly in the mood for a celebration and I shouldn't think you'd be either,' she reproached.

'I'm hungry. I'll settle for a sandwich and a cup of tea in the arcade if you won't go anywhere else.'

'Why won't you tell me why you did it?' She recalled his reticence the week before when they had called into the store.

'This has something to do with what happened last week. You said that you'd quarrelled with Geraint then.'

'I can't talk about it,' he pleaded.

'Won't, more like.'

'Can't,' he corrected, 'and as you only get one day off a week, let's not spoil it.'

'Just answer me one thing.' She laid her hand on his arm, and stopped him in the middle of Market Square. 'Is it about a girl?'

'I made someone a promise,' he hedged.

'A girl someone?'

'Not a girl I've gone out with or even looked at in the way I've looked at you.'

'I didn't think there was a girl left within a ten-mile radius that you haven't gone out with.'

'I swear I have never regarded this one as my girlfriend, not even for a second.'

'And telling me more would break your promise to her?'

'Yes,' he confessed miserably.

'Why did you promise her anything if she means nothing to you?' When he didn't answer her question, she said, 'Only last week you made me a solemn promise. Do you make a habit of going around promising girls whatever they ask of you?'

He gripped her by the shoulders and pulled her into the shelter of a doorway. 'I made you a promise. I won't and haven't broken it. And I'll swear that on the Bible if you want me to. What happened between Geraint and me is nothing to do with any girl that I've ever gone out with.'

'You mean it?'

His eyes were dark, anguished. 'Yes.'

'If I ever find out that you've lied to me, Joey, I'll walk away from you and keep on walking. There'll be no second chance.'

'I know.'

'Let's go to the New Inn and have lunch.'

'And then we'll go back to Tonypandy and see Father Kelly about booking the wedding before visiting Victor and Megan.'

'Yes.' She tried to smile, but a tiny maggot of doubt wormed at the back of her mind, poisoning her thoughts and magnifying every reservation she'd ever had about accepting Joey's proposal.

'A visit from my sister. I am honoured,' Geraint watched his housekeeper pour, sugar, milk and stir his tea, before taking a piece of toast from the rack she had set on the table. 'I take it you haven't come for breakfast?' he enquired caustically when Sali shook her head at the housekeeper's offer of refreshments.

'No, I haven't, Geraint.'

'I'll ring if I need anything else, Mrs Andrews.' He dismissed the elderly housekeeper, who left the room and closed the door behind her.

Knowing that if she waited for an invitation to sit down she'd wait for ever, Sali sat opposite her brother at the table. 'By the look of you, you've fully recovered.'

'No thanks to your thug of a brother-in-law.' He picked up his knife and fork and cut into the bacon and eggs Mrs Andrews had put in front of him.

'You still refuse to tell me why he hit you.'

'Does a ruffian like him need a reason? After growing up in the gutter and working in a colliery before you pulled strings to get him a position in Gwilym James, he probably thinks beating a man senseless is an acceptable pastime.'

Sali flinched at the insult, aimed not only at Joey, but Lloyd's entire family. It wasn't easy to ignore, but having discovered from past and unpleasant experience that a shouting match with Geraint would achieve precisely nothing, she continued. 'Joey wouldn't have hit you for no reason.'

'That's right, take the side of the dirt you married into.'

A steely note crept into her voice. 'I didn't come here to have an argument with you, Geraint, but another comment like that and I will.'

'Why did you come?' he demanded belligerently.

'You haven't been in work since last Tuesday.'

'I had concussion.' He set down his fork, buttered two pieces of toast and cut them into triangles.

119

'You're up, you're dressed and you look perfectly fit to me now.'

'Monday is my day off. I have an important engagement.'

'Can I tell Mr Horton that you'll be in work tomorrow?' she persisted patiently.

'You can tell him what you damn well please.'

She found it difficult to ignore his swearing, but not wanting to get sidetracked from the purpose of her visit, refrained from reproaching him. 'He won't be pleased if he sees you walking around town today.'

'Now you're threatening to dismiss me from Gwilym James?'

'As you well know, hiring and firing is Mr Horton's prerogative, not mine.'

'Come on, Sali, drop the pretence.' He picked up his fork. 'Mr Horton's your lap dog. He wouldn't dare be anything else when it's your son who owns the business.'

'If he ever hears you saying that, you will be out of the door,' she informed him coldly. 'I have no more influence than any of the other trustees over Mr Horton.'

'Has he been complaining to you about my work?' There was an edge to Geraint's voice and Sali hoped that he was disturbed by the thought of losing his only income.

'I'm your sister, not your guardian. If you're worried about your position in the company, I suggest you talk to Mr Horton about it. That's if you do condescend to work tomorrow.'

'You can tell Mr Horton I'll be in,' he conceded abruptly.

'Tell him yourself,' she said wearily. 'There's one more thing. The trustees have asked me to remind you that Mother died six months ago.'

'And you want me out of your house.' He tossed his napkin over the uneaten food on his plate.

'The trustees want you out of *Harry's* house,' she corrected. 'You requested one month's grace; you have been given four. I asked them to pay the wages of the nurse and housekeeper and the running costs of this annex so Mother would be cared for during her lifetime. They felt that they couldn't do any less for Harry's grandmother and, while she was alive, they were happy for you to live with her.'

'And now she's dead they're happy to put Harry's uncle out on the street?' he challenged.

'They're not happy about the situation, Geraint. But, unlike Mother, you are able-bodied. And for the last three years you have been promising me and the trustees that you will look for other accommodation, rather than be a burden on your nephew's estate.'

'If I'd found anywhere suitable, I'd be there,' he snapped.

'It costs a great deal to keep this wing open. There are coals, electricity and gas to pay for as well as Mrs Andrew's wages and the meals Mrs Williams sends over from the main kitchen. I told the trustees I'd talk to you one more time before—'

'Before what, *dear* sister? They send me an eviction notice?' he cut in.

'It's not my decision.'

'No, only one-twelfth of your decision. I'll look for lodgings but have you considered Llinos and Gareth?' He referred to their younger brother and sister. 'Where are they supposed to go when they visit their home town? Judging by the way you treat me, I can't see you making them welcome in your house.'

'Gareth and Llinos know that they can stay with us in the main house any time they choose.'

'But I can't!'

'Not permanently, no.' She struggled to contain her temper. 'Holidays are different, and if you were living away like them you'd be welcome to visit – for a week or two,' she added pointedly.

Gareth's inheritance had been invested in property, which their uncle had been unable to plunder. He had an income of four hundred pounds a year, which had covered the cost of his education, enabled him to set up a modest saving account and enrol in Sandhurst after he'd left school. Llinos's education had been paid for by Harry's trustees and they had, at Sali's instigation, also advanced Llinos a loan so she could take a position as a 'working' pupil in a language school in Switzerland with a view to becoming a lady's travelling companion. But Sali knew her sister's sole ambition was to marry well and wealthily. Laudable or not, at least Llinos had an ambition, whereas Geraint appeared to have none.

'You'd be happy to see me living in some ghastly run-down lodging house with colliers, wouldn't you?' Geraint taunted.

'I'd be happy seeing you living anywhere where you weren't a burden on my son's estate,' Sali replied tartly. 'Plenty of men are paying mortgages and bringing up families on less than you earn. You've had absolutely no living expenses for the past three years. Surely you've saved something?'

'I've had to buy my clothes . . . my . . .'

Loath to listen to more of her brother's excuses, Sali left the table. 'It would be embarrassing for the trustees and me if you force us to serve an eviction notice on you, but we will if we have to. Please, be out by the end of the month.'

'And if I can't find anywhere?'

'Mrs Jenkins at the lodge has a spare room.'

'You expect me to move into the lodge!' Geraint was horrified by the thought.

'It's clean and it's comfortable.'

'It doesn't even have an inside bathroom.'

'No, but the spare bedroom has a washstand. Mrs Jenkins charges seventeen shillings and sixpence a week for accommodation, breakfast, supper and personal laundry. If you don't move in voluntarily, I will arrange to have your things taken over there on the last day of this month. You will have to be out by then because a builder is coming in on the first of next month to carry out repairs to the chimney and annex roof. Should you find somewhere else before then, I would appreciate it if you would let me know, so I can give Mrs Andrews notice.'

'Believe you me, I'll do my best to find something better than the lodge.'

Hurt by his ingratitude as much as his anger, Sali drew comfort from the thought of Lloyd and his family's love and support when she returned to the main house. They had helped her to see her brother for what he was: a snobbish, discontented man, hopelessly shackled by bitter resentment. Their uncle had not only lost Geraint's money but also destroyed his integrity and self-respect.

Geraint hated having to work in the store. He hated being subservient to Mr Horton, he hated having to be polite to people he regarded as beneath him, and he hated being beholden to Harry's trustees for the roof over his head. Yet he continued to remain sunk in the rut he had fallen into, making no effort to move out or find a position more suited to a man of his education and intelligence.

Their father had made great plans for all of them when they'd been children. When he'd been alive, Geraint had been interested in the collieries their grandfather had sunk and their family had still owned. But his plans to study engineering in university had dissipated along with his money. If only he would realize that his self-pity was wasting and destroying his life and his talents.

She wanted to tell Geraint that he wasn't alone; that, whatever else, she loved him because he was her brother, and she would do everything she could to help him, short of supporting him in a lifestyle he could no longer afford. But while he remained consumed with anger, she couldn't even talk to him, let alone give him the encouragement he needed to change his life.

Geraint cringed when he saw Julia step off the Cardiff train. She had bought a new outfit. A light-grey coat, matching skirt and wide-brimmed hat trimmed with ostrich feathers. He recognized it as part of the latest spring range from the most expensive French fashion house that supplied Gwilym James. On most women of Julia's age, it would have been stunning. But instead of resembling a fashion plate she reminded him of a clumsy adolescent at the 'ugly age' who had dressed up in her mother's best clothes. No amount of money or careful cut of cloth could disguise Julia Larch's thick-set figure, or plain face.

'That is a lovely coat you are wearing. Light colours suit you,' he said insincerely, when she reached him.

'Thank you. This is the first time I've left off mourning since my mother died.' Unused to receiving compliments, she coloured in embarrassment.

'Where shall we lunch?' He offered her his arm.

'My father always takes us to the Angel Hotel when we come to

Cardiff.' She wished the words back into her mouth the moment she had spoken them. From the time she had realized the importance of money she had been given a generous allowance, which her father had increased annually until her twenty-first birthday when she had been allowed control of the trust fund her grandfather had set up for her. When she and her brother had inherited her mother's estate, they both went from being comfortably off to wealthy, by anyone's standards. As a result, she hardly ever thought of the cost of her purchases relative to a working man's wage.

'The Angel Hotel it is.' His voice, flat, devoid of emotion, made her feel even worse.

'Only if you let me pay.'

'I wouldn't hear of it,' Geraint said stiffly.

'You can pay for the theatre afterwards.'

Geraint did a rapid mental calculation. He would get very little change from fifteen shillings if they had a bottle of wine with their lunch in the Angel Hotel. The best seats in the theatre would cost him half-a-crown for the two of them, he had to pay his train fare and possibly even buy tea in a teashop after the show. He was earning three pounds a week; a weekly outing like this could easily cost him half his wage. Swallowing his pride, he said, 'I'll compromise with you, Miss Larch. I'll pay this time, you can pay next.'

Julia was elated by the thought that he was already planning their next outing, but she tempered her enthusiasm. First, two outings didn't constitute a full courtship. And secondly, even if Geraint Watkin Jones was prepared to marry her for her money — and that was a big 'if' because she was nowhere near as attractive as Elizabeth Hadley — much as she couldn't wait to escape from her stepmother, she didn't want to exchange Mabel for someone who might prove even more difficult to live with. And, unlike a stepmother, a husband would have legal control over both her and her money.

She took his arm. Geraint Watkin Jones might be doing his utmost to charm her, but she was astute enough to know that his attitude towards her might change, especially if he began to suspect that she needed him to gain her independence every bit as much as he needed her money. Also, should things progress between them to the point of marriage, she wanted to be certain that he would treat her with respect, if not affection. And that it would be possible for them to build comfortable, if separate lives, and, for propriety's sake, under the same roof.

Chapter 8

RHIAN DROPPED THE ironing basket on to one of the kitchen chairs, lifted out a table napkin, laid it on the table, dipped her fingers into a bowl of lavender water and sprinkled it liberally over the creased damask linen. She rolled it up, set it to one side and picked up another.

'Rhian, leave that.' Mrs Williams bustled in with a basket of the family's mending. 'Mrs Larch wants her shoes picked up from the cobbler's, immediately, if not sooner. So, apron and cap off.' The twinkle in her eye belied the sharp tone of her voice.

'Yes, Mrs Williams.' Rhian tore off her cap before she reached the door to the servants' staircase.

'Wear your coat not a cardigan, it may be spring but it's cold out there. And,' Mrs Williams lowered her voice, 'no more than twenty minutes in Gwilym James.'

Rhian ran all the way to Dunraven Street to save an extra five minutes to add to the twenty. The cobbler's was full but she managed to attract the attention of an apprentice who had a soft spot for her and less than two minutes after walking in there she was at the door of Gwilym James.

'Mr Evans is in his office, Miss Jones.' The doorman gave her a sly wink.

Joey was on his feet before she was even halfway down the aisle to his office, he grabbed his suit jacket from the back of his chair, shrugged it on over his waistcoat and shouted to his assistant manager, who was re-arranging the window display of leather goods, 'Hold the fort for me for quarter of an hour, Sam.'

'The Irish linen rep will be in any minute,' Sam called back.

'Give him a cup of tea and a chocolate digestive. Two if you have to.' Joey grabbed Rhian's hand. 'Thank Mrs Williams for me.'

'Why?'

'I saw her coming out of Rodney's this morning and asked if she could find you an errand.'

'You're right, she must be getting fond of you.' Rhian was amazed that the housekeeper had agreed to Joey's request. 'Where are we going?'

'It won't be a surprise for long.' He led her across the road to the jeweller's.

The manager dropped the newspaper he was reading when he saw them coming. He disappeared into the back room and emerged a moment later with a velvet-covered tray that he set on the glass counter in front of them.

'Shall I tell her, Mr Evans?' he asked Joey.

'No, Mr Stephens. Let her guess.'

The manager whipped off the velvet cloth and Rhian looked down on a glittering array of wedding bands.

'They're new designs that came in yesterday. I wanted you to have first pick, before they went,' Joey explained.

'You've already chosen one, haven't you?' Rhian said.

'Yes, but saying that, you can have any of them, or we could look elsewhere if you prefer.'

Rhian studied the rings. Some were embossed with patterns of flowers and leaves, some engraved with abstract designs, but she was drawn to the plain gold bands. A few were so thick and heavy they looked as though they'd be uncomfortable to wear, others were so thin and light she thought they'd snap if they were subjected to continuous use. She found herself returning to one particular ring midway between the two extremes. She pointed to it.

'You were right, Mr Evans.' The manager lifted it from the bed. 'That's the exact ring Mr Evans said you'd choose, Miss Jones. Would you like to try it on for size?'

'It will fit her perfectly.' Joey took it, slipped his mother's regard ring from Rhian's finger and put on the band.

'How did you know the size?' she asked.

'From my mother's ring. You really do like this one?'

'It's beautiful.'

'That's it then, Mr Stephens. You'll engrave it *Joseph and Rhian Evans, 1 August 1914*?' He looked to Rhian for confirmation. She nodded.

'I'll make a note of it, Mr Evans.' The jeweller opened a drawer in the counter and removed an individual ring box. He slipped the ring into it, scribbled a note on a pad, tore off the piece of paper and folded it on top. 'And the engagement ring, Mr Evans?'

'I don't want one,' Rhian protested.

'I know you said you didn't but I thought you could at least look at them. There's a solitaire . . .'

'I don't want to see it.' Rhian shook her head determinedly

'Most girls insist on the most expensive in the shop, Mr Evans, so if I were you I'd quit while you are ahead and be grateful for an undemanding fiancée.'

'I'm that all right.' Joey wrapped his arm around Rhian's shoulders. 'Can I pick up the ring next week?'

'It will be ready on Monday, Mr Evans.'

'You didn't say anything about getting the ring so soon.' Rhian linked her fingers into his when they left the shop.

'I told Mr Stephens I wanted to get you something special and when he showed the tray to me last night, I couldn't wait for you to see it. Now I feel as if we really are going to be married. Have you time to go to the teashop?'

'Mrs Williams is kind, but she'll never hear the end of it if the mistress finds out I've been there in my uniform in the middle of the day.'

'Kiss then?' he asked hopefully.

'In the middle of the street?'

'You'd prefer my office?'

'I only have ten minutes left of the twenty Mrs Williams gave me.'

'It only takes one to draw the blinds. That gives us nine whole minutes,' he grinned, 'and if I'm not going to see you again for twenty-four hours, I intend to make the most of them.'

*

'Have a good journey to Pontypridd and enjoy your suffragette meeting.' Geraint showed his platform ticket and walked Julia to the Pontypridd train.

'I will. Thank you again for a lovely day,' Julia gushed.

'Goodbye.' He halted outside the open door to a first-class carriage.

'Goodbye,' Julia echoed, leaning towards him.

He hesitated for the barest fraction of a second before ignoring her proffered cheek and holding out his hand. 'Same time and place next week?'

She broke into a radiant smile. 'Yes, please.' She stepped inside the train, the stationmaster blew his whistle and the guard slammed the doors shut. Geraint stood back and watched the train chug out of the station.

Although it was only their first outing, there was a barrier between them; one he recognized of his own making. Julia Larch had responded to his compliments with blushes, listened attentively to every single word that he had said, allowed him to hold her hand the entire time the picture house had been plunged into darkness, when he had imagined that he was with Tonia, and even leaned towards him in expectation of a kiss when they'd parted.

She met all the criteria he had dreamed of finding in a wife. She was wealthy, of age, independent from her family and had a pleasant and equitable nature. But he had found it almost impossible to conceal the fact that she repelled him physically.

With the deadline to leave Ynysangharad House looming, he had to secure his future as a matter of urgency and, as there was only one other woman in comfortable, if not independent circumstances who had responded to his attentions, he found himself questioning the veracity of what Joey had told him about Rodney's stores. The more he considered the idea that Connie Rodney's father had left the store to his nephew, not daughter, the more he wanted to dismiss the idea. But he was realistic enough to know that Tonia, not common sense, was his motive for questioning Joey's assertion.

The thought of Julia naked revolted him, the idea of sharing a bed with her made him feel nauseous. Whereas Tonia . . . He smiled when he recalled how accommodating she had proved during their shared afternoons in the privacy of the stockroom before Joey had burst in on them.

He needed to know more about Connie Rodney's finances, but he could hardly go up to Tonypandy and start asking question about her shop, assets and bank account without raising suspicions. And even if Connie was as wealthy as Julia Larch, which he doubted, there was no guarantee that she'd give her daughter a penny or consent to his marriage to Tonia unless, as Joey had so shrewdly pointed out, he made Tonia pregnant.

If he did, would Tonia's mother sit back and watch him and Tonia struggle to bring up her grandchildren in poverty? Or if she did deign to help them, would she expect him to help her in her shop, because much as he hated working in Gwilym James, he most certainly didn't want to exchange his position there for an assistant's job in a grocer's shop. And even all these 'what ifs' were dependent on him getting Tonia to speak to him after the scene outside the stockroom.

He'd missed her, or rather their stocktaking sessions the last week. But if he was going to resume his relationship with her, he couldn't allow the situation between them to fester for much longer. He was dreading returning to Gwilym James in the morning. Because no matter how much he tried to hide in the office and the stockrooms, sooner or later he was going to have to walk on to the shop floor. And, at that moment, he didn't have a clue what he could possibly say to her.

'Did you have a good time yesterday, Miss Julia?' Rhian asked when she brushed her hair the following morning.

'Yes.' Julia held her finger to her lips. 'Open the door,' she whispered urgently.

Rhian did as she asked and looked up and down the landing. 'There's no one out there.'

'Whenever we talk in here I have the feeling that Mrs Larch is standing outside with her ear pressed to the keyhole.'

'She's downstairs, checking the menu for next week's Ladies' Circle tea party with Mrs Williams.'

'Before breakfast?' Julia asked in surprise.

'She's been up early every day since the coffee morning.'

'I heard it was a great success.' Julia tried not to sound disparaging.

'We were talking about yesterday. Are you going to see your young man again, Miss Julia?' Rhian asked, unable to contain herself a moment longer.

'Yes, next Monday.' Julia smiled.

'What is he like?'

'Tall, dark, handsome, well read, well educated, polite and charming.'

'A real gentleman.'

'In every way,' Julia concurred.

'Where did he take you?'

'We lunched at the Angel Hotel in Cardiff then visited a picture house and afterwards we had tea in one of the small shops in the arcade before he walked me to the station.'

'That sounds as if you had a good time.'

'The best.' Julia smiled at the memory.

'Are you going to see him again?'

'Next week. Where is your Mr Evans taking you today?' Julia had said more than she'd wanted to about Geraint. She trusted Rhian implicitly, but her courtship with Geraint was very new and hardly normal and she couldn't bear the thought of anyone, especially Rhian, of whom she was really fond, criticizing it at this early stage.

'To Victor and Megan's for lunch and Sali and Lloyd's for tea. We do go to other places sometimes, but we both like seeing the children.'

'You are lucky that your Mr Evans has a large family. It must be lovely to have nieces and nephews.'

'They're not my real nieces and nephews yet, but yes, it is nice.' Rhian pushed the last pin into Julia's chignon and combed the loose hair from her brush.

'All I know about young children and babies is what I can remember from Gerald's childhood. And because there are eleven years between us, to be truthful I wasn't very interested in him at the time. Do you want children?'

'Joey has already told me that he hopes we'll have babies.' Rhian smiled self-consciously.

'In the plural.'

'When I look at Sali's three and Victor's twins I agree with him. It must be wonderful to be part of a large family.'

'You've never talked much about your childhood. Was it happy? Did you have brothers and sisters?'

'Two brothers, both years older than me. They are dead now.'

Ever sensitive, Julia recognized something in the tone of Rhian's voice that warned her not to pry further. 'I'm going to miss you and our chats when you leave to get married.' Julia untied the cape she wore when Rhian did her hair.

'I'm not marrying for months yet and the way things are with your young man, you may be walking up the aisle before me.'

'And I think you're building a very large castle on the foundation of one outing.' Julia reached for the locket on her dressing table.

'It will be two next week. And you do like him?' Rhian fished, sensing that something wasn't quite right between Miss Julia and her young man.

'Oh, yes.'

'And you think it will lead to marriage?'

'I hope so.' Julia didn't dare confide the identity of her secret 'admirer', not that she felt entitled to call Geraint that, when it was her money that he admired.

'Then if you don't mind me saying so, why don't you bring him to the house? Your father is a kind man—'

'And Mrs Larch?' When Rhian remained silent, Julia added, 'I want to keep him to myself until we get to know one another really well.'

'I can understand that.'

'Rhian?'

'Yes?' Rhian twisted the loose hair from Julia's brush into a spiral and dropped it into her hair tidy.

'Your Mr Evans is quite comfortably off, isn't he?' Julia really wanted to ask her maid's opinion on the idea of marrying solely for money but she thought the direct question would shock her.

'Joey earns a good wage, a lot more than me of course, and his father owns houses,' Rhian began earnestly. 'But that isn't why I'm marrying him.'

'I wasn't suggesting for one minute that it was. It's just that – and I'm talking about myself – it's not easy when one person is much wealthier than the other.'

'Megan had nothing when she married and Victor had the farm but that didn't seem to bother either of them. And although I've never talked to Sali about it, I don't think Lloyd was keen to move into Ynysangharad House, but he put up with it for her and Harry's sake.'

'And there're no problems?'

'With Sali and Lloyd, and Victor and Megan? Not that I've ever seen. I only hope Joey and I will be as happy.' Rhian hung her mistress's cape away in the wardrobe. 'This young man of yours,' she ventured. 'He doesn't have as much money as you?'

'No,' Julia said quickly, not wanting to give Rhian a clue that might identify him.

'But money isn't what's really important. And your father is reasonable and easy to talk to. I'm sure once he realizes how much you love him, he will give you permission to marry.'

'Even if he doesn't, I am of age and I can marry without it.'

'You wouldn't do that, would you, Miss Julia?' Given how close her master and the young mistress had been, especially before the old mistress had died, Rhian couldn't bear the thought of an estrangement between them.

Julia rose from the stool. 'It's early days. Promise me, Rhian, that you won't breathe a word of this to anyone. So far as you know, Monday is my suffragette day.'

'I promise, Miss Julia.'

'Thank you for taking the time to do my hair. Enjoy yourself today.'

'I will.'

'And, before I forget, I caught Mrs Larch looking in my drawers. When she saw me watching her, she commented on how tidy they were, so I told her that my wardrobe needs sorting out and I'd asked you to see to it this week. So next time you sneak away to read in here, take some of the clothes out of the wardrobe and put them on the bed.'

'I will. Thank you, Miss Julia.'

'Thank you,' Julia smiled, 'and hurry. You don't want to keep your Mr Evans waiting.'

'Mr Watkin Jones, sir?'

'You spoke to me, boy?' Geraint glared at the lad. In all his time at the store he had never known a lift attendant address him by name.

'Yes, sir.' The boy faltered, amazed at his own temerity. 'I spoke to Mr Evans, the manager of the Tonypandy store, the other day,' he began hesitantly.

'I do know who Mr Evans is,' Geraint barked brusquely. The mention of Joey didn't exactly endear the boy to him.

'I told him that I wasn't happy working on the lifts and I'd like a trainee assistant's job. He suggested that I speak to you about it, sir.'

'Did he now?' Geraint mused, his temper rising.

'You, or Miss Gulliford, sir. Do you think that I could get a trainee assistant's job, sir? My brother Geoff works in the stock-room in Tonypandy, and Mr Evans has promised to look at his work record in four months and, if it's good enough, give him a trial. That's all I'm asking for, sir, a trial.'

'You live in Tonypandy and travel down every day?' Geraint asked.

'Yes, sir, in Primrose Street, not too far from Mr Evans. Of course, his father owns his own house.' Wary of putting himself on the same social level as the manager of the Tonypandy store, the boy felt the need to explain his background. 'We rent from Mrs Rodney.'

'Mrs Rodney of Rodney's Provisions?' Geraint softened his voice.

'Yes, sir, she owns most of the houses in our street, sir. Al-though from the way her daughter behaves you'd never think it.

134

She always has time for a kind word, sir.' The lift reached the top floor, the boy opened the doors but Geraint didn't step out.

'So, how many houses would you say that Mrs Rodney owns?' he asked thoughtfully.

'Hundreds, sir. It's not just Primrose Street; she has houses all over Pandy. She even employs her own rent collector. About the job, sir—'

'Tell you what I'll do . . . what is your name?'

'Mike, sir, my mother called me Micah after one of the Old Testament kings but I prefer Mike. You won't tell anyone, will you, sir? Most people think I'm Michael.'

'I won't tell anyone – Mike. I'll talk to Mr Horton and see about moving you into the stockroom. If you do well there for a month or so, I'll consider you for the first trainee assistant vacancy.'

'Thank you, sir.' Mike gazed at Geraint as he strode up the corridor. Mr Evans had been right. All he'd had to do was talk to one of the managers. And it had been so easy the only wonder was that he hadn't plucked up the courage to do it before.

'Miss Adams?' Geraint waylaid the supervisor when she returned from her lunch break. 'Could you spare Miss George for an hour when she has finished serving her customers? Mr Horton has ordered an intensive stocktake to ensure that we don't overbuy for the next three months before the July sale. Your department in particular had more out-of-season reduced goods than were strictly needed last January.'

Taking Geraint's comment as he'd intended, as an adverse reflection on her inability to control her stock, Miss Adams replied, 'Of course, Mr Watkin Jones. Please, keep Miss George for as long as you need her.'

Tonia was showing a selection of straw hats to a woman and her two young daughters. Although apparently engrossed in her task, she'd heard every word Geraint had said.

Like everyone else in the store she knew that Geraint hadn't been in work because he'd been suffering the after-effects of Joey's assault, but unlike everyone else she knew why Joey had hit him.

As Geraint hadn't attempted to see her privately or contact her since Joey had walked in on them in the stockroom, she had assumed that Joey had been right and Geraint was after her mother's money, not her.

The knowledge hurt and she had determined, even before Joey had hit him, that if she could make Geraint Watkin Jones suffer for what he had done to her – she would.

Geraint answered Tonia's knock on the stockroom door ten minutes later. 'Miss George, thank you for coming so promptly.' He looked up and down the empty corridor before admitting her. 'My dear Miss George.' He locked the door and kissed her.

Tonia pushed him away and kicked his shins with all the force she could muster. 'You beast!'

'Ow! That hurt!'

'It was meant to.' She lifted her foot, intending to kick him again, but he retreated behind a pile of stock to rub his wounds.

'Why so vicious?'

'How can you ask that question after what you did to me?'

'Darling—'

'Don't "darling" me. Joey was right; you're only after my mother's money.'

'Surely you didn't believe him?' Geraint countered indignantly, still massaging his aching leg.

'Of course I did,' she retorted fiercely.

'Tonia, Tonia, look where I live, and the way I live. Not to mention how I dress.'

'Everyone knows that you lost your money.'

'But I earn a decent wage. Granted, it's not what I'm used to, but I have the wing of Ynysangharad House, expense-free for as long as I need it, or I will have when the repairs are completed on the roof next month,' he lied. 'And when I marry, I'll move my wife in there. It's fairly modest, but there are four bedrooms, a bathroom, drawing room, dining room and study, all fully furnished. And I and my future family have use of the grounds, garden, carriages and car.'

'Really?' she questioned suspiciously.

'Tonia, everyone knows that my nephew is going to inherit the store. You don't think he'd allow his uncle to live like a pauper, do you? Besides, I have shares in the company,' he elaborated, moving further into the realms of fantasy.

'Then Joey was wrong, you're not after my mother's money.'

He stepped out from behind the boxes, linked his arms around her waist and pulled her close to him. 'I'm after your mother's daughter, not her money, darling.' He nuzzled her neck.

'But Joey—'

'I thought you'd realize that I was afraid he'd tell your mother about us. The last thing I want is for her to interfere in my plans for our future. I meant what I said about us eloping, Tonia. But if your mother found out about us before I have time to arrange everything, she might lock you up or send you away and then I'd never find you.'

'You'll still take me to Gretna Green?'

'Of course, darling. We'll be off the minute the repairs are completed on the roof of the annex of Ynysangharad House. I'm moving into the lodge temporarily, and I can hardly take you there to live in one room after we're married, now can I?'

'No.' She thought about what he'd said. It made perfect sense.

He released her, checked the lock on the door and jammed a wooden wedge beneath it. 'Not that I'm expecting Joey Evans to come back but someone else might take it into their head to visit here.'

'The stocktake—'

'I did it earlier.' He pulled her blouse from the waistband of her skirt, slid his hands inside her bust-shaper and drew her behind a mountain of hatboxes. 'I love you, Tonia; there'll never be anyone else for me.' Lifting her skirt, he pushed her gently down on to an old curtain he'd laid out on the floor. 'You believe me?' He stroked her leg and pulled down her drawers in one easy movement.

'Yes.' She kissed him. 'Yes, Geraint, I do believe you.'

'I love you, darling, only you.' He unbuttoned his flies. 'God, you're so beautiful, you've no idea how much I've missed you this last week.'

She locked her arms around his neck as he entered her. 'I love you too, Geraint,' she murmured, her mind busy painting pictures of the perfect life they would lead in Ynysangharad House.

'Only two and half weeks to go before you become Mrs Joseph Evans. Aren't you excited?' Julia and Rhian were in Julia's bedroom, and although it was Rhian's day off, as usual, she'd gone to Julia's room first thing to dress her hair.

'I am excited but it seems unreal,' Rhian brushed Julia's hair. 'You're absolutely sure about the style?'

'As firm and tight a bun as you can make. I don't want a hair to move until I take it down before I go to bed tonight.'

'You're going to see *him* on a Tuesday?' Rhian asked in surprise.

'I am.' Julia smiled as she always did when she thought of Geraint. They had dropped the formal 'Mr Watkin Jones' and 'Miss Larch' on their second outing and had spent every single Monday together for the last thirteen weeks. Before he had walked her to the station to catch her train late yesterday afternoon she had asked him to meet her in the Angel Hotel for dinner that night.

She had a plan. If it didn't work she would resign herself to life with her stepmother and, given her father's increasingly frequent absences, without the comfort of his presence. If, by some miracle, her scheming did come to fruition, her entire life would change, but there would still be problems, not least Geraint himself. Although he had become increasingly considerate and sympathetic over the months, she felt that something was missing from their relationship.

He listened attentively to everything she said and made the correct remarks in the correct place. He complimented her on her clothes and choice of reading material, agreed with the aims of the suffragette movement without condoning their more extreme methods of attempting to achieve them, such as the recent attack on Buckingham Palace. He repeated every respectful and admiring comment he'd heard about her father and when she couldn't refrain from mentioning her stepmother, added implied but never outright criticism of Mrs Larch. He offered her his arm when they

walked together, opened doors for her, helped her on and off with her coat — and never touched her other than in the way a respectful nephew would an elderly maiden aunt.

She picked up a pair of gold earrings from her dressing table and fiddled with them. 'Can I ask you something, Rhian?'

'About the wedding?' Rhian mumbled absently, her mouth full of hairpins. All she seemed to talk about was her coming wedding. With Mrs Williams, who had bought a new hat and outfit for the occasion. With Sali, who'd refused to listen to her and Joey's plans to hold their reception in the Catholic Hall, instead insisting that she and Lloyd, with Mari's help, provide the wedding breakfast in Ynysangharad House. And with Joey, who rarely mentioned the actual ceremony but was completely obsessed with their honeymoon. But no matter how long the conversations, she never grew tried of the subject.

'No, not about your wedding.' Julia locked her fingers together on her lap and stared down at them. 'Do you allow Mr Evans to kiss you?'

'I have trouble limiting Mr Evans to just kisses,' Rhian answered dryly. 'If it was up to him we'd honeymoon before the wedding. But then, from what Mrs Williams says, every girl has the same problem.'

Julia blushed. 'I just wanted to know how far . . . I mean . . .'

'If I was engaged to anyone other than Joey I might allow him to take more liberties,' Rhian interrupted, anxious to spare Julia's embarrassment. 'But given Joey's past I warned him that I would make him wait until our wedding night, and so far I've succeeded.'

'Are you frightened?'

'Of the wedding night? No.' Rhian smiled. 'After all the kissing and . . . other things, I'm rather looking forward to it. You?'

'I think you and your Mr Evans are further along than me and . . .' Julia smiled self-consciously. She had already said more than she had intended.

'I am dying to find out who he is. Do I know him?'

Julia watched Rhian push the last pin in her hair. 'Sort of. I won't say any more until I am sure of his feelings towards me. But

I promise you that if I do marry him you will be one of the first to know who he is.'

'Are you madly in love with him?'

Julia hesitated again before deciding there was no harm in Rhian knowing exactly how she felt, especially as it was highly unlikely that she would meet Geraint in the future. 'Completely.' Until that moment she hadn't realized just how much she meant it.

'And he loves you just as much?'

'I don't know.'

'Men aren't like us. They have trouble expressing their feelings.'

'Is that right?' Julia grasped at the straw of comfort Rhian offered.

'Do you want me to come in tonight and brush out your hair?'

'No, you'll be tired after your day with Mr Evans.' Julia handed Rhian a copy of Bennett's *Anna of the Five Towns*. 'Let me know what you think of it?'

'I will.' Rhian hid the book in her handbag. 'See you in the morning.'

'Enjoy your day.'

Julia looked around her room after Rhian left. Her stepmother had wanted to redecorate it but she hadn't allowed her to touch a thing. As a result it had changed very little since her childhood. The simple pinewood furniture and cream wallpaper were both over twenty years old. She had removed her toys from the shelves either side of the fireplace and used them to store her books and display some of the photographs her father had taken. Carefully-posed studio shots with her mother and Gerald, taken at various stages of their childhood, outdoor snapshots of her and Gerald playing tennis and cycling, and the last photograph he had taken of her with the staff on New Year's Eve.

Leaving the stool, she opened her wardrobe and lifted out the Gladstone bag she had used to carry documents to and from suffragette meetings for the last few weeks, or so her father and stepmother thought.

She packed a new nightgown and negligee in the bottom, placed a brand-new set of toiletries on top and a plain hairbrush and comb. The photographs were difficult and she took a few moments to choose them, eventually settling on one of her mother, one of her parents, Gerald and her that her father had taken with an experimental timer and one he had taken of her and Rhian last summer. She wrapped the frames in a towel to protect them and placed them in the bag.

She added a change of underclothes, stockings, a lightweight summer dress and a pair of shoes. She had problems closing it, and the leather sides bulged. Hoping that no would pay much attention to it when she left the house, she opened her casement window wide, moved her chair in front of it and began to re-read her favourite book, *Wuthering Heights*. Her sympathies oscillated between Cathy's mad passionate love for Heathcliff, and a desire to shake the woman for not appreciating her safe, boring husband, Edgar Linton, and the secure life he gave her.

Chapter 9

'I AGREE, JOEY, there's always wars going on "down there in the Balkans" as you put it. But I've a feeling that this one is going to spill over and reach here.' Billy Evans took a cheese scone from the trays of cakes, scones and sandwiches Megan had put on the table and set it on his own plate.

'Surely it won't affect Tonypandy?' Megan glanced instinctively at the twins. She couldn't bear the thought of violence marring their childhood.

It was three o'clock in the afternoon, and the air was still, uncomfortably warm even within the stonewalled farmhouse. They were eating tea, and because of the early hours Victor kept, a full hour earlier than it would be served in polite circles.

'I'm afraid it might, Megan.' Billy tapped the copy of the previous Saturday's *Rhondda Leader*. 'It says here that the Admiralty wants the mineworkers in the pits that supply the Navy with coal, to work through their summer holidays.'

'The South Wales Miners' Executive Council have declared that it is not necessary for Britain to interfere in a war between Austria and Serbia,' Joey chipped in.

'Unfortunately the Miners' Executive Council doesn't run this country, or have any more influence than the International Miners' Congress. They adopted a resolution condemning the war between Serbia and Austria and demanding their members do everything they can to stop their respective governments from going to war. But only an incurable optimist would believe that resolution will have the slightest effect.' Billy spread butter on his scone.

'So what are you saying, Dad?' Victor asked. 'We're powerless to prevent it?'

'As ordinary working men, yes. The capitalists have decided to go to war for their own selfish ends, which have everything to do with making money for the arms manufacturers and nothing to do with freedom, common sense or the comfort of ordinary people and their families. And because they want it, they'll engineer it no matter what.'

'They've been preparing for it for years,' Betty Morgan declared. Betty's husband, like Billy Evans, had been a Communist and miners' leader, and unlike most women of her class, she had developed a keen interest in politics. 'Why else is the Kaiser about to launch the world's biggest ship, the Bismarck, if he doesn't intend to start a naval war?'

'You only have to read the papers.' Billy pointed to the neat pile in the alcove next to the stove. 'The Kaiser's reaffirmed Germany's alliance with Austria, the Russians have warned that they won't sit back and watch Serbia be invaded, so you've four countries hell-bent – sorry, ladies but I couldn't think of another word to use – on wasting the lives of their young men. And once they start firing shots at one another, more will join in. That kind of guts and glory killing has always been infectious in the past.'

'But Britain will stay out of it.' Megan looked to her husband for reassurance.

'For now, Megs. Cut me a slice of that apple pie, please.' Victor held out his plate.

'Don't worry, Megan, nothing's going to happen in Tony-pandy.' Joey dropped a spoonful of clotted cream on the last piece of fruit scone on his plate.

'I thought that right up until the day I saw troops marching down Dunraven Street.'

'That was the strike, Dad.' Victor could see that Megan was really upset.

'And you think the miners' refusal to work holidays isn't reason enough for the government to send the soldiers back into the Rhondda?'

'Let's hope not.' Victor pushed his chair away from the table.

'In the meantime I've a herd of cows to bring in and milk. Coming, Dad?'

'Aye.' Billy picked up his cap and pushed it on to his head. He and Victor kissed Rhian's cheek and shook Joey's hand when they left the table to say goodbye. 'Enjoy the show in the New Theatre.'

'We will.' Joey said goodbye to the twins and the women and followed his father and Victor into the farmyard. 'You don't really think that Britain is going to get involved in this war, do you, Dad?' Unlike his father and Lloyd, he had never been a political thinker or interested in anything that took place outside of his immediate circle.

'I can't see into the future, but I don't mind telling you I'm worried. Particularly when I look at the newspaper reports. Truth seems to have given way to flag-waving and patriotism of the worse kind.' His father laced on the dusty working boots he'd left outside the kitchen door.

'The Evans family will just have to remain neutral,' Victor said loudly for Megan's benefit when she pushed the twins' pram out into the sunshine. 'Hoping they'll sleep for an hour, Megs?'

'Betty said she'll keep an eye on them for me while I clear the dishes and start cooking supper.'

'And Betty has the best end of the bargain.' The elderly widow carried a chair and her knitting into the yard and sat next to the pram. 'See you next week, Rhian, Joey?'

'And then in church,' Joey smiled.

'I'll get there early. Half the Rhondda will be wanting to see Joey Evans walk up the aisle.' Betty shook her head in wonder 'I never thought I'd live to see the day.'

Rhian slipped her arm around Joey's waist as they made their way along the track that led from the farm to Tonypandy. The heat of the day was slowly giving way to balmy early evening warmth, and she felt blissfully happy and contented.

'Tired?' Joey asked when she yawned.

'Maybe, just a little. All of us have been working harder and longer hours than usual. Mrs Larch has organized a series of garden parties in aid of the hospital fund. I'm glad to be missing one today.'

Joey slipped his arm around her shoulders and pulled her close to him as they walked. 'I wish I could see more of you.'

'Then you feel as though we haven't had enough time to talk the last couple of months as well?'

'Yes, but I'm not complaining. I like visiting Victor, Megan and the twins and Sali, Lloyd and their children, and,' he gave her a slight squeeze, 'it won't be for much longer. Another two and a half weeks and we'll have all the time in the world. A two-week honeymoon in my aunt's cottage on the Gower followed by a lifetime. We could even have a little more now, if you took Sali's advice, handed in your notice to Mrs Williams and moved into Ynysangharad House.'

'I told Mrs Williams that I would work until the twenty-sixth of this month and I will,' she countered firmly.

'That will only give you five days to prepare for the wedding,' he warned with mock solemnity.

'You know Sali and I have everything in hand.'

'There's always last-minute panics with a wedding,' he pronounced authoritatively.

'And how would you know that?'

'I was at my brothers'.'

'So was I, and everything went smoothly.'

'They both married in the register office. We're marrying in church.'

'And everything is ordered, booked and sorted. If I gave up work any earlier I'd have nothing to do except sit around Ynysangharad House and annoy Sali.'

'You could never annoy anyone.' He bent his head and dropped a kiss on to the nape of her neck below her upswept hair. 'You said that Mrs Williams has already engaged your replacement.'

'She doesn't start until Friday and she'll need training in the mistress's ways.' Rhian stopped when they reached the summit of the mountain and looked down. Distance and sunlight lent enchantment to the living map spread out below them. The river sparkled as it wound its way over the floor of the valley and she reflected that if she had only seen it from this distance she might have believed its blackened, filthy and debris-strewn waters to be clean.

To her right the pithead gear of Pandy Colliery dwarfed the surrounding terraces. The banging of wagons being shunted in the sidings of the goods sheds echoed upwards, accompanied by the cries of a crowd of boys who were playing football with a stuffed haversack on the flattest area of mountain above the houses.

The fine weather had enticed people out of their homes. The mountain was covered with miniature figures. Young girls holding hands and skipping behind groups of mothers, carrying babies Welsh-fashion. Colliers crouched in circles, smoking their pipes and, judging by the shouts she could hear even from that distance, arguing politics. Courting couples edging away from the crowds and heading upwards in search of privacy.

'You sure I can't persuade you to hand in your notice now?' Joey dropped his arm to her waist. 'I could visit Ynysangharad House every day after work.'

'Even on a Thursday, Friday and Saturday when you close the store at ten o'clock?'

'Sali has enough bedrooms. She'd let me stay over and we could breakfast together.' He pulled her back, just over the brow of the hill where they couldn't be seen, and kissed her long and thoroughly.

She grew weak and began to tremble as she always did when he kissed her. She wrapped her arms around his neck, pulling him to her until their bodies meshed so close she could feel his heart beating against hers.

He moved his head back, linked his arms around her waist and looked down into her eyes. 'I love you.'

'I love you too.' Her senses heightened by the passion he'd evoked, she breathed in the scents she had come to associate with him: Kay's toilet soap, Cherry toothpaste, tobacco, the sweet, seductive almond aroma of the Macassar Oil he used on his hair.

'Oh, hell!' He stopped abruptly.

'Something's wrong?'

'You may be about to become a virginal bride, but you can't

be that innocent. Have you any idea what you've just done to me?'

She didn't want to, but she couldn't stop herself from glancing at his crotch. 'I'm sorry.'

'So am I. It's times like this that make me wish I hadn't made you one particular promise.'

'When you kiss and touch me the way you just did, so do I.'

'It's nice to know you're suffering too.' Keeping his distance, he bent his head and kissed the soft skin just below her ear. She clamped her hand over his when he reached for her breast and moved it away before he touched her. 'The past four months have lasted for ever, but the next two and a half weeks are going to be an eternity,' he complained.

'For me too,' she said quietly.

'Do you mean that?'

'You have no idea of the number of nights I have lain awake imagining that it's you, not Bronwen sleeping beside me. I can't wait to be close to you every minute of every night and to wake in the mornings knowing that the first person I will see when I open my eyes will be you.'

'Truly?' he asked seriously.

Deciding that as she had gone this far, she may as well confide the rest of her thoughts. 'And wondered what you look like without your clothes on because I've never seen a man naked.'

'You had but to ask,' he teased.

'I was afraid of what it might lead to.' She felt the colour flooding into her cheeks.

'Afraid?' He fell serious again.

'Only because I don't want to get pregnant before we're married.'

'The wedding is so close, it hardly matters now.'

'I know,' she whispered.

Wary of pressurizing her, he said, 'Unlike women, men aren't beautiful without their clothes on. That's why most artists paint female nudes,' he added, forestalling any comment on his past.

'I can't wait for us to be married so we can make love without

147

worrying about having a baby because our baby would be a blessing like Victor and Megan's twins. But most of all I want to touch you the way you touch me and find out what it will be like when we do go to bed together for the first time.'

'It will be wonderful – if we're not too tired after our wedding and travelling down to Gower,' he added wryly.

'Joey . . .' she faltered and fell silent.

'Yes.' He sensed what she was about to say.

'With the wedding so close we don't have to wait any longer.'

She had spoken so low he wondered if he had dreamed her reply. He said the first thing that came into his head. 'We have tickets to see Chung Ling Soo in the New Theatre.'

'If you'd prefer to see the show—'

'With my father and Betty Morgan still living at the farm and the house empty apart from me – and you, if you care to visit – the only magician I want to see is you,' he whispered huskily.

'What's the time?' Before he could move, she opened his jacket and slipped his watch from his waistcoat pocket without unclipping the chain.

'Almost four.' He closed the watch and took it from her fingers. 'We can be at my father's house in twenty minutes but I don't want to force you into doing anything you don't want to,' he said soberly. 'I promised you that I'd wait for you until our wedding night and I will, if you'd still prefer it to be that way.' He lifted her hand to his lips. 'Because the one thing that I am certain of is that you're worth waiting for, Rhian.'

She took his hand and led the way back to the summit. 'You couldn't force me, Joey, because suddenly I want this to happen as much as you do.'

'Father, I am sorry to disturb you in the office.'

'Julia, this is an unexpected pleasure.' Edward rose from his chair behind his desk and greeted his daughter. 'Would you like some tea?'

'If you're having some and you have time.'

'Sit down, I'll ask Miss Arnold to bring in a tray.'

Julia glanced around the room. Her father's office hadn't changed since she was a child. Same brown-varnished dado below a cream-painted upper wall hung with a framed copy of his law degree and various other certificates. Four glass-fronted barristers' bookcases stacked with law books. A filing cabinet and low cupboard that presumably held his clients' papers. But something was different, she was sure of it. She simply couldn't see what it was.

'I didn't mean to interrupt you,' Julia apologized when Edward returned and moved a pile of papers to the side of his desk to make room.

'I'm not dealing with anything urgent, just a will. Did you just call in on the off-chance that I'd be free or did you want to talk about something in particular?'

'Something in particular.'

Miss Arnold brought in a tray and set it on Edward's desk. 'It is nice to see you, Miss Larch. Will there be anything else, Mr Larch?'

'Nothing, thank you, Miss Arnold. My daughter will serve us. As soon as you have finished typing the rental agreement on Mr John's shop you may break for your own tea.' Edward waited until his secretary left the room before broaching the subject uppermost in his mind. 'I know that things have been particularly difficult at home between your stepmother and me lately, and I haven't been spending much time in Llan House—'

'That's not why I called, Father,' Julia interrupted before he launched into revelations that would embarrass them both. 'It's about this garden party.' She opened her shopping bag and removed one of the cards her stepmother had ordered from the local printer and she had offered to pick up.

Her father took the fine white board from her and ran his finger over the letters, confirming his suspicions that they were engraved. The process was much more expensive than printing. He had given Mabel an adequate allowance, but it wouldn't allow for extravagances on this scale.

Mr and Mrs Edward Larch at home.
6.00–8.00 p.m. Saturday, 25 July.
Llan House, Tonypandy.
Dress formal. Canapés and Champagne.

RSVP

'Mabel asked you to order these?'

'She ordered them; I volunteered to pick them up.'

'And how much did they cost?' he enquired sharply, doubting that Mabel had budgeted for them. The costs of her recent parties had exceeded her allowance and he'd already given her two warnings about excessive expenditure.

'Three guineas for sixty.'

'She's invited sixty people to the house!'

'Probably more, if she's had sixty invitations printed. But she did discuss it with you at breakfast a week ago. I was there.' She prompted his memory.

'As I recall, she mentioned a garden party but she said nothing about engraved invitations or sixty people.' He leaned back in his chair and pressed his fingertips together. 'Damn the woman, I wish I'd never set eyes on her,' he muttered feelingly.

'I wanted to ask your permission to invite a friend.'

'It's your stepmother's party,' he pointed out. 'If it were up to me it wouldn't be held.'

'She'd refuse me permission.'

The moment had arrived that he'd been dreading for weeks. 'You want to introduce me to Geraint Watkin Jones?'

'You know?' She felt as though her heart had leapt up her throat and stuck there.

'I know that you've been seen in Cardiff with him. Julia—'

'Before you say anything about him, I know he only invited me to spend time with him because I have money.'

'And that doesn't bother you?' Edward questioned incredulously.

'I'm not pretty.'

'Your stepmother has a cruel, vicious streak, particularly when it comes to you. I think she's jealous—'

150

'She is also realistic,' Julia cut in calmly.

'Have you fallen in love with this boy?' He drummed his fingers impatiently on the desk, dreading her reply.

'No more than you did with my stepmother when you first met her,' she answered evasively, wondering if she had fallen prey to the same blind infatuation that had flared so briefly in her father when he had first met Mabel at a family wedding shortly after her mother's death.

'Then you'll get over it. Don't expect me to say I'm sorry and not just because he's after your money. Harry Watkin Jones was a fine man and he gave that boy a good education. I was sorry to hear that Harry's brother-in-law turned the family into paupers, but Geraint was of age. He could have done something other than turn to his eldest sister to bail them out.'

'I may not be in love with Mr Watkin Jones, Father, but that doesn't mean I won't marry him.'

Shocked, Edward knocked over his teacup and tea flooded his desk. Julia whipped the cloth from the tray and stemmed the flow before it reached his papers.

'You are that unhappy living in the same house as Mabel?' he asked her seriously.

'Yes,' she replied honestly.

'This is my fault. I never should have married her.'

'It's not your fault, Father. Even if you hadn't remarried, I'd consider marrying Mr Watkin Jones.'

'And burden yourself with an idle husband for the rest of your life?'

'An idle husband is a small price to pay for the respect that comes with being a married woman. You have no idea of the contempt spinsters are held in. Everyone assumes they are un-loved, unwanted and useless. Think of the life I'd lead if I didn't marry. Growing old in your house because it's unthinkable for an unmarried woman to live alone, even if she has the means to buy and run her own house.'

'Women can do more than run a house these days, Julia,' he said impatiently. 'We are in the twentieth century.'

'We are, but I'm not bright enough or trained to do anything other than run a house.'

'I take it that Geraint Watkin Jones has proposed and you've made up your mind to accept him, which is why you want my approval to bring him to Mabel's garden party?'

'He hasn't proposed.'

'Thank heavens for that,' he said feelingly.

'But he will.'

'What can I say, other than by all means, bring him to Mabel's garden party.'

'You want me to see how other people treat him,' she asked suspiciously.

'I'll not deny it.'

'And then you'll try to persuade me to change my mind about him.'

'You can't stop me from voicing my opinion.'

'No, Father, I can't. But I rather think you already have.' She set her teacup back on the tray. 'You're dining at your club in Cardiff tonight?'

'Yes. Are you going to your evening suffragette meeting?'

'I am,' she confirmed. 'I'm just going back to the house to change before taking the train to Cardiff.'

'Then I'll see you at breakfast.'

'Goodbye, Father.' She studied the door set in the back wall of his office. It had been carefully painted with the same brown paint as the one that led into the passage. But the paint was marginally brighter than that on the dado and skirting board. If she hadn't visited the office constantly as a child she might never have noticed the new addition.

She wasn't the only one whose secret had been discovered. People liked to talk. She didn't doubt that whoever had told her father that they had seen her with Geraint Watkin Jones had enjoyed tittle-tattling. Almost as much as Mr Hadley when he'd asked her if her father had stopped visiting his club in Cardiff because her stepmother was keeping him home at nights.

Ironically for two people who'd agreed that they never had enough

152

time to talk, Rhian and Joey walked the rest of the way into Tonypandy in silence. Joey waved to and returned the greetings of his friends, but they didn't stop to talk to anyone. By tacit agreement they approached the house through the building site of the new school. And, although the street was deserted, they walked around the side of the house and in through the basement door just in case any of the neighbours were watching the front.

Heart pounding, Rhian followed Joey up the stairs into the kitchen. He helped her off with her cardigan. While he hung it together with his jacket in the hall, she unpinned her hat and set it on the table.

She glanced at her hair in the small shaving mirror on the window sill. It was coming loose and she pulled out the pins. It cascaded in a tangled mass of blonde curls over her shoulders to her waist. She continued to stare into the glass, barely recognizing the pale-faced girl who stared back at her. She couldn't believe what she was about to do after all the resolutions she had made and everything she had said to Joey about waiting until she had a wedding ring on her finger.

She heard his footstep. She turned and he was in the doorway watching her.

'Leave your hair just as it is,' he said, when she pulled it back away from her face.

'It's a mess.'

'It's a lovely mess.' He held out his hand, she took it and he led her up the stairs and opened his bedroom door. She had seen the room once, before Victor had married Megan and he and Joey had shared it. But since then she had spent hours imagining his life at home, if anything, even more since his father and Betty Morgan had moved into the farm. But the reality took her by surprise.

'It's so neat, tidy and clean. Of course, Mrs Hopkins comes in.'

'Not any more.' He froze momentarily at the memory of his neighbour walking in on him and Tonia.

'You do your own cleaning?'

'You think men can't clean?'

'If I didn't, I know different now.' The room smelled pleasantly of fresh air, lavender water and toilet soap. The brass bed and oak furniture gleamed in the muted light that filtered through the lace at the window. The high bed was covered with a hand-crocheted white cotton spread. And beside the oil lamp next to the bed was a silver frame containing the photograph of herself that she'd given him.

He saw her looking at it. 'I told you I'd kiss it every night before I go to sleep and I do.'

She heard the key turn in the lock and saw him move away from the door.

'I couldn't take the key from the front door,' he explained.

'People would talk if they saw it missing,' she agreed.

He folded back the bedcover, revealing white, starched bed linen and grey striped Welsh flannel blankets. Sitting on the bed, he unbuttoned his jacket, pulled it off and draped it over a chair. 'You're still sure?' He looked up at her.

She unclipped the cameo brooch he had given her from the high neck of her white lawn blouse. He took it from her fingers and set it on the bedside cabinet. Slowly and with a patience she would never have suspected him of possessing after what had happened on the mountain, he slipped the row of tiny pearl buttons on the front of her blouse. When he finished, she unbuttoned her cuffs. He slid the blouse from her shoulders and draped it next to his jacket over the seat of the chair.

'If we are going to do this, there is something you should have.' He opened the drawer in his bedside cabinet and removed a ring box. 'Recognize this?' He held out the wedding ring.

'I can wait two and a half weeks.'

'You don't want to wear it now?'

'No, it would bring us bad luck.' She turned her back to him, unbuttoned her cream linen skirt and stepped out of it. She heard the swish of cotton and linen as he undressed behind her. When she had stripped to her petticoat, she stopped.

'I'll clear off for ten minutes, if you like,' he offered.

'No. This is something I . . . we . . . are going to have to get used to.'

He stepped in front of her and her heartbeat quickened at the unexpected impact of seeing him dressed only in a thin pair of summer cotton drawers.

'Here, let me help you.' He untied the strings on her petticoats and helped her out of them. After she laid them over her skirt he unhooked the bust-shaper on her corset.

Nervous, she said the first thing that came into her head. 'You're an expert on women's underclothes.' She could have bitten her tongue when she remembered how he had acquired his knowledge.

'Only yours and the ones we sell in the store from now on.'

She set her foot on the edge of the chair, loosened her garters and rolled her stockings from her legs, before peeling off her corset. She faced him in her camisole and drawers. He slipped down the straps on her camisole, exposing her breasts.

'You are even more beautiful than I imagined and I imagined a lot.' He slid his hands down the side of her body, and it took a few seconds for her to realize that he'd removed her two remaining garments. Lifting her into his arms, he carried her to the bed and set her on a towel that he'd placed over the bottom sheet.

After kicking off his drawers, he lay next to her, exploring her breasts with his fingertips and lips, teasing her nipples to firm peaks with his tongue before moving down her body. Pushing her legs apart with his knees, he stroked, teased and caressed every inch of her, evoking new and overpowering emotions.

All thoughts of right and wrong, his past, the future dissolved in the intensity of the passion he unleashed. She clung to him, digging her nails into his shoulders, wanting what he was doing to her to last for ever, right up until the moment when she could stand it no longer, and he, sensing her crisis, finally penetrated her body with his own.

Afterwards, when she lay, spent and exhausted in his arms, she remembered his other women. She opened her eyes. He was lying back, his head on the pillow, his dark curls tousled, his eyes closed. And she wondered how anyone could do what they had just done without being totally, completely and utterly in love.

'I wish it too.'

'What?' she asked, startled because she had assumed he was sleeping.

He opened his eyes and cupped her breast. Lowering his head, he kissed each of her nipples in turn before meeting her steady gaze. 'That I'd waited so this could have been the first time for both of us. But then this has been a first for me too. The first time I've made love when I've been in love.'

'I can't imagine doing that and not being in love,' she murmured with more honesty than thought for his feelings.

'It's like the difference between watching a colourless silent film and experiencing reality.'

She sat up. 'I have to wash.'

'I'll do it for you.'

'No, you will not.' Suddenly and absurdly shy considering what had happened only moments before, she grabbed the sheet and pulled it to her chin. He took it from her fingers and gently tugged it away.

'As you said earlier, my love, we are going to have to get used to this, and "this" includes me treating your body as my own.'

He left the bed and padded naked on bare feet to the washstand. He filled the toiletware bowl with cold water from the matching jug. Picking up his soap and sponge, he carried them over to the bedside cabinet, soaked the sponge and rubbed soap on to it. Tenderly, lightly, as if he were washing a child, he sponged first her face and neck and then her breasts.

'Do you think that you will get used to me?'

She smiled up at him. 'Eventually.'

He kissed her. 'I am looking forward to loving you for the rest of my life.'

'I was so surprised when you asked me to meet you here tonight; I forgot to ask how you intended to get away.' Geraint shook his napkin out after the waiter had taken Julia's bag and shawl and shown them to the table she'd booked in the Angel Hotel.

'I told my father and stepmother that I was attending a regional suffragette meeting. There isn't one but my stepmother is so disinterested in events outside of Tonypandy, she won't find out.'

'And your father?'

'He rarely dines at home these days but I called into his office this afternoon. He knows we meet.'

'You told him?' The memory of the confrontation he'd had with Mr Hadley had remained fresh in Geraint's mind, and he baulked at the thought of facing another angry father.

'We were seen by someone who couldn't wait to give him the news.' She picked up the menu and proceeded to study it.

His face darkened. 'You don't have to tell me; the expression on your face says it all. He doesn't think that I am a suitable companion for you.'

'Is that all we are, Geraint? Companions?' she asked boldly.

'For the moment,' he answered carefully.

'And the future?' she pressed.

'I would like to talk to you about that sometime soon.'

'And I would like to talk to you about it now.' She leaned back so the waiter could set her napkin on her lap.

The waiter, who had come to know them well over the preceding months, brought a bottle of Geraint's favourite Moselle.

'Your usual, sir?' he asked.

'Please,' Julia answered.

He uncorked it at their table and poured a little into Geraint's glass. Geraint sipped it and nodded without really tasting it.

Julia looked up. 'I'll have the set dinner please, Mr Edwards.'

'You, sir?' The waiter stood with his pen poised over his notebook.

'What is it?' Geraint suspected that he was about to eat his last dinner with Julia and he wanted it to be a good one.

'Iced grapefruit, lobster soup, sole in aspic, chicken mousse, roast lamb, mint sauce, new potatoes, asparagus, fruit salad and whipped cream.'

'Make that two set dinners, Mr Edwards.' Geraint handed his unopened menu to the waiter. He had long since stopped even the pretence of protesting at Julia's insistence on footing the bill when they ate in the hotel. Especially since, employing a tact and diplomacy he was beginning to recognize as typical of her, she slipped the money surreptitiously into his pocket so it would appear that it was he who was paying.

'You know that I am financially independent,' Julia said after the waiter left.

'Yes,' Geraint answered cautiously.

'And, having no illusions about my appearance, I realize that my money is the only reason you invited me to spend time with you.'

Speechless, he sat back in his chair.

'Our outings have been interesting, Geraint. I have enjoyed them.'

Unable to bear the suspense a moment longer, he said, 'But you don't want to see me any more?'

'On the contrary, I want you to marry me.'

He picked up his wine and downed the glassful the waiter had poured. Choking, he turned aside and coughed into his hand-kerchief before running to the gentlemen's toilets. He leaned over a sink and gulped in great breaths of air. He thought he had been clever in being kind to Julia, listening to her long, boring con-versations about women's suffrage and the interminable number of classic and romantic books she read. And all the while she'd known that he was only after her money. And now *she* had the gall to propose to *him* when he was still torn between deciding whether or not he'd be able to live with her as his wife and give up Tonia, or if it would be worth him persevering with Tonia in the hope of squeezing a house and money out of Connie Rodney. Discreet enquiries had confirmed the lift boy's revelations, but they had also enlightened him as to Tonia's mother's distrust of, and hardened attitude towards men.

He took half a dozen breaths to steady himself and returned to their table. The waiter had brought the iced grapefruit and Julia was sitting calmly, eating it.

'This is excellent.' She took her bread roll, broke it into small pieces and buttered them.

He lifted his napkin from his chair and sat down.

'Are you all right? You look very pale,' she enquired solici-tously.

'Did I hear you correctly?' he murmured hoarsely.

'If you heard me propose marriage to you, yes.' She pushed her empty bowl aside, removed her napkin from her lap and dropped it on to her bread plate.

'I intended to propose to you,' he mumbled reproachfully.

'After you found out how much I was worth?'

'Julia, I wouldn't have invited you to go out with me if I didn't like you. I am very fond of you—'

'Can we be honest with one another, Geraint? You may have been the one to ask me out, but we both know that I was the one who did the manoeuvring. I couldn't have been more obvious if I had written "spinster wants presentable husband" on my forehead. I heard that you invited Elizabeth Hadley to the moving pictures after she came into her inheritance and that her family had prevented you from pursuing a courtship. So, I hoped you'd consider me instead.'

'I liked Elizabeth. It wasn't the money . . .' The excuses sounded lame even to his own ears.

'You are well educated, more than presentable, you have a degree in English from Balliol College, Oxford, and you intended to live the life of a gentleman on the income from your investments before your uncle embezzled and lost your inheritance. It is hardly surprising that you're looking to repair your fortune through marriage.'

'You are remarkably well informed,' he said resentfully, conveniently forgetting that she had only researched his background with considerably more success than he had hers.

'You are the subject of a great deal of gossip among women with daughters of marriageable age in Pontypridd.'

'So it would appear.' Seeing the waiter staring at them, he picked up his spoon and began to eat his grapefruit.

'From appearances, I'd say that you hate working in Gwilym James.'

Deciding that he had nothing further to lose by being honest, he replied, 'I do.'

'And I hate living with my stepmother. I want my independence, Geraint, and I would have that if you married me. As my husband, you would be in control of my money. We would have to live together if we wanted to be accepted in decent society, but it wouldn't have to be a marriage in anything other than name. And we would both be extremely comfortable. I have fifty thousand pounds invested in gilt-edged stocks as well as an income of four thousand pounds a year from rents on properties that my grand-father left me. I also have a sufficiently large float of capital in my bank account to buy, furnish and run a substantial house.'

Geraint's mouth dropped open. He had heard that Julia Larch was wealthy, but this was wealth on a scale that overshadowed his vanished inheritance.

'You can live like a gentleman with nothing more onerous to do than manage my affairs. All I ask is that we share my four thousand pounds a year income and you leave my gilt-edged stocks intact to accrue interest.'

'You would give me an income of two thousand pounds a year if I marry you?' he asked in disbelief.

'Less your share of the cost of running our home, which, even if we live well, shouldn't come to more than eight hundred pounds a year and that would be split between us. I would like to manage the household.'

'Naturally.' He was so taken aback he barely knew what he was saying.

'You can choose where we live, the house and the furnishings. But I would appreciate it if you lived your life discreetly without causing any scandal or gossip that might reflect adversely on me. So, what do you say?'

The waiter took advantage of the silence to clear their plates and bring the lobster soup.

'I do care for you, Julia?' Geraint said after the waiter left.

'I believe you do – a little.' Even as she said it, Julia knew that she was deceiving herself.

He laid his hand over hers on the table. 'How soon do you want to marry?'

'Immediately.'

'I will hand my notice to Mr Horton tomorrow morning.'

'I thought if you were agreeable, we would elope tonight. There are places in Scotland where we could marry tomorrow.'

'We have no luggage,' he pointed out practically.

'I have a few essentials packed in the Gladstone bag I handed the waiter, including a spare toothbrush for you. A sleeper is leaving Cardiff station for Carlisle in two hours. From there it is a short train journey over the border to Gretna Green. I have a hundred pounds in my purse, as well as my cheque and bank books and the key to my safety deposit box in the Capitol and Counties Bank in Pontypridd. I have left letters in Llan House that will be found if I don't return there tonight. I think that covers everything, don't you, Geraint?'

Chapter 10

'YOU LOOK AS though you've lost a guinea and found a penny, Edward,' Mr Larch's junior partner, Cedric, commented when he joined him in his office at the end of the working day. 'Trouble with the Morton Lewis will?'

'Sorry, did you say something?' Edward glanced up from the documents in front of him.

'I asked if there were any problems with the Morton Lewis will.'

'None, it's perfectly straightforward.'

'So it should be. I drew it up.' Cedric stretched out in the visitor's chair in front of Edward's desk. 'So, if it's not the will it must be something else.' He waited a few moments and when Edward didn't volunteer any information, he said, 'Miss Arnold mentioned that Julia called.'

'She came to tell me that she has been meeting Geraint Watkin Jones.'

'You didn't tell her that I'd seen them lunching together in the Angel Hotel?' Cedric removed two cigars from his top pocket and placed one on Edward's desk.

'No.' Edward rolled the cigar between his fingers and thumb, and sniffed it before slipping it into the top pocket of his suit. 'Thank you, I'll smoke it after dinner.'

'Are you worried about her?' Cedric lit his cigar.

'A little.'

'That frown on your forehead, cuts deeper than "a little" worry warrants. You and Mabel still not getting on too well?' he enquired intuitively.

Edward dropped his pencil and sat back in his chair. 'I don't want to talk about her.'

'When you stop complaining, it has to be bad,' Cedric declared.

Without thinking, Edward repeated the observation he'd made to Julia. 'I wish I'd never set eyes on the woman.'

'You can't say that I didn't—'

'Warn me? I should have listened to my friends at the time, but I didn't.' Edward left his chair and walked over to the empty fireplace, which was screened by a tapestry that Amelia had stitched. He stared dejectedly down at it.

'What's done is done.' Cedric blew a perfect smoke ring. 'You went crazy after Amelia died.'

'I certainly behaved like a lunatic,' Edward agreed miserably. 'Marrying the first woman who smiled at me. Julia saw through Mabel right away. She begged me to wait before rushing her to the altar but I wouldn't listen. And now not only me, but Julia and Gerald are suffering for my impulsive behaviour. All Mabel wanted was her own establishment and a place in a Ladies' Circle. Well, she certainly has that. And all I have is the expense of keeping her. Between her clothes, extravagances and the amount of entertaining she insists on doing, she costs me a bloody fortune.'

'You were lucky that Amelia had her own money and unlucky that she left it to the children.'

'My share of the business would keep any normal wife and family in luxury.'

'Why don't you hold back Mabel's allowance until she unlocks the padlock on her drawers?'

'You know what's really bloody awful, Cedric?'

'Tell me?' The fact that Edward had sworn twice in the space of a few sentences spoke volumes for his state of mind.

'Even if she let me, I couldn't bear to touch her, not now.'

'Really?' Cedric was surprised. 'She's not bad-looking. A bit prim and proper and plump for my taste, I never did go a bundle on women who look as though they are about to burst out of their corsets, but when needs must, I assumed she'd do. And you obviously must have thought so when you first met her.'

'That was before I found out what she was really like.' Edward couldn't bring himself to confide the story of Mabel's attack on Rhian, even to Cedric. He abhorred violence of any kind in women. And the sight of his wife slapping a helpless maid and blaming her for an accident had destroyed the pathetic remnants of the feelings he'd once had. Feelings he now knew had been rooted in grief and loneliness not fondness for Mabel.

'So, you're saddled with a miserable, frigid woman.' Cedric was bored with the conversation. 'You're not the first man to find himself in that predicament and you won't be the last. Getting maudlin won't help, but I know what will.'

Regretting the whisky-sodden evening that had ended with him confiding the details – or rather lack of details – of his and Mabel's married life, Edward snapped, 'You think a visit to Mrs Smith's brothel can cure everything.'

'Not everything, just one small problem,' Cedric replied evenly. 'And, it's not a brothel, it's a—'

'Bordello?' Edward suggested.

'Mrs Smith prefers "Gentleman's Club". You really didn't give it a fair try, Edward. Just a single brief visit when you were feeling particularly low after Amelia died.'

'I should have never allowed you to talk me into going with you,' Edward countered.

'The trouble with you is you don't know how to enjoy yourself.'

'I know when I'm not and I can't understand why you go there. You have a wonderful marriage with Elizabeth. And it's not as if she isn't attractive.'

'She is and I love her dearly.' Cedric studied his manicured nails. 'But she's also a wife and in my, granted, limited experience, because I've only had one, wives simply don't have the same repertoire as whores, or the willingness to experiment.'

'When I was married to Amelia I never wanted to look at another woman.'

'But Mabel isn't Amelia.'

'You can say that again,' Edward muttered sourly.

'So, why don't you come with me? As it happens, I'm visiting

164

there tonight and Mrs Smith will be pleased to see and accommodate you.'

'No.' Edward's refusal was final.

'In that case, try looking close to home. You've two cracking maids in your house.'

'I would never touch one of the servants!' Edward was horrified by the suggestion.

'Then all I can say is more fool you. As you pay their wages, they're already beholden to you, and a couple of guineas on the side works wonders. I make a point of bedding ours – the young presentable ones, that is – before they've been in the house a month.'

'Under Elizabeth's nose!'

'Not literally. I wait until she's out of the way, visiting someone, or occupied in another room.'

'And she's never suspected anything?' Edward asked.

'She accepts that I'm a man, and as such, I have more pressing needs than her. But if one of the girls gets too cocky after I've had them, she sacks them. Two went last year. Since then she's hired ones that are built like dray horses and look about as appealing, which is why I now make two visits a week to Mrs Smith's.' He gazed thoughtfully at his cigar. 'Do you think Elizabeth could have hired those ugly girls on purpose?'

'Probably.' Edward gave a wry smile.

'Damn her.'

'Perhaps you're not as clever as you thought.' Edward sat back behind his desk. 'I could never visit Mrs Smith's again. I'd be too terrified of meeting someone I knew there. A client or a business associate.'

'If you did, they'd be there for exactly the same purpose as you, so they'd hardly think any the less of you for being there. Actually, in my experience it can be a social icebreaker. I hardly knew Judge Davies until I saw him leaving the room next to mine in Mrs Smith's one evening. Now Elizabeth and I dine regularly at his house.'

'Judge Davies!'

'You'd be surprised at the people who frequent Mrs Smith's.

I'm getting the five o'clock train down to Cardiff. She has four new girls, country stock from Brecon.' Cedric left his chair. 'For the sake of your health and your sanity, I suggest you come with me. Shall I send in the boy so he can take a message to Llan House to say you're dining out?'

'I'm not expected home this evening.'

'So you'll come with me?'

'I really have made arrangements to dine out tonight.' Edward picked up his pencil.

'You'd be better off with Mrs Smith than Maisie,' Cedric ventured. 'At least Mrs Smith's girls have weekly medical checks.'

'What do you mean?'

'I know all about the rooms next door and Maisie, Edward, but before you panic, I doubt anyone else does except the old woman you put in there to clean them for you.'

As denial was futile, Edward said, 'How did you find out?'

'I went to see how the builder was progressing. He's done a good job, and a quick one. He told me another week will see it finished. And your elderly widow is ecstatic with her job and accommodation. I believe the local vernacular is "she thinks she's in God's pocket."'

'She told you about Maisie?'

'Good heavens, no. She couldn't have been closer-mouthed than a nun on silence. Maisie told me she has a weekly appointment with you. In fact, she was complaining it's not often enough for her purse or liking. In case you didn't know, she's very fond of her gentlemen.'

'Damn her,' Edward said feelingly, wondering just who else Maisie had spoken to.

'Don't tell me that you didn't know Maisie has a loose tongue?'

'I've suspected it.'

'She's particularly garrulous after she's been drinking. A couple of gins and she'll not only give you a full client list but any secrets men have been stupid enough to entrust to her. She'll service anyone who'll pay her a shilling, and in the street if there's nowhere better. You're taking a risk with her.'

'So are you by the sound of it.' Edward shuffled the papers back in front of himself. 'If I'm going to have this ready for the typewriter tomorrow morning, I need to get back to work.'

Accepting that Edward had dismissed him, Cedric went to the door. 'You know what they say: all work and no play makes Edward a dull boy.' He glanced at the clock on the wall. 'Don't keep at it too late, will you, there's a good fellow? You'll make me feel guilty if you do.'

At half past six Edward finished drafting his last letter, left his desk and opened the door in the back wall of his office that connected the building with the one next door. His father had bought both when they were new. He'd rented the second to a corn and seed merchant who had signed a maintenance lease only to allow the place to fall into disrepair during the last few years of his tenancy. Edward had meant to set it to rights when the merchant retired, but there had always been more pressing business that demanded his attention. Shortly after his first wife's death he had received a notice from the council saying that they were 'concerned' about its rundown state, but rather than tackle the problem, he had boarded up the windows.

His single unhappy foray to Mrs Smith's, coupled with Mabel's continued refusal to sleep with him after the disastrous experience of their wedding night, when she had screamed every time he had tried to touch her, had given him the impetus he'd needed to engage a builder to convert the building into three separate sets of rooms. There was a shop on the ground floor with living accommodation behind, which was almost ready to be advertised. He'd rented the second floor to a collier's widow in exchange for cleaning duties, the third floor he'd earmarked for his own use.

He walked into a windowless corridor and switched on the electric light, installed as part of the refurbishment, before opening the door to the first of four rooms he'd had decorated to his own specifications. It was a spacious and comfortable, if somewhat old-fashioned, sitting-cum-dining room. The wallpaper was plain light cream, the woodwork brown, the chaise-longue, easy chairs and sofa upholstered in a dark-green William Morris chintz that had been popular a quarter of a century before. The faded curtains and fire screen were of the same material. The bookcase in the alcove alongside the hearth held a selection of his favourite novels. A solid oak table, upright chairs and sideboard were set in front of the window and the general impression was of a room that belonged in a late Victorian rather than Edwardian home. Mabel would have hated it.

He walked through to a tiny kitchen that held a zinc-topped cupboard, a small scrub-down pine table, two chairs, a Belfast sink and gas cooker. He sniffed the air, and his mouth watered. His dinner had been carried over from the White Hart and Mrs Ball, the miner's widow, had put it in the oven to keep it warm.

Taking a cloth from the table drawer, he lifted out the plate and set it on a tray that had been laid with a knife and fork, glass and bottle of beer. Removing the plate that had been placed on top of the food to stop it from drying, he smiled. Steak and kidney pie, cooked with plenty of onions, and served with lashings of mashed and roast potatoes, cabbage, cauliflower and gravy; a substantial, heavy meal and one he never failed to enjoy.

He returned to the passage and opened another door that led to a bedroom and adjoining bathroom with plumbed-in bath, sink and toilet. The alterations had cost a small fortune, but not as much as the 'improvements' Mabel had made to Llan House, and on that basis he had decided to indulge himself. After washing his hands and face and checking the bedroom to make sure that the bed had been made, he returned to the kitchen to pick up his tray. He felt perfectly at home. But then he should. Everything in the rooms had come from the cellar he'd used to store the furniture he and Amelia had chosen together when they'd married, and Mabel had so summarily discarded.

He took his time over his dinner, eating slowly, savouring the food whilst reading *The White Peacock*, a novel by a new young writer, D. H. Lawrence, that a member of his club had recommended on one of his increasingly rare visits. He enjoyed his solitary dinners, preferring the selfish luxury of his own company and the plain substantial cooking of the White Hart, to the strain and formality of eating the fancy nine-course dinners Mabel ordered. He felt guilty at leaving Julia alone to face her stepmother at meal times but not enough to join them.

The last time he had dined at home, Mabel had invited Mrs Hodges and Mrs Hadley of the Ladies' Circle, and their respective husbands to join them for what was probably the most expensive meal that had ever been served at Llan House. Mrs Williams constantly complained to him about the cost of caviar and buying exotic fruit, fish and game out of season. Even Cook had asked to see him privately so she could grumble about the time it took her to prepare delicacies alien to her repertoire: Italian, French and Spanish sauces, cocktails, fancy cake decorations and icings. She'd also voiced her objections to being ordered to produce four times her usual quota of chutneys, pickles, preserves and mustards so Mabel could donate the extra to Mrs Hodges and Mrs Hadley's endless bazaars and bring-and-buy sales. Eventually, between the servants' moans, Julia's increasing reserve and Mabel's icy politeness, these rooms had become more his home than Llan House.

He finished his meal, stacked the tray with his dishes and carried it through to the kitchen. Taking a glass and a decanter of brandy from the sideboard, he poured himself a large measure and settled in an easy chair with his book. But not for long. At eight o'clock he was disturbed by a knock at the door. He shouted, 'Come in.'

Mrs Ball peeped around the door. 'I've shown Maisie into your bedroom, Mr Larch. Will there be anything else that you want doing tonight?'

'Only the removal of my dinner dishes, Mrs Ball, thank you.'

He didn't leave his chair until he heard the old woman walk down the stairs, then he went into the bedroom where Maisie was sitting wrapped in her cloak on an upright chair.

If Maisie had another name, he didn't know it. She had told him she was eighteen. She looked forty. Her hair was badly bleached and had the texture of straw. Her cheeks were heavily rouged, her eyelids painted bright blue and her face blotted in a thick layer of powder, all of which presumably helped to announce her profession to the world.

Returning late one night from a business meeting in Pontypridd, he had seen her outside the station. He had watched her approach three men, all of whom had walked away, before inviting her to share a glass of brandy with him in his office. She had wanted him to take her to one of the pubs that let out rooms to prostitutes but he had insisted on his office or nowhere.

That first meeting had led to others. She now visited him twice a week. The widow let her in and it was a discreet but unsatisfactory arrangement. He had been terrified of catching a disease from her even before Cedric's warning, and no matter how many times she assured him that she was 'clean' he was acutely aware of her other 'clients'.

Dirty, grubby men who thought nothing of using a dozen prostitutes in a week, men who went to women who were possibly incubating both kinds of pox that Maisie could pass on to him – or already had.

'You're ready?'

'Yes, sir.' She left the chair and removed her cloak, a sober garment that could have belonged to any respectable woman in the Rhondda. She stood before him, naked apart from a pair of red silk stockings and showy black and gilt garters. 'On the bed or the chair, sir?'

He stared at her. Try as he may, he couldn't feel anything for the girl. If he'd asked, he didn't doubt that she would tell him some horrendous hard luck story about her descent into prostitution, but he couldn't escape the fact that he didn't given a damn about her. The simple truth was he needed the relief she gave him while despising himself for being reliant on it.

'Or do you want to take some photographs of me, sir?' she said archly. There was a camera permanently set up in the corner of the room and he had once paid her two guineas for an hour's posing. Money she had used to clear her rent arrears and buy her cloak and a black silk frock, because her better-class 'gentlemen' preferred her quietly dressed.

'No photographs.' He had paid her to pose but had scarcely looked at the results. Instead of exciting him as he'd hoped, they'd disgusted him and he had shoved them into a drawer and forgotten them. He loosened his belt, unbuttoned his trousers and lay on the bed. She climbed up next to him and her scent wafted thick and overwhelmingly sweet, making him nauseous. 'I wish you'd use a better perfume.'

'Most of my customers like this one, sir.'

He flinched at the mention of customers.

Realizing she'd made a mistake, she tried to reassure him, only to make things worse. 'They're all gentlemen like yourself, sir. There's nothing wrong with me, or them, sir.'

'Just get on with it, Maisie,' he said sharply.

She opened his drawers. Slipping her hands between his thighs she fondled his erection, swiftly and expertly bringing him to a climax.

He opened a drawer in the bedside cabinet, removed a handkerchief and cleaned himself up. 'Your money is on the mantelpiece, Maisie.'

'Thank you, sir.' She picked up the ten-shilling note, slipped her cloak back over her shoulders and pushed the note into her handbag.

'You came here like that?' he asked, shocked at the thought of her walking naked beneath her cloak around the streets.

'My clients like me naked, sir, and it saves time. Tuesday and Thursday are my nights for home visiting.' The casual mention of 'home visiting' made her sound like a district nurse.

'Have you thought what would happen if the police stopped and searched you?'

'The station is my last stop, sir. Same time as usual on Thursday, that's if there is nothing more that I can do for you now?'

Revolted to the pit of his stomach, he said, 'I may be busy Thursday. I'll send for you when I next want you. You're living in the same room?'

'I am, sir. Look, sir, if I've done anything to upset you I'm really sorry. Your ten bob a week is the only real regular money I can rely on getting. So if there's anything else that I can do to please you, just ask, no matter how funny it is. Nothing's peculiar to a girl like me, sir. I've seen it all.'

Ghastly images of all kinds of unnatural practices flooded his mind. 'I don't doubt you have, Maisie. But if you'll excuse me, I have things to do.'

'Yes, sir.' Holding her cloak around herself, she left. He rose from the bed and went into the bathroom. He lit the geyser above the bath, put the plug in and ran the water so hot it spurted from the pipe in great boiling dollops. Topping it up with a thin trickle of cold, he stripped off his clothes and gingerly lowered himself in. He added more hot water until his skin burned bright red and scrubbed himself with a stiff-bristled, unvarnished wooden brush and carbolic soap. But it was useless. The more he scoured himself, the less clean he felt, and before he had finished washing he had to clamber out of the bath to vomit the meal he had enjoyed, down the toilet.

He only wished he could as easily rid himself of the revulsion he felt at using a girl like Maisie.

Sali and Lloyd were sitting, curled together on the garden bench outside the French windows of the drawing room in Ynysangharad House, sipping Mari's homemade parsnip wine, breathing in the heady midsummer flower perfumes and watching the sunset, when the butler, Mr Jenkins, coughed discreetly in the room behind them.

'I'm sorry to disturb you, Mrs Evans, Mr Evans, but Mr Geraint is on the telephone. He would like to speak to you urgently, Mrs Evans.'

'Thank you, Mr Jenkins.' Sali swung her feet down on to the gravel path and felt for the shoes she had kicked off earlier.

'After the last time you two talked, it might be better if I spoke to him,' Lloyd suggested.

'He's my brother and he hates me. But for absolutely no reason that I can fathom, he hates you more.'

'Don't let him upset you again,' Lloyd warned.

'I'll try not to.'

'Can I get you anything before I lock up for the night, Mr Evans?' Mr Jenkins asked after Sali left for the hall.

'Nothing, thank you, Mr Jenkins. When Mrs Evans returns we'll probably go to bed. I'll lock the French doors when we come in.'

'In that case I'll say goodnight, Mr Evans.'

'Goodnight, Mr Jenkins.'

The old man left the drawing room and Lloyd reflected that they had come a long way since his first visit to Llan House before he had married Sali. Then the butler had made it clear that working-class men should use the tradesmen's entrance.

A mutual respect had developed between them but it had been a slow and occasionally painful process. The butler had found it demeaning to recognize him as master of the household, and Lloyd had found it just as difficult to set aside his 'every man is equal' Marxist principles and live in a house staffed by a butler, house-keeper, cook, footman, coachman/chauffeur and maids. But he had been forced to accept that everyone in the house had a job to do for wages they needed to support themselves, and, in some cases, their families. However, he still found it difficult to give any of the servants a direct order, and he would far rather get himself a drink, or serve himself at table than have someone do it for him.

'Is Geraint all right?' he asked when Sali returned.

'He couldn't be better.' Sali joined him again outside. 'He was telephoning from Cardiff station. He and Julia Larch are eloping to Scotland.'

'Edward Larch's daughter? The red-head the gossips say has inherited a fortune?' Lloyd stared at her in disbelief.

'That's what he said.'

'But she's . . .' he faltered.

'Plain,' Sali supplied succinctly. 'But as Geraint is marrying her, I think we can take it the gossips are right about her fortune. He's been trying to marry into money ever since he lost his own. Remember how he tried to court Elizabeth Hadley?'

Lloyd re-filled their glasses from the bottle he'd balanced against the leg of the bench. 'I only hope Miss Larch realizes that it's her bank account Geraint loves, not her.'

'So do I, but their elopement when she is of age suggests that Julia Larch doesn't think her father will approve of Geraint as a son-in-law.'

'Having money again might make Geraint less aggressive.'

She sipped her wine. 'It might.'

'Do you think we should try to stop them? I have Edward Larch's telephone number.'

'Geraint said they were catching the ten o'clock sleeper to Scotland. It's ten minutes to ten now. Even if we telephone Edward Larch, there is nothing that he can do at this short notice. And if we telephoned the railway station or the police, they couldn't stop them. She may be foolish and Geraint avaricious, but they are both over twenty-one. Besides,' she added, 'as Geraint just pointed out to me, Julia Larch's reputation will never survive if they don't marry now. He also said that eloping was her idea.'

'Then she definitely knew that her family wouldn't approve. Did he say anything else?'

'He asked me to give his apologies and his notice to Mr Horton and Mrs Jenkins in the lodge. And to turn his Gwilym James staff account into a personal shopping account, which he'll clear when he returns from honeymoon.'

'Look on the bright side, sweetheart.' Lloyd rose to his feet and offered her his hand. 'He'll never annoy you or Mr Horton in work again.'

'It's not me or Mr Horton I'm worried about, it's Julia Larch.'

'You know her?'

'I've met her at the suffrage meetings. She may not be pretty, but she's sharp, intelligent and incredibly well read.'

'Then all I can say is for an intelligent woman she's picked herself a dolt for a husband. But you're right, there's nothing we can do about that now. I'll telephone Edward Larch first thing in the morning. Meanwhile, let's go to bed.' He raised his eyebrows before kissing her.

'I know that look, Lloyd Evans. We'll have a son nine months from now.'

'No, we won't,' he contradicted, 'we'll have another daughter, and we'll call her Maggie.'

'We'll call him Glyn after my grandfather.'

'She won't like it.' He took her empty glass from her. 'You go on upstairs and check Bella, Edyth and Harry; I'll take these into the kitchen.'

'I love having Harry home.'

'So do I, sweetheart, but much as I hate to admit it, your Mr Richards was right about Harry settling down in school. After the Christmas holidays I was sure he wouldn't, but did you hear the way he was talking about his cricket and tennis lessons and the school picnics?'

'Yes, and I hate the thought of losing him.'

'You won't,' he assured her. 'He'll always be our Harry, no matter how much he enjoys school and being with his new friends.'

'I hope you're right.'

'I am. See you upstairs in five minutes.'

Sali said goodnight to Mr Jenkins, who was locking and bolting the front and porch doors, and made her way up the sweeping staircase to the nursery. A shaded nightlight burned in the corner nearest to Mari's door. She crept in and pulled the blankets over Bella, who had kicked them off in her sleep. Tucking her favourite brown teddy bear that Victor and Megan had bought her under her daughter's arm, she tiptoed across to Edyth who was lying curled on her side, her face flushed with sleep, her tiny fist curled loosely above her head.

She slipped out of the room, closed the door silently behind her and walked down the landing to the bedroom she had prepared for Harry as a summer holiday surprise. He too was fast asleep, a comic book open on the pillow beside his head, his small, slight figure lost in the depths of the double bed.

She picked up the children's paper, which was illustrated with pictures of Cowboys and Indians, and realized that Joey must have given it to him on his last visit. She left it open on the bedside table and stole back along the landing to her own bedroom.

'If we have any more children, it will take you until dawn to check them all,' Lloyd teased.

'Only in the school holidays because they will all be boys.' She unbuttoned her blouse and dropped it into the linen bin. 'I wonder what Geraint and Julia are doing now.'

He unclipped his pocket watch from his waistcoat and opened it. 'Speeding north, I'd say.'

'I hope he'll have the sense to make her happy.'

'So do I, sweetheart, but knowing Geraint, I doubt he'll even try.' He tossed his shirt on top of her blouse.

Sali thought about Julia as she continued to undress. She liked and admired the girl and resolved to write her a letter to welcome her as a sister-in-law. But she also couldn't help agreeing with Lloyd: Julia Larch had chosen a dolt for a husband.

Feeling too sick and tired to make his way home, Edward Larch threw on his dressing gown and returned to his office. He telephoned Mrs Williams at Llan House, told her that he'd been unavoidably delayed in Cardiff, was staying at his club and would be home in the morning. He set down the receiver before giving her a chance to ask any questions.

He locked the connecting door behind him when he returned to his rooms. Slipping between the sheets of the bed, he rested his head on the pillow, closed his eyes and took solace in recalling every detail about Amelia. The way her blonde hair had curled around her forehead. Her seductive smile when she undressed. The sensuous feel of her skin, as she had lain naked next to him night after night in their big brass bed. The loving look in her eyes when she first caught sight of him after every absence, no matter how brief.

Remembering brought pain as well as pleasure, and, not for the first time since she had died, he wished himself under the same stone slab in Trealow cemetery. If there was an afterlife he'd be with her, and if there wasn't, at least what little remained of him would be beside her. But there was Julia and Gerald and, quite apart from his reluctance to leave Gerald, who was underage, to Mabel's mercies, he was too much of coward to kill himself, because he hadn't entirely given up hope that somewhere in the world he would find another woman a little like Amelia who would make life tolerable and, who knew, maybe even almost happy again.

'Who is it?' Julia sat up quickly, hitting her head on the window sash of the train.

'Geraint.'

'Just a minute.' She reached for the burgundy velvet robe she had bought along with her lavishly-embroidered silk nightdress. Tying the belt of the robe loosely around her waist, she splashed on a dab of essence of violets before opening the door.

'I wanted to make sure that you are all right, have everything you need and to thank you for the toothbrush and powder.'

'I am fine, thank you.' She leaned towards him, willing him to kiss her, or ask if he could spend the night with her. But he stepped back into the corridor.

'Don't forget to lock your door. You can never be sure who is on a train.'

'I will.' She closed the door, pushed the bolt across and leaned against it. Geraint didn't love her, but he had to care for her. Why else would he have knocked her door and checked that she was all right?

Besides, he was only following the guidelines she had set down for their relationship. Financial and personal independence for both of them, separate lives lived discreetly under the same roof. It was what she wanted. She would never have told him otherwise if she didn't. Would she?

Edward rose early and left the office as the shopkeepers in Dunraven Street were opening their shutters and carrying their wares out on to the pavements. He tipped his hat to the manager of Oliver's Shoes, and Mr Davies the ironmonger, but he didn't stop to talk. The milk train from Cardiff reached Tonypandy station at five o'clock. He hadn't seen anyone around who could challenge the story that he had concocted for Llan House. He had arrived in town on it, and gone straight to his office to do a couple of hours' work before going home for breakfast.

Mrs Williams opened the door before he'd mounted the short flight of steps and one look at the expression on her face told him that something was very wrong.

'Miss Julia?' he asked, truly indifferent to his wife.

'She didn't come home last night, sir. Mrs Larch asked me to check her room at ten o'clock in case she'd come in and gone straight upstairs. There was a letter on her pillow addressed to you.' She didn't tell him about the second letter addressed to Rhian, which she had passed on and the maid had shown her. It was short but shattering to someone who didn't even know that Julia had been seeing a man.

> Dear Rhian,
>
> I promised I'd tell you his name as soon as I knew what was happening between us. If you read this I will be eloping with Mr Geraint Watkin Jones, your friend's brother. Pray for me and wish me well,
>
> Love, as always,
> Julia

'We telephoned your club.' Mrs Williams lowered her voice discreetly when Bronwen crossed the hall behind her. 'They said you weren't there, sir.'

'I had to go out for a couple of hours to see a client. He – the client – was busy. He could only see me late at night.' Edward realized that in elaborating he had only succeeded in making the lie more obvious.

'When we couldn't find you, sir, Mrs Larch opened the letter.'

'A private letter addressed to me by my own daughter!'

'It was either that or call the police to search for Miss Julia, sir.'

'Edward, you've deigned to come home.' Mabel left the dining room.

Mrs Williams glanced from her master to the mistress. 'If you'll excuse me, sir, ma'am, I have things to attend to in the kitchen.'

'You are excused, Mrs Williams.' Edward took off his hat.

'If you are in the slightest bit concerned as to what's happened to your precious daughter, you'd better read this.' Mabel pulled an envelope from her pocket and thrust it at him.

Edward took it from her. He glanced at the handwriting. There was no doubt; it was Julia's.

> *Dear Father,*
>
> *Thank you for talking to me today but I made the decision to marry Geraint Watkin Jones months ago. If you are reading this, it means that I have eloped with him tonight. Please do not try to find us. Only marriage can restore my reputation now.*
>
> *Love as always,*
>
> *Julia*
>
> *Do not blame yourself. If there is fault or guilt, it is entirely mine.*

Chapter 11

'HAVE YOU HEARD about Mr Watkin Jones?' Rosie Dyer from women's corsetry whispered to Tonia when they left the shop floor and walked upstairs to the canteen for their lunch break.

'No, is he ill?' Tonia had missed him that morning, because he usually commandeered her on Wednesdays to assist him in 'special duties', which invariably resulted in what he referred to as 'alone time' for them in the stockroom. She had even splashed out a week's wages on new French silk underwear for the occasion.

'No,' Rosie giggled. 'Miss Prendergast overheard Mrs Evans talking to Mr Horton in the office this morning. Mr Watkin Jones has left the store.'

'He has another job? Did they say where?' Tonia asked excitedly. Geraint had talked about finding another, better-paid position that would enable them to elope in style before returning to live in the newly-repaired annex of Ynysangharad House.

'Not another job, he's gone and eloped with Miss Larch. Mrs Evans told Mr Horton that he wouldn't be coming back – ever – and to turn his staff account into a customer account.' Taking Tonia's silence as bewilderment, Rosie continued, 'You must know Miss Larch, Miss Julia Larch. She's that ugly, fat . . . well, not exactly fat, but square customer. Apparently she has pots and pots of money. A man like Mr Watkin Jones would never marry an ugly woman like her if she weren't rich, but I still wonder if she has enough to keep him on the straight and narrow.'

'What do you mean?' Tonia whispered faintly, too shocked to fully comprehend what Rosie was saying.

'Come on, you must have heard what he's like. He's had the

knickers down of three assistants from ladies' fashions that I know of.'

'Who?' Tonia asked faintly.

'You know that blonde girl who works on shoes, and Barbara from gloves and Judith from skirts.'

'Are you sure?'

Rosie spat on the tip of her finger and waved it over her chest. 'Cross my heart and hope to die. I saw him with Judith myself and the liftboy told me about the other two. Well, not me exactly, but he told his sister and she told me. They live next door to my Auntie Bess—'

'Eloped,' Tonia repeated feebly, as the enormity of what Geraint had done sank in. If he really had run off with Julia Larch, he would *never* marry her.

'To Scotland, that's what Mrs Evans said,' Rosie babbled. 'They took the sleeper train from Cardiff last night. I think it's incredibly romantic. Do you think he sneaked from his carriage into hers in the night? Mind you, as Annie Harris said, he'll have to wrap a blindfold round his eyes and think of a bucketful of sovereigns to get into bed with that one. What a sight to wake up to every morning. Talk about beauty and the beast . . .'

Tonia didn't hear any more. She gripped the rail for support, as stairs, girls and ceiling whirled in a montage of black-and-white uniforms, black-and-white floor tiles and black iron banisters. Geraint was married! After he had promised to marry her. She'd be a laughing stock.

Joey would point a finger and tell the world that she'd allowed Geraint Watkin Jones to – what had Rosie said? – 'pull her knickers down in the stockroom.' It sounded so sordid and crude. And it wasn't what had happened at all. Geraint had made love to her gently and tenderly; he'd made her feel as though she was the only girl in the world for him. He had been as much in love with her as she him – she was sure of it. And now! He had left her for an ugly woman like Julia Larch just because she had more money than her.

She thought of what she'd allowed him to do to her and began to panic. He'd promised her that she wouldn't have a baby. He'd used something he called a French letter, but what if it hadn't worked and she did have a baby? And even if she didn't, she was still ruined. No man wanted damaged, second-hand goods for a wife.

Joey knew what she'd done, he'd promised not to tell. But supposing he broke his word? And if he didn't, the next man she went out with would find out eventually. Even if she made him wait until their wedding night to make love, he still could leave her, perhaps divorce her . . .

'Tonia, you all right? You've gone terribly pale.' Rosie took her arm and steered her to the nearest free table in the canteen.

Tonia almost fell into a chair.

'Is it that time of the month?' Rosie asked sympathetically.

'Yes.' She grasped at the straw Rosie offered.

'You sit there and I'll get your food.' Rosie looked at the board, although she didn't need to. The subsidized meals the management in Gwilym James arranged for the staff never varied from one week to the next in a season and Wednesdays in summer meant cold ham, potato and lettuce salads, followed by gooseberry flan and custard.

Tonia stared at the girls lining up at the counter with their trays and tried to think. Would Geraint and Julia Larch set up home in Pontypridd or Tonypandy? He had said that he wanted his account turned into a customer account. That meant he intended to visit the store. Of course he did, no one who was anyone in the valleys would shop anywhere else in Pontypridd. And how could she serve him and Julia and call him 'sir' and her 'madam' after what he'd done to her.

And if she was having a baby! She'd had one scare already. He'd promised to take care of her if she did fall pregnant but how could he if he was married to Julia Larch? And Joey – he was getting married a fortnight Saturday to that awful goody two shoes Rhian. Everyone was getting married except her! She'd be left on the shelf, a spinster – no, worse, a bad woman like the horrible girls who lined up behind the Empire Theatre after the shows.

She sank her head into her arms.

'Tonia, are you ill?'

Her supervisor was standing over her.

'I don't feel well, Miss Adams,' she croaked.

'I can see that. I think you should go home in case you are sickening for something contagious. The last thing we need is a bout of summer influenza in the store.' She looked around. 'I'll get one of the other girls to accompany you.'

'There's no need, Miss Adams. I can make my own way.'

'I'll at least get a cab to take you to the station.'

'That is very kind of you.'

'I'll ask Mr Horton for some money from petty cash so you can take a cab from Tonypandy station to your mother's shop. It isn't far, is it?' she enquired cautiously.

'No, not far at all, Miss Adams.'

Joey would be working in the Tonypandy store. She would call in and see him. And perhaps even find a way out of her predicament that wouldn't make her a laughing stock after all.

Mrs Williams checked the dining-room chairs and floor for crumbs while Bronwen and Rhian cleared the dishes from Mrs Larch's lunch table. When they'd finished, she replaced the Irish linen cloth with a 'show' crocheted lace cloth that matched the curtains, set in the centre a silver rose bowl, which Mrs Larch had spent all morning filling with buds, and closed the door.

'Leave the dining-room door, Mrs Williams, I'll inspect it before I go upstairs.' Mrs Larch crossed the hall from the library. 'You've prepared the trolleys for afternoon tea?'

'Yes, ma'am.'

'Nine kinds of sandwiches and six kinds of cake?'

Mrs Williams gritted her teeth; the first Mrs Larch had never thought it necessary to inspect the rooms after she had seen to them or enquire after menus once she'd ordered them. 'Cook has followed your instructions, ma'am.'

'Caviar, salmon mayonnaise, lobster, *pâté de foie gras*, cream cheese and cucumber savoury sandwiches, strawberry and banana, chocolate and Neapolitan sweet,' Mabel reminded her, although she written out the menu for the housekeeper two days previously.

'And make sure the sweet sandwiches are made with Madeira, not sponge cake like last time.'

'Yes, ma'am.' Mrs Williams took care to remain outwardly impassive and deferential, which wasn't easy. She had seen the sweet sandwiches Cook had made – with sponge cake.

'Lemon cheese cakes, Madeleines, iced honey cakes, macaroons, queen cakes, cherry cakes plus a selection of buttered fruit breads and plain and cheese scones, all homemade. I want nothing served this afternoon that has come from a baker's shop. And I can tell the difference, as can all the ladies on the committee,' she warned.

'Nothing will be served from the baker's, ma'am,' Mrs Williams reassured.

'Everything is under control, isn't it?' Mabel enquired suspiciously. 'I don't want any repeat of the mistakes Bronwen made at the last committee tea. No sloppy service or damp sugar in the bowls. Every detail must be absolutely perfect, Mrs Williams. In fact, on reflection, it would be best if Rhian and yourself served the ladies, and Bronwen cleared away the dirty dishes.'

'I will take care of it, ma'am.'

'See that you do. The girls cannot be trusted to work un-supervised.' Mabel entered the dining room. She ran her finger above the doorframe and checked the mantelpiece ornaments for dust before walking slowly around the table. The housekeeper braced herself for criticism but although Mabel pursed her lips she made no comment. She left the door open and returned to the hall.

'I am going upstairs to rest before the ladies arrive. You will call me with a cup of tea at a quarter to three. Not one minute after.'

'Yes, ma'am.' Mrs Williams glanced at the clock. It was just after one. She headed for the back staircase and the kitchen. Cook's voice wafted up to greet her, high-pitched and fractious.

'That new mistress has a heart of stone,' Cook said to no one in particular when Mrs Williams walked in on her and the maids. 'I don't know how she can contemplate holding her precious committee tea with Miss Julia missing, the Lord only knows where with that awful man, and the master gone searching for them. As if

184

we haven't enough upset in the house without her entertaining her ladies, today of all days.'

'There's going to be even more upset if we don't carry out her orders to the letter.' Mrs Williams thrust the tablecloth she was holding at Mair. 'Shake that out of the back door and fold it properly, there's a good girl.' She turned to Cook. 'The mistress has run through the menu with me and insisted the sweet sandwiches be made with Madeira cake.'

'I've never heard of such a thing. The last mistress, God rest her soul' – Cook, who was of Irish extraction and a practising Catholic, crossed herself – 'always wanted them made with plain brown bread and butter and very good they were too. Then this one comes along and it has to be stale sponge cake. So, I have to bake perfectly good sponge cakes only to let them go hard. And now Madeira . . . I'm telling you, Mrs Williams, more waste has gone on in this house since that one married the master, than in any other in the Rhondda. And that includes Mrs Hodges and Mrs Hadley's. Well,' Cook crossed her arms across her white-aproned bosom, 'I'm not making any Madeira cake now, no matter what she says.'

'You haven't time.' Mrs Williams looked to Rhian, who was eating her midday dinner of faggots and peas. The mistress had lunched on hors d'oeuvres of the same salmon mayonnaise that had been used to make the savoury sandwiches, cold roast chicken, salad and fresh cherry compote. In the late Mrs Larch's time, the servants had eaten more or less the same meals as the family with the exception of the fancier trimmings. Now there were two entirely different menus and the mistress had cut the one served to the staff to the cheapest, barest minimum.

'There's nothing for it, Rhian. As soon as you've finished eating you'll have to go into town to buy a couple of Madeira cakes from Rodney's. But mind you're not seen carrying them by any of Mrs Larch's "ladies". Tell whoever serves you to wrap them up well and take a teacloth to put over the basket.' Mrs Williams took the folded tablecloth from Mair.

'And be quick about it,' Cook warned. 'I need them by half past two at the latest if we're going to get the tea trolleys set up the way she wants them.'

'I'll run there and back.' Rhian spooned the last of her peas into her mouth and pulled her maid's cap from her head.

'You've more than enough time, so don't go breaking your neck. Tell Mrs Rodney to put them on the household account. And,' Mrs Williams lowered her voice, 'no more than five minutes in Gwilym James, even if it is a certain person's dinner time.'

Rhian fetched a basket from the scullery and took a clean Irish linen teacloth from the drawer.

'Get me a penny bar of Fry's chocolate when you're there, please, Rhian.' Mair handed her a penny from her pocket.

'And me.' Cook rummaged in her pocket and found a silver joey. 'Get me three. The way the mistress works us I can't see any of us going out again before our days off.'

'Unless we run out of one of her fancy wishes again,' Mrs Williams muttered under her breath.

'Bronwen, you want anything?' Rhian checked her reflection in the small mirror. Her face was clean and shiny, but there was no time to powder it. And because she had washed her hair the night before, her curls were more unruly than ever.

'No thanks, Rhian. It's going to take me the rest of the day to digest these faggots. I only hope I don't burp at the mistress's tea party. If I do I'll never hear the end of it.' Bronwen wiped her mouth on a napkin.

'Never mind your own shopping, Rhian, off with you now, and be as quick as you can.' The brief exchange with the mistress had made Mrs Williams short-tempered.

'I'll be back before you know it.' Rhian grabbed her straw boater, stripped off her apron and secreted the coins Mair and Cook had given her deep in the pocket of her grey-and-white striped uniform dress. She opened the back door, stepped outside and her spirits soared.

It was a glorious day. The sun shone from a clear, cloudless, blue-washed sky. The trees were clothed in their full summer garb of leafy green and the scent of the enormous cream cabbage roses, the pride and joy of the part-time gardener, filled the air. She ran down the drive to the gate, arms and legs flying, not caring how she looked.

Only two and half more weeks and she'd be walking away from Llan House for good. And, although she'd miss Mrs Williams, Bronwen, Mair and Cook, she didn't mind half as much now that Miss Julia had left. Six and a half more days and she'd spend her next day off with Joey. She smiled when she thought of what had happened between them the day before. Joey . . . her smile broadened as an image of him came to mind. Handsome, smiling, his dark eyes filled with love – and mischief.

If she hurried, she could walk to Dunraven Street and back in just over half an hour. Cook said she wanted the cake by half past two. If there wasn't a queue in Rodney's and she was served quickly, she could afford to steal ten not five minutes and pop into Gwilym James. She knew that more often than not Joey's dinner was a sandwich at his desk.

Holding her boater on her head with one hand, she picked up her skirts with the other and quickened her pace.

Tonia was on her feet before the train stopped at Tonypandy station. Bracing herself for the judder when the driver hit the brakes, she stood impatiently in front of the door. Nausea, dizziness and shock had been superseded by a burning desire for revenge, not only on Geraint for rejecting and betraying her, but also on Joey for telling him that her mother didn't own Rodney's. If Joey hadn't said anything, Geraint may never have looked at Julia Larch because the only possible reason he could have for marrying a woman as ugly as her was money.

Consumed by a rage that had been fuelled rather than assuaged by Miss Adams's compassion and sympathy at her supposed 'illness', she was no longer capable of logical thought. She only knew that she wanted to wound both men as she had been wounded.

She jumped down from the train as soon as it stopped. Oblivious to the attention she was attracting, she ran, skirt and petticoats flying to her knees, all the way from the station to Dunraven Street. The sun burned and suffocated her, dressed as she was in her Gwilym James uniform of black twill skirt and high-necked, long-sleeved cotton blouse. She loosened the tie on her collar and unbuttoned her cuffs, earning herself a glare of disapproval from the vicar's wife.

The street was packed with people. Children out from school for the summer holidays ran wild, dodging between trams, delivery carts, carriages and pedestrians as they played 'chase and catch'. The landlord of the Dunraven Hotel was standing on his front doorstep in shirt sleeves, smoking a pipe and exchanging news with the local constable, who was keeping a watchful eye on a couple of young boys hanging around the back of the baker's cart.

She stepped up on to the pavement and pushed past mothers carrying babies in shawls slung around both child and their own bodies as they walked slowly, measuring their steps to those of their toddlers. Two massive shire horses waited patiently in harness in front of a brewery dray parked outside the White Hart. The potman was assisting the draymen in rolling barrels down through the steel trapdoors set in the pavement that led to the public house's cellars.

A crowd of small boys had clustered around the posters pasted in front of the Empire Theatre that advertised the current variety show playing there. An elegantly-dressed lady in a fine white lawn skirt and blouse was leaving Owen Jones's milliner's shop with three hatboxes and Tonia suddenly wished with all her heart that she could be that woman. Rich and idle enough to buy three hats at once in the middle of the working day, and pretty enough to attract attention and turn men's heads. *She* would never have given herself to a man capable of betraying her by running off with another woman.

An overpowering smell of warm ham filled the air and she halted, her nose barely an inch away from a smoked pig carcass that hung outside the doorway of the New Market. Swerving to avoid it, she ducked into the empty doorway of the cobbler's when she spotted her mother's delivery boy ferrying boxed orders from the shop into the back of his cart.

Across the street, the front of Gwilym James was crowded with window shoppers trying to read the sale tickets that had appeared on the remaining summer stock. A tram rattled past at speed.

Pulling her hat down low over her eyes, she fastened the buttons she had loosened on her blouse and marched towards the front door.

'Good afternoon.' She acknowledged the doorman, who recognized her from the time she had worked in the store.

'Good afternoon, Miss George.'

'Is the manager in?' Her voice sounded odd, high-pitched, and she took a deep breath to steady herself.

'Mr Evans is in his office, Miss George. It is his lunch break. Would you like me to announce you?'

'That won't be necessary. My cousin is expecting me.' Looking neither left nor right, Tonia made her way down to the back of the store and Joey's office. The blinds had been closed on the window that overlooked the shop floor. The door had an opaque etched-glass panel that blocked out everything except the light. She stood before it and listened hard for a moment. Hearing only silence, she knocked.

'Unless the store's on fire, I'm not here.'

Recognizing Joey's drawl, she opened the door. Joey was sitting alone in shirtsleeves and waistcoat, his feet propped on his visitor's chair, a cup of tea and a half-eaten cheese and tomato sandwich on the desk in front of him.

He frowned when she closed the door behind her.

'I had to see you,' she gasped, her resolve wavering now she was actually alone with him.

He kicked his feet from the chair, folded the copy of the *Rhondda Leader* he'd been reading and set it aside. 'Leave the door open.'

'So everyone in the store can hear what I have to say to you? Not likely.' She dropped her handbag on to a chair and walked towards him. He rose to his feet and moved in front of his desk.

'You have nothing to say to me that other people can't hear.' He tried to pass her but she blocked the narrow gangway, trapping him between his desk and the wall.

'That's what you think.'

He stared at her. She glared back at him. Hoping to avoid a

scene, he sat on the edge of his desk, crossed his arms across his chest and faced her quietly. 'What's this about, Tonia?'

'You and me.'

'There is no you and me.'

'You've forgotten what you said to Geraint Watkin Jones in the stockroom in Gwilym James in Pontypridd?' she challenged.

'Completely,' he said flatly.

'I bet you think it's funny. Enjoying a good laugh at my expense?' she hissed.

'I have no idea what you are talking about,' he protested.

'You haven't heard that Geraint's run off with Julia Larch.'

'Oh, that. It's all over Tonypandy.'

'So everyone knows.' A tear fell from her eye and rolled down her left cheek. She didn't attempt to wipe it away and he recalled all the times she had run to him and his brothers when they'd been children. Remembered the schoolyard battles he'd fought on her behalf and the times she'd sneaked chocolate from the shop to pay him back afterwards.

Feeling sorry for her, he opened his arms and she fell into them. 'I'm sorry, I really am, Tonnie.' He reverted to her childhood nickname. He stroked her hair, she shuddered and her tears trickled hot and wet through his thin shirt on to his shoulder. 'Geraint may be Sali's brother but they're chalk and cheese. I knew what he was like. I should have warned you before you left here to go to the Pontypridd store. If I had, you might never have got involved with him in the first place and saved yourself all this heartache.'

'I thought he loved me,' she sobbed.

'I know,' he consoled clumsily. 'But he's not worth crying over. There's a right man out there for you, Tonnie, and you'll find him.'

'Whoever he is, he won't want me now. Not after what I've done with Geraint,' she wailed.

'No one need know about that.'

'You know. Geraint knows, and I do and I can't forget it—'

'Tonia, please, don't upset yourself any more. Not over Geraint Watkin Jones. He isn't worth a single one of your tears. I feel sorry for Julia Larch getting stuck with him. I bet she'll soon start feeling sorry for herself too, when she finds out what he's really like. Come on,' he tried to hold her at arm's length but she fought him. 'Let me take you home.'

'No!' Her crying escalated to hysteria. 'Not home, I don't want my mother and Annie to see me like this.'

He glanced up at the clock. 'I have to go back on the shop floor in ten minutes.'

'Please, Joey, just hold me.'

He reached for his handkerchief and gave it to her. 'Dry your eyes and sit down. I'll ask Miss Robertson to bring you a cup of tea. Then you can stay here until you are fit to go home.'

She locked her arms around his neck and refused to let him go. 'Just another minute, Joey, please.'

'One minute, Tonia, and then I'll fetch Miss Robertson to see to you.'

'You're lucky, Rhian, these are our last two Madeiras until tomorrow's delivery. Will there be anything else?' Annie O'Leary wrapped the cakes in brown paper bags and put them in the bottom of Rhian's basket.

'No, thank you, Annie.' Rhian folded the cloth over them.

'I'll see you in church on the first of August.'

'I'll probably be in here again before then.' Impatient to see Joey, Rhian was already at the door.

'The way you lot from Llan House are bobbing in and out of here these days, you're more than likely right,' Annie shouted after her.

Clutching her basket, Rhian dashed across the road, narrowly missing a boogie cart, created imaginatively but not soundly from firewood and balanced on pram wheels. It hurtled past her, its small driver and three even smaller passengers screaming as they crashed into a lamppost.

'Any bones broken?' Father Kelly lifted the most vociferous casualty from the wreckage.

'Are they—'

'They're fine, Rhian,' he reassured. 'I've seen them do this a dozen times a day. When are you going to get yourself a boogie with brakes, Sean?' he asked the driver. He'd noticed the direction Rhian was walking in and guessed from her uniform that she was stealing five minutes out of her working day to see Joey. 'I can see you're in a hurry, Rhian.'

'I am, Father Kelly. Bye and thanks.'

The doorman lifted his hat to her. 'Good afternoon, Miss Jones, Mr Evans is in his office.'

'Thank you.' Rhian saw that the blinds were drawn on Joey's office window. Assuming he was still eating his lunch, she knocked once and opened the door. Then froze.

Joey was leaning with his back against his desk. Tonia was standing in front of him, her head resting on his shoulder, one arm wrapped around his neck, the other around his waist.

Rhian dropped her basket. It crashed to the floor. The Madeira cakes and teacloth rolled out on to the lino.

Joey saw the shock register in Rhian's eyes, watched her hand fly to her mouth. 'Rhian, this isn't what it looks like—'

'You promised!' Rhian's voice fractured with emotion. 'You made me a solemn promise!'

'Tonia was upset.' He pushed his cousin away from him. 'Tonia, tell her what happened.'

Tonia looked from him to Rhian. 'Tell her what, Joey? That you and I are lovers and I'm having your baby?'

Rhian turned and fled blindly through the store. She was vaguely aware of crashing into display stands and knocking them over. Of barging into shoppers. Of people staring.

'Mr Evans!' Miss Robertson's voice rang loud and high-pitched in shock. Rhian stopped and looked back through misted eyes. Joey was in his office doorway and she knew why the supervisor had shouted. His flies were unbuttoned, his shirt-tail poking out of his open trousers. Fumbling with his buttons, he charged after her, only to slip on one of the cakes. She didn't wait to see any more. Picking up her skirts, she darted into the street.

A horse whinnied, a barrel crashed down the chute into the cellar of the White Hart. People shouted behind her but she didn't stop. She dived up a side street and from there into a lane. She ran to the end. A garden gate was open. She went in, crouched behind it and gulped in great mouthfuls of air. She needed to get her breath before she went . . . to where?

Sali, she could go to Sali. Or could she? Sali was Joey's sister-in-law. She couldn't ask her to take sides. No more than she could Megan. It would split the family in two. They had all warned her against going out with Joey, his own brothers as well as Sali and Megan. Even his father had tried to tell her what he was like. But after that first wonderful day they had spent together, she had refused to listen to anyone except Joey. And now . . . now she knew that even when he had given her his mother's ring he had lied to her. Her own voice echoed in her mind.

But it's not the past that concerns me, Joey, it's the future. Can't you understand that?

I solemnly promise you, Rhian, that if you marry me, I will never do anything to hurt you.

Never?

Never.

She had wanted to believe him enough to allow him to deceive her, or had she simply deceived herself?

Handsome is as handsome does.

She knew exactly what handsome Joey Evans had done before he met her – and to dozens of girls. He hadn't changed, and that knowledge hurt more than she would have believed possible.

She couldn't return to Llan House to face Mrs Williams and the other girls and confirm that they'd been right to distrust Joey all along. She wouldn't even be able to hide what had happened. Even if news didn't reach them from the store right away, they only had to take one look at her to realize that something was very wrong. Besides, she didn't even have the cakes . . .

Tonia and Joey! How could she have been so blind? She closed her eyes against the image of them embracing in front of his desk. Of Joey standing in the doorway of his office, Tonia behind him, his flies unbuttoned. A baby! Tonia said she was having his baby!

In the space of a few short minutes her entire world had fallen apart. And she was on her own with absolutely no one to turn to.

*

Cook opened the kitchen door and looked into the back yard. 'Where can that girl have got to?'

'If they didn't have any Madeira cake in Rodney's she could have gone to another shop. You know what the queues can be like in James Cole's and the Maypole.' Mrs Williams's excuse was weak and she knew it. She checked the clock for the tenth time in as many minutes. Rhian was always so reliable, but she had left the house at a quarter past one and it was half past two. She had taken an hour and a quarter for what should have been a forty-five-minute errand.

In another quarter of an hour, the mistress would have to be woken, and an hour after that the tea trolley would have to be taken upstairs. Everything had been prepared except the sweet sandwiches and she knew that if Rhian didn't turn up in the next five minutes, Cook, who could be difficult at the best of times, would refuse to make them on principle. And if she made them, Cook would create an almighty fuss and tell the mistress that she was trying to take her job.

'Bronwen, make a pot of tea and wake the mistress with a cup at a quarter to three.' Mrs Williams joined Cook in the opened doorway.

'Yes, Mrs Williams.'

'Here she comes now,' Cook sighed impatiently when they heard the crunch of footsteps on gravel on the lower part of the drive.

'That's not a her it's a him.' Mrs Williams squinted into the sunlight when a figure walked around the side of the house. 'What are you doing here at this time of day, Joey Evans?' she barked.

'I need to see Rhian.'

'She's not here,' Cook snapped. 'She went into town over an hour ago and she's not come back.'

'That wouldn't have anything to do with you, now would it?' Mrs Williams demanded suspiciously.

It choked Joey to admit it. 'Yes.'

'And?' Mrs Williams glared at him when he didn't elaborate.

'I've looked for her everywhere I can think of in the last hour,' he pleaded. 'I've been from one end of Tonypandy to the other and there's no sign of her in any of the streets or on the mountain. No one's seen her anywhere. Please, Mrs Williams, if she is here, let me see her,' he begged. 'There's been a dreadful misunderstanding.'

'Knowing you, Joey Evans, one involving another girl.' When Joey didn't contradict her, Mrs Williams set her mouth in a grim line. 'You may as well tell me what's happened so I'll be prepared for the worse.'

'She saw me with Tonia.'

'Your cousin?'

'It wasn't what it looked like,' Joey protested earnestly. 'Tonia was upset, she was crying on my shoulder.'

'And what was Tonia upset about?'

'I can't say.' Joey had never been so reluctant to keep a secret.

'I see. And what happened after Rhian saw your cousin crying on your shoulder?' Mrs Williams turned bright red, a sure sign to those who knew her that she was having trouble keeping her temper.

'She ran off.'

'When was this?' Cook asked.

'About an hour ago.'

'Then the mistress can kiss her Madeira cake goodbye.' Cook sounded almost triumphant but, Mrs Williams reflected sourly, she wasn't the one who'd be facing Mrs Larch's temper.

Joey recollected Rhian dropping her basket in his office and him slipping on something that had fallen out of it afterwards.

'I've taken the mistress her tea, Mrs Williams. She wants to see you.' Bronwen lifted her lace 'afternoon' apron and cap from the peg where she'd hung them earlier.

'And I have some news for her.' Mrs Williams glared at Joey. 'Don't you have a job to go to?'

'You'll tell Rhian—'

'I'll tell Rhian nothing, young man. I warned her what you were like before she walked out with you. We all did, but would she listen? No, not her. Well, it looks like she's found out the hard way what you are. And if she has any sense she'll stay away from you.'

'You'll tell her I called,' Joey pleaded, looking over the housekeeper's shoulder to Bronwen and Cook.

'Clear off, we're busy.'

Joey walked slowly down the drive, looking behind every bush and shrub as he went. If only he had insisted that Tonia leave the door open as he had asked her to. If only he had felt her unbuttoning his flies. If only he'd had the sense to walk away from her when she'd started crying instead of offering her sympathy. If only he had caught up with Rhian when she had run off. And the biggest 'if only' of all – if only Rhian would listen to him when he finally did find her. But he had a numbing, blood-chilling feeling that she wouldn't.

Chapter 12

'TONIA, IF YOU won't tell me what's happened, I can't help you,' Connie said irritably. An impatient mother on the infrequent occasions when everything was going smoothly between her and Tonia, she wasn't sure whether she should hug or slap her daughter out of her hysteria.

She and her live-in assistant Annie had been serving in the shop when they'd heard Tonia thundering up the side staircase that led to their living quarters. Assuming that her daughter had been taken ill in work, she'd left Annie in charge of the shop, and rushed upstairs to find Tonia sprawled on her bed, howling like a toddler locked into a tantrum. And she had continued to respond to all her questions with incoherent sobs since.

'Tonia, please . . .'

Tonia shrugged off her mother's restraining hand and crawled under the bedclothes. Fighting Connie's efforts to expose her head, she crouched on her hands and knees, covered herself completely with the bedspread and pinned it firmly to the mattress beneath her.

'You haven't played at being a tortoise in a shell or a caterpillar in a cocoon since you were a child, Tonia,' Connie shouted in exasperation. 'Don't you think you're being absurd?'

'Connie, the Cadbury rep is here,' Annie shouted up the stairs. 'Do you want to order in extra for miners' fortnight?'

'I'll be there in a minute,' Connie yelled back. She slapped the lump on her daughter's bed. 'Sooner or later you are going to have to come out from under there, Antonia, and tell me what you've done to get yourself into this state.'

Tonia heard her mother leave the room and slam the door but she didn't move. When she had thought through what she was going to do on the train journey up from Pontypridd, it had seemed so simple. Excite Joey the way she did Geraint, allow him to make love to her and then, afterwards, if he refused to marry her, threaten to tell her mother and his father what he had done. She knew her mother and Uncle Billy would march him up the aisle, at knifepoint if necessary.

Joey might not have the same finesse or education as Geraint, but he was a husband worth having. Good-looking and with a well-paid job. She'd be envied, but more importantly, Joey was one of the only men in the Rhondda who couldn't throw her indiscretions with Geraint back at her, because he'd done worse himself.

She'd scarcely given a thought to Rhian when she'd made her plans, other than to recall that she disliked her for attracting Joey at a time when she'd wanted Joey to notice her.

She'd grown up with Joey, and knew him so well she was confident she'd make him a better wife than a maid from Llan House. But the expression on Rhian's face when she had seen her and Joey together had terrified her. She had never seen such naked pain in another person's eyes. And far from marrying her as she'd intended, Joey had looked as though he could have killed her there and then in his office.

If anything happened to Rhian . . . if she did something silly . . . she pushed the unpalatable thought from her mind. Rhian would be all right. She simply had to be, because the alternative was too horrible to contemplate.

'Joey, I don't know what else we can do or where else we can look.' Lloyd returned to their table in the back bar of the White Hart after telephoning Sali.

Joey pushed one of the two pints of beer he had bought across the table towards his brother. 'Sali hasn't seen her?'

Lloyd shook his head. 'She telephoned Llan House again half an hour ago. Edward Larch isn't home but she spoke to Mrs Williams. The housekeeper said they've searched everywhere around the house, including the outbuildings and garden.'

'That's it,' Joey said excitedly. 'The outbuildings around Victor and Megan's farm.'

'Didn't you hear Victor's farmhand tell him no one was in them? And if Rhian had gone there we would have seen her walking on the mountain, either on our way to, or back from the farm. Besides, it's like I said before we went. Given our relationship, I don't think Rhian would put Sali or Megan in the embarrassing position of having to take sides in this stupid situation you've got yourself into, by appealing to either of them for help.'

'She doesn't know any one else.' Joey stared wretchedly into his beer. As a last resort before going to the pub, they'd called into the police station to report Rhian missing, only to be treated in a cavalier fashion by the duty constable who'd already been given an embellished version of the afternoon's events in the store. He told them that young girls were always running off, especially from service, and if Rhian was still missing in two weeks he might 'just might' consider filing a missing persons' report. But he hadn't been able to resist a final jibe: 'Who could blame a girl for running away from her fiancé after she'd caught him making love to another woman less than three weeks before their supposed wedding?'

'I can't just sit here doing nothing.' Joey pushed his half-finished pint away and rose to his feet.

'Tell me where we can look, and I'll take you there,' Lloyd said evenly.

Joey closed his eyes for a moment then sat back down. He had searched everywhere he could think of, and asked just about everyone he knew if they had seen Rhian, before catching a train to Pontypridd and soliciting Lloyd's help. If Rhian had left Tonypandy by either train or tram, she had done so without any railway official, tram driver or conductor seeing her. No assistant or manager in any of the shops in Dunraven Street had seen her, and he had offended Connie by point-blank refusing to discuss what had happened between him and Tonia to make Rhian run off.

'Do you know she only had fourpence in her pocket?' Joey muttered.

'So Mrs Williams told Sali when she telephoned Llan House,' Lloyd reminded him patiently.

'If anything happens to her, I'll never forgive myself.'

'Is it too much to ask, even at this late stage, why you and Tonia were in your office with the blinds drawn and your flies undone?' Lloyd asked.

'I've told you.'

'And I told you that I don't believe a word of it. Tonia would never set you up that way.'

'There's something you don't know about our charming little cousin.' Joey scraped his chair over the flagstones. 'I'm going to check the streets again.'

Lloyd glanced at the clock behind the bar. 'Want me to come with you?'

Joey shook his head. 'You go home.' Sensing that Lloyd was about to insist on accompanying him, he added, 'I'd rather be on my own.'

'You'll telephone Ynysangharad House if you find her or hear anything?'

'I will.' Joey walked through the blue, smoky atmosphere of the pub to the door. He opened it and left.

Edward Larch had come to the end of an overly long, unpleasant and tiresome day. He had spent the morning in Pontypridd, met with Lloyd and Sali Evans who had offered him their sympathy and, despite their guarded comments, confirmed his worse suspicions about Geraint Watkin Jones's character and motives for eloping with Julia.

He had returned to his office and combed through all the papers relating to Julia's trust fund, in what he knew from the outset to be a futile exercise. There was no legal way that he could safeguard his daughter's inheritance from her unscrupulous and conniving future, if not actual, husband.

And then, to top it all, he had received a telephone call from Mrs Williams, distraught for the first time since he had known her, to inform him that the prettiest and most reliable maid in his household had disappeared, apparently after an argument with the feckless and unfaithful fiancé she had been due to marry in less than three weeks.

And when he had finished speaking to the housekeeper, Mabel had come on the line demanding that he dine at home that evening to silence rumours that had reached the inner sanctum of the Ladies' Circle. Talk that suggested he had set up a separate establishment for himself in the house next door to his office. He was angry with Mabel, but even more furious with himself for not being more careful.

Mabel had then gone on to demand he dismiss all the indoor servants, including Cook and Mrs Williams, because they had made a mockery of the tea party she had given for the Ladies' Circle. The mention of the tea party, which he regarded as trivial in comparison to everything else that had happened in the last twenty-four hours, was the final straw.

He told her he'd return for supper at ten-thirty and she could have half an hour and not a minute more of his time then. Ignoring the work piled on his desk and the ringing telephone, he had locked himself in the sitting room next door to his office for what remained of the afternoon and the evening. He felt odd. Tired yet curiously restless, he couldn't settle to anything, including the meal he asked Mrs Ball to order in from the White Hart.

Not wanting to walk home, or run the risk of getting Mabel on the line again by ringing Llan House and asking that Harris bring the carriage down to his office, he told Mrs Ball to order him a brake, one of the carriages that had been built specifically to cope with the steep hills of the Rhondda Valleys. It was due to pick him outside at a quarter past ten but she knocked on his door a full ten minutes earlier.

'If that's the brake, tell the driver to wait, Mrs Ball.' He couldn't bear the thought of exchanging the luxury of solitude for his wife's company a moment before he was forced to.

'It's not the brake, sir. I heard a noise out the back. I thought it might be a stray dog, but it was a young girl. She's huddled against the wall of the yard and refusing to move. Shall I call the police?'

He left his chair. 'No, Mrs Ball. There's no need to call the police. I'll go down and see to her myself.'

'And, as you have formally declared in front of these two witnesses your intention to live as man and wife from this day forward, I formally declare you as such in law. Congratulations, Mr and Mrs Geraint Watkin Jones.' The 'anvil priest', hired by the landlord of the hotel Geraint had booked himself and Julia into that afternoon, kissed Julia's cheek and shook Geraint's hand.

'Don't we get a certificate?' Julia asked in confusion. Since they had left the sleeper that morning, first to change at Crewe then Carlisle to take the slow local train to Gretna Green, she had been in a daze. Geraint had taken charge of everything, including the money, bank and chequebook she had brought. He'd insisted they stop and outfit themselves with new clothes and luggage at Carlisle before lunching in a grand and expensive hotel.

When they'd reached Gretna Green he had asked the station-master to recommend the best hotel in the town and left her to rest in the suite he'd booked, while he arranged their wedding with the hotel manager.

'Of course you get a certificate, Mrs Watkin Jones.' The 'anvil priest' handed Geraint a sheet of paper. 'Take that along to the register tomorrow morning, the receptionist will tell you where it is, and you can formally register your marriage, although as I just said, you are already man and wife in law.'

The landlord and his wife who had stood witness applauded briefly. Geraint kissed Julia's cheek and she glanced at their reflections in the mirror above the fireplace. Geraint stood next to her, handsome and resplendent in a pale-grey suit, high-collared white linen shirt and grey silk tie. In unflattering contrast she resembled a photograph of the elderly Queen Victoria stuffed into a vast and shapeless crinoline. Only where the old Queen's gowns had always been black, hers was white, covered in frills and topped by a hat the size of a small umbrella. The only good thing that could be said about it was that it hid her hair, which she'd never been able to manage without Rhian's help.

'Mrs Watkin Jones.' Geraint held out his arm and she realized that she had done what she had set out to do. She had bought herself a presentable and good-looking husband.

'Dinner is being served in the dining room, Mr Watkin Jones, but if you and your wife would prefer to eat in your suite I could arrange to have it brought up to you.'

'No, thank you, Mr Hamilton.' Geraint answered without referring to Julia. He led her into the dining room where half a dozen inquisitive couples glanced at them. The other ladies were elegantly – and comparatively plainly – dressed in summer lawns and linens, making Julia wish that she hadn't given in to Geraint's persuasion to buy the white lace outfit in Carlisle.

Geraint studied the menu while the waiter pulled out Julia's chair and settled a napkin on her lap.

'Shall I order for you, Julia?'

'No, thank you, Geraint.' Julia felt that if she didn't make a stand, she'd never make another decision for herself in her married life.

'If I might make a suggestion, sir, madam, we have some fine fresh salmon cutlets and fillets of beef.' The waiter stood next to Julia's chair, pencil in hand.

Geraint continued to study the menu. 'I'll start with the olive croutons, followed by the salmon cutlets with mayonnaise sauce, the ham soufflé, roast duck, with four vegetables and strawberry cream. And to drink . . .' He studied the wine list. 'A bottle of champagne. Do you have Moët et Chandon?'

'But of course, sir.'

'We'll have a bottle with the entrée, but we'll start with hock.'

'Very good, sir.' The waiter noted his order. 'Madam?'

Tired out by her disturbed night and confused day, Julia wasn't hungry. She picked out the two lightest dishes she could see on the menu. 'I'll have the sole in aspic followed by fruit salad, please.'

'I am sorry, you must be feeling tired, I didn't think. Perhaps we should have eaten in our suite after all.'

She found Geraint's concern irritating as well as tardy. 'It would have been nice to have been consulted.'

'We have only just ordered. I am sure that they will take our meals upstairs if we ask them.'

'There's no need to put anyone to any bother.'

'I'm sorry; this is hardly a good start to our married life. Rushing across half of Britain in a sleeper train, having to change trains twice on the way, buying new wardrobes and then marrying in a hotel sitting room with strangers as witnesses. I'll make it up to you when we return to Pontypridd. Have you any thoughts on where you'd like to buy a house?'

'None.' She watched the waiter pour their hock. 'We don't have to live in Pontypridd,' she ventured, thinking of her stepmother. Her father might come round to what she had done. Mabel never would.

'My brother Gareth is a professional soldier, he also has business interests in the town – owns properties that my uncle couldn't sell without attracting the attention of our bank. Given all this talk of war, he may soon be seeing active service so he'll need someone to oversee his interests.'

'And you think you should volunteer your services?'

'Both our families live close by,' he reminded her.

'I wouldn't count on my father or stepmother being too friendly after what we've just done,' she warned.

'Other than school I haven't lived anywhere else.'

'We could travel for a while, see if there's anywhere we prefer?'

'You have somewhere in mind?'

Was it her imagination or did he sound unenthusiastic. 'No, but I have always wanted to live by the sea.'

'We'll discuss it.' His croutons arrived. 'These look delicious, Julia. Are you sure you don't want to try one?'

'No, thank you.' Her heart sank. *We'll discuss it*. She had wanted a husband who would give her financial and personal independence. The ink was scarcely dry on the marriage certificate and she was beginning to wonder if she'd have either.

Edward stepped out of the back door of the shop on the ground floor. Twilight had fallen and he looked twice around the yard before he made out the outline of Rhian huddled in the corner between the house and the steps at his feet. He held out his hand to her. 'Half of Tonypandy is out looking for you.'

She stared up at him blankly, white-faced and shivering despite the warm air.

He reached down and tried to lift her by the shoulders. 'Come on, let's get you in the house where Mrs Ball can look after you.'

She shook her head violently from side to side.

'You can't stay out here all night.' Recognizing she was in shock, he pulled her up forcefully. 'At least come inside. Mrs Ball can make you some tea.' He turned to the woman behind him. 'Run upstairs and get the bed ready please, Mrs Ball, and then fetch the doctor.'

'No! No doctor!' Rhian screamed. 'Please, Mr Larch, sir, I don't want anyone to know where I am, please . . .'

'Leave the doctor for the moment, Mrs Ball.' He lifted Rhian into his arms. 'But I will call him if you don't do as you're told,' he warned.

Two glasses of hock, three of Champagne, a brandy and a Scottish whisky liqueur on top of very little food had set Julia's head spinning.

'Another brandy?' Geraint asked.

'No, thank you.'

'If you don't mind, I will.' He signalled to the waiter.

'I'm tired.'

'Why don't you go on up to bed?' he suggested.

'I think I will.'

He left his chair. 'I'll take you up.'

'There is no need, enjoy your brandy.'

She walked slowly up the stairs and went into the bathroom at the end of the corridor. Taking advantage of the plumbed-in bath, she returned to her room and gathered her toiletries, nightdress and negligee. Wishing that she could ring for Rhian, she struggled out of her elaborate lace dress and underclothes.

She caught sight of herself in the mirror opposite the bath as she lowered herself into the water. Geraint was handsome and she was fat and ugly, her skin freckled, her hair redder than ever under the bright electric light. Trying to forget her shortcomings, she washed and dried herself with care. Afterwards she applied a lavish sprinkling of a new range of scented toiletries the assistant in the chemist's in Tonypandy had recommended, Cleaves 'White Lilac'. Paying particular attention to her breasts, she sprinkled her skin with powder, dabbed scent behind her ears, under her armpits and in every fold of her skin from her elbows to the back of knees.

She stood naked in front of the mirror and brushed out her long hair. It was difficult to study her body objectively, but the images she'd dreamed, cultivated and cherished of her sitting next to Geraint in theatre boxes, restaurants and walking into ballrooms holding on to his arm, were already dissipating. Instead she imagined the sniggers and whispered comments when people saw them as a married couple.

She has money. Tens of thousands apparently.

So sad, he lost his. He would never have considered marrying her otherwise.

Such an odd pair.

She didn't get on with her father's new wife and he was on the lookout for any girl with a decent income. Mr Hadley had him thrown off his doorstep when he came sniffing after his daughter.

Everyone knows he doesn't give a fig for her but who can blame her for deluding herself. He is very good looking.

Do you think that he – they – share a bed?

Do you think . . .

She slipped on her gown and negligee. She wasn't pretty but she was clean and she smelled good. Picking up clothes and her toilet bag, she made her way back to her bedroom, smiling self-consciously at a young couple who came up the stairs arm in arm together.

She went into the suite, switched on the light and packed away her hat and dress, determined never to wear either again. She folded her linen, rolled her stockings neatly, and, when the room was tidy, crept into bed. The suite had a sitting room with a smaller second single bedroom off it where Geraint had placed the bag of new clothes he'd bought. Would he sleep there? Or with her?

She lay rigid with her arms at her side and waited. The small sounds of the hotel echoed through the doors and walls. People walking up and down the corridor outside. Climbing the stairs and moving about in the rooms overhead. Snatches of voices drifted in, a trolley rattled as it was pushed past her door.

She reached for the watch she'd placed on a side table. She had been upstairs for over an hour. The last thing she remembered looking at before she went to sleep was the wedding ring that Geraint had bought with her money in Carlisle and placed on her finger that afternoon.

'She's had a warm bath, drunk a glass of brandy and I've tucked her up in bed, Mr Larch. I hope you don't mind but I gave her one of your clean nightshirts.'

'That's fine, thank you, Mrs Ball.' Edward dropped his book on to the floor next to his chair.

'She's asking to see you, sir.'

'I'll talk to her, Mrs Ball, but I'll leave the door open. Do you mind seeing to her if she should need you in the night? I'll pay you for your time.'

'There's no need, sir. I have nothing else to do.'

Edward rose from his chair and, careful to leave both the sitting-room and corridor doors open, went into the bedroom. Rhian was lying in the centre of the large double bed, still pale and trembling despite Mrs Ball's ministrations.

'You do realize that you've had people out looking for you all day.' He sat on the chair in the corner of the room.

'I can't face anyone. You won't tell a soul where I am, will you, sir?'

'I have to tell them you're safe. Mrs Williams said that Mr Evans has called at Llan House several times today and Mrs Evans has telephoned—'

'Please, sir. You won't tell anyone?' Her eyes rounded in agitation. 'I'll leave first thing in the morning.'

'To go where?'

'I don't know, sir. But it doesn't matter so long as it's away from Tonypandy and somewhere I can find work.'

'We'll talk again tomorrow. Mrs Ball's rooms are on the floor below these should you need anything in the night. I'll let everyone know you're safe but I won't say where you are, is that all right?'

She nodded dumbly.

'And you promise to stay here until I come back in the morning? If you're still determined to leave Tonypandy then, I'll pay you what you're owed, so you'll have some money behind you.'

'Thank you, sir. You're very kind.'

He left his chair. 'Sleep well. Hopefully everything will look better in the morning. We'll talk then.'

'Don't worry, sir, I'll look after her,' Mrs Ball said, as he returned to the sitting room. 'I told the driver of the brake to come back at eleven.'

'It's that late now?'

'Ten minutes before, by the clock, sir.'

Edward picked up his jacket. If Mabel were still up she'd be furious. But he realized with a start that without Julia in the house, he had no reason whatsoever to continue calling Llan House home – or even to visit there.

Edward went into his office and locked the communicating door behind him. He picked up the telephone book from his secretary's desk, looked under E and dialled Lloyd Evans's number. A butler answered and he breathed a sigh of relief, he didn't feel up to conversation. He left a message to say that Rhian was well, safe and in good hands, but didn't want to see anyone for a day or two.

The brake was waiting in the street and he settled back in the seat, trying not to think about what his daughter might or might not be doing with Geraint Watkin Jones at that very moment.

The driver stopped in the drive of Llan House. Edward alighted and was almost bowled over by Joey Evans who hurtled out of the shrubbery to meet him.

'Mr Evans, a strange time for a social call, don't you think?' Edward brushed off the pollen Joey had deposited on his jacket.

'Mr Larch, have you seen, Rhian?' Joey demanded breathlessly.

'You've saved my coachman a trip, Mr Evans. I would have sent him round to your house as soon as I got in. Miss Jones is in safe hands, but she doesn't want to see anyone for a few days. I telephoned your brother's house earlier and left a message.'

'I must see her. You know where she is—'

'I've told you all that I can, Mr Evans. Now if you'll excuse me, I haven't been home all day.'

Joey blocked Edward's path. Edward stared back at him in the gloom and Joey realized that he had no right to demand any more of him.

'Thank you, Mr Larch. I'll call back tomorrow, if I may.'

'Please don't, Mr Evans. She knows where to get in touch with you if she wants to.'

'She won't. Can you get a letter to her?' Joey asked as an afterthought.

'Yes, Mr Evans. I will be able to arrange that.' Edward looked up. The curtains were open in the drawing room and he could see Mabel pacing in front of the window. 'Good evening, Mr Evans.'

Joey watched Edward walk into his house before turning towards home. He had done all he could – for tonight.

Half an hour later he turned the key in the lock of his father's house, went into the hall and switched on the light. Before he had time to walk down the passage, the kitchen door opened and his father limped out.

'Did you find Rhian?'

Wretched, sunk too deep in his own misery for anything outside of it to register, Joey wasn't even surprised to see his father home for the first time in months. 'I saw Edward Larch. He said Rhian is safe but she doesn't want to see me.'

'I'm not surprised.'

'You've seen her?' Joey whirled around eagerly.

'No,' his father interrupted tersely. 'Connie's here, she came to see me in Victor's house.'

Joey set his hat on a coat hook. 'What does she want?'

'What do you think she wants?'

Joey looked at his father for the first time. 'You and Connie believe Tonia, don't you?'

'At the moment I'm not sure what to believe.'

Joey walked past his father and went into the living room. Connie was sitting next to a small fire his father had lit. A cup of tea stood on the shelf next to her but she was nursing a glass of leftover Christmas brandy.

'We can't believe Tonia,' she informed him coldly, 'because Tonia hasn't said a single word since she came home this afternoon. But the customers who called into the shop said plenty.'

'I can imagine.'

She glared at Joey. 'I need to know, Joey. Were you two alone together in your office with the blinds drawn and the door closed?'

'It wasn't what it looked like.' Joey had said the words so often he was sick of them.

'No?' she questioned sceptically.

'No,' he repeated emphatically.

'And when Rhian opened the door and surprised you, your trousers weren't unbuttoned.'

'They were, but as I keep saying, it wasn't what it looked like,' Joey repeated wretchedly.

'Then my customers weren't *all* lying?'

Joey ran his fingers through his hair, ruffling his curls. His father recognized the gesture. Joey had done it since babyhood whenever something upset him.

'If there is an explanation other than the obvious, I'm listening.' Connie sat back in her chair and waited. Joey heard the tap of his father's walking stick and the springs creak on his chair when he sat in the chair behind him.

'I'll not say any more without Tonia in the room.' Joey sat at the table and sank his head into his hands.

'For pity's sake, Joey,' Connie raged. 'Isn't any woman safe from you? Antonia's your cousin, your younger cousin,' she emphasized. 'You two were brought up so close you could almost be brother and sister.'

'Which is why I've never regarded or treated Tonia any

differently to the way I would have a younger sister.' He dropped his hands from his face and parried Connie's glare.

Billy looked at his youngest son for a moment before turning to Connie. 'It's late and without Tonia we'll never resolve this tonight. I'll walk you home. We'll talk about this tomorrow.'

'When? It's Pandy Parade tomorrow night. Joey and I have to work until ten o'clock.'

'I'll come down to your house first thing in the morning. The sooner the mud's cleaned from my name, the sooner I can get back to finding Rhian.' Joey left his chair. 'And I'll see you home, Connie, not my father. If you walked here from Victor's, Dad, you've done enough hiking for one day.'

'You're not walking anywhere with me, Joey,' Connie refused curtly.

'Then I'll walk behind you.'

'After what's happened today I'd be more frightened of you attacking me than one of the drunks leaving the Pandy.'

'That's a vicious thing to say.'

'Not after what you've done to Tonia.'

'Stop it, the pair of you,' Billy ordered brusquely. 'Sniping at one another isn't going to help. I'll walk you back, Connie, and before you say another word, Joey, Victor brought Connie and I back here in his cart. Get some sleep, boy,' he added, not too unkindly, before following Connie out.

Mabel stood quivering with rage as she faced Edward across the drawing room. 'I asked you a question, Edward. And, as your wife, I demand an answer. Is what Mrs Hodges said true? Have you fitted out rooms for your own use in the building you've renovated next door to your office?'

'At the risk of repeating myself ad nauseum, Mabel, yes, I have fitted out a shop and three sets of rooms in the building. And, as you're so adamant on knowing every detail of the arrangements, yes, I have furnished the rooms on the second floor to my own personal taste.' Edward sat on the sofa, slipped his hand into his inside pocket and pulled out his cigarette case.

211

'You know my rules. I won't have any smoking in the drawing room.'

'It was your insistence on laying down rules as to how I should live in my own house that drove me to furnish those rooms, Mabel.' Edward lit his cigarette.

'Have you any idea how it feels to have someone tell you that your husband is leading a double life?'

'Am I your husband, Mabel?' He stared up at her questioningly.

'We're married . . .' She faltered under his steady gaze.

'Standing up together in church doesn't constitute a marriage, Mabel.'

'How can we have a marriage when you are never at home?'

'How can we have a marriage when you won't let me touch you, and refuse to share my bed?' He continued to look at her but she turned away.

'Married couples of our class always have separate bedrooms.'

'Amelia and I never did.'

'Then she was very different to me.'

'She was,' he concurred.

'Are you trying to tell me that she liked the disgusting things men want to do to women?'

'I'm not a violent man, Mabel,' he broke in harshly, 'but you say one more word about Amelia, not just now – ever – and I'll hit you, and harder than you hit Rhian.'

'That's what this is all about, isn't it?' She grasped the excuse to move away from the subject of their non-existent intimate life. 'My punishing a stupid maid.'

'The sight of you slapping an innocent girl may have woken me up to the person you really are, Mabel. But that is not what this argument is about. Hasn't it occurred to you that details of our family affairs come to you as complete revelations from strangers because you've done your damnedest to destroy my family life? And, as for a double life, I wouldn't call anyone's existence in this house a life, which is probably why Julia has sought escape by eloping with a fortune-hunter and Gerald wrote to tell me that he would prefer to spend the summer in France with his friend's family than come home. It's certainly the reason why I've gone to all the expense of setting up a separate establishment.'

'That is a despicable thing to say after all the care and attention that I've lavished on this house.' Her temper escalated to meet his.

'That's exactly it, Mabel. You've turned my and my children's home into a house. A cold, unwelcoming place presided over by a woman who cares more for the Ladies' Circle than the family she married into.'

'Just because I have some consideration for appearances—'

'Consideration!' he sneered. 'Well, I have consideration too. For myself, and you. Because if I spent any more time in this house I would probably end up harming either one or both of us. Would you like to know what I do in the rooms I've furnished?' He inhaled his cigarette before continuing. 'I sit alone. I dine alone. I eat simple food and read books, enjoying my own company, which I find infinitely preferable to yours.'

Devastated, Mabel sank down on the nearest chair.

'And before you ask the obvious question, no, I am not always alone. I do have the occasional visitor, but then you've forced me to go elsewhere for the pleasure and comfort you've denied me.'

'Mrs Hadley said you had a woman there. But Mrs Hodges said she was a respectable, elderly widow. And to think that I chose to believe Mrs Hodges. You . . . you . . . beast!'

'The Mrs Hodges and Mrs Hadley seem to spend a great deal of their time watching my movements,' Edward observed coolly.

'You are shameless and disgusting. Have you no thought for my reputation?'

'On the contrary, I thought you were trying to preserve one as a vestal virgin.' Edward couldn't resist smiling when he thought of Mrs Ball. She would never see her sixtieth birthday again, but if Mrs Hadley had heard that he'd employed a female caretaker-cum-housekeeper he had no doubt she'd put two and two together and made a dozen. Women like her loved scandal. On the other hand there was enough truth in the gossip Mabel had heard for him to appreciate just how closely they had been watching him.

Suddenly, he remembered Rhian, and in the light of Mabel's

accusations, just how much he'd compromised her reputation by allowing her to sleep in his rooms.

'How can you sit there smiling . . . Edward, I am talking to you,' Mabel shouted when he jumped to his feet. 'Where are you going?'

'Out!' He flung the word back at her before slamming the door.

Chapter 13

EDWARD STOOD OUTSIDE his offices in Dunraven Street. No lights burned in the building or the one next door, but his bedroom was at the back. If Rhian was going to preserve her reputation, he had to get her up, dressed, and ask Mrs Ball to call a brake and take her down to Ynysangharad House quickly, and more importantly, without anyone connecting her disappearance with him.

He opened his office door, locked it behind him and ran lightly up the stairs. He walked through the connecting door to his rooms. A strip of light showed beneath his bedroom door. He knocked.

'I'm fine, Mrs Ball.'

'It's not Mrs Ball, it's Edward Larch, Rhian.'

'Mr Larch, sir?' Rhian opened the door. Her slim figure was swamped by the voluminous folds of his blue-and-white striped flannel nightgown. The sleeves hung loose, inches below her fingertips; the shirt-tails flapped around her ankles.

'You have to leave, now.'

'But it's the middle of the night, Mr Larch.' Her speech was slurred, her eyes clouded, and he recalled Mrs Ball telling him that she had given her a glass of brandy.

'I've just discovered that my wife and her cronies in the Ladies' Circle know about these rooms. There's been gossip. She's heard that I employ a woman to look after the place. Mrs Ball is a respectable elderly widow. No one would dare talk about me and her in the same breath. But if anyone should find out that I allowed you to stay the night here, you would be ruined.'

'There's no need to worry about my reputation, Mr Larch. Not now.' Rhian staggered back sluggishly and fell on to the bed. She pulled the bedspread modestly over her bare legs before pushing the sleeves of his nightshirt to her elbows. It was then that he noticed she wasn't wearing her ring.

'Maybe your fiancé wasn't the man you thought he was, but there'll be others,' he consoled clumsily. 'You're a young girl . . .' Completely forgetting what he was talking about, he gazed at her dumbly. In the intimacy of the bedroom, surrounded by the furniture Amelia had chosen, Rhian's resemblance to his late wife was more evident than ever. The same golden curls, slender figure, enormous blue eyes . . .

He looked into them and saw such intense pain he longed to scoop her into his arms and rock her to sleep the way he had Julia and Gerald when they had been babies. Only Rhian wasn't a baby. She was a grown woman who had been engaged to be married. And his feelings towards her were hardly paternal.

'You have to get dressed. You shouldn't be here,' he said abruptly, not trusting himself to remain alone with her a moment longer. 'Mrs Ball can take you to Mrs Evans in Ynysangharad House.'

'I can't go to Sali. Her husband is Joey's brother.'

'There must be someone you can stay with?' he said impatiently.

'There isn't, sir. My only friends are Joey's family and the ones I've made in Llan House.'

'I can hardly take you back there in the middle of the night without arousing my wife's suspicions.'

'No one saw me come in except Mrs Ball, sir. And I'll leave first thing in the morning before anyone else sees me.'

'I can't just let you walk out of here when you have nowhere to go.'

'I'll get another situation, sir. I'll be fine, unless . . .' She thought of Bronwen's sister Jinny, and closed her eyes tightly.

'Unless?' he prompted. When she remained silent, he asked, 'Are you pregnant?'

'It only happened once, sir, last week,' she whispered,

embarrassed to be discussing such an intimate subject with her employer. 'I was engaged. I thought I'd be married.' She looked down and he saw tears fall from her eyes on to the sheet.

Her pitiable state roused emotions in him that he'd assumed had died with Amelia. For the first time since he had buried his wife he felt sorrow and compassion for another human being. And his awakening from the trance-like state that had settled over him, numbing his senses and dulling his mind, was acutely painful.

He thought of Maisie and how she had been reduced to selling herself, very probably as the result of a situation similar to the one Rhian was in now. He couldn't countenance the thought of such a young, beautiful and innocent girl — it was strange but even after what Rhian had just told him he couldn't think of her as anything less — ending up in a house like Mrs Smith's to be used and abused by wealthy, jaded middle-aged men.

'I have a shop downstairs that I was going to advertise for rent next week,' he said hesitantly, trying to think the idea through as he was speaking. 'You could run it for me if you don't want to go back to Llan House. In fact, it would make sound business sense. The profit of a shop is likely to be double the rent I'd get. And there are rooms behind it that you could live in.'

'Sir? She looked up at him blankly and he realized she was in no state to understand what he was saying, let alone plan her future.

'You understand what I told you about your reputation, Rhian? That it might not survive if it ever became common knowledge that you spent the night in my rooms?' He stepped towards her and saw that her eyes were closed. He lifted her legs gently, and slid her back into the bed. It would have been so easy to lift the gown and look at her body, but, summoning all his powers of self-control, he tucked the sheets around her and tiptoed from the room.

Pulling the door to behind him, he stole quietly into the living room and poured himself a large glass of brandy before sitting in the comfortable chair next to the fireplace and considering Rhian's position. The last thing he wanted to do was seduce or exploit the girl. But on her own admission she wasn't a virgin.

He had a good income, and a house with three sets of rooms

that he didn't need to let out. He could fit out and stock a shop on the ground floor as a tobacconist. He was tired of walking to the other end of Dunraven Street for his cigars and cigarettes and there was good profit in tobacco. Rhian could move in and run it for him. Of course there would be talk, particularly as news had already reached the Ladies' Circle of his rooms in the building, but with Mrs Ball in his pay and living on the premises, he could counter any gossip with the assertion that she was Rhian's chaperon. No one would believe it, but, on the other hand, if he was discreet they wouldn't be able to prove anything either.

Mabel would be furious, but he wasn't in the least concerned with her feelings. In fact, after the way she had behaved, upsetting her would be a bonus. He recalled the way Rhian had looked when she'd sat on the edge of the bed, her hair tousled, her figure slim, curvaceous and eminently desirable even beneath his flannel nightshirt. He imagined what it would be like to undress her, take her in his arms, smother her with kisses . . .

Restless, he left the chair, walked to the table and refilled his brandy glass. If only he had listened to Julia and Cedric's cautionary warnings he could have married Rhian instead of Mabel. She might be only a maid, but she had been prepared to give herself to a man willingly before marriage and he had no doubt that she would have made a damned sight better wife.

But would she be prepared to sleep with him so soon after breaking off her engagement? She might be angry with her fiancé now, but would she change her mind in the morning and forgive whatever it was that he had done to her? And if she didn't, would it be so very wrong of him to offer her a position as his mistress?

He could take care of her, give her all the things women wanted and she'd never had. Fine clothes, jewellery, outings to restaurants and hotels away from Tonypandy, he would shower her with gifts and good times, and in return . . .

And in return, he would enjoy her gratitude, the happiness in his domestic life Mabel had denied him and perhaps even the physical closeness he had missed and craved throughout all the long lonely days since he'd lost Amelia.

*

218

'You look like you've just come off a double shift down the pit,' Billy Evans said to Joey when he walked up from the basement in his dressing gown.

'I couldn't sleep, so I went downstairs for an early bath.' Joey had hung his jacket over one of the kitchen chairs and reached into a pocket for his cigarettes.

'A cold one?'

'I don't see the point in lighting the range in summer.' Joey struck a match and lit his cigarette.

'You don't cook for yourself?'

'We have a staff canteen in store. And after we close, I eat in one of the cafés.'

'Well, as I've lit this stove up here this morning, would you like tea?'

'If it's made,' Joey answered absently.

'Do you want to talk?'

'Would you listen?'

'Try me?' Billy poured two cups of tea and sat at the table.

Joey took his and put it on the mantelpiece. 'I'd prefer to wait until after I've seen Tonia.'

Billy looked at his son. 'For what it's worth, I really believed that you'd settle down with Rhian.'

'I want nothing more.'

'Then why play around with Tonia?' Billy asked irritably.

'I didn't, Dad,' Joey retorted vehemently.

'I'd like to believe you.'

'But you don't.' Joey's hand trembled as he drew on his cigarette.

'Appearances are against you. And, much as I hate to say it, you have always been an expert liar. How many times have you sworn blind to me and your brothers that you weren't having an affair with a married woman, only to get caught out in her bed afterwards?'

Joey sipped his tea, made a face and replaced the cup on the saucer. 'I'm going upstairs to dress, then I'm going down to Connie's.'

'Do you want me to come with you?'

Joey almost said 'please yourself' but recalling the look on Lloyd and Sali's face when he had told them why Rhian had disappeared the night before, he decided he needed all the friends he could get. And his father had always proved to be a friend, even when he'd been furious with him.

Freshly bathed, shaved and wrapped in his bathrobe, Edward walked into the bedroom where Rhian lay asleep in the middle of the double bed. Her blonde curls tumbled in disarray over the pillow; her cheeks were flushed with sleep. She looked beautiful, perfect – and innocent, that word again. He set the cup of tea he had made for her on the bedside cabinet, sat down and continued to watch her.

Rhian moved and opened her eyes. She stared at him uncomprehendingly for a moment then looked around the room.

'How do you feel this morning?'

'A little tired, sir.'

'Stay in bed. I'll get Mrs Ball to bring you breakfast.'

'I can't stay in bed, sir. I am used to being up at five and cleaning the house before breakfast.'

'Mrs Ball does all the cleaning that needs doing here. You don't want to put her out of a job, now do you?'

She shook her head.

He pointed to the cabinet. 'I brought you tea.'

'Thank you, sir.' She sat up, her golden hair haloing her face.

'Do you remember anything about last night?'

'Not much, sir.'

'Do you remember me coming back and asking you to leave because I was afraid that your reputation might not survive if anyone found out that you'd stayed the night in my rooms?'

'Vaguely, sir.'

'Really?' he pressed sceptically.

Realizing that he didn't believe her, she replied truthfully, 'No, sir, I don't. I'm sorry, sir, I've put you to an awful lot of trouble.'

'You haven't.' He took the cup of tea from the bedside cabinet and gave it to her.

'Thank you, sir.' Acutely conscious of and embarrassed by Mr

Larch's state of undress, and being in the peculiar and somewhat ludicrous position of being served morning tea by the master, she sat and took the cup.

'Is your head clearer now?'

'Yes, sir.'

'Last night, I asked if you'd like to stay here and manage a shop for me that I intend to open downstairs.'

'Me, sir? Manage a shop?'

'Why not? You're bright and you'll soon pick it up. If you're worried about taking on a job you're not used to, I can always get someone in to help you until you feel more confident about it.'

'Where would I live, sir?'

'I have three sets of rooms here.'

'But everyone knows that you own the building, sir. I'm not thinking of myself, but Mrs Larch . . .'

'Damn Mrs Larch!' he cursed feelingly. 'Dear God, looking at you sitting there, Rhian, I wish I'd married you instead of her.'

'Sir?' Stunned, she couldn't believe she'd heard him correctly.

'Why not?' he smiled. 'You're sweet natured, beautiful . . .'

'And a maid, sir,' she reminded him. 'Gentlemen don't marry maids.'

'Damn people and damn gossip! You would have made a better wife than Mabel.' He paced to the window and back. 'Will you marry your fiancé if he apologizes to you?'

'No, sir. Not now,' she said finally.

'You're sure about that?'

'I've never been more sure of anything, sir. I warned him that if he ever went back to his old ways and started seeing other girls again, I'd leave him. And I have.'

He lifted a chair close to the bed and sat on it. 'So, would you consider remaining in Tonypandy and managing the shop for me?'

'I don't want to remain close to Joey, but it would be better than trying to make a new life for myself among strangers, sir. I've never been further than Cardiff in my life, and after yesterday I realize just how few people I can turn to for help.'

'Then that's settled. You'll stay here and manage the shop for me.'

'Sir, you won't tell anyone that I'm here, will you?' she pleaded.

'People will have to find out where you are eventually, Rhian.'

'I know, sir. But not just yet.' Tears started into her eyes.

Afraid of losing control if he tried to comfort her, he left the chair, opened the wardrobe door and lifted out a set of clean underclothes, a shirt and suit. 'I'll dress in the bathroom. We have a lot more to discuss. Spend the morning in bed. I'll join you for lunch. We'll talk some more then.'

'Yes, sir, and thank you.'

'You have nothing to thank me for, Rhian. Not after everything you have done for my family during the years you've worked for us. Try to get some sleep.' He smiled at her and left the room, closing the door behind him,

'Come in, Uncle Billy.' Connie left the breakfast table when Annie showed the men into the dining room.

'Tonia not up?' Billy noticed that the table was set for three but one place setting was untouched.

'I'll get her.' Annie left and a few seconds later they could hear her hammering on Tonia's door.

'Would you like tea or shall we go into the drawing room?' Connie continued to ignore Joey.

'In the other room, I think, Connie,' Billy suggested. Joey hadn't said a word since they had left the house, and he continued to remain silent, his brooding presence heightening the fraught atmosphere.

'Sit down.' Connie took one easy chair, Billy the other. Joey went to the window. Brushing aside the net curtains, he stared down at the street. The ash cart was out, and men were emptying dustbins into the back, clattering and banging when they returned them to the pavement.

The door jerked open and Tonia stumbled into the room. Annie followed and it was obvious that she had pushed Tonia in. The dark circles beneath Tonia's red-rimmed eyes were even more pronounced than Joey's. She was wearing her Gwilym James uniform, but it was so creased and crumpled it looked as though she had slept in it.

'Antonia,' Connie turned to her daughter, 'I went to see Joey last night—'

'He told you, didn't he?' Tonia burst out hysterically. She turned on Joey. 'You promised you wouldn't tell! You promised!' Then, realizing what she'd said, she screamed, 'It's all a pack of lies! You can't believe a word he says! You can't! You can't—'

Connie left her chair and went to her daughter. 'Pull yourself together, or I'll slap you.'

Tonia buried her face in her hands and her screams subsided into soft whimpers.

'What did Joey promise you and what is all a pack of lies?' Connie demanded. 'Answer me, Tonia.'

'Why ask me? You were the one who spoke to him.' Tonia's voice wavered precariously.

'I didn't tell your mother anything last night, Tonia, but after what you did to Rhian and me yesterday I will,' Joey said quietly.

'I didn't do anything—'

'You came crying to me because Geraint Watkin Jones had eloped with Julia Larch.'

'What's that got to do with Tonia?' Connie asked in bewilderment.

'Do you want to tell your mother, Tonia, or shall I?' Joey asked.

Tonia sank down on the floor, curled into a ball, wrapped her hands around her knees and buried her face in her arms. She began to cry again, not the high-pitched hysterical screams of when she had first entered the room, but self-contained, throat-rasping sobs that racked her shoulders and sent shudders through her body.

'Tonia,' Connie said angrily, 'I will have the truth.'

Tonia clamped her hands over her ears in a final, last-ditch attempt to block out what Joey was about to say, and she remained on the floor while Joey told her mother, Annie and his father how he had stumbled across her and Geraint making love in the stockroom in Pontypridd. How Tonia had pleaded with him not to

223

tell anyone and the promise he had made to her that he had regretted making several times since. How she had visited him in his office the day before. And when, against his better judgement, he had offered her a shoulder to cry on, she had unbuttoned his trousers and told Rhian they'd been having an affair and she was carrying his baby.

When Joey finished talking, no one said a word. He turned back to the street. Silence grew in the room, dense and oppressive.

'Is this true, Antonia?' Connie asked, finally breaking the tension.

Tonia whimpered like a puppy being whipped.

Joey turned around. 'I have told you the truth, Connie, but frankly, I don't care what you think of me. The only person I care about right now is Rhian and I'm going to see Edward Larch. If he won't tell me where she is, I'll give him a letter I wrote to her last night. Hopefully, she will read it and believe my side of the story even if none of the rest of you do.' He left the room and closed the door behind him.

'Tonia? Is what Joey said true?' When her daughter didn't answer, Connie yanked her violently to her feet.

Tonia stared at her mother, burst into tears and ran from the room. Her bedroom door slammed and the key turned in the lock.

'I take it that's a yes.' Billy reached for his stick and rose stiffly and awkwardly to his feet.

'This isn't just Tonia's fault,' Connie said defensively. 'If Joey hadn't behaved the way he has over the years, none of us would have believed that he'd assaulted Tonia in the first place.'

'Are you making excuses for your daughter's behaviour, Connie?'

Ashamed, Connie fell silent.

'It seems to me that neither of them has behaved particularly well, Joey for years and Tonia yesterday afternoon. But just when I hoped that Joey was finally putting his past behind him, it looks like Tonia might have put paid to his future. I won't argue that Joey had a right to the happiness he found. I've always thought that Rhian was too good for him, and that's coming from a father who loves all his sons, even the wayward one. But one thing that I am certain of is that Rhian didn't deserve to see the pantomime Tonia staged for her benefit. No wonder she's hiding. The poor girl must be crushed by the thought of Joey's betrayal. I'll see myself out, Connie, Annie. Between the shop and Tonia it looks as though you're going to have a full day.'

At one clock, Edward Larch left his desk and walked through the connecting door into his rooms. He smiled when he entered his sitting room. The table had been laid for one and there was a cold ham, a bowl of salad, a loaf of fresh bread and a half a pound of butter set out on a clean, pale-green linen cloth. Rhian walked out of the kitchen with a jug of barley water and a glass.

'Thank you for laying the table.'

'The boy brought the food an hour ago, sir. Mrs Ball took the hamper in. All I had to do was set the table.'

'There's just one thing wrong, Rhian.'

'What, sir?' she asked apprehensively.

'It's set for one, not two.'

'I couldn't eat with you, sir. It wouldn't be proper.'

'Proper or not, I won't eat without you. We have a lot to discuss and talk is always better accompanied by food, so the sooner you get yourself a plate, knives and a fork, the sooner we can begin.' Feeling as though he'd come home after a very long journey, Edward removed his jacket, hung it on the back of a chair, unbuttoned his waistcoat and sat at the table. Then he remembered the visitor who'd called into his office that morning. He felt in his jacket pockets and removed the envelope Joey Evans had given him to pass on to Rhian. He set it in front of her plate.

She picked it up, visibly flinching when she turned it over and recognized the handwriting.

'He came in the moment the office opened. He wants to see you.'

'You didn't tell him where I am?' she asked in alarm.

'No, but as I said earlier, if you stay in Tonypandy you are going to have to face him sooner or later.'

'I know.' She stared at the envelope, before slowly and deliberately tearing it in two. Aware that Mr Larch was watching her, she continued to tear it and the paper it contained into tiny shreds. She didn't stop until it was no more than a pile of confetti. Only then did she scoop the fragments into her hand. Leaving the table, she carried them into the kitchen and dropped them in the waste bucket.

Her smile was too bright, too brittle when she returned, but he didn't pass comment. Instead he changed the subject.

'This looks a fine ham; would you like two or three slices?' He waited until they had finished eating and she had made and served coffee before broaching the subject uppermost in his mind. 'As I said, we have a lot to discuss. Starting with your salary for managing the shop.'

'I'd be happy with whatever is the usual rate, sir.'

'Two pounds a week.'

'Two pounds a week, sir?' she gasped.

'Plus free accommodation and food. Is that all right?'

'It is too generous, sir.'

'Then it's settled.'

'There's nothing I can say except thank you, sir.'

'I have been thinking about another vacancy that you might consider. And before I tell you what it is, I want you know that I won't withdraw the offer to manage the shop or think any the less of you if you refuse it. You know what my marriage is like. There's no need to be coy,' he added, when she blushed. 'The way Mabel behaves, everyone in Llan House knows it barely exists in name, let alone anything more intimate. I decorated these rooms so I could have some peace, and also so I could meet women here. I never thought of setting up another permanent establishment but if you were willing to live with me, I would take care of you. Good care.' He stopped talking, scarcely believing that he'd found the courage to say what he just had to her.

She was staring down at her hands and he found it impossible to gauge her reaction. 'You do understand what I'm suggesting, Rhian?'

'Yes, sir,' she mumbled.

'If I've offended you, tell me and I'll never broach the subject again. If you decide to accept this – extra position,' he said hesitantly, 'I would like you to live in these rooms with me. If you decide against it you can live in the rooms behind the shop.'

She finally raised her head and looked at him. 'People would find out, sir.'

'They might guess but they wouldn't know. Not for certain, if we were discreet. There's a communicating door between this building and my office so I could see you any time I wanted without having to go to into the street. And although all I am free to offer you is a position as my mistress, I'd treat you like a wife. I'm comfortably off. I could give you everything you've ever wanted. And, if it worked out between us, you'd never have to worry about me looking at another woman. I loved my first wife.' His voice wavered when he thought of Amelia.

'The first Mrs Larch was lovely, sir.'

'Yes, she was. And she'd be horrified if she'd heard the proposition I've just put to you.'

'You wouldn't have made it if she'd been alive, sir.'

'No, I wouldn't,' he said slowly. 'And I've said more than enough for now. I'm truly sorry if I've shocked you. The last thing I want to do is hurt you, or force you into doing anything that you don't want to.'

He used almost the same words as Joey when she had offered to make love to him for the first time. She swallowed her tears.

'I'm sorry. I shouldn't have said anything. You're a decent young woman.'

'If you want me, sir, I'll run your shop, keep your rooms and sleep in your bed. But I told you that I've been with Joey. If I have a child it might not be yours, sir.'

'I wouldn't care.' He left his chair, took her in his arms and helped her up. The feel of his hand on her head as he stroked her hair was warm and comforting and she allowed herself to relax enough to rest her head on his chest.

'There's all the time in the world, Rhian,' he murmured, fighting the urge to carry her into the bedroom. 'I don't want to rush you into anything. We'll talk again tonight. In the meantime, think about my offer, but remember the last thing I want to do is take advantage of you after everything that's happened in the last two days. I wouldn't have said anything to you now if I hadn't seen you tear up that letter.'

She recalled asking Joey how he could make love to someone he wasn't completely in love with. 'I don't have to think about it, sir.' Lifting her face to Edward's, she kissed him.

Edward tasted the salt tears on her lips, luxuriated in the sensuous feel of her smooth young body.

'No . . . not yet . . .' He tried to back away, but she kissed him again.

'Rhian, I warn you, it's been a long time for me, you have no idea what you are doing to me.'

Wanting to hurt Joey as he had hurt her, she whispered, 'Yes, I do, sir.'

He finally picked her up and carried her into the bedroom. Dropping her on the bed, he kicked off his shoes, lifted his legs on to the bed and lay beside her. She helped him off with his jacket and shirt; he unclipped his braces and unbuttoned her dress. She lifted it over her head but there was no time to remove all her clothes.

He pulled her petticoats and bust-shaper above her waist, tugging at her corset laces to expose her breasts. Yanking down her drawers, he pushed her legs apart with his knees and abandoned himself to a passion that he hadn't experienced since Amelia had died.

Rhian lay back and absorbed the sensation of committing the ultimate intimate act with a man she didn't love. Even now, when she was practically naked in bed with him, she couldn't think of him as anything other than Mr Larch. He was skilled and considerate. His kisses were tender; his thrusts urgent. He whispered no endearments but his touch was gentle and she knew that he would keep his promise and take care of her.

It's like the difference between watching a colourless silent film and experiencing reality.

Joey was right, making love without being in love was just as he had described. But Mr Larch needed her, and she needed to be loved by someone who would never lie to her or betray her again.

So she returned the master's caresses, telling herself that she did so out of respect and gratitude. But even as she kissed and held him, she knew that she was being driven more from an all-consuming, burning desire to wound Joey as deeply as he had wounded her, than any consideration for Edward Larch.

Afterwards, Edward stripped Rhian of the rest of her clothes, lay back on the pillows and held her close beneath the single sheet that was all the cover they needed given the warmth of the afternoon. He didn't doubt that the world would see him as the wealthy middle-aged roué who had seduced a sweet young girl and reduced her to the ranks of fallen women. Yet he didn't feel guilty enough to regret what had happened. And certainly not enough to want to forget the experience, or send her away. He couldn't wait to repeat it – and often.

It wasn't as though he had forced Rhian to do anything she hadn't wanted to and they hadn't caused anyone pain by making love except perhaps Mabel, Joseph Evans and propriety. And it could be argued that Mabel and Joseph Evans deserved to be hurt. As for propriety, he'd never been one to live his life by the rules drawn up by narrow-minded church ministers and old wives. So why shouldn't their liaison continue?

Was it selfish of him to want a quiet life in these rooms with all the pleasures that Rhian could give him instead of the fraught life of Llan House? The only wonder was that he thought so little of his marriage vows to Mabel to break them so soon after taking them. But then he'd observed them when he'd been married to Amelia. And hadn't Mabel broken her vows first? *Love, honour and obey.* Mabel certainly didn't love him, he had seen no sign of honour, only contempt and she had never obeyed him in the bedroom.

'Are you all right?' He looked at Rhian attentively.

'Yes, sir.'

'Given the circumstances, don't you think that you should call me Edward?'

'That will be difficult after years of calling you sir, sir.'

'And you will be happy to stay here and take both positions I offered you?'

'Yes, sir.'

'Are you sure?'

She plucked nervously at the bedclothes. 'Yes, sir.'

'And if your young man should want you back?'

'I told you, sir, I would never go back to him, not after seeing him and Tonia together.'

'Then, if you're sure, I'll see about getting stock for the shop. And if you feel up to going out, you could go shopping for clothes for yourself.'

'I'd rather not, sir.'

'You are going to have to leave here sooner or later.'

'I know, sir. Just not today,' she pleaded.

'I'll send up to Llan House and ask Mrs Williams to pack your things and give them to Harris to bring down here. I'll tell her that you are going to live here and run the shop for me.'

'Please, sir. Not just yet,' she begged. 'Can't I stay here just for a little while longer without anyone knowing where I am?'

'I told Mrs Williams and the two Mr Evanses last night that you are safe and being looked after. I suppose we could keep it quiet for another day or two,' he conceded.

'Thank you, sir.'

'In the meantime, I'd better go back to work.' He left the bed, but he didn't stop looking at her even when he picked up his clothes. 'When your things come, you can hang them next to mine in the wardrobe. There are two empty drawers in that chest, should you need more space . . .'

'I won't, sir,' she interrupted. 'I have very few clothes apart from my uniform.'

'Then we'll have to get you more.' He bent over the bed and kissed her gently on the lips. 'I would give a great deal to get back down there with you for half an hour.'

The painful memory of seeing Tonia and Joey in one another's arms had seared into her memory. Without hesitation she said, 'Why don't you, sir?'

'As I don't have any appointments until three o'clock, I suppose I could spare another half-hour.' He pulled the sheet back and exposed her naked body.

For a few seconds he saw her through his photographer's eye.

He even went so far as to imagine the erotic picture she'd make in black and white. A perfect female nude. Alabaster skin lightly shadowed with pale grey, as if an artist had drawn a brush lightly below her curves to emphasize their perfection.

The stirrings of desire brought him crashing back to reality. His gaze lingered on her nipples, the triangle of curly golden hair between her thighs, the soft swelling of her breasts. He lay back beside her and touched the flat of her stomach. 'You're cold.' He pulled the sheet over her.

'No, sir . . .'

'And no more sirs, Rhian. Not ever again. Why don't you call me Eddie?' It was a name no one had used since Amelia had died.

Chapter 14

THURSDAYS AND FRIDAYS were the longest retailing days in Tonypandy. Gwilym James opened at eight, as it did every morning, but unlike the other four days it closed at ten not seven o'clock in the evening. Joey had been in the habit of taking a walk in the quiet hour after lunchtime or locking himself in the office to 'do paperwork', which the staff knew was an excuse that enabled him to take a short nap, or time out to read the paper. But that Thursday he couldn't settle to anything. Even when he was forced to go into his office to answer the telephone, he left the door open so he could continue to watch the main door.

Edward Larch had promised to deliver his letter to Rhian and he kept expecting her to walk in at any minute, or at the very least send a messenger with a reply to the heartfelt outpourings that had taken him all night to compose.

But as the morning wore on into the afternoon and finally the evening, and there was still no word, he didn't know what to think. Then, the idea came to him when he was closing the store and preparing the day's takings to put in the bank's night safe. She could have gone to his house! He seized on it because it was preferable to the alternative, that she still believed the allegations Tonia had made.

He locked up in record time, entrusted the takings to Sam for the first time since he had managed the store and ran all the way to his father's house. His spirits soared when he opened the door and heard voices. Rushing down the passage, he threw open the kitchen door.

'Lloyd, Sali, Dad?' The disappointment was evident on his face when he looked around and saw no one else. 'You've heard from Rhian?' he asked Sali, brightening at the prospect.

'No, we hoped you would have. Dad said you were going to talk to Edward Larch.'

'He won't tell me where she is.'

'He wouldn't tell me either,' Sali divulged. 'All he would say is that she's safe and being well looked after and she'll contact us when she's ready. I went up to see Mrs Williams at Llan House afterwards. She told me that Rhian had sent for all her things.'

'She's given up her job?' Joey took off his hat and dropped it on the table.

'Mr Larch told Mrs Williams that she wouldn't be coming back.'

'I gave Mr Larch a letter for her. I hoped she'd answer it.'

'But she hasn't?' Lloyd said shortly.

'No.'

'Bit of a mess all round,' Billy said superfluously.

'It is.' Suddenly and desperately tired, Joey sank down on a chair.

'All you can do is wait.' Lloyd laid his hand on his brother's shoulder. 'If we can do anything to help, you know where to find us.'

'Thanks,' Joey mumbled disconsolately.

Sali kissed Joey's cheek. 'Just give Rhian time; she'll come round when she finds out the truth about you and Tonia.'

'I hope you're right, Sali.'

'And I hope it's in time for two weeks Saturday,' Sali said thoughtfully. 'Otherwise there's going to be a stunning dress and an awful lot of wedding cake going begging.'

The next day was the longest of Joey's life. Expecting Rhian, or at the very least a reply to the letter he had sent her, to arrive in the store at any moment, seconds dragged like minutes, minutes became hours and hours crawled the length of days. Unable to settle, he paced between the counters nearest to the front door until Miss Robertson asked if he was trying to wear out the floorboards.

He retreated to his office, piled suppliers' catalogues on his desk and pretended to study them, but he kept his door and the blinds on his internal window open. And every time an assistant or customer obstructed his view of the front of the shop, he leapt to his feet.

By closing time he was physically and emotionally drained with barely enough energy left to walk home. The last thing he felt like was company – apart from Rhian's – and when he saw Connie and Tonia sitting with his father in their kitchen he retreated before crossing the threshold.

'Joey, you'll want to hear what Tonia and Connie have to say to you,' his father called after him.

He returned to the doorway and not trusting himself to look at Tonia, spoke to Connie. 'Have you seen Rhian?'

'No.' Connie gave her daughter, who was on the verge of tears, a warning look. 'But we would like to talk to you.'

'I said all I had to say to you yesterday morning.'

'You mentioned that Mr Larch offered to give Rhian a letter from you. If he can deliver one, I thought he might be able to deliver another.' Connie handed him an open envelope. 'Tonia's written to her to explain what happened in your office.'

Joey pulled a kitchen chair out from under the table and sat down. 'Is this explanation anywhere close to the truth?'

'Tonia!' Connie prompted brusquely. 'Answer Joey's question.'

'I'm sorry I said what I did to Rhian, Joey,' Tonia mumbled. 'I didn't want everyone pitying me because Geraint had run off with Julia Larch.'

'I was the only one who knew about you two,' he reminded her bitterly.

'I thought if I had a husband it would prove to Geraint that even if he didn't love me, someone did.' Her eyes welled, but a glare from Connie stayed her tears.

'And any husband would do,' Joey observed acidly. 'What have I ever done to you, to deserve what you tried to do to me?'

'Nothing,' Tonia whispered.

'And Rhian? Didn't you spare a thought for her? We're engaged and just about to get married and you tell her that you're having my baby! For God's sake, Tonia, the most I've ever done is kiss you on the cheek in front of people!' Joey clenched his fists in an effort to contain his anger. 'When I think that you would have palmed Geraint Watkin Jones's baby off as mine—'

'I took Tonia to the doctor's this morning. There is no baby,' Connie broke in. 'But given what happened in Gwilym James on Wednesday afternoon, Tonia's reputation is in tatters.'

'As is mine,' Joey pointed out coldly.

Connie couldn't resist the jibe. 'You didn't have one to begin with.'

Joey left the chair and turned his back on her.

'Joey, please, what I meant to say is that there's no point in trying to salvage Tonia's reputation. And she wants to make amends for the trouble she's caused.'

Joey turned around and held up the envelope. 'Can I read this?'

'That's why we left it open.'

'Did you or Tonia write it, Connie?' Joey asked.

'Tonia, but I helped phrase it.'

Joey extracted the single sheet of paper. Tonia must have been crying when she had written it; the paper was crinkled and blotched with stains that had made the ink run, but he could decipher the words.

Dear Rhian,

I am sorry for what I did to you and Joey. Joey saw Geraint Watkin Jones and me making love in the stockroom in Gwilym James and I made him promise that he wouldn't tell anyone. When I heard that Geraint had eloped with Julia Larch I didn't want anyone pitying me because I'd been jilted so I went to Joey's office to try to trick him into marrying me. I picked Joey, because of his reputation. I thought no one would believe him if he tried to tell the truth. I unbuttoned his trousers when he was trying to stop me crying. He didn't even notice what I was doing. I thought . . . I didn't think. You don't have to forgive Joey, Rhian, because there's nothing to forgive him for. He's never even tried to hold hands with me, or kiss me properly. That's the truth. I'll swear it on the Bible if you want me to,

Tonia

Joey had never backed down from a confrontation when he was growing up, despite the best efforts of his father and brothers to teach him to control his rage. But his fights had always been with boys and men his own age or older. He had never felt angry enough to want to harm a woman – until Tonia had told Rhian that they were lovers. And then, he'd been too concerned with running after Rhian to think of his cousin. Now Tonia looked so cowed and miserable he almost pitied her.

Connie was as tough in her private life as she was in business and, given the uncompromising tone of the letter and Tonia's dejected state, he suspected that she had meted out as much, if not more, punishment than her daughter could take. He folded the sheet of paper back into the envelope.

'Where are you going?' Billy asked when he replaced the chair beneath the table.

'To deliver this to Edward Larch's office.'

'You must be hungry, boy.'

Joey shook his head.

'You look as though you haven't eaten or slept in a week,' Connie said solicitously.

'That's hardly surprising given the circumstances, Connie. Don't worry, Dad, I'll be straight back.'

Tonia burst into tears when they heard the front door close.

Connie growled, 'Shut up!'

Tonia covered her face with her hands and fell silent.

'I hope Rhian gets that letter and reads it.' Connie picked up her handbag and adjusted her hat.

'So do I,' Billy said feelingly.

'Uncle Billy—'

'There's no point in talking what's happened to death, Connie,' Billy said wearily. 'What's done is done. All we can do now is see what tomorrow brings.'

'Don't move, Uncle Billy, we'll see ourselves out. Tonia!' Connie called her daughter to heel like a dog. Head down, hands folded in front of her like a novice nun, Tonia followed her mother out of the room.

*

Rhian stared at the words. Scarcely daring to believe what they said, she read them a second and a third time.

You don't have to forgive Joey, Rhian, because there's nothing to forgive him for. He's never even tried to hold hands with me, or kiss me properly. That's the truth. I'll swear it on the Bible if you want me to, . . .

'There's no stamp. It must have been delivered by hand last night after the office closed.' Edward picked up one of the fresh bread rolls he had bought from the baker's that morning and buttered it.

'It's from Joey's cousin, Tonia.' Rhian volunteered the information because she sensed that although Edward was curious, he wouldn't ask her for it. She folded the letter, lifted the teatowel she had pinned around her waist because she didn't have an apron and pushed it into her skirt pocket.

'The girl in his office? The one he was having an affair with?'

'According to this, they weren't having an affair. She tricked him,' she divulged.

'Why on earth would she do that?'

'Because she'd been jilted by another man, and wanted a husband to prove to him and herself that she could get one. I know it doesn't make sense, but when a woman thinks she's in love, she tends not to think straight.'

'I won't argue with you. Not after the way Julia's behaved.'

Edward had told her how unhappy he was at his daughter's choice of husband. The last thing Rhian wanted was to make him even more miserable by revealing that Geraint Watkin Jones had been having an affair with another girl right up until the day he had eloped with Julia. She forked four pieces of bacon on to Edward's plate.

He frowned at her. 'This letter changes everything.'

'It changes nothing,' she contradicted.

'Yes, it does. You still love Joey Evans.'

'And for a thousand and one reasons, most of which have nothing to do with this girl,' she brushed her hand against the letter in her pocket, 'I won't marry him. And that is why I said yes when you asked me to become your mistress.'

'I should never have propositioned you. I feel as though I've ruined your life.'

'You've probably saved me from a disastrous marriage.'

'Rhian—'

'Please, I don't want to talk about it. Unless that is, you're unhappy with my being here and want me to leave.' After an afternoon and a night spent in his bed she was confident of his reply.

He laid his hand around her waist and pulled her to him. 'I haven't been happier in over a year.'

She poured the tea and sat at the table. After only three meals together, they had earmarked two of the four chairs as 'theirs', his on the right nearest the door, hers on the left in front of the fireplace.

'Are you going out today?' He deliberately changed the subject.

'No.'

'You can't stay here cooped up for ever.'

'I know, but I can stay here for a little while longer. I have some serious thinking to do. I need to sort out what I'm going to say to Joey when I do eventually face him.'

'I only want your happiness, and for us to always be honest with one another,' he said earnestly. 'Promise me that when you do meet Joseph Evans, whatever decisions you make will be for yourself alone without any consideration for me. I may not want to, but I will survive without you if I have to.'

'Thank you . . .' She hesitated, still finding it difficult to call him anything other than 'Mr Larch' or 'sir'. 'I would be lying if I told you that I was happy right now. But I will try to be once I've talked to Joey and settled things between us.'

'You won't be bored while I work?' he asked.

'How could anyone be bored in this room?' Her eyes were suspiciously bright and he couldn't bear to look into them, knowing he'd caused her another problem. 'When I've finished my thinking, there are some marvellous books on those shelves that I've never read.'

'If you make a list of the things you need, I'll get them

delivered. Mrs Ball can take them in so you don't have to see the errand boys.'

'Groceries?'

'Anything, clothes, groceries, whatever,' he offered generously.

'Will you be eating your meals here?'

'All of them,' he smiled. 'Unless you object. And if you don't feel like cooking, Mrs Ball will have them sent in from the White Hart.'

'I like cooking.' She returned his smile. 'After we've finished breakfast I'll plan some menus.'

'Plain food. No smoked salmon or little fancy iced cakes and absolutely no caviar.'

'Sausage and mashed potato,' she joked.

He finished his last bacon roll, dabbed his mouth with his napkin and kissed her. 'That, my sweet, sounds absolutely perfect.'

Joey sat in his office, staring at the calendar. It was eleven o'clock in the morning on Wednesday, 29 July, two weeks to the day since Rhian had run out of the store and disappeared, and three days to the hour, to the wedding he and Rhian had planned. A wedding that, against his father and brothers' advice, he had categorically refused to cancel.

'Joey? Joey!' Sali called his name twice before he saw her standing in his office.

'Sorry, I was miles away.'

'I saw.'

He left his chair and pulled the visitor's chair into the centre of the room. 'What brings you to Tonypandy?'

'Your father is worried about you,' she said. 'As are your brothers and Megan.'

'While you, of course, are not?'

'I wouldn't be here if I wasn't. We drew straws to see who should talk to you. I lost. That, in case you didn't realize, is a joke. But you don't have to smile.'

He reached for the cigarette case on his desk and took one. 'I feel as though I've slipped into another country. It's similar to the one I was living in and most things are recognizable. I meet people

I know and I visit familiar shops to buy my tobacco and news-papers. I go home, my father is there and the furniture is where it's always been. People speak to me in a language I hear but don't quite understand because nothing makes sense. Not without Rhian. I find myself storing up things to tell her on her day off. I write to her at the end of every day, just as I've done since we started to go out with one another in January.'

'But she hasn't written back?'

'No, and Mr Larch said there was no point in forwarding any more of my letters to her after I gave him the third. He pointed out that if she wants to get in touch with me she knows where I am.'

'Joey, about the wedding—'

'I won't cancel it!'

He was so vehement she didn't dare broach the subject again. 'You do know that you can take as much time off work as you want.'

'I have a two-week holiday starting on Monday.' He gave her a cold smile that didn't reach his eyes. 'My honeymoon, remember?'

Sali plucked up courage to ask the question uppermost in all the family's minds. 'Joey, what are you going to do if she doesn't turn up?'

'Keep waiting. What else can I do?' He lit his cigarette. 'If you have another suggestion I'm willing to hear it.'

'I only wish that I did have one to give you.'

'Are Lloyd and the children all right?'

There was real concern in his voice and she was touched that he could think of them given his present wretched state. 'Edyth is teething but otherwise they're all fine. Harry's been asking after you.'

'Tell him I'll come and see him as soon as I have time.'

'I will.' She picked up her bag and left the office. She wished she could say something to comfort him, but if there were words that would help, she simply didn't know what they were.

Edward waited until he and Rhian were drinking their after-lunch coffee to broach the subject that was never far from his thoughts. 'Mr Evans called into my office again this morning.'

'You said he calls in every day.'

'Twice a day most days, and he watches the front door of my office from the store in between.'

'I will see him soon,' she promised.

Edward almost asked, 'Will you?' but the words remained unspoken. The last thing he wanted to do was question his good fortune, but the insecurity that had plagued him since he had lost Amelia, suddenly and without any warning, made him do exactly that. Before Rhian had moved in, the rooms had been a retreat, but she had transformed them into a home that he missed the minute he walked away from it.

He often thought of her during his working day. He liked to imagine her sitting in the living room, reading, or cooking in the kitchen, waiting for him to join her and, as a result, he had taken to calling in on her unexpectedly whenever he had a few free minutes.

He adored seeing the expression on her face when he brought her flowers, chocolates, or expensive silk lingerie that he suspected gave him more pleasure than her. He looked forward to meals as he hadn't done in over a year. But no matter how often Rhian reassured him that she wouldn't leave him, he couldn't quite believe that his new and blissful domesticity wasn't doing to disappear just as abruptly as it had done once before. And the main cause of his misgivings was Rhian's continued avoidance of the world outside of the building.

The weather was hot even for July, the rooms stifling, no matter how wide they opened the windows, but Rhian made no attempt to go outdoors, not even as far as the backyard. Joseph Evans was persistent and very obviously deeply in love. He recognized his devotion because he had felt the same way about Amelia before they'd married, and he simply couldn't bear the thought of Joseph snatching Rhian back just after he'd found, if not happiness exactly, the peace and contentment that had eluded him for so long.

Almost as if she sensed his thoughts, Rhian moved closer to him on the sofa. 'I saw Mrs Ball today; she said the shop is ready to open.'

'It is. I've been meaning to talk to you about it. I could get it stocked and ready for customers in two days.'

'Why don't you?'

'You haven't stepped out of these rooms in two weeks. I didn't want to rush you into something you weren't ready for. Managing the shop means meeting people and having to talk to them. If you've had second thoughts, I could find someone else to run it.'

'I haven't had any second thoughts.' She finished her coffee and set her cup aside. She knew that Edward was aware that Saturday was to have been her wedding day. 'If I give you a letter for Joey, will you see that he gets it?'

'Of course. But aren't you going to see him?'

'Yes, I'll write to ask him to meet me somewhere public but quiet.'

'The tea shop might be a good place.'

'It might,' she replied.

'If you prefer privacy with people within earshot, you couldn't do better than his office. He's there when I unlock the office door at eight and he's still there when I lock up in the evening. I warn you now, he looks dreadful.'

'You think I'll go back to him, don't you?'

'I'd hate to lose you, but should you decide to go ahead with your wedding to him after all—'

'I won't,' she interrupted vigorously.

'But if you should,' he repeated, 'I don't want you to feel that you owe me anything.'

'We've talked about this, and I've made up my mind.'

'Then go and see him tomorrow. I'll take a letter if you want me to.'

'I do. He might have meetings booked with suppliers or someone else. It would be embarrassing for both of us if I had to sit around waiting for him to finish. I'll suggest I visit the store at lunchtime. I hope he's free, because only half the staff are on duty then, so it should take twice as long for any gossip about my reappearance to circulate around the town,' she added dryly.

'About the shop.'

'Yes, please, let's talk about the shop.' She snuggled her head down on his shoulder.

'I thought I might postpone the opening until the end of the miners' fortnight holiday, which will take us to Monday, the tenth of August. That will give us a week's grace. If you're agreeable we could go away. The seaside is glorious when the weather is like this.'

'Go on holiday, with you?' Her eyes rounded incredulously.

'Yes, with me. The Lord only knows you need a break. You've been cooped up for so long in this house I think you've forgotten what fresh air is like. I thought we'd go to a hotel.'

'A hotel? You'd take me to a hotel?'

'Somewhere where no one who knows us is likely to go. Brighton or the Isle of Wight, perhaps. I'll book us in as Mr and Mrs Edward Larch.'

'And your wife?' she asked in amazement.

Edward had only visited Llan House twice in the last two weeks, but Rhian could imagine Mrs Larch's fury if she discovered that her husband had taken her former maid to a hotel.

'It's a matter of the greatest indifference to me whether she finds out or not but it's important we keep up appearances as long as we can for the sake of my practice. Mrs Ball can hire a brake to take you and your luggage to the station. You'll have to change trains at Cardiff, and I'll meet you there. I'll book seats for us when I book the hotel. We'll have a week with nothing more onerous to do than go for walks on the sands, eat cream teas, breathe in fresh air and do some shopping for you. You're in desperate need of new clothes.'

Rhian thought of the trousseau she and Sali had chosen with such care, which was still in Gwilym James in Pontypridd. 'Me, in a hotel! Being waited on hand and foot!' She was stunned by the thought.

'You in a hotel.' He smiled at her astonishment. 'But first, promise me that you'll see Joseph Evans.'

It was then that she realized the trip was to be a reward for breaking the final, tenuous ties that bound her to Joey. Despite everything she'd said to the contrary, Edward was still worried that she'd leave him, and he wouldn't be certain she'd stay until she had seen Joey again – and returned to him.

'A letter has just come for you, Mr Evans.' Miss Robertson knocked Joey's open door.

Joey's heart beat a tattoo. He jumped up and took it from her. 'Who delivered it?

'The doorman gave it to me.'

Recognizing Rhian's writing, Joey tore the envelope open. 'Send him in, Miss Robertson.' He had to rub his eyes to stop the letters dancing on the page.

Mr Larch has told me that you call in the office every day to ask about me. If you want to see me, send a message to Mr Larch's office, saying when and where, but it has to be a public place and I warn you, no matter what you say, it will be for the last time.
Rhian

'Not even Dear Joey . . .'

'Miss Robertson said you wanted me, Mr Evans,' the doorman muttered diffidently.

'Yes. Who brought this?' He held up the envelope.

'Mr Larch's messenger boy five minutes ago, Mr Evans.' He waited. When Joey didn't say anything else, he asked, 'Will that be all, Mr Evans?'

'Yes.' Joey sat at his desk, picked up his pen and dipped it in his inkwell.

Dear Rhian
The sooner the better. Is my office public enough? I will leave the door open and I will be here for as long as the store is open.
All my love, as always,
Joey

Thursday mornings were the quietest in Dunraven Street. Thursday evenings were bedlam because they were pay nights and the miners and their families swarmed into town to do their weekly shopping and pay off their 'slates' in the provision shops.

The first Thursday morning of the miners' fortnight holiday was the quietest of all. Unless they had several boys of working age, most miners' families lived from hand to mouth. But the majority still managed to scrape together enough money to pay the train fare to a relatives' house for one week, if not two. Some worked on farms for their keep, regarding two weeks in the open air as holiday enough, and even the poorest of the poor were taken on chapel-and-church-sponsored day trips to Pontypridd Park, Barry Island or Porthcawl.

Joey's reply to Rhian's note had been delivered to Edward Larch's office less than ten minutes after Edward had sent out the messenger boy. He took it into Rhian and told her he was lunching with a client so she wouldn't have any excuse not to see Joey right away. At ten minutes to twelve, she went into the bedroom and opened the wardrobe door. She had sent her uniform dress back to Llan House via Mrs Ball and Harris, Edward's coachman. Since then she had worn a blue cotton skirt and white blouse, and when they were in the wash, a grey cotton skirt and cream cotton blouse, which were the sum total of her summer wardrobe apart from her 'best outfit,' a plain cream linen skirt and the silk blouse Sali had given her.

She put them on, wound her curls into a bun at the nape of her neck, pinned on a straw hat and after glancing in the mirror to check that her face was clean and there were no marks on her clothes, left Edward's rooms for the first time since he had carried her up the stairs. She knocked on Mrs Ball's door on her way down.

'Rhian, you look pretty,' Mrs Ball exclaimed in surprise.

Rhian thought she detected a note of condemnation in the widow's voice, and wondered if she were being over sensitive. Mrs Ball had confided that she had been one day away from the workhouse when Mr Larch had offered her a job, so she was hardly likely to risk her home and livelihood by passing judgement.

'I'm going out, but I won't be long. Mr Larch has given me the front door key.'

'I'll put the groceries in your kitchen when they come, shall I?'

'Please.' Rhian ran down the remaining stairs and stepped out. She felt odd, almost as though she had been ill and this was her first outing after being incarcerated in a sickroom. Only she hadn't been sick – unless heartsick counted, she thought bleakly.

She faced the road. The street seemed bigger than the last time she had been in it, the trams, carriages, bikes and carts, noisier. Pungent scents wafted from the shops and the road and she breathed in the smell of raw and smoked meats, shoe leather, lamp oil, freshly baked bread, overripe cheeses and horse manure. A van rattled past with an unsteady load and she jumped, startled by the noise.

She faced Gwilym James. Pretending not to hear the whispers of her fellow pedestrians or notice the stares of the doorman and staff in the store, she headed straight for it and didn't stop walking until she reached Joey's office.

He had seen her and was standing, waiting in front of his desk. Edward hadn't exaggerated about the change in him. He had lost an alarming amount of weight and looked as though he hadn't eaten or slept since she'd last seen him.

'Please, sit down.' He offered her a chair. 'Would you like something? Tea? Coffee?' He was so polite; he might have been talking to a stranger.

She shook her head. Tears burned at the back of her eyes and a lump rose in her throat, preventing her from speaking. She pulled the chair away from the front of his desk and sat down.

'I got your letter. Did you get mine? That is a stupid thing to say,' he said quickly. 'Obviously you've read my letter. If you hadn't, you wouldn't be here. Did you have to come far?'

'Across the road.'

'You've been in Edward Larch's office for the last two weeks?' He lowered his voice at a noise outside his door.

'I've been living in rooms in the house next door to his office.'

'The house that Michaels the builder has been renovating?'

'Yes.' They were exchanging words, but she was aware that neither of them was saying what they wanted to.

'Rhian, what you saw – me and Tonia – it wasn't what you thought.'

'I read Tonia's letter.'

'And it didn't make any difference?'

'I meant what I said in my note, Joey, this is the last time that I'll see you alone like this.'

'Why, when—'

'Please let me speak, Joey. I have had two weeks to think about what I'm going to say to you, and it's not going to be easy to remember it all. When I saw you holding Tonia and she told me that you'd been having an affair and she was carrying your baby, I believed her. Until that moment I didn't think a heart could break but I felt as though mine had cracked.'

'I have felt that way for the last two weeks.'

'I loved you so much . . .'

Loved – past tense. Joey gripped the edge of his desk until his knuckles turned white but he didn't interrupt her.

'. . . And then, when I received Tonia's letter and she said that she'd lied, that the secret you'd kept from me was that she'd been having an affair with Geraint Watkin Jones, I realized it didn't make any difference. I loved you, I should have believed in you but I didn't.'

'Because of my past?' he questioned.

'Doesn't it bother you, that I was so ready to believe the worse of you? A wife should stand up for her husband no matter what he's accused of. Murder, robbery, rape . . . all Tonia accused you of was loving and sleeping with her and I believed her.'

'So you're saying that we should end our engagement just because you believed Tonia's lies?' he demanded incredulously.

'Yes.'

'Oh, no, Rhian! I'm not going to allow something so stupid and vicious to end what we have.'

'You have no choice.'

'Yes, I do. Do you think for one minute that I'd stand back and let you walk away without a fight?'

'There's nothing left for you to fight for, Joey.'

'You've stopped loving me?' he challenged.

'Love is nothing without trust and we've proved that I don't trust you. Don't you see that if we married, I'd turn into a nagging, jealous wife?'

'Providing you were my nagging, jealous wife, I wouldn't mind.' He smiled, a ghost of his old mischievous smile, and it was as though someone had stabbed her and twisted the knife.

'You would mind in time, because you would learn to hate me and I couldn't live with that.'

He propped his elbows on the desk, sank his chin on to his hands and stared at her. 'I can understand you wanting to postpone the wedding after what has happened, but if we continued to see one another—'

'No, Joey, I'll not lay myself open to your persuasion a second time,' she countered firmly.

'Mrs Williams told Sali that you'd left Llan House.' He had to ask the question, although he dreaded the answer. 'Are you moving from the Rhondda?'

'No, Mr Larch is opening a shop in the building he's had renovated. I am going to manage it for him.'

'Then we will see one another.' He continued to clutch at the hope, unwilling to let it go.

'There's something else that you should know, Joey.' She glanced uneasily at the open door.

'Shall I close it?'

She looked at the window that overlooked the shop floor. Everyone there could see them, but they wouldn't hear anything that she and Joey said if the door was closed. 'Yes, please.'

He left his seat and walked past her chair to the door. He had to tense his muscles to stop himself from reaching out and embracing her. She was like a magnet drawing him inexorably towards her, and he couldn't bear the thought of never being able to touch her again. Of never making love to her . . .

He closed the door.

She stared at his back, so broad and finely muscled beneath his shirt and waistcoat. Noticed the way his hair curled above his collar. Traced the line of his jaw . . .

He turned and walked back to his chair, taking a detour around hers. 'What is this other great revelation, Rhian?'

'I have become Edward Larch's mistress.'

He stared at her dumbfounded for a full minute and when he found his voice it was hoarse from shock and anger. 'He took advantage of you!'

'If anything, I took advantage of him,' she said quietly. 'When I ran from here I didn't know where to go. Mr Larch has always been kind to me so I hid in the yard behind his office.'

'In the hope that he'd find you?'

'I wasn't thinking that clearly.'

'But he did find you.'

'The woman he pays to look after his offices and the new building did. She fetched him.'

'And then you went to bed with him.' Joey left his desk and pulled the blind on his window.

'Mr Larch wanted to take me to Ynysangharad House. I wouldn't go. And I refused to return to Llan House. I didn't want to talk to anyone. I wanted to be alone. He asked the woman to take care of me then went home to Llan House.'

'And afterwards? How long was it before you jumped into bed with him?'

'What difference does that make?' she asked uneasily.

'I have a right to know when you are engaged to me.'

'I made love to Mr Larch when I realized that I didn't trust you and never would, and that was no basis for a marriage.'

Joey turned his back to her and ran his hands through his hair. 'Do you love him?'

'No.'

'Does he love you?'

'I don't think he's capable of loving anyone other than his first wife.'

'You don't love him, he doesn't love you and yet you're prepared to remain his mistress? Why?' he demanded harshly.

'Because we respect one another. And because we don't care deeply enough about one another to inflict pain. I know I'm being selfish, Joey, but I feel safe with Mr Larch. I can be totally honest with him knowing that he'll take care of me, no matter what I do.'

'You trust and respect him? A married man who sleeps with you instead of his wife, and yet you leave me because you think that I *might* cheat on you? I promised you I wouldn't—'

'But your promise wasn't enough to make me believe you,' she reminded. 'Mr and Mrs Larch's marriage is a disaster. It was from the outset. He spends more time with me than his wife.'

'Then why did he marry her?'

'Because he went insane with grief after his first wife died.'

'If I lost you I'd go insane too.' He looked into her eyes.

'I'm sorry, Joey.'

'The day after tomorrow is our wedding day.'

'You haven't cancelled it.' She paled at the thought of all the hours he'd waited for her to return.

'No.'

'But you will?'

'Only if you make me.'

'I won't be at the church, Joey.' She gripped the back of the chair for support as she rose to her feet. 'It's time I went.'

He blocked the door. 'Your sleeping with Edward Larch makes no difference to me, Rhian. I love you. I still want to marry you.'

'It would make a difference in time, Joey. And I've told you why I can't marry you. If you want me to see Sali, Megan, your brothers and your father to explain the way I feel, I will.'

'I'll do all the explaining that has to be done.'

'Then I'll write to them.' She opened her handbag and removed the handkerchief containing his mother's ring. She untied the knots and laid it carefully in the centre of his desk.

'You may as well keep that; I won't be giving it to any other girl.'

'I couldn't keep it, Joey. Not now. Please, try to understand, if I wasn't so afraid of being hurt again or turning into a shrewish wife I would . . .'

'Marry me?'

She shook her head. 'Goodbye, Joey.' She stood in front of him and he stepped aside.

She walked past him and he reached out and gripped her hand.

She returned the pressure of his fingers for a few seconds, then opened the door and walked away. She didn't look back, not even when he finally released her.

Chapter 15

EDWARD LARCH WAS sitting in the living room, ostensibly reading a book, when Rhian returned from the store. He watched her remove her hat and gloves, walk into the hall and put them away in the cupboard. She returned, sat on the edge of the chair opposite his and stared into the empty fireplace. Disturbed by her silence, he asked her a question he already knew the answer to, because he had seen her enter Gwilym James from his office window.

'You saw Joseph Evans?'

'I returned his ring, and told him that I couldn't see him alone again. I also said that I was going to manage your shop for you and,' she raised her chin defiantly, 'that I am your mistress.'

Shocked, he said, 'I know we may not succeed in keeping the rumours at bay, but is he likely to tell anyone?'

'After this afternoon I doubt that Joey will want to mention my name to anyone ever again.'

She looked so crushed and devastated that he longed to gather her into his arms and offer her comfort, but he sensed it was too soon. 'I'm sorry; it must have been difficult for you.'

She continued to stare at the vase of dried flowers that filled the grate.

'You look exhausted. How about we send out to the White Hart for dinner tonight?'

'If you like,' she answered carelessly. It made no difference whether she opened or closed her eyes; the desolate expression on Joey's face had imprinted itself on her mind. She could still feel his hand burning hers. Hear the emotion in his voice as he had pleaded with her to reconsider. She loved him! She'd even told him she loved him! Why had she walked away?

Then she recalled the agony of seeing him with Tonia. The way she'd felt afterwards. And she knew she had done the right thing. She was hurting, but she knew from the painful experiences of her own childhood that time was a great healer. Whereas marriage to a man like Joey would be interminable torture because she would never be able to trust him out of her sight.

'If you pack, we could leave first thing in the morning. It would give us an extra day.'

'Leave?' She looked blankly at Edward.

'That holiday we delayed the opening of the shop for. The one we're going on this Saturday, remember?'

'I remember,' she murmured distantly.

'I checked the railway timetable.' He switched the conversation to practical matters in the hope of gaining her attention. 'There's a train leaving Cardiff at nine o'clock tomorrow morning for London. We can change there for Brighton.'

'Don't you have to work tomorrow?'

'I only have two appointments. I'll ask my secretary to cancel them, clear my desk, then go to Llan House and pack. I'll stay here tonight and leave an hour before you in the morning. I'll buy our tickets at Cardiff station and meet you there. We'll breakfast in the dining car on the train.'

'Won't Brighton be full at this time of year?'

'The cheaper boarding houses perhaps, but not the best hotels.' He left his chair, leaned over her and stroked her cheek with the back of his fingers. 'Get some rest. I'll be back for dinner. Do you have a suitcase to pack your things?'

'Mrs Williams sent my clothes down in an old Gladstone.'

'Use it. We'll buy you new luggage in Brighton when we buy you a new wardrobe.' He looked back at her from the doorway. He knew she was going to start crying once he left, and he was coward enough not to want to see her tears.

The pang of guilt he had felt when she had told him about Tonia George's letter intensified. For all her protestations to the

253

contrary, he suspected that she would have married Joseph Evans, if he, Edward Larch, hadn't made love to her.

But he would make it up to her next week. He had already made enquiries. One of the largest seafront hotels had an expensive suite with a balcony vacant. He would book it by telephone that afternoon and introduce her to a life of luxury she had never experienced. He'd take her to the best restaurants, theatres and shops that Brighton had to offer, buy her clothes, perfumes, jewellery and books – anything she wanted. Give her all the things he had longed to lavish on Amelia when they had honeymooned, and he hadn't been able to afford as a young man. He was determined to make it a perfect holiday, one they would both remember for the rest of their lives.

'When Sali last called into the store, she told me that I could take as much time off as I wanted to. And with it being miners' fortnight, Dunraven Street's never been quieter. Sam's ambitious, he won't want to remain an assistant manager for ever, and there won't be a better time for him to learn to run Gwilym James on his own.' Joey dropped the small suitcase he'd packed inside the kitchen door and set his straw boater on top of it.

'I can understand you wanting to get away, but wouldn't it make more sense to wait until morning?' Billy Evans was concerned by Joey's abrupt decision to leave. His son had walked into the house unexpectedly in the middle of the afternoon and informed him that he'd finally seen Rhian. He said she'd broken their engagement, returned his mother's ring and asked him to cancel the church and the other arrangements that had been made for Saturday. But he'd refused to elaborate as to why she wouldn't marry him.

'I want to go now,' Joey said flatly. 'Will you do me another favour, please?'

'If I can.'

'Write to Aunt Jane and tell her that I won't be needing the house on the Gower for the next two weeks, but I'll be happy to pay her the rent if she can't let it to anyone else.'

'I'll write, but I doubt she'll need your money. There are

always people looking to rent places down there at this time of year.' Billy reached for his walking stick. Leaning heavily, he levered himself to his feet. 'Is it too much to ask where you're going?'

'Swansea. Being a port town it's livelier than the Gower villages and far enough from here for me not to meet too many people I know. It has a beach I can sit on, pubs I can drink myself stupid in and music halls if I feel like being entertained.'

'Sounds to me as if you may need some help to guide you back to your bed at night. Want some company?'

'No thanks, Dad.' Joey's refusal was firm. 'I'll be all right,' he added unconvincingly. 'I just need some time on my own.'

'You going for the full two weeks?'

'Yes.'

'And when you come back?'

'I'll live here and carry on working in Gwilym James. What else do you expect me to do?'

Billy laid his hand on his son's shoulder. Sali and Megan were the demonstrative ones in the family, kissing everyone indiscriminately on the cheek, men as well as women. He and his sons rarely embraced one another. 'If you don't look after yourself you'll have me to answer to when you do get back, boy,' he warned gruffly.

'I know.' Joey tried to smile, but it was a shadow of his usual roguish grin. 'Say goodbye to Victor, Lloyd and the girls for me, kiss my nieces and nephews, and tell them I'll be back with sticks of rock.'

'Do you have enough money?'

'More than enough, Dad. I'll send you a postcard.' Joey picked up his straw boater, pushed it on his head without checking the angle in the mirror and walked out through the door.

Hearing noises in her husband's dressing room, Mabel Larch crept out of her bedroom, stole along the landing and froze when she saw that the doors to Edward's dressing room and bedroom were open.

Edward walked through the inner door that connected the two

rooms and dropped half a dozen starched white shirt collars into a suitcase that lay open on the day bed in his dressing room. He glanced up and saw her watching him. 'Careful, Mabel, you're almost in my private quarters. You may see something that will bring a maidenly blush to your cheek.'

'This is the first time you've been home in four days and you're packing.'

'I have business in London.'

'You're leaving tonight?'

'In the morning.' He went to the tallboy, opened it and removed two piles of drawers and undervests.

'You are staying here tonight.' It was an appeal more than a question.

'No.' He dropped a boater into his hatbox, closed the lid and fastened the leather strap. 'I have an early start and I wouldn't want to disturb you. I have ordered Harris to pick me up at my rooms in Dunraven Street.'

'You will at least stay for dinner.' She was almost begging him. And not only because Mrs Hodges and Mrs Hadley had taken her aside to warn her that she wouldn't remain respectable for long if her husband persisted in living apart from her.

Since Julia and, more especially, Edward had moved out of Llan House, she was lonely. She had discovered that fundraising coffee mornings, charity bazaars, bring-and-buy sales and afternoon teas with the Ladies' Circle were no substitute for family meals, even ones fraught with tension. And perfectly-decorated rooms were simply empty spaces when she didn't have anyone to share them with.

'I have ordered dinner to be brought to my rooms from the White Hart.'

'How long will you be gone?'

'I will return to Tonypandy one week Sunday.' He flicked through the ties on the rack in his wardrobe and chose two.

'To here?'

He turned and gave her a cool smile. 'No.'

'This is your home. You haven't slept here—'

'I did warn you, Mabel,' he cut in dispassionately.

'You could at least try to keep up appearances.'

'I'm here now, aren't I? I haven't thrown you out on the street. I give you personal and housekeeping allowances.'

'We're married—'

'I think not, Mabel, and that's not an invitation to discuss the subject. You know my feelings.'

'I miss you.'

'Really?' Sock-suspenders and braces in hand, he stared at her in astonishment.

'I'll do anything—'

'Then open that door for me, please. I asked Mrs Williams to bring up the rest of my laundry. But, as it happens, I don't need it. There are more than enough clean clothes here to last me the week.'

'Edward, please. I am trying.'

He couldn't help but contrast her clumsy attempt to make amends with Rhian's effortless lovemaking. 'As you don't want to obey me and open that door, I'll take the opportunity to tell you something before you hear it from Mrs Hodges or Mrs Hadley.' He dropped a bundle of socks into the suitcase, snapped it shut, lifted it down to the floor and set it beside his hatbox. 'I have a mistress, we live in the rooms next door to my office, she has made me very happy and no, she is not Mrs Ball, the elderly widow I employ to clean the building.'

'You have another woman!' She couldn't have looked more pained if he'd struck her.

'It shouldn't come as a surprise after I told you that I would look elsewhere for what you wouldn't give me.'

'And you're happy living in sin, knowing that you will go to hell for turning your back on God and the Christian way.'

'Much happier than I was living in respectability with you,' he divulged frankly. 'When I return from . . . my business trip, I will examine my finances. You brought very little into our marriage, but I will make a settlement on you, and a more generous one than the allowance your father gave you before you left his home. However, there is a condition. You will have to return to Carmarthenshire to live with your parents for the greater part of the year. We could let it be known that your father or mother is in ill-heath and you're needed to look after them.'

'You are talking about a separation and I have been an exemplary wife.'

He lifted his eyebrows. 'Really, Mabel, we both know that is not true, as do the servants. And witnesses are forced to swear the truth and the whole truth so help them God in court.'

'You would bring up our private life in court?'

'Eventually, in ten years or so, when I retire from business.' He was polite, icily so. He'd answered every question she'd asked him. He'd left her nothing with which to reproach him, no cause for criticism other than his absence from the house and her life.

'Edward, please—'

'Think about what I've said, Mabel. This house is expensive to maintain. If I reduce the staff and close up most of the rooms, it will mean more money in your pocket. And if we handle our separation discreetly, no one need know how final it is until I retire.' He checked his reflection in the mirror, straightened his tie and smoothed the grey hairs back above his ears.

'But if you cut back on the staff and close up most of the house, I won't be able to hold my head up in Tonypandy or the Ladies' Circle ever again.'

'That is the least of my concerns.'

'How can you say that when the Ladies' Circle is so influential and we all live here!' she exclaimed.

'I doubt Julia will come back to Tonypandy. Hopefully, she is a respectable married woman by now. And no matter what we may think of her choice of husband, I am confident that he won't want to settle too close to her family.'

'There's Gerald.'

'Who was only too glad to accept his friend's invitation to holiday in France because it meant that he didn't have to come home and face you this summer.' Edward's voice was neutral but, rightly or wrongly, he blamed his children's problems and his estrangement from them on his disastrous marriage. 'And, as he spends most of his time away at school and will soon go on to university, any alteration in our domestic circumstances will have very little impact on him.'

'I live here,' she reminded him in a small voice.

'The way we are at the moment, I am sure that you would be happier returning to your father for most of the year. You could assist him with his work just as you did before. Think about it, Mabel.' He retrieved his cases. 'We will discuss the subject on my return. Please open the door.'

She swallowed hard and tensed herself as though she were preparing to jump into a pool of icy water. Stepping quickly inside the door, she closed it behind her. 'I could try . . .' Colour flooded her cheeks as words failed her.

'Try what, Mabel?' he grinned, amused by her embarrassment.

'To do whatever it is that you want me to. I could . . . I could undress, if you like,' she stammered.

'Now, here?'

Closing her eyes, she unfastened the buttons at the neck of her blouse. She pulled it free from her skirt. Shivering, but not from cold, she dropped it to the floor. She unbuttoned her skirt, allowed it to fall and stepped out of it. She kept her eyes closed as, one by one, she removed the rest of her garments.

As a child her father had always taken her into his study and stripped her before slapping her buttocks with his bare hands to punish her for her misdemeanours. She had felt totally mortified and humiliated, but not as much as when he had rubbed goose grease on to her skin to take the sting from his blows later. And there were things . . . other things that he had done to her, things that he had insisted she'd made him do, although she hated him touching her that way. And he had warned her not to tell a living soul about them on pain of far greater punishments from heaven than he could ever mete out.

Still keeping her eyes closed, she dropped her final garment, her drawers. She continued to stand, shamed and waiting. 'I'm naked, Edward.'

'So I see.'

She opened her eyes. He was staring at her. 'This was what you wanted me to do, wasn't it?'

'Maybe on our wedding night, Mabel.' He couldn't help comparing her to Rhian – his wife's body was plump and flabby, her breasts sagging – but he couldn't resist dropping the cases he was holding, reaching out and touching . . .

She turned aside and vomited over her clothes when his fingers brushed her bare skin. He took his winter robe from his wardrobe and handed it to her. 'I think you've just proved that it's a bit late for you to be taking wife lessons, Mabel.' Retrieving his cases, he walked into his bedroom and left by the other door.

*

Owing to a summary rejection by the German Government of the request made by His Majesty's Government for assurances that the neutrality of Belgium will be respected, His Majesty's Government have declared to the German Government that a state of war exists between Great Britain and Germany as from 11.00 p.m. on 4 August 1914.

'You reading about the war?' the plump young barmaid asked Joey.

'I was.' Joey folded the two-day-old newspaper and pushed it back into the corner of the saloon bar where he had found it.

'We'll show them bleeding Huns they can't order Britain about. Just you wait until our Welsh boys get over there. They'll give them what's what.' She pulled a second pint of beer and set it on the tray next to the shorts he'd ordered.

Joey almost reminded her that it was the Belgian Government that the Germans were ordering about, not the British, then he reflected that the last thing he wanted to do was start an argument about the war with a patriotic barmaid. In the three days since it had been declared, he'd heard enough people's opinions on the conflict to last him a lifetime. The sight of a uniform of any description was enough to set men, women and children cheering and waving the flags that had miraculously appeared overnight on every souvenir stall in Mumbles and Swansea. Military bands had taken to marching up and down the main thoroughfares as well as occupying the bandstands as part of a recruiting drive. And to his disgust, that morning, he'd even caught himself humming "Soldiers of the King" when he was shaving.

'How much is that?' he asked the girl.

'Two double whisky chasers and two double gins and peps, at

sixpence each and two beers at sevenpence, that'll be three shillings and twopence, sir.' She held out her hand. He flicked through his change, and to her disappointment handed her the exact money. He knew she'd been hoping for a tip, but his holiday was proving expensive enough without treating barmaids.

However, he hadn't bargained on meeting Effie and Susie or Frank, although in all fairness to his new friend Frank, he paid his corner. He picked up the tray and pushed his way through the crowd to the table where a stocky young man with brown hair was sitting next to a couple of attractive brunettes.

His train had pulled into Swansea station at ten o'clock at night eight days before. The hotels he'd tried in town had been full, so he'd caught the train to Mumbles. His determination to spend his two weeks holiday alone had crumbled in the face of the village's shortage of accommodation. Everywhere he went it was the same story; town and village were bursting at the seams with holiday-makers. Eventually a landlady had offered him a half-share in a double bed. The other half had been taken by Frank Badham, a miner from Ammanford, and at breakfast the next morning they had found themselves sharing a table with two sisters, Effie and Susie, housemaids from Llandaff, whose employers had gone to Torquay for a fortnight.

'Ooh, you bought us large ones, you naughty boy, Joe.' Effie dug Joey in the ribs when he sat on the bench seat next to her. 'Well, I'm telling you now, you'd be better off asking me for whatever it is you want, than trying to bribe me with gin. I can drink any girl and most men, under the table.' She batted her eyelashes, which she'd smudged with boot black.

'Perhaps that's exactly where I want both of us, Effie. Under the table.' Joey winked suggestively. It was the kind of flirtatious banter that had come easily to him before he had begun to go out with Rhian, and he was amazed at how quickly he had slipped back into his old, shallow ways.

'Ooh, and I thought you were such a nice boy. I can read the wicked thoughts in your mind.' She turned to her sister. 'You were right about Joe, Susie. He has designs on me.'

'Is that designs or desires?' Frank interposed.

Effie gave a noisy, throaty giggle that sounded as though she were gargling with salt water. Susie whispered something in Frank's ear and they both burst out laughing.

Excluded from her sister's conversation, Effie grabbed Joey's arm and whispered breathlessly, 'So why *did* you buy me a double gin and pep?'

'To save going up to the bar twice before we go on to the People's Bioscope Palace, that's if you still want to go.' He took a long thirsty pull at his beer.

'Want to go!' Susie shouted in Frank's ear, making him wince. 'You heard those boys at the bar. They're showing pictures of what's going on in Belgium. We'll see guns and soldiers and fighting—'

'It's too soon for fighting,' Frank curbed her enthusiasm.

'But we'll see the boys marching in,' Effie enthused. 'I so-o-o love a man in a uniform,' she sighed theatrically.

'I'll warn all the tram conductors in the town then, shall I?' Joey said dryly.

'Ooh you, I've never known a card like you, Joe.' She elbowed him again and he spilled his beer.

'Steady on.' Joey pulled his handkerchief from his pocket and mopped his trousers.

'You think any more about what I said?' Frank looked at Joey over Effie's head.

'About what?' Joey made a grab for Effie's hand. She was scrabbling around the top of his thighs under cover of the table.

'Enlisting, of course. I told you, my brother's in the South Wales Borderers. He could have a word with his sergeant and we'd be in before the big rush starts. If it's going to be over by Christmas, there won't be that much time for us to do our bit, let alone win any medals.'

'I'm on holiday, Frank. It's the only two weeks I get off a year and I intend to enjoy both of them.' Joey succeeded in pinning Effie's hand to his knee.

'A week can be a long time in a war that's only going to last a few months. I'm going to write to my brother tonight. Come on, it'll be fun to go with a mate.'

'We've only known one another a week,' Joey protested.

'But I feel as if I've known you all my life.' Frank downed his whisky chaser in one and made a face. It was obvious he didn't enjoy the taste.

'So do I.' Effie slipped the buttons on Joey's flies with her free hand. He lifted the hand he was holding on to the table, and held it there. Grabbing her other hand, he pinned it together with her first, while he refastened his buttons.

He saw Frank wriggling. Judging by the colour in his cheeks, and Susie's look of studied innocence, he wasn't the only one to have his flies opened in the saloon bar of the Grand Hotel.

'Spoilsport,' Effie whispered in his ear.

'Drink up.' Joey lifted his whisky chaser. 'If we're going to the Bioscope we'd better get a move on.'

'I think we should go home.'

'Home?' Julia repeated in bewilderment. She and Geraint were dining in the conservatory of a country hotel two miles outside York. He had insisted on making what he referred to as a 'wedding trip,' not honeymoon, and they had left Gretna Green for Dumfries, followed by Edinburgh, Glasgow, Berwick, Newcastle and Scarborough, where they had stayed an entire week before travelling on to York. But she had come down to breakfast that morning to find Geraint studying a railway map of Britain, and as the first question he had asked her before she'd even sat down was 'Would you like to see Leeds before we go on to Manchester?' the last thing she'd expected him to say was, 'I think we should go home.'

'Yes, home – Pontypridd,' he clarified, realizing how odd it was to say 'home' when they didn't have a house to call their own. 'I've been reading the papers and I think the editorials are right, this war is changing everything. If Great Britain as we know it is to survive, every man must do what he can, volunteers as well as professionals.'

'And you are thinking of volunteering?'

'They are already shipping soldiers out to France. The army needs a hundred thousand men. I'm guessing that Kitchener intends to deploy them on garrison duties in Ireland and the colonies to free the professionals for the fighting. They are especially short of officers. I received some military training at school and university so I'm guaranteed a commission.'

'I see,' she murmured, not quite sure what else to say.

'If I didn't go, I don't think I'd be able to hold my head up in years to come.'

'If you feel that way, then you should certainly enlist.' She drained her wine glass. They had been married for over three weeks, shared meals, trips, travelling, spent almost every waking hour except late in the evening together, slept in the best hotel suites their current town or city had to offer – Geraint always insisted on a suite with a sitting room and two bedrooms – and he had never once shown her any more affection than he would have his sister.

Attributing his disinclination to touch her to her lack of looks, she hadn't brought up the subject of the intimate side of marriage and, as a result, developed a more formal version of the relationship that she had with her brother.

'It would mean leaving you to do everything on your own.'

'What everything?' she enquired.

'Finding, buying and furnishing a house.'

'Even if you volunteered your services, it wouldn't necessarily mean that you'd have to leave immediately.'

'I don't think we could count on my being around for long.'

The waiter removed their plates. The wine waiter replenished their glasses and held up the empty bottle.

'Yes, please, we'll have another,' Geraint said, 'and Champagne with the *entrée*. And could you ask the receptionist to check the times of the trains and details of the connections we'd have to make to reach Cardiff tomorrow?'

'Of course, sir.'

Geraint smiled at Julia. 'Thank you for making it easy for me to go.'

'As we have a long journey ahead of us, perhaps we could pass the time by discussing what kind of house you would like and how you would like me to furnish it.'

'The house would have to be detached and in its own grounds with two master suites of bed and dressing rooms. An indoor, plumbed bathroom is essential and at least six guest bedrooms. I'd prefer completely separate servants' quarters and staircase. In addition to drawing, morning, breakfast and dining rooms, I think we should have two studies and a library . . .'

As Julia continued to listen to Geraint's very definite ideas on furniture and decor, she felt as though he were describing an actual house not an ideal. But she had no idea that he *was*. Apart from the addition of a modern bathroom, he was describing Danygraig House, the family home his grandfather had built, where he had grown up, which had been sold by his uncle and demolished by the purchaser to make way for the YMCA building in Pontypridd.

'I find it odd to think that we are at war.' Rhian clung to Edward's arm as they walked the length of Brighton pier. Night had fallen, the lamps had been lit and the warm breeze carried snatches of music from the concert party playing in the theatre.

' "Land of Hope and Glory" ' Edward remarked. 'Now that the first shots are about to be fired I believe we're in for a severe dose of patriotism.'

'You don't approve of the war?'

'I don't approve of any war. Neither did my father. His brother thought it would be a lark to enlist when we were fighting the Crimean War. He was killed two days before his twenty-first birthday. As my grandfather said at the time, and excuse the language, "It was a bloody awful waste of a promising young life." '

'It must have been dreadful for your grandmother.'

'She died shortly afterwards. My father said of a broken heart.'

'You won't enlist, will you?' She was alarmed by the thought of losing the one person left in her life.

'They don't want old men. Only young healthy ones who can run fast enough to dodge bullets.'

'You're not old.'

'I am nearly fifty but thanks to you I haven't felt so young in years.' He smiled at her. 'Would you like to go back to the hotel for supper and a nightcap?'

'I couldn't eat another thing after that dinner.'

'Not even ice cream? One of those deliciously cold raspberry sundaes covered in whipped cream and nuts?' He mentioned the delicacy on the hotel menu that had become her favourite.

'I'll burst.'

'No, you won't, and you can wash it down with an apricot brandy.' They leaned on the rail and gazed down at the sea.

'I'd seen pictures and postcards of course, and when I lived close to the River Taff I used to pretend it was the sea. But nothing prepared me for the real thing. I never imagined it was so beautiful, especially at night. Always moving, shimmering even in the dark, and the scent.' She breathed in deeply. 'It's like God packed all the oxygen in the world above it and sprinkled it with salt.'

'And the aroma of fish,' he laughed. 'Why didn't you tell me that you'd never seen the sea before we came here?'

'Because I didn't want you to think that I was ignorant.'

'Given the number of books you've read and the speed with which you tackle a new one, I could never think that.' He offered her his arm again and they resumed walking.

'Home tomorrow,' she said wistfully.

'I'll bring you here again next year,' he promised, 'and in the meantime we'll have weekends away — lots of them — in places nearer home like Penarth, Porthcawl and Barry Island.'

'Someone might see us and tell your wife.'

'I told Mabel that I had a mistress.'

'But you didn't tell her who I was.'

'I will when we go back.' He covered her hand with his.

'Thank you for bringing me here.' She lifted her long skirts in preparation to walk up the short flight of steps to the hotel entrance.

'And thank you for bringing happiness back to my life.' He kissed her hand. 'Do you want the ice cream and apricot brandy in the supper room, or our bedroom?'

'What do you think?' She gave him a smile he had come to know well during the past week.

'You go on up; I'll order it.'

*

'Poor darling.' Lloyd dipped his fingers in the glass of brandy on his bedside cabinet and rubbed them lightly over Edyth's gums. She stopped crying and looked up at him, tears sparkling in her eyelashes, a wan smile on her face.

Sali unbuttoned her blouse and draped it over a chair. 'You are a wonderful father, Lloyd.'

He chose to ignore her ironic tone. 'Aren't I?' he echoed smugly from the depths of their four-poster bed, where he was nursing Edyth who had been unusually fractious, even for a teething day.

'But I wish you'd realize that brandy isn't the cure for every childhood ailment.'

'Edyth Evans, your mother is a mean spoilsport,' he said solemnly to the baby before lifting her on to his bare shoulder and patting her back.

Sali watched the baby's eyelids droop as she gradually relaxed against Lloyd.

'Almost ready to put down?' Lloyd whispered.

'By the time I've finished undressing she will be.' Sali unrolled her stockings and dropped them into the laundry bag.

'I bet you a pound to a penny she'll sleep through tonight.'

'The amount of brandy you've given her, she'll probably wake with a hangover in the morning.' She took Edyth from him, and set her down in the cot they'd moved out of the nursery into their bedroom.

'I doubt she even tasted it.' He held back the bedclothes while she slipped off her drawers and chemise. When she climbed into bed, he lifted his arm, draped it over her shoulders and pulled her close.

'She tasted it all right. Didn't you see the way she smiled when you rubbed it on to her gums a second time? That was a drunken Evans smile if ever I saw one. And I should know, I've seen it on you, Victor and Joey often enough.'

He reached out with his free hand and turned down the wick on the oil lamp, plunging the room into darkness. The trustees were about to extend the electric lighting circuits to the upstairs of the house, but the work wasn't scheduled to start until after the holidays.

'You're worried about Joey, aren't you?' Sali asked as he lay back beside her.

'Only because he hasn't been in touch after he promised my father that he'd send a postcard.'

'Perhaps one will come tomorrow.'

'If he hasn't been too busy chasing women to write,' he countered cynically.

'It will take him a while to get over Rhian.'

'My point exactly. Since the day he was born, my baby brother's always acted before he's thought. You knew how besotted he was with Rhian. There's no saying what losing her will do to him.'

'I wish I knew where she was. I could explain about Tonia.'

'My father said the letter Tonia wrote to Rhian explained everything.'

'Then I can't understand why Rhian called off their wedding.'

'You can't make the whole world happy, sweetheart,' he dropped a kiss on her forehead, 'so you'd better just get used to making me and the children happy.'

'I can't bear the thought of Joey and Rhian being apart. They belong together and no matter what their problems are, I'm sure they could work them out if they went the right way about it. I wonder what they're both doing now.'

'I have no idea.' He kissed her again. 'But I know what I would like to be doing, sweetheart. Could you try to put Rhian and Joey's problems out of your mind, just for a little while?'

Rhian lay soaking in hot, violet-scented water in the private bathroom in the luxurious suite Edward had engaged for them. Her hair, cut and set at the beginning of the week by the hotel's hairdresser who had finally succeeded in taming her unruly curls into an elegant style, was loosely knotted on the top of her head. At Edward's instigation, her finger and toenails had been mani-cured at the same time and she lifted her hands and feet out of the water to admire their perfect oval shapes and glossy French polishing. She felt privileged, pampered and, after the raspberry sundae and apricot brandy, pleasantly tired, full and relaxed.

Edward wandered in, two brandy glasses in hand. He had taken off his jacket and waistcoat and was in shirtsleeves, his braces dangling over his trousers. 'Would you like a brandy?'

'I'll be seeing double if I drink one that size.'

'It tastes so much better after the glass has been warmed in a bath.' Edward handed one to her. 'Want me to wash your back?'

'Please.' She sat up and leaned forward.

He squeezed a sponge in the water, rubbed a bar of purple, violet-scented soap over it and gently massaged her shoulder blades, trickling water down her spine.

'You said my back,' she protested when he sponged her nipples.

'A man would have to be made of stone not to stray. And bathing you is like . . .' A strange expression she couldn't quite decipher clouded his eyes.

'What?'

'Like all the dreams and fantasies I had as a young man come true. You're not only beautiful, you're uninhibited. Have you any idea how rare that is in a woman who isn't . . .' He'd only just stopped himself from saying 'a whore'.

'A wife,' she finished for him.

'Exactly.' Taking her glass from her, he set it together with his own on the window sill, before sliding his hands beneath her and lifting her from the water.

'Edward, you'll get us both soaking wet.' She laughed as his sodden shirtsleeves dripped rivulets of scented water over both of them.

'Then we'll play at being sea creatures. I'll be the octopus.' Setting her down on the bath mat, he wrapped a towel around her and blotted her skin as tenderly as if she were a baby. 'I love seeing you like this.'

'Naked?'

'I wish you'd never wear clothes again.'

'Pass me my robe, please.'

'Let's stay here a while longer.' He lowered her to the floor, before stripping off his clothes. She closed her eyes, knotting her fingers gently into his hair, as he smoothed scented cold cream over her skin.

'I'll be as slippery as a—'

'Mermaid.' He began to caress and explore her body with his fingertips and lips, teasing and tantalizing her until she began to writhe in unrequited passion.

'Please, Edward, let's go to bed.'

'Not yet.'

She returned his caresses with a technique born of intuition and practice. In the last few weeks she had come to know his body well. The touches that roused him and gave him pleasure, the places he liked to be kissed, the responses she could expect to provoke. But she still kept her eyes closed.

Edward was similar to Joey in some ways; in others they couldn't have been more unalike. When it came to lovemaking, Edward felt and tasted different, his cologne was sharper, more astringent, but by shutting her eyes she found it easier to ignore the differences between her two lovers and imagine herself with Joey.

She hoped that a time would come when she would want to stop pretending and that, until that time came, Edward wouldn't discover her deception.

'My love . . .'

Guilt prompted her to murmur, 'Eddie.'

'Amelia . . .'

It saddened more than shocked her to realize that she wasn't the only one who was pretending. Edward Larch was considerate, affectionate – and using her to fool himself that his first wife had come back from the grave. But was his self-deception any worse than hers?

And was it so terrible to use someone if they, in their turn, used you?

Chapter 16

'COME ON, JOE, be a sport,' Frank coaxed.

Because he couldn't bear the thought of any other girl calling him Joey, he had told his new friends in Swansea to call him Joe, with the result that it took him a few seconds to realize that Frank was talking to him and not the barman in the Mermaid Hotel. 'I'm not putting up with Effie in our room all night, just because you want to sleep with Susie.'

'We can hardly chuck the poor girl out and expect her to roam the streets until morning,' Frank pleaded. 'Please, Joe, the land-lady's as blind as a bat and deaf as a post. She'll never cotton on if one of us switches with one of the girls. And, unlike you, Effie, Susie and I are leaving in the morning. We've only one night left, and it was bloody uncomfortable on the beach last night. Susie moaned like hell about the places the sand had got into. And I've a rash on my knees from kneeling on seaweed.'

'The answer is no,' Joey said obdurately.

'It's not as if I'm asking you to make a great sacrifice. Susie was only telling me tonight that Effie's more than willing to give you a lot more than you've taken so far. She's really disappointed that you haven't made a real play for her. A few kisses are all right, but why stop there when the lot is on offer?'

'Hasn't it occurred to you that I might not want more of what Effie's offering?' Joey suggested.

'Is there something wrong with you?' Frank gave Joey a sideways look.

'Now I have to have something wrong with me, just because I don't want to sleep with a tart?'

'Quiet, the girls are coming.' Frank smiled as the sisters left the Ladies and headed towards them. Both girls had combed their hair, and, as they came closer, it was obvious that they had split the best part of a bottle of Attar of Roses between them. But their bright red lipstick was smudged and the boot black on Effie's eyelashes had fallen below her eyes, making her look as though she was in the final stages of consumption.

Their trip to the bioscope had been followed by a visit to a Swansea café for a fish and chip supper and more drinks in Swansea's oldest pub, the Cross Keys. The fresh air had hit both girls when they'd taken the train back to Mumbles and, against Joey's advice, Frank had insisted on buying a last drink for everyone in the nearest hotel to their lodgings, which the girls had been angling to visit all week because it was the best and most expensive in Mumbles.

'They're calling last orders,' Frank said as a bell rang. 'You two want a gin nightcap or something else?'

'Any more gin and you'll be wheeling me home.' Susie grabbed the bar for support.

'Last time I looked, you had legs not wheels under your skirt, Susie,' Joey said with a straight face.

'Eh?' Susie tried and failed to focus on him.

'Take no notice of Joe; he's trying to be funny again.' Effie tossed her head in the air. She was cross with Joe. They had spent almost the whole week together and apart from a couple of quick goodnight kisses, he hadn't touched her. Whereas Susie had hit the jackpot with Frank, a working miner who lived with his widowed mother, and knowing Susie's luck, one who'd welcome a daughter-in-law into her ready furnished home. It was Susie who'd suggested she unbutton Joe's flies under cover of the table in the Grand to 'get him going'. But all she had succeeded in doing was annoying him at the expense of bruised fingers.

The one thing she and Susie wholeheartedly agreed on was that they were sick and tired of service. They had scraped together every penny they could lay their hands on to holiday in Swansea because two chambermaids they knew had met a couple of miners there. They'd had a double wedding less than two months after they'd returned, and, like them, she wanted her own place, her own man and a wedding ring on her finger.

'You girls find a table. Joe will give me a hand with the drinks.' Frank waved his hand to attract the barman's attention.

'Get singles for the girls and put plenty of water in them,' Joey advised. 'Effie's had enough to put her on her back as it is and I'm too tired to carry her to our lodgings.'

'If you won't spend all night with Effie, how about an hour?' Frank cajoled. 'Susie's promised me an eyeful, but only if we're in a bedroom.'

'If you've seen one girl naked you've seen them all, unless she weighs over twenty stone,' Joey replied flippantly.

Frank fell serious. 'I've never seen one in the buff. Not off a picture postcard.'

Frank's reply took Joey aback. 'You have to be joking?'

'It's not that I haven't done it, I have, plenty of times,' Frank boasted. 'But without somewhere to go, the girls won't take more off than they have to.'

'You've had girlfriends before Susie?' Joey looked him in the eye. 'The truth, Frank?'

'Not before Susie,' Frank muttered shamefaced.

'And you used a French letter?'

'A what?'

Joey had a sudden insight into how Lloyd and Victor must have felt when they'd tried to give him advice. 'A French letter. You put it over the vital part before you go visiting the lady, if you get my meaning. And that way you'll ensure there'll be no little Franks to send Susie scurrying round to your door with a maintenance order nine months from now.'

'The way she behaves when we're alone I wouldn't mind if there was a baby,' Frank declared recklessly. 'It's time I settled down and found a wife.'

'There's a lot more to marriage than taking a woman's clothes off.' Joey made a face as he saw the irony of him of all people lecturing someone on marriage.

'I never thought any girl – decent girl that is – would behave like Susie. I could live with a lifetime of that every night.'

'It doesn't last beyond the honeymoon.'

'I don't believe you. If anything, she likes it more than me.'
Frank reddened when he realized what he'd said.

'Frank,' Joey shook his head, 'you're a lost cause.'

The barman leaned over the counter and whispered, 'If you're after French letters I can sell you a couple for five bob.'

'How about it, Joe, want to go halves?' Frank asked eagerly.

'I have no use for one, mate.'

'Half a crown for one?' Frank added two shillings and sixpence to the coins he'd placed on the bar to pay for the round.

'Three bob,' the barman snapped.

'That's a tanner over the odds.' Joey eyed the barman sternly. 'You're making a tanner profit as it is.'

'All right, half a crown.' The barman thrust his hand under the counter and handed Frank a small packet.

'This is no use without the room,' Frank murmured mournfully, pushing the packet into his trouser pocket.

'You can have our room for one hour,' Joey capitulated. 'But not one minute longer. I'll go for a walk.'

'You'll take Effie?'

'That I draw the line at, but I will see her back to the lodging house. She can go to the girls' room.'

'Susie did say that Effie's been wondering if there's something wrong with you,' Frank ventured.

'A lot,' Joey replied with mock seriousness. 'But nothing that I want to go into. The sooner we get these drinks into the girls the sooner you can get started on the Susie road to heaven.'

Effie watched Frank and Susie run into the house and up the stairs. She closed the porch door behind her and joined Joey on the doorstep. 'You're not coming in?' She moved in front of him, hoping he'd kiss her.

'Not yet.'

'You going somewhere?'

'For a walk.'

'I'll come with you.'

'I wouldn't be good company.'

'You don't like me, do you?' Effie wailed, the combination of gin and rejection making her tearful.

'You're a great girl, Effie, just not my type,' Joey answered evasively.

'I have the same as every other girl and plenty of it. And I know how to use it. I'm not shy about coming forward.'

'You proved that tonight in the Grand Hotel.'

'Not that you took advantage of me.' She swayed drunkenly. He grabbed her when she fell backwards into the door. She caught his hand and clamped it on one of the breasts spilling out of her low-cut blouse.

'No, Effie.' Joey withdrew his hand as if it had been scalded.

'Why not?' she demanded belligerently.

'Because, although I like you, I don't want you that way. Can't we just be friends?'

'You're married, aren't you?' She peered up at him through red-veined eyes. 'No, you're not,' she frowned as the fug of alcohol lifted slightly from her mind. 'The married ones can't wait to pull a girl's drawers down.'

Joey knew it was irrational for a man who had been drunk more times than he could count in his life to be revolted by the sight of an inebriated woman, but he couldn't stop himself from feeling disgusted. Or sickened by her crude language and manners, which were so different from Rhian's.

'So, if you're not married, what's wrong with you?' she demanded when he stepped away from her.

He said the first thing that came into his mind. 'I have a disease.'

'A disease.' She slurred the syllables. 'You mean . . . Susie! Joe's diseased. I kissed him! I could have caught it!' She barged back through the door and charged up the stairs.

Reflecting that it was just as well that Effie and Susie were leaving first thing in the morning, Joey thrust his hands into his pockets and walked down Mumbles Road.

Music drifted from the Pavilion where Tom Owen's Pierrots played Wednesday and Saturday afternoons and twice nightly. When he drew nearer he recognized the chorus of "Rule Britannia" being belted out by the audience as well as the players. He crossed the road and headed for the beach. Lighting a cigarette, he sat on the sea wall and allowed his mind to drift over the past week.

He should never have become involved with Susie, Effie and Frank. He should have stuck to his original plan, remained aloof and holidayed in solitary misery. Eaten all his meals alone, drunk alone, visited the theatre alone and . . . what? Played the part he was playing now. That of voyeur? A man who spent all his time watching others, because he no longer had a private life.

He looked over the sands towards the sea. The beach was full of shadowy figures merging, separating and melting into the darkness. He could hear the quick short gasps of heavy breaths intermingling with lighter ones. The rustle of linen and cotton accompanied by soft mews of discomfort and pain that he attributed to seaweed and sand after Frank's confession in the Mermaid. A slap rent the air followed by a masculine cry of pain.

A female voice distracted him. 'All on your own?'

The nearest street lamp was some distance away but even in the darkness he recognized the cheap scent and direct approach of a professional. 'Waiting for someone,' he answered.

'I can keep you company until she comes.' She leaned on the wall next to him.

He almost told her he had a disease until he thought of an even better excuse that would keep not only her, but any other watching professional, at bay. 'You're the wrong sex, love.'

'I should have known, you pretty ones are always bloody pansies.' She flounced off.

He jumped down from the wall, and walked further up the beach towards a rotting wooden breakwater. The sands had given way to a pebbled foreshore and he stood listening, mesmerized by the sound of the waves sucking in and out of the stones. The moon hung low, an enormous silver-gold orb suspended above a streak of black horizon; its broken reflection dancing and shimmering on the navy-blue surface of the sea.

A party of noisy drunks stumbled noisily along the pavement behind him, singing.

Rule Britannia,
Britannia rules the waves
Britons never never never shall be slaves.

Damned war or 'damned capitalist war', as his father would say. 'A war engineered by brainless aristocrats, speculators and arms manufacturers out to make a fortune from young men's blood and wrecked lives.' But then his father was steeped in the rhetoric of workers' rights.

He had talked to enough people besides Frank in the last week to realize that young men were answering Kitchener's call because war offered adventure, escape and a chance to cover themselves with glory, as well as an opportunity to abdicate all personal responsibility and the dreary routine of everyday life. He had no doubt that was why Frank wanted to join up, and probably would, if Susie didn't stick her claws into him first.

The thought occurred to him that if he enlisted he wouldn't have to make another decision for himself until the peace treaties were signed. He wouldn't have to go back to Tonypandy, or sit in the store every day, or come to terms with the fact that Rhian was living and working across the road from him – and sleeping in Edward Larch's bed.

The last few weeks without her had been torture and proof that he was finding it impossible to distance himself emotionally from her. Perhaps it would be less painful if they were separated by hundreds of miles. And it would be so simple. All he'd have to do was pay his bill in his lodgings in the morning, cut his holiday short by a week and head for Pontypridd and the Drill Hall where they recruited soldiers.

It was a tempting prospect. Mulling it over, he walked down a slipway to the beach and headed for the sea.

Sali left the breakfast table and walked into the library where she spent most of her mornings answering correspondence and study-ing buyers' catalogues. She picked up the post that Mari had placed on her desk and flicked through the letters. She recognized Rhian's writing on an envelope, but the postmark, Brighton, surprised her. With some trepidation she slit it open.

Dear Sali,

This is a hard letter to write, but I wanted to explain why I couldn't marry Joey. I will understand if you don't want to see me again and I am sorry to have put you to all the trouble of organizing a wedding for nothing, but after seeing Tonia in Joey's arms I couldn't stop picturing him with other girls. You know what he's been like . . .

'I know,' Sali murmured feelingly, thinking of all the times that she had lectured Joey on his behaviour.

. . . and I was afraid that if I did marry him I'd turn into a nagging, jealous wife who wouldn't allow her husband out of her sight. That I'd end up spending as much time in the store as him, watching his every move and suspicious about every woman he spoke to.

Holding the letter, Sali walked to the window. She understood exactly how Rhian felt. When Lloyd had been given the post of colliery manager, his father had told him that he'd inherited all the brains in the family. Lloyd had replied that if that was right, then Victor had been given all the strength and practical ability, and Joey enough charisma and looks not to need anything else. Everyone had laughed at the time; now it didn't seem so amusing.

She picked up the letter again.

When I ran away from Joey's office I hid behind Mr Larch's office. He found me and I have become his mistress. I don't love him and he doesn't love me, but he is kind. I am going to manage a shop for him. It is a sort of business arrangement. I made it when I thought that Tonia was having Joey's baby and I didn't really know what I was doing but that is not Mr Larch's fault, it's mine.

I tried to explain my reasons for the decisions I've made to Joey. He thinks Mr Larch took advantage of me. But he didn't, Sali. I promise you, he didn't. What happened is, if anything, more my fault than his.

Thank you for everything you have done for me. I will always love and be grateful to you. Kiss the children for me and tell them whatever you think best. I won't try to see any of you again. Please

tell Lloyd, Victor, Megan and Joey's dad as much of this as you think
they should know and please, please, be kind to Joey. He needs all
the love and support that you can give him. Thank you for being
such a good friend. Love and kisses to you and the children,
     Rhian

Sali stared out into the rose garden but all she could see was
Rhian's face, pale and serious, as she must have looked when she'd
penned the letter, which was as selfless and caring as she.

'Rhian,' she murmured softly. 'What have you done?'

'Your cab is waiting, sir.'

Geraint nodded to the doorman of the New Inn Hotel in
Pontypridd, stepped down on to the pavement and spoke to the
driver who was holding the cab door.

'The Drill Hall on Broadway.'

'Yes, sir.' The driver closed the door, slipped the car into gear
and pulled away.

They drove slowly down the main road that led from
Pontypridd to Cardiff but long before they reached the Drill Hall
they passed an enormous queue of men that snaked along the
pavement facing the direction of the hall. They were all waiting,
some more patiently than others. Geraint was amazed to see boys
who couldn't have been more than fifteen or sixteen years of age
standing next to grizzled pensioners who looked well past the enlistment ceiling of forty-four.

He left the cab, told the driver to wait and after a brief, 'Excuse
me,' to no one in particular, pushed past the line of men to the
door of the hall.

A non-commissioned officer stepped smartly in front of him.
'You will have to join the queue, sir.'

Geraint gave the recruiting sergeant a withering look. 'Major
Smythe-Davies is expecting me.'

'Yes, sir. Sorry, sir.' The sergeant saluted. 'Inside, sir, second
door on the left.'

Geraint went ahead and tapped the open door. He'd never met
Paul Smythe-Davies but he had been at school with his brother

John, and a chance meeting in the 'Gentlemen's Only' bar in the New Inn with John the night before had resulted in this interview.

A thin man looked up from a desk smothered with papers. 'Yes?' he barked impatiently.

'Watkin Jones, your brother's school chum.'

'Oh yes, he mentioned you to me this morning. I told my orderly to give you a bell in the New Inn. Glad to see you could make it.'

'It's good of you to see me at such short notice, Major Smythe-Davies.'

'Not at all.' The major left his office and looked down the corridor to the rooms where the recruiting officers were sifting through and swearing in the new recruits. 'What price this?' He pointed with his pen at the men queuing out of the door. 'Kitchener will soon have his hundred thousand volunteers. But between you and me, I think he's going to need a lot more. I spoke to my CO about you this morning on the blower. You can have a commission, as a second lieutenant, effective immediately.'

'I can't thank you enough,' Geraint said sincerely.

'You won't be thanking me when you're doing your basic training. Those sergeants can be swines, and they like nothing better than giving officers stick while they have the chance.'

'So when do I leave?'

'Eight o'clock train tomorrow morning, start training the day after.' The major opened a drawer in his desk and extracted an envelope. 'Travel orders. You'll need a uniform and other things. I've put my tailor's card in there. He's a good chap and as reasonable as any of them. But he doesn't press his bills as hard as some,' he added in a whisper.

'That was thoughtful, thank you again.'

'Please stop thanking me, old boy; we need all the good chaps we can get in the regiment. Rumour has it we'll be in France next month. You'll be joining us there as soon as you're ready.'

'I'll look forward to it.' After weeks of travelling with Julia, Geraint was hungry for masculine company. 'If you can get away, I'd like to buy you lunch.'

'No chance, old man, up to my eyes in it. Next time perhaps.'

The major slapped Geraint's shoulder and they stepped outside his office. Geraint started and retreated.

Joey Evans stood in the corridor in front of a desk, the pen in his hand poised above a sheaf of papers.

'Geraint.' Joey looked him coolly in the eye. 'You're the last person I expected to enlist.'

Drawing confidence from the major standing next to him, Geraint said, 'I've just been commissioned.'

Joey looked up at the recruiting sergeant who was swearing him in. 'Whatever regiment he's in,' he indicated Geraint, 'make sure I'm put in a different one. If I'm not, another war will break out in our ranks. And there'll be blood.'

'You threatening me, Evans?' Geraint blustered.

'Just a joke, Geraint.' Joey looked from the sergeant to the major. 'We're related. Sort of brothers-in-law.'

'Sort of,' Geraint concurred warily.

'I see.' The major looked doubtful. 'Then you'll want to be in the same regiment after all.'

'No,' Joey broke in. 'If we're in different ones, we'll have each other's letters to look forward to. Don't forget to give Sali your address, Geraint. I'll send you a card as soon as I'm settled into my cosy barracks.'

'Joey, what a lovely surprise.' Sali ran down the stairs after settling Bella and Edyth in the nursery for their afternoon naps. She hugged him. 'Harry will be mad, Robert's just taken him off for a riding lesson but he'll be back in an hour. We've all been so worried about you. And you're here safe and sound. Your father and brothers will be pleased. Leave your case in the hall, come into the drawing room. Are you hungry? But what a stupid question, you must be. I'll ring for Mari.'

'Tea and sandwiches would be great, I haven't eaten since breakfast.' Joey followed Sali into the drawing room. 'Where's Lloyd?'

'At a meeting between colliery management and naval representatives in the New Inn. They've been ordered to step up production to meet the military's increased demand for coal.'

'If I know my communist pacifist brother, he won't be happy working for the war effort,' Joey commented.

'He's not.' Sali sat on the sofa and patted the cushion beside her. 'But what have you been doing with yourself this last week?'

'Enjoying a holiday in Mumbles.'

'By yourself?' she probed tactfully.

'I met some people.'

'You had a reasonable time?'

'As reasonable as I could without Rhian and I don't want to talk about her or the wedding that wasn't, Sali.'

Sali had been about to mention the letter she'd received from Rhian that morning, but instead she said, 'I can understand that.'

'Thank you.'

'Mari, look who's here,' Sali said to the housekeeper who had answered her ring. 'Do you think you could get some food for Joey, please?'

'Enough to tide him over until tea,' Mari said flatly. 'Have you any special requests, Joey?'

Joey wondered if it was his imagination, or if Mari really was cooler towards him than she had been the last time she'd seen him, when he and Rhian had still been engaged. 'Tea, a sandwich or a piece of cake would be great, please, Mari. But don't put yourself or anyone else to trouble on my account.'

'Seeing as I have to galvanize someone to make an effort, you may as well choose what you want to eat. Ham or chicken sandwich?' Mari barked.

'One of each?' Joey ventured.

'That's you; always want one of every sort that's going.'

'Mari!' Sali reprimanded.

'Sorry if I spoke out of turn, Miss Sali, but I'm very fond of Rhian.' She glared at Joey. 'My sister and I warned her about this one, but would she listen? Oh no! And it ended in tears, just as we said it would.'

'Not only Rhian's tears, Mari,' Joey said quietly.

'Yes, well, as my sister is so fond of saying, handsome is as handsome does and you've never been very good at doing handsome, only being it.'

'That's enough, Mari,' Sali interposed sharply. 'Whatever happened, happened between Joey and Rhian and is their, and no one else's, business.'

Mari was fond of Rhian but she was fonder still of Sali. 'I'll see what food I can come up with,' she said in a marginally softer tone. 'Would you like anything, Miss Sali?'

'Just a cup of tea to keep Joey company, please, Mari. And if that is Lloyd,' she added as the front door opened, 'you'd better bring three cups.'

'I may as well bring a full tea in early and make fresh for Master Harry when he comes in from his riding lesson.'

Lloyd walked in still wearing his hat, his face grim, his dark eyes glittering with anger.

'Lloyd, whatever's happened? Is it Harry?' Sali leaped to her feet.

'He's fine,' he reassured her quickly. 'I saw him and Robert in the field down by the river when I drove in.'

'Then the meeting—'

'The meeting went as well as any meeting between representatives of His Majesty's Services and their despised suppliers could. After it, I was enjoying a quiet drink in the bar with two of our engineers when I saw Geraint.' He turned to his brother.

'Geraint's back?' Sali asked.

'Back, married and staying in a suite in the New Inn with his wife until tomorrow morning, when he's catching a train to an army camp to begin his basic training. He even unbent enough to speak to me long enough to tell me that he's been commissioned as a second lieutenant and his regiment is being posted to France next month.'

'So soon.' Sali paled. With Gareth in Sandhurst she'd been forced to come to terms with the idea of having one brother drafted into the war, and, despite her differences with Geraint, she couldn't bear the thought of both of them being sent to the Front.

'After the brainwashing of patriotism, King and country Geraint was subjected to at public school, he sees it as his duty to serve. From the way he was talking, you'd think he was off on a jaunt not a killing field.' Lloyd took off his hat and dropped it on a chair. 'You'd better remind me to have a few quiet words with Harry before he reaches military age.'

'It will be over by the time Harry comes of age, won't it?' Sali asked anxiously.

'I hope so, sweetheart. However, given the size of the Kaiser's standing army, I wouldn't bet on it. But then, Geraint's not the only one who has enlisted. Is he, Joey?' When Joey didn't answer him, he added, 'There's no use denying it. Geraint told me that he'd seen you in the Drill Hall.'

Sali looked from her husband to his brother and sank slowly back down on the sofa.

'Joey, how could you?' Lloyd railed. 'You know how our father feels about the war. This will kill him and almost certainly you. Of all the stupid, hare-brained, idiotic things you've done in your life, this has to be the worst.'

'When do you leave?' Sali asked Joey in a small voice.

'The eight o'clock train tomorrow morning.'

'You've seen the newsreels of the Kaiser's army. It's better equipped than ours and it's huge. Fritz is going to make mincemeat out of Jacques and Tommy. It's not going to be a war, it's going to be a bloodbath and you couldn't wait to jump into it.' Lloyd turned away from his brother in disgust. When he spoke again his voice was terse, and Sali knew he was having a problem controlling his temper. 'Give me one reason, just one reason why you signed your life away? And it had better be a good one.'

'Because the army promised to make a man of me.' Joey's stupid quip fell leadenly into the heavy atmosphere.

'None of your idiotic jokes, not now.'

Seeking support, Joey sat on the sofa besides Sali. She reached for his hand and held it. He looked at her then at his brother. 'I think you know why I joined up, Lloyd.'

'You've thrown your life away over a –' Lloyd remembered that he was talking about Rhian and curbed his language – 'a girl. Joey . . .'

'A special girl, Lloyd. Rhian meant – means – as much to me as Sali means to you or Megan means to Victor.'

'And now it's over between you two you've decided to commit suicide?' Lloyd stated acidly.

'Not all soldiers get killed in battle. I came here before going home because I hoped that you two would understand why I enlisted, and travel up to Tonypandy with me. I want to explain why I did it to Dad, and say goodbye to him, Megan and Victor.'

'I'll drive you, and Sali if she wants to come, up to Tonypandy. I'll even go into Victor's house with you. But when you tell our father what you've done, you'll be on your own. I won't stand by you, and I doubt Victor will either.'

'It's wonderful to see all of you, especially you.' Megan ran up to Joey as soon as he stepped out of the car. 'We've all been so worried about you, and you look so fit, well and suntanned. Isn't it a gorgeous day? Betty and I have been picking the last of the French beans in the kitchen garden while the twins have been enjoying the air in the pram you bought for them, Sali. I had no idea you could get one that big.'

'It was a special order but we didn't have too much trouble tracking it down. We'll come and help you pick beans.' Feeling like a coward, Sali turned to Harry. 'Run ahead and take Bella to see the twins, but be careful not to wake them.'

'They are awake, Harry, so you don't have to be quiet,' Megan called after him.

'Where are Dad and Victor?' Lloyd asked.

'In the milking shed.' Megan frowned at the expression on Lloyd's face. 'Is something the matter?'

'Joey and I'll go and see Victor and Dad.'

'Sali?'

'Sorry to descend on you without any warning,' Sali knew she was talking too quickly, but she didn't want to say anything about Joey in his, or Lloyd's, earshot. 'I hoped you'd invite us for supper. I asked Mari for a hamper.' Sali handed Edyth to Megan and lifted the box Mari had packed from the back of the car.

'You know you don't have to bring food when you come here, Sali. This is a farm, we have plenty.'

'Mari wanted to give you some of her special preserves, two

285

of her fruit cakes and one of her home-cured hams.' Sali dumped the basket on the garden table outside Megan's back door. She watched the men enter the milking shed. 'Besides, this meal is going to be something in the nature of a last supper. Joey enlisted this morning. He's leaving tomorrow.'

'Because of Rhian?' Megan asked.

'I can't think of any other reason why he'd do something so stupid and drastic.' Lloyd wasn't the only one who was having a problem controlling his anger over what Joey had done.

'If I put Edyth in the twin's indoor cradle, will you help me with the tea, please?'

'Of course,' Sali agreed. Megan's approach to Joey's devastating news was sensible and eminently practical. She only hoped that they could continue to ignore the war, until the day he would come marching home – if he survived.

'Aren't you going to say anything, Dad?' Joey had left the milking shed with his father after he had broken the news of his enlistment to him and Victor. They were standing at the entrance to the farmyard, looking over the mountain towards the town.

'What do you want me to say?' Billy asked flatly.

Too old for a beating – not that his parents had given him many, and none undeserved when he'd been growing up – Joey had expected his father to curse, shout and swear when he told him he'd enlisted. But he hadn't been prepared for the awful resignation in his voice.

He wished Lloyd and Victor would finish in the milking shed and join them. But he sensed that his brothers would hide in there until he and his father joined the women in the house. And he couldn't blame them. If he were in their shoes he would do exactly the same thing.

'Anything would be better than nothing, Dad.' Joey felt as though he were tempting the devil. Whatever his father said wasn't going to be good.

'What is there to say, Joey? You've done it. Go back on your word now and they'll shoot you like a dog. Like they did the strikers in Llanelli.'

'This isn't a strike, Dad. This is about peace. About building a better world, and a better future, for all of us.'

'You joined up believing their lies.' Billy's eyes were cold, dead.

'Yes . . . No, I joined up because I wanted to get away from Tonypandy – and Rhian.'

'She's staying in the town?'

'She has another man.'

'That's a reason for joining up that I can at least understand. The thought of you succumbing to this ridiculous patriotism that's infected the country is more than I can stomach.'

'I won't be gone long, Dad.'

'You'll be gone for years, boy, and I dread to think of the state you'll be in if you are one of the lucky ones who comes back. That's my last word on the subject. I'll not say another. Now I suppose we'd better go in and eat this supper the girls have prepared for you.' He grasped Joey's neck and leaned close to him for a moment.

When he released him Joey's collar was wet with his father's tears.

Chapter 17

'MRS WATKIN JONES has arrived, Miss Sali.'

'Will you show her out here, please, Mari?' Sali rose from the rug she'd spread out on the grass for Edyth, and dusted off the daisies Bella had strewn over her hair and skirt. When Julia appeared, she held out her hands and embraced her. 'Julia. I hope I may call you Julia?'

'Of course, and thank you for inviting me to dinner. I hope I'm not too early. You did say five o'clock in your letter.'

'I thought you might like to meet your nieces and nephew before we ate.' Sali picked up the rattle Edyth had dropped on the rug and returned it to her. 'Bella,' she called her eldest daughter who was still picking daisies, 'Come and meet your new Auntie Julia.'

Bella obediently started running, her short, chubby legs pumping up and down like engine pistons.

'Have you a kiss for your Auntie Julia?' Sali prompted. Bella lifted her face expectantly and handed Julia the damp bunch of daisies she was holding.

'For me? Thank you, Bella, and I have something for you.' Julia opened a carrier bag and lifted out two stuffed toy dogs, a dachshund and a Welsh terrier. 'One for you and one for your sister. If you press the lever under their chins, they bark.' She demonstrated as she handed them to Bella.

Bella opened her arms, took the dogs and lisped, 'Thank you, Auntie Julia.'

'And because you're the oldest I think you should decide which is the most suitable for Edyth.'

Bella immediately carried the dogs over to Edyth.

'I wasn't sure what to get Harry. Geraint told me he's seven, so I asked the assistant in the toyshop for suggestions. He thought this might be suitable.' She removed a metal moneybox in the shape of a Humpty Dumpty from the bag.

'I'm sure he'll love it but you really shouldn't have bought so many presents,' Sali protested in embarrassment. 'The children will think it's Christmas and Lloyd and I haven't even bought you and Geraint a wedding present yet.'

'Well, it was hardly a normal wedding.' Julia took a box of Rowntree's chocolate almonds from her bag and laid it on the wrought-iron garden table. 'These are for you and your husband.'

'Thank you.' Sal smiled conspiratorially. 'Shall we open them now?'

Mari emerged from the house with a tray. 'I thought you two ladies might like a glass of my lemonade.'

'Mari, this is my sister-in-law, Mrs Geraint Watkin Jones. Julia, this is our housekeeper and valued member of our family, Mrs Williams.' Mari had become increasingly outspoken of late, and Sali hoped that she would keep her opinions on Geraint and his failings to herself.

'You are so like your sister, our Mrs Williams,' Julia said in surprise.

'She's told me a lot about you over the years, Mrs Watkin Jones. Congratulations on your marriage,' Mari said formally.

'Thank you.'

'I have brought some lemonade for you, Miss Edyth, but I can see that you have new toys.' Mari went over to admire the dogs.

Sali touched her glass to Julia's as they sat at the table. 'It's funny when you think of all the times we've met at the suffrage meetings. I had no inkling that one day you would be my sister-in-law. I do hope that you and Geraint will be happy.'

'Thank you.' Julia was finding it increasingly difficult to respond to people's congratulations on her marriage when it was so obviously one of convenience on both sides.

'Have you seen your father yet?' Sali asked. 'He came to see us the day after you eloped. He was very worried about you.'

'I hope he didn't put you to any trouble.'

'Not at all. He – we were all concerned by the suddenness of your decision. None of us had any idea that you and my brother even knew one another . . .' Realizing how this might be misconstrued, Sali fell silent. She had already heard ladies whispering in the corners of the suffrage meetings, discussing possible reasons for Julia and Geraint's elopement, and none of them had been charitable. Half the ladies thought poverty-stricken Geraint had turned 'poor plain Julia's head' with his good looks. The other half had decided he'd seduced her and there was already a baby on the way.

'I intend to visit my father tomorrow.' Julia opened her handbag and removed a handkerchief. 'Given his reaction when I told him that I knew Geraint and was seeing him, it might be as well that Geraint's enlisted.'

'Your father disapproves of your marrying my brother?'

'He knows that Geraint married me for my money.'

Sali was so shocked she dropped her glass. It fell on to the grass, spilling the contents, but it didn't break.

'After losing his inheritance, Geraint was determined to marry into money. I have money and I'm of age, in fact three years older than him, so there are no parental complications. From Geraint's point of view, it's a perfect arrangement.'

'For Geraint perhaps, but what about you? What on earth will you get out of the arrangement?' Sali was finding it difficult to recover from the shock of Julia's frank appraisal of Geraint's motives.

'Independence, for one thing. Things have been impossible at home lately. I dislike my stepmother's company almost as much as she dislikes mine. I would have preferred to have moved into my own house but it's difficult for a single woman to live alone, even when she can afford her own establishment. I knew that if I asked my father's permission, he would refuse because it would reflect badly on his ability to keep the women in his family in order.'

'Does Geraint know that you're aware he only married you for your money?' Sali asked cautiously.

'Of course. I told him that I wanted us to be always totally honest with one another when I proposed to him.'

'You proposed to him!' Sali repeated in astonishment, wondering what other shocks Julia had in store.

'He said that he intended to ask me to marry him very soon; I didn't want to wait.'

Sali smiled as Bella made both toy dogs bark for Edyth's benefit. 'You bought them the perfect presents.'

'I am so glad they like them. I have no experience of children, but I hope yours will accept and be tolerant of a trainee aunt.'

'I rather think you're already accepted.' Sali fell serious. 'Julia, you do know that relations between Geraint and I have been strained since Lloyd and I married?'

'No, I didn't. Geraint's hardly told me anything at all about you. He's mentioned your brother Gareth a couple of times, but he's said very little about you and your younger sister.'

'Llinos,' Sali murmured absently. 'Do you mind if ask you a personal question?'

'Not at all.'

'Do you love Geraint?'

'I don't even know what love is,' Julia answered evasively. 'No, that's unfair; I do know what it is because my parents were happy until my mother died. My father's second marriage is a disaster.'

'I'm sorry.' The words sounded trite but Sali didn't know what else to say in the face of such unreserved honesty. And her compassion for Edward Larch didn't extend to forgiving him for seducing Rhian when she was at her most vulnerable.

'That's your husband, isn't it?' Julia asked, when a horse and rider approached the house from the direction of the river.

'Yes, and that's my son Harry, and Robert who works for us riding behind him. Harry's having riding lessons and, as Lloyd never learned, he decided to join him.'

'You're lucky.' Julia looked from the girls sprawled on the rug, to the approaching riders. 'You have three lovely children.'

'And a wonderful husband.' Sali didn't know what kind of husband Geraint would make, but she suspected rather a selfish one.

291

'It's strange, Geraint insisted that we make our home in Pontypridd, and yet no sooner do we arrive than he enlists, leaving me to buy a house and furnish it.'

'Geraint told you that he wants to live in Pontypridd?'

'You're surprised?'

'Frankly, yes.'

'He said something about being on hand to oversee your brother's investments because he is in the army.'

'Gareth's just left Sandhurst and stationed with his regiment in Kent, but he wrote to me last week. He's expecting to be sent to France very soon.'

'And you don't want him to go?' Julia questioned intuitively.

Sali shook her head. 'I can't bear the thought of either of my brothers fighting at the Front.'

'And your sister?'

'Is in a school in Switzerland. We haven't heard from her for a month, but that's hardly surprising given what's going on in France. We hope she'll stay there and not attempt to come home until the war is over.'

'I'm not quite sure where I am going to find a house like the one Geraint wants me to buy without building one to his specifications.'

'Geraint has given you details?'

'As detailed as an architect's specifications can be without the drawings.' Julia opened her handbag and handed Sali a notebook. Sali flicked through the pages, in increasing amazement. Geraint had described the outside and inside of Danygraig House meticulously even down to the type of ashtrays in the study, the china patterns he wanted for the dining and breakfast rooms and the style of furniture; mahogany in the dining room, oak in the library, walnut in the two master bedrooms – and satinwood in the others. Feeling as though she was prying, Sali closed the book and handed it back to Julia.

'You are right; it is going to be difficult to find a house like that. Perhaps you ought to look at the ones that are being built just outside town on the Common. One of the builders might be prepared to adapt an existing design.'

'That's a good idea, thank you, I will.'

'Would you like to meet Lloyd and Harry? They're riding into the stable yard.'

'I'd love to,' Julia said enthusiastically.

'Mari, would you keep an eye on the girls for me, please?' Sali asked the housekeeper.

'Their dogs are guarding them,' Mari joked.

Sali led the way around the side of the house. Julia was so forthright and open, she felt as though she had known her for years. And, although her new sister-in-law was undoubtedly plain, what she lacked in looks she more than made up for in integrity and honesty. Whichever way she viewed Geraint's marriage, she couldn't help feeling that, given his recent behaviour, he had definitely married a woman a great deal better than he deserved.

'I hate having to leave you here, Rhian, but for the sake of my practice we'd better keep up the pretence of employer and employee.' Edward left his seat and retrieved his suitcase from the overhead luggage rack. 'You have enough small change to tip the porter to carry your cases from the Cardiff to the Tonypandy train, and to pay a porter and a cab in Tonypandy?'

'I do.' Rhian removed her glove and pulled off the wedding and engagement ring he had given her when he'd met her on Cardiff station at the outset of their holiday. 'You'd better have these back.'

He folded her hand over them. 'I promise you that you will need them again and soon, so keep them safe.' He lifted down the set of matching green leather luggage that he had bought for her and stacked it together with her two new hatboxes next to the door.

She opened her handbag, and tucked the rings into an inner pocket. 'You should never have given me so many things. I feel guilty for accepting them.' She felt more than guilty, she felt as though Edward had 'paid' her with his lavish and extravagant gifts. And that put her in the same bracket as the women who plied their trade at the back of the Empire Theatre.

She had spent a week doing things a woman of her class and

station in life could only dream of on a maid's wage. Travelling first class on a train, spending a week in the best hotel in Brighton and acquiring more clothes and jewellery than she could possibly wear in a year. Edward had also insisted on opening a bank account in her name and depositing a hundred pounds of 'just in case' money. All of which compounded the feeling that she had accepted payment for 'services rendered'.

'I bought you no more than you deserve. That was one of the best and certainly the most relaxing week of my life.' It was true; he hadn't felt so well or rested since Amelia had died. He lifted a corner of the blind that he had drawn on the window and eyed the backs of the buildings coming into view. 'Another few minutes and we'll be in Cardiff. I'll go out ahead of you and send a porter for your luggage. Don't bother to cook tonight, order in dinner from the White Hart. We'll have a quiet evening.'

'You're not staying in Llan House?'

'After this week,' he stooped down and kissed her, 'I never intend to spend a night there again. And you should rest while you can. Don't forget that you're going to be busy next week getting the shop ready for the opening.'

'I'm looking forward to working again.'

'I'm not sure that I am. Another week like last week would have been perfect. Next year we'll go away for a fortnight.'

'That would be greedy.' She smiled.

'It would but it would also be rather wonderful. Have a bath when you go in and dress in the white silk gown and robe, and,' he lifted his eyebrows, 'no underwear.'

Rhian suspected that Edward derived more pleasure from buying her clothes, and choosing what she would wear, than she did. Especially the outfits she wore in the evening when they were together in private. 'Have you any preference for dinner?'

'You know my tastes, the simpler the better.' The train began to slow down. 'Don't open the blinds on the window or the corridor. Someone who knows me may see me walking out, look in and see you.' He jammed his trilby on his head, draped his coat over his arm, picked up his suitcase and left the carriage, sliding the door shut behind him.

A few minutes later the train juddered to a halt. Rhian slipped on the brown silk coat that matched her skirt. When she judged it safe, she went to the window and peered through the side of the blind. She saw Edward leave the train and watched his tall, slim figure stride assertively through the crowd. He hailed a porter and waved him in the direction of the carriage. Then she spotted Harris walking up the steps on to the platform, and ducked back out of sight.

'You wanted a porter, madam?' The porter knocked and opened the door.

'Yes, please.'

He gazed in dismay at the pile of cases next to the door. 'Are all these yours, madam?'

'Six cases and two hatboxes,' she confirmed.

'I'll need help with this lot. Where you going, madam?'

'Tonypandy.'

'All I can say is that I hope someone is meeting you the other end.'

It was then Rhian realized that while she remained with Edward and he insisted on remaining 'respectable', there'd never be any-one meeting her. So far as the world was concerned, she was a single woman without family. And, given her secretive relationship to Edward, which she didn't doubt would eventually lead to gossip, estranged from her friends.

Edward adored her. He couldn't get enough of her company – now. But after Joey she knew what it was to be in love and she was realistic enough to accept that Edward was no more in love with her than she with him. Their relationship was purely physical, rooted and based in lust. They both derived enjoyment from it, but it was also fraught with guilt; his for using her, which was why he insisted on showering her with expensive presents, and hers for accepting them because it made her feel like a whore.

She wondered what he would do if he tired of her. He'd made no secret that there had been others before her. If another girl caught his eye, would he ask her to move out of the rooms so he could move her successor in? Would she lose her position as manager of his shop?

The uncomfortable thought occurred to her that should Edward ever discard her, she would find herself more alone than she had ever been in her life. Without Sali, Megan, Mrs Williams or, given that she was Edward's daughter, even Julia to turn to. Her position as Edward's mistress had effectively isolated her from her previous life, as much as a move to the colonies of Canada or Australia would have.

Lloyd refilled Julia and Sali's wine glasses and then his own. 'Will you carry on working for the suffragette cause, Julia?' he asked.

'Now that the King has given a complete and general amnesty to all suffragettes being held in prison, as well as all strikers convicted of assault, I think the war has temporarily pushed both the suffragette and workers' rights campaigns into abeyance. Besides, my first priority must be to look for a house. I can't live in the New Inn for ever.'

'Why don't you move in with us? Sali asked impulsively. 'We'd love to have you, wouldn't we, Lloyd?'

Lloyd shot her a warning glance and Sali knew what he was thinking. Julia was delightful company but unless she found a place and quickly, Geraint would be likely to spend his leaves with them and that would put them all under enormous strain.

Knowing what they were thinking, Julia asked, 'Is it possible for me to find a house in six weeks? Geraint may or may not get leave then, but he certainly won't get any before.'

'If you don't, you could always move back into the New Inn for however long Geraint's leave lasts, and back here when he returns to his regiment,' Lloyd suggested.

'After getting to know both of you this evening, I am sorry that things are strained between you and my husband.' Julia handed her empty plate to Sali.

'So are we,' Lloyd replied deprecatingly. 'You do know that things between my younger brother and your husband are even worse. On occasion they have become – shall we say – somewhat physical?'

'Geraint did mention it.' Julia allowed herself a small smile.

'So, what do you say, Julia?' Sali asked. 'Would you like to stay with us?'

'I warn you that our service isn't up to the standard of the New Inn but it is cheaper if you don't persist in buying the children toys.' Lloyd smiled.

'Yes, please.' Julia returned his smile, feeling as if she had found herself the second family that she had been looking for.

'Home, sir.'

Edward woke with a start, opened his eyes and to his amazement discovered that his carriage was outside Llan House. 'We're here already, Harris?'

'You fell asleep before we left Cardiff, sir.' Harris opened the door and folded down the steps. 'I'll bring in your luggage.'

'Thank you.'

'Sir?'

'Yes, Harris?' Edward's limbs were heavy from sleep and he moved awkwardly as he stepped down from the carriage.

'I would like to hand in my notice so I can enlist, sir. My brother's going and we want to join up together.'

'This rather leaves me in the lurch, Harris,' Edward said irritably.

'I did wait until you came back, sir. If it had been up to my brother we would have signed up last Monday.'

'Isn't this a sudden and irresponsible decision of yours, Harris?'

'I don't think so, sir. I'll be sorry to leave Llan House, you've been a more than fair employer, but well, the way my brother and me see it, our country needs us more than anyone else right now. So, if it's all right with you, I'd like to pack right away and leave tonight.'

'And the horses, have you thought what's going to happen to them?' Edward was furious at being saddled with practical problems the minute he'd returned to Tonypandy.

'I'll stable them as usual tonight, sir. The oldest Jones boy said he'd see to them in the morning and I've made enquiries. There's room in the stables in town.'

'You've taken a lot upon yourself, Harris.'

'I wanted to make sure that they would be all right, sir. About my wages . . .'

'Come into the house after you've packed.'

'Thank you, sir.'

'Just one thing, Harris. I know that some people would see what you're doing in a heroic light, but I have to be practical. I can't pay your wages while you're in the army.'

'I wouldn't expect you to, sir.'

'And I can't guarantee that you'll have a job to come back to. I'll need to employ another coachman and I can hardly fire him when the war is over, especially if it lasts any length of time.'

'I understand, sir.' Harris returned to the box and drove the carriage around the back of the house.

Edward walked up the steps and Mrs Williams opened the door.

'I trust you had a good journey and a successful trip, sir?'

'I did, Mrs Williams.' Something in the expression on her face made him uneasy. 'Is everything all right?'

'Not exactly, sir. I was hoping to have a word with you.'

Sensing trouble of his wife's making, he braced himself. 'I'll see you in my study in ten minutes, Mrs Williams. Is my wife in?'

'She's at church, sir. Can I get you anything?'

He shivered, suddenly cold after his sleep although the evening was warm. 'Hot coffee, please, Mrs Williams. My letters are in my study?'

'On your desk, sir.'

'Most of the clothes in my suitcase can be sent to the laundry.'

'I'll see to them, sir.'

Edward retreated to his study and poured himself a brandy. He checked the time. Seven o'clock. With luck, Mr Hadley would preach a long sermon, in which case Mabel wouldn't leave church for another half-hour. And as she usually spent another ten minutes gossiping outside afterwards, it would give him ample time to go through his mail, pack clean clothes and be long gone by the time she came home.

A pile of envelopes had been stacked neatly to the side of his blotting pad on his desk. Taking his brandy, he sat in his chair and flicked through them before picking up a silver sword letter-opener that had been a gift from Amelia.

'Your coffee, sir.' Mrs Williams brought a silver pot and porcelain cup in on a tray.

'Bills, bills and more bills.' He studied the grocer's invoice. 'Ground almonds, salted almonds, French cheeses, eight pints of fresh double cream?' He looked questioningly at Mrs Williams.

'The mistress has been doing a great deal of entertaining, sir.'

He opened the fishmonger's bill. 'Caviar, smoked salmon, lobster, shrimp, prawns.' He moved on to the greengrocer's account 'Grapes, asparagus, pineapple, melon . . . The food bill for the last month is the highest it's ever been and for most of that time my wife has been living alone.'

'Yes, sir,' Mrs Williams agreed shortly. 'But if you'd like to see the household accounts, you'll note that the food bill for the servants has been halved.'

'You don't follow the same menu?'

'It's smoked salmon on Melba toast upstairs and bloater paste on dry bread downstairs, sir.'

'Have you complained to my wife?'

'Not only me, sir, but also Cook.'

'And her reaction?'

'She said there has been a great deal of waste in the house, sir.'

'I'll go along with that,' he agreed caustically. 'But from what I can see it's none of yours or Cook's doing.' He took a large envelope from his desk drawer and pushed the bills into it. He intended to check them all meticulously against Mabel's allowance. And if, as he suspected, she'd exceeded it, he'd force her to cut her expenditure until she'd made good the deficit.

'There's something else, sir.'

Edward slipped the envelope into his inside pocket and turned his chair to face the housekeeper. 'If there's any more bad news, Mrs Williams, I may as well hear it all at once.'

'There's been talk in the town, sir. Rhian was seen leaving the house next door to your office.'

'She is renting rooms there and I have offered her a job managing a shop I am opening on the ground floor.' Unable to meet Mrs Williams's penetrating gaze, he turned away.

'It is not for me to criticize, sir—'

'But you are,' he interrupted.

'As I said, sir, there's been talk. I thought you should be aware of it.'

'I was aware that it would start, Mrs Williams. I didn't think you would subscribe to the gossip.'

'I took Rhian on as a trainee when she was barely fifteen, sir. She is a decent girl. I feel responsible for her. I have grown very fond of her—'

'I too, am fond of her, Mrs Williams,' he cut in.

'I wasn't happy when she got herself engaged to Joey Evans, but I could see that she was head over heels in love with him and it was pointless saying anything against him. Then when he showed his true colours and she ran off I don't mind telling you that I was worried sick. When you said she was somewhere safe, I never dreamed for one minute that it was with you.'

'Rest assured, I will take care of her, Mrs Williams,' he said firmly.

'But you can't buy her respectability.' When he didn't comment, she added, 'Can I be blunt, sir.'

'I thought you were being exactly that, Mrs Williams.'

'May and December never work, sir. Half a century and nineteen are thirty years too far apart.'

'There's blunt, Mrs Williams, and there's overstepping the mark with an employer.'

She poured his coffee. 'Not for much longer, sir. I am handing in my notice.'

'Because of Rhian?'

She didn't answer him. 'I have a cousin who owns several houses, including one in Pembrey. The government has taken over a factory down there to make munitions. My cousin has asked me if I'd run his Pembrey house as a boarding house for the workers.'

'And you would prefer to work for him after working for me for nearly thirty years?'

'Frankly, yes, sir. This is no longer a happy house. The mistress has made it plain that she's not satisfied with my work and I am certainly not satisfied with her attitude towards me or the rest of the staff.'

'I see.' Edward couldn't imagine Llan House without Mrs Williams and Harris. 'Happy or not, there is no way that it can be run with just Bronwen, Meriel and Mair.'

'It could if you promoted Bronwen to housekeeper and shut up everything except the drawing and dining room and the mistress's bedroom, sir.'

'Would you consider staying on as a special favour to me, until I can make alternative arrangements.'

'No, sir. I'm needed in the boarding house right away.'

'Surely you can spare four weeks after the length of time you've worked here?'

'No, sir.' Her reply was final and Edward realized there was no point in pressing her further. 'Will there be anything else, sir?'

'No.' Edward rose to his feet. All he wanted to do was pay Harris his wages, plus a week extra in view of his patriotic gesture, pick up clean clothes and take refuge with Rhian in the comfort of his rooms in Dunraven Street before Mabel returned.

Mrs Ball left her rooms when she heard Rhian turn her key in the front door. 'Some letters have come for you, Miss Jones. I've put them in your living room.'

'Thank you, Mrs Ball.' Rhian took her hatbox from the cabman who was unloading her suitcases on to the pavement. 'Could you please carry these up to the second floor?' She handed him a shilling as an incentive.

'I'll watch these, while you go on up,' Mrs Ball offered.

Rhian picked up her second hatbox, ran up the stairs, left the boxes in the bedroom and picked up her letters from the table. One was from Sali; the other was addressed to her in Joey's hand. Lacking the courage to open Joey's, she opened Sali's first.

Dear Rhian,

I want to say so much more to you than I can put in a letter. I love you like a sister and always will. Please come and see us as soon as you can. If it isn't easy for you to get away, let me know when it will be convenient for me to call.

The children miss you and can't wait to see you. I warn you that there is no way they, Lloyd or I will allow you to leave our family,
    Love as always,
    Sali

'Where do you want these suitcases, Miss?'

Rhian stared blankly at the cabman.

'The cases, miss?' He held one of them up.

'Please put them in the bedroom, it's the next door on the left.'

While he returned downstairs to fetch the rest of her luggage, she pushed her thumb under the flap of the second envelope and opened it.

Dear Rhian,

You don't have to worry about seeing me around Tonypandy because I have enlisted. If you think that I have joined the army because of what happened between us, you'd be absolutely right. I don't wish you ill, but I'll never understand why you wouldn't marry me after reading Tonia's letter. It will be a long time, if ever, before I forgive you,
    Joey

The cabman carried the last of the cases upstairs and left. Rhian was only vaguely aware of his presence and the front door closing a few minutes later.

She sank down on a chair. And that was where Edward found her an hour later, dry-eyed, white-faced and still holding Joey's letter.

'I'll have three boxes of safety matches.' Mrs Williams dropped four pennies and a halfpenny on the counter of the tobacconist's that Rhian had been managing for over three weeks.

Flustered, Rhian turned her back to the housekeeper and looked along the shelves although she kept all the safety matches under the counter.

'Rhian?'

'Yes, Mrs Williams.' She turned and looking down, lifted three boxes on to the counter, took the fourpence halfpenny and dropped it into the cash drawer.

'Can we go to a tea shop for half an hour?' Mrs Williams asked.

'I'm not sure . . .' Although Mrs Ball was standing beside her behind the counter and there were no other customers in the shop, Rhian made a great show of looking at her watch.

'I can take over here, Miss Jones,' Mrs Ball offered in response to a signal from Mrs Williams. 'We won't get busy for another hour or so until the shops start their lunch hour.'

'Then we'll go next door, Rhian.' Mrs Williams went to the door and held it open.

Realizing that the housekeeper wasn't going to take no for an answer, Rhian unbuttoned her khaki overall, went into the stock-room and hung it on a peg. Picking up her coat, hat and gloves, she returned to the shop. Mrs Williams was still holding the door. She walked through it.

'Tea for two, and two chocolate éclairs,' Mrs Williams ordered the waitress in the tea shop without asking Rhian what she wanted.

Rhian sat at a table and, not knowing what to say, waited for Mrs Williams to open the conversation.

'Did Mr Larch tell you that I'd handed in my notice?' Mrs Williams began.

'Yes, he did. Did you get my letter?' Rhian asked tentatively.

'Yes, and what was all that stuff and nonsense you wrote me and Mrs Evans about understanding if we didn't want to see you again?'

'My circumstances have changed,' Rhian said quietly, aware that one or two of the women sitting around them were staring.

'So Mr Larch told me. But he's tight-lipped when it comes to strangers, and gossip doesn't constitute hard fact. From what I've heard, whatever's being said about you hasn't affected trade in the shop you manage.'

'It hasn't,' Rhian confirmed. 'Mr Larch is pleased with the turnover.'

'I bet he is pleased and not only with the turnover.'

Rhian steeled herself to look at the housekeeper after their tea and cakes arrived. 'Are you leaving Llan House because of me?'

'Why do you think I would do that?'

Rhian lowered her voice. 'What happened isn't Mr Larch's fault.'

'I suppose it's yours.'

Rhian nodded. 'I took the easy way out of a difficult situation.'

'Do you really believe that?' the housekeeper questioned searchingly.

Rhian picked up a sugar lump with silver tongs and dropped it into her tea. 'What's done is done.'

'No doubt Joey Evans is saying much the same thing.'

'You know someone who's heard from him?' Rhian asked eagerly.

'Only Mrs Evans, and as we didn't discuss him other than to comment on his enlisting when she called in on me yesterday afternoon, I don't have any fresh news, not about him. I wanted to see you to give you this.' Mrs Williams pushed a folded piece of paper across the table. 'It's my address, in Pembrey. I'm going to run a boarding house for my cousin. It's a nice spot by the sea. So if you fancy a holiday, or need a friend, or just somewhere to stay for a while, you know where to find me.'

'Thank you.' Rhian raised her eyes to meet the housekeeper's gaze. 'I didn't expect everyone to be so kind. You, Sali, even Victor and Megan have written to me.'

'Yes, well.' Embarrassed by being thought of as kind, Mrs Williams spread her napkin on her lap and picked up her cake fork. 'Eat up. A lot needs doing before I leave Llan House in the morning so I can't waste all day sitting here talking to you. I'd rather do that later on when you come and visit me.'

Chapter 18

JULIA LEFT THE train at Tonypandy and walked briskly towards Dunraven Street. When she reached the area in front of the station reserved for cabs, she saw the driver of a brake help Mrs Williams on to the pavement before proceeding to unload an assortment of suitcases, bags and boxes. The housekeeper was preoccupied with paying the man and Julia had to tap her shoulder to gain her attention.

'Miss Julia!' The housekeeper embraced her and dropped her purse.

'Here, let me.' Julia picked up the purse and the coins that had rolled from it.

'I am so glad to see you. I thought I'd have to leave without saying goodbye.' Mrs Williams brushed aside a tear, took her purse from Julia and handed the driver a sixpence.

'You're going on holiday?'

'I'm leaving, Miss Julia.'

'Tonypandy?' Julia asked in astonishment.

'And Llan House for good,' Mrs Williams added, to ensure that Julia understood the situation.

'I am so sorry to hear that, Mrs Williams. Father will miss you.'

'So he says,' the housekeeper said cynically, 'but I can count on one hand the number of times he came home in the last month, and then it was only to pick up clean clothes or books.' She lowered her voice although the driver had already returned to his cab. 'He hasn't eaten a meal or slept in Llan House since he came back from a trip away in August. Excuse me.' She hailed a porter who was standing, hands in pockets with his back to the wall.

'I do hope your decision didn't have anything to do with my leaving home,' Julia said softly.

'A little.' Mrs Williams pointed out her luggage to the porter, who took one look at it and disappeared to fetch a trolley. 'If I'd known where to find you, I would have written. I really do need to talk to you, Miss Julia,' she said seriously.

'We could go to the Ladies' waiting room,' Julia suggested.

Mrs Williams glanced at the fob watch pinned to her lapel and gazed at the sea of luggage around her. 'I have barely ten minutes and it will take me that long to get these on the train, even with the porter's help. Have you come to Tonypandy to see your father?'

'Yes, but he isn't expecting me.'

'He took your elopement hard,' Mrs Williams reproached. 'So much has happened since you left, but I dare not miss this train. I'm not just going to Cardiff. I have to change trains there for Swansea and again in Swansea for Burryport.'

'Why Burryport?'

'I have taken a position as housekeeper in a Pembrey boarding house owned by a cousin of mine.'

'He's a lucky man.'

The housekeeper frowned. 'There are things that you really should know—'

'My father can tell me about them,' Julia interrupted.

'I doubt he'll tell you anything, Miss Julia.'

The housekeeper looked so grave Julia made a swift decision. 'Do you have your ticket?'

'No, and I'd better get one.' Mrs Williams turned to the porter who was piling her luggage on to a trolley.

Julia walked to the ticket office, opened her purse and slid a sovereign across the counter. 'One first-class single to Burryport, please, and one first-class return to Cardiff.'

'Not first-class, Miss Julia,' Mrs Williams protested.

'Call it a goodbye present, Mrs Williams.' Julia pressed the ticket into the housekeeper's hand. 'And if you want to talk, we will get more privacy in a first-class carriage.'

Sali smiled when she read the letter from her sister. If she hadn't seen it in black and white in Llinos's own hand she might not have believed it.

Dear Sali,

Just to let you know that I am safe and well. I have left the finishing school and no longer need an allowance from Harry's estate because I have accepted a salaried position as an interpreter with the French High Command. All those French, German and Italian lessons have proved good for something, and I am glad to be in a position to be able to contribute to the war effort. There is no need to worry about my safety as I am miles behind enemy lines and, as I work with the top-ranking military personnel, we are kept well away from any danger . . .

'A letter from Master Gareth?' Mari asked, recognizing the French postmark.

'Llinos,' Sali answered. 'She is working as an interpreter for the French army.'

'Miss Llinos, working?' Mari placed a sceptical emphasis on the last word.

'She says that she is glad to do her bit for the war effort.'

'And this wouldn't have anything to do with the officers working for the French army?'

'I've no doubt there's a few bachelors among them,' Sali commented wryly.

'And knowing Miss Llinos, she's already sorted the wheat from the chaff, or should I say the well-to-do from the poor. Well, I've always said that one would land on her feet.'

'So you have,' Sali agreed.

'But you didn't always believe me.'

'The way Llinos and Gareth behaved after Uncle Morgan lost Father's money, can you blame me?'

Mari cleared an empty teacup from Sali's desk. 'No word from Master Gareth or your brother-in-law yet?'

Sali shook her head. 'I would have told you if Gareth had written and I'm surprised to hear you ask after Joey.'

'Yes, well, whatever I think of what he did to poor Rhian, I don't wish the boy ill,' Mari sniffed.

307

'What happened was as much her fault as his, Mari. From what I can gather, Rhian saw Joey with Tonia and assumed the worst.'

'So my sister wrote in her last letter. She said the whole of Tonypandy is talking about it, and what Rhian has become.'

'That is just gossip, Mari,' Sali said firmly, in the hope of putting an end to the conversation.

'You don't believe that, Miss Sali, any more than I do.'

'Rhian's young——'

'And she's made a very wrong decision on the rebound. Mr Larch is old enough to be her grandfather let alone father.'

'Not quite, Mari, and whatever she did is done now. She needs our love and support more than ever and when she comes here again, as I hope she will very soon, I trust that you will treat her no differently than you did before.'

'You'd invite her to this house?' Mari was clearly shocked at the thought.

'Of course.'

'You're more forgiving than most, that's all I can say, Miss Sali. And don't go forgetting that you've daughters to consider.'

'Who both adore Rhian,' Sali reminded the housekeeper forcefully.

Realizing that she wasn't going to alter Sali's opinion, Mrs Williams changed the subject. 'You'll send my best wishes and congratulations to Miss Llinos on her new job when you write back, Miss Sali.'

'I will, Mari.'

'Just one more thing, Miss Sali.'

Sali looked up, expecting Mari to pass another comment on Rhian.

'Will you be in for lunch?'

'Not today, Mari. I have to go up to the Tonypandy store to see how the assistant manager is getting on.'

'Joey's left a big hole behind him.'

'And not only in the store, Mari,' Sali murmured thoughtfully, gazing at the photograph of Lloyd and his brothers on her desk.

'You're sure about this, Mrs Williams?' Julia asked carefully.

'Your father didn't even try to deny it when I told him there was gossip about him and Rhian. Everyone in the town knows that they are both living in the building he owns next door to his office. And she's managing a tobacconist's he's opened on the ground floor.'

Julia leaned back against the seat of the train. She had slipped the porter an extra sixpence to find an empty carriage and so far they were the sole occupants. 'I knew he was unhappy with my stepmother – but Rhian. She is only nineteen!'

'And your father is nearly fifty,' Mrs Williams pointed out superfluously.

Before her mother's death, her father had been a hero to Julia. If they had drifted apart afterwards, she felt it was down to the almost insupportable grief of losing someone they had both loved so dearly. The thought of him living as man and wife with Rhian appalled her. She felt physically ill when she imagined her father embracing, kissing – or worst of all – sharing a bed with Rhian. It was a complete betrayal of all the ideals about living a decent life that he had instilled in her.

'When I saw Rhian yesterday, she insisted that your father hadn't seduced her,' Mrs Williams revealed.

'You asked her outright?'

'More or less.'

'And you believe her?' Julia said acidly.

'From all the accounts I've heard, she was devastated when she found her young man in the arms of his cousin. Most people in Tonypandy now seem to believe that Mr Evans's cousin set it up to look as though there was something between them when there wasn't. But the truth hardly matters now that Rhian is with your father and her young man has joined the army.'

'And everyone in Tonypandy knows that she and Father are living together?'

'There's gossip because they live in the same building, but there's no real proof. Everyone knows that your father split the house next door to his office into three sets of rooms, and he put a woman in one set to take care of the building. For all that anyone knows, Rhian could be in another set of rooms and he could be living in the third, so no one can say anything against either of them for definite. But it is common knowledge that he has left Llan House and rarely visits there except to fetch something in the middle of the day when it is more likely than not that your stepmother will be out.'

'How is my stepmother?' Julia was anxious to change the subject. She was glad that she had met Mrs Williams and had decided to accompany her to Cardiff. The news that her father was living with Rhian had come as a shock, but it would have been much more of one if she had discovered it accidentally.

'Mrs Larch is the same as she was when you were living at home, Miss Julia. All she thinks about is her precious Ladies' Circle. I for one don't blame your father for not wanting to live with her.'

'Does she know about my father and Rhian?'

'She knows that your father has set up a separate establishment in the rooms next door to his office. As for Rhian, I couldn't tell you. But she is unhappy about your father's decision to live apart from her.'

'She must be sorry to be losing you as housekeeper.'

'If she is, she hasn't shown any signs of it to me. Harris has left as well; he enlisted in the second week in August.'

'You'll all be hard to replace.'

'Your father isn't replacing any of us. He has sold the horses and carriage and bought himself a car that he garages behind his office. And he's promoted Bronwen to housekeeper. He's shut up all the rooms in the house except for the dining and drawing rooms, the servants' quarters and your stepmother's bedroom.'

'I almost feel sorry for Mrs Larch,' Julia murmured absently.

'Pardon?' Mrs Williams stared at her as if she had taken leave of her senses.

'She told me that the life she had in Tonypandy wasn't what my father had promised her.'

'Your father didn't get what she promised him in church when she agreed to be his wife either,' Mrs Williams observed caustically. 'And what did she expect? To be presented at court. Didn't she know that there isn't one in Tonypandy?'

'I think she expected to be the centre of attention.'

'Your father did more for her than most men would have done for a second wife. He let her refurnish and redecorate the entire house, and buy whatever she wanted in the way of clothes and knick-knacks. And in return she behaved like a nun. Someone should have told her before she married that when a man gives all his worldly goods he has the right to expect a bit of loving kindness in return.'

Julia thought of her own unconsummated marriage. She had given all her worldly goods and received nothing in return. But then, unlike Mabel with her father, Geraint had never even tried to pretend to love her.

'How are you enjoying married life, Miss Julia?' Mrs Williams enquired as if she'd guessed her thoughts.

'Geraint has enlisted,' Julia divulged. 'I'm looking for a house for us and in the meantime I am living with my sister-in-law.'

'Miss Sali?' Mrs Williams smiled for the first time since they had met. 'My sister thinks the world of her, and from what I've seen she is a lovely lady. You will be all right with her.'

'I am.' Julia managed to return the housekeeper's smile.

'Are you happy, Miss Julia? But then, what am I saying? No bride could be happy with her husband gone to war. Well, I'll say the same to you as I said to Rhian: if you want a holiday, or a break, or a few days away, come and see me. There's lovely country around the boarding house.' She opened her handbag. 'Let me give you the address, but it might be best to write and let me know if you do decide to visit. If Rhian is with me, you might not want to stay. Not the way things are between her and your father.'

'Second post, Mr Larch.' Miss Arnold set Edward's mid-morning cup of tea on to his desk and stacked the letters next to it.

Edward gazed at the pile of buff-coloured envelopes. When he had returned from Brighton with Rhian, he had arranged to have all his post re-directed from Llan House to his office.

He picked up the first envelope, slit it open and removed an unpaid bill from Gwilym James's ladieswear department that

311

exceeded his wife's monthly allowance. Sorting out the rest of the bills, he consigned them to his inside pocket. He really couldn't afford to put off confronting Mabel any longer.

The last envelope he looked at was addressed in a strange hand and bore the crest of Gerald's public school. He felt horribly guilty and neglectful. He and his son had never been the best of correspondents but their sporadic contact had become even more sparse and perfunctory since last Christmas.

> Dear Mr Larch,
>
> I regret alarming you, but Gerald, along with five other senior boys from his house, left school sometime late last night and have not returned. The boys were present at final roll call before the doors were shut for the night, and found to be absent at breakfast this morning.
>
> They left a note in one of their studies stating that they intended to enlist. Please be assured that we are doing all we can to trace them. The headmaster has forwarded their names and correct ages to the relevant authorities. However, as the local recruiting offices are not demanding to see birth certificates or proof of age, they could have volunteered under false names, so it may take us some time to find out if they have in fact enlisted, and if so, what regiment they have joined.
>
> I repeat, we are doing everything in our power to find them. I trust that you will contact me immediately should you hear from Gerald. I will keep you informed of any new developments,
>
> Yours faithfully,
> Anthony Mayfield, Housemaster

Edward gazed at the photograph of Amelia, Julia and Gerald on his desk. Gerald had been fifteen when he had taken it. He compared the way Gerald looked there to when he had last seen him. He was tall and broad-shouldered; any recruiting sergeant anxious to boost his regiment's numbers would accept the boy without asking too many questions.

But that didn't alter the fact that Gerald wouldn't be seventeen until January. The fool! The damned stupid fool!

But how much was he to blame when his son's last holiday at home had been blighted by the strain between him and Mabel and embarrassment at Mabel's assault on Rhian. He couldn't even remember the last real conversation they'd had together. He tried to recall the content of the last letter he'd received from his son. It had been a thank you for sending him a cheque to cover his term's allowance, after the family Gerald had summered with in France had been forced to cut their holiday short because of the war.

He opened his desk drawer and rummaged through the small pile of personal correspondence he kept there. Notes from Amelia, the letter Julia had left on her pillow before she'd eloped. He found Gerald's letter and read it again.

> *Dear Father,*
>
> *Thank you for the cash and the extra ten pounds, which I will put to good use. France was excellent and we were sorry to have to leave three weeks before we planned to, but we are now back in Windsor and Michael's mother and housekeeper are helping us pack for school. I am replacing everything that I have grown out of and the store has agreed to forward the bills to you. Hope that is agreeable.*
>
> *See you at Christmas. Give Julia my love.*
>
> *Your son,*
>
> *Gerald*

'Mr Edwards, sir,' Miss Arnold tapped his door. 'Your wife is here.'

'Have I any appointments?' he barked brusquely, concern for Gerald and anger at Mabel's spending making him abrupt.

'Not until eleven-thirty, sir.'

'Show her in, and make my apologies to the clients if we run late.'

'Yes, sir.'

'Mabel, take a seat.' He didn't rise when his wife entered his office.

Miss Arnold hesitated at the door. 'Would you like tea, Mrs Larch?'

'No, she wouldn't, Miss Arnold. Close the door behind you.' Edward studied his wife. She looked tired, her face was drawn and there were dark circles beneath her eyes. He felt that he should have a certain amount of sympathy for her after leaving her to live

313

alone in Llan House, but after reading the letter from Gerald's housemaster all his compassion was for himself. 'To what disaster do I owe this unexpected pleasure?' he enquired frostily.

'I need to talk to you, Edward. You never come home, you never—'

'I am well aware of my faults, Mabel. There is no need to catalogue them.'

She swallowed hard and straightened her back. 'Bronwen and Cook gave me a month's notice this morning. I contacted the Labour Exchange but they said they have no suitable replacements. I need your permission to advertise.'

'It's not worth advertising, you won't get any applicants.'

'I pay the going rate—'

'*I* pay the going rate, Mabel,' he corrected her heavily. 'But you treat servants like slaves. Word gets around, especially in a place like Tonypandy. And with the employment situation the way it is, any intelligent, capable woman can earn twice as much in a month in a factory as I pay in a year.'

'What factory?' she asked blankly.

'I suggest you read a newspaper, Mabel. It might prove an enlightening experience.' He picked up a copy of *The Times* from his desk and tossed it towards her. 'With so many men answering Kitchener's call there is an acute shortage of labour. Women are needed to take their place in factories, offices and shops and that's without the recruitment drive for munitions and land workers.'

'What will I do if I can't get anyone?' She looked horrified at the prospect.

'Return to Carmarthen,' he suggested.

'I will not go back to my father's house.'

'The only alternative is for you to do your own dirty work.'

'Are you suggesting that I scrub floors, wash clothes and clean the house myself?'

'Other women do it.' He thought of Rhian, walking upstairs to cook their meals and clean their rooms after putting in a full day's work in the shop. He had wanted Mrs Ball to do their cleaning. But Rhian had insisted she didn't mind doing it, and it gave them more privacy if she, not Mrs Ball, did most of it.

'You can't expect me to—'

'I don't expect you to do anything, Mabel,' he cut in ruthlessly. 'I'd like you to return to Carmarthen but I have no desire to argue with you about it. And, as you're here, you've saved me a trip to Llan House. I gave you an allowance and I warned you to stick to it.' He removed the bills from his pocket. 'On my rough calculations you have already exceeded it by fifty pounds this year.' He had pulled the figure from the air, but she didn't contradict him. 'If you do not retrench over the coming months to pay back your overspend, I will place that newspaper advertisement I warned you about, and absolve myself of all liability for your debts.'

'All I have done is a little entertaining. You want me to live like a nun?'

'I thought you were.'

She blushed hotly. 'I offered—'

'Too little, too late, Mabel. And you have done a lot more than "a little entertaining". You forget that I have seen the bills. And it is not only entertaining, you have also been shopping.' He threw the bundle of envelopes at her and they fell, scattering over his desk and the floor.

Her face contorted, ugly in rage and intensity. 'I know all about Rhian,' she hissed. 'An uneducated maid. A slip of the girl younger than your own daughter—'

'As you are, Mabel.'

'You're perverted, disgusting, dirty—'

'If you force me to call for help to eject you from my office, that would give the Ladies' Circle something to talk about.'

'You wouldn't dare!'

He sat back in his chair and crossed his arms. 'Please leave, Mabel. Now.'

'Christmas is in a couple of weeks. You have to come home then.'

'I won't.'

'Gerald—'

'Has enlisted.'

'He's not old enough.'

'It's amazing what my children will do to get away from you,

Mabel: Gerald enlisting, Julia eloping.' Tired of arguing with her, longing for the peace and quiet of his sitting room next door so he could think out what he should do about Gerald, he said, 'My next appointment will be here any minute.'

'You still haven't told me if I can advertise for replacement staff for the house.'

'If you must, but as I said, you won't get any takers.' He watched her leave the chair. 'Go back to your father for Christmas. Stay there and I'll clear your bills, Mabel.'

'I can't go back because my parents are coming to spend Christmas in Llan House.'

'Your father won't leave his parish.'

'His curate is taking over. And I have invited the entire Ladies' Circle and their husbands, over fifty people, for supper on Boxing Day.'

'How brave of you without a cook or housekeeper.'

'I'll get them and I need a host, Edward. Let me down, and I'll see that your business suffers.'

'I'll sell it before I spend another night under the same roof as you.'

She glared at him for a moment, then left, slamming the door behind her. Edward sat, staring at the door before picking up his pencil. He opened a notebook and wrote a heading across the top of the first page: *Last Will and Testament*.

'Come on, Rhian, come to Pembrey with us,' Bronwen coaxed. She and Cook had called into the tobacconist's unexpectedly at midday and persuaded Rhian to join them in the tea shop for a lunch of sandwiches, tea and cakes.

'We're going to lodge in Mrs Williams's cousin's boarding house,' Cook added persuasively. 'It will be all of us together, just like old times.'

'Except we'll be earning decent money for the first time in our lives,' Bronwen crowed. 'Jinny wrote and told me that she made two pounds seven shillings last week. And Mrs Williams only charges seventeen shillings and sixpence a week for full board, lodge and washing. Think of all the money we'll save.'

'Your sister Jinny is working in the munitions factory in Pembrey?' Rhian asked.

'Yes, she had her baby adopted.'

'No, she didn't.' Cook contradicted. 'She left it in the workhouse.'

'It could be adopted by now,' Bronwen countered.

'But the munitions factory just doesn't take on anyone,' Cook explained. 'You have to be British born of British parents, physically fit and have good eyesight. Bronwen and I had physical examinations last week.'

'And we both passed with flying colours. But then, if we weren't fit, we'd be dead the way the mistress works us,' Bronwen complained. 'I swear she's got ten times worse since we've given in our notice. Old witch!'

'And you have to supply four references,' Cook continued. 'Mrs Williams and the doctor have given us two and I asked the minister and my old schoolteacher for the others.'

'Not Mrs Larch?' Rhian poured herself another cup of tea from the pot on the table.

'No fear.' Cook opened her ham sandwich and spread mustard over it. 'We were frightened she'd give us a bad one in the hope they'd turn us down. She hasn't had a single application from anyone who wants to fill our posts.'

'She'll be left all alone with Mair, that's if she stays.' Bronwen added another lump of sugar to her tea. 'And there's no way that girl can run Llan House on her own.'

Rhian wondered if Edward knew what was happening in Llan House. He'd hardly mentioned the house or Mrs Larch in months but then he had been preoccupied with trying to find Gerald. Not that he or any of the masters at Gerald's school had succeeded in tracing any of the boys who'd enlisted.

'Jinny said it's hard work. They have to work a full ten-hour day, starting at eight in the morning and grafting right through to half past six at night with only an hour for lunch and no other breaks at all. But they work two weeks on and one week off and get paid for the one off.'

'She wrote and told Bronwen she'd turned yellow,' Cook laughed.

Wondering if Cook was joking, Rhian looked to Bronwen for confirmation.

'It's something in the stuff they use to make the pellets or put in the shells. Gunpowder, or TNT or whatever it is, turns their skin yellow and their hair gold and apparently it doesn't wash off,' Bronwen corroborated. 'It's even caused some of the girls to break out in a rash.'

'If you worked there your hair would probably turn green, Rhian.' Cook finished her tea and stacked her cup on her empty plate. 'Jinny said in her letter that the girls with fair or grey hair go that colour.'

'If that's the case, then it might be as well I'm not going with you. I don't fancy green hair.' Rhian reached out impulsively and gripped Bronwen's hand. 'I know I haven't seen much of you lately, but I'm going to miss you when you've gone.'

'You did well to get out of Llan House when you did.' Cook earned herself a disapproving look from Bronwen. They had argued for some time about whether or not they should say goodbye to Rhian. Eventually, Bronwen had agreed they could go, but only on condition that Cook didn't mention Rhian's situation with Mr Larch.

'You will write to me,' Rhian pleaded as they left the table.

'Of course, and we'll call in the shop again before we leave town,' Bronwen promised. 'But we have to get back to the house before Mrs Larch comes home from her shopping trip.'

'Why?' Cook demanded mutinously. 'The worse she can do is sack us, and I wouldn't mind going down to Pembrey a week early. I know it's freezing cold but Mrs William says there are lovely walks around there and you can see the sea from the windows of the house.'

'You've lost weight, Cook,' Rhian said in surprise when her friend put on her coat.

'The way Mrs Larch has cut down on our rations, we're all shadows of what we were.' Cook kissed Rhian's cheek. 'And, as from the end of this week, I won't be Cook any more, just plain Meriel, munitions worker. I can't wait.'

Bronwen kissed Rhian's cheek. 'Take care of yourself and if you want to do your bit for the war, you know where to come.'

'You'll be the first one I'll write to.'

Rhian went to the coat rack and retrieved her coat. The tobacconist's was doing well and she and Edward had slipped into a comfortable domesticity. But much as she hated to admit it, even to herself, her life was beginning to pall. Apart from the customers, who were friendly enough but barely passing acquaintances, she never saw anyone to talk to other than Edward and Mrs Ball. Her days were: leave bed in the morning, bath, make breakfast and eat it with Edward, go from rooms to shop to serve customers until lunchtime when she and Edward ate together and, at the end of the day, shop to rooms to cook, clean and return to bed.

She was hungry for more news than Megan and Sali put in their letters. To be specific, news about Joey. She needed to know that he was if not safe, at least well. But despite Sali's letters and invitations, she lacked the courage to go down to Ynysangharad House and ask after him. And not just the courage, she reflected as she made her way back to the shop. The only day off she had was Sunday, and Edward commandeered every minute of that.

'Edward?' His junior partner, Cedric, knocked the door and walked in. 'Bad news?' he asked, seeing the stricken look on Edward's face.

'Another letter from my son.' Edward folded it carefully and placed it in his desk drawer.

'He still hasn't said where he is?'

'No, but the postmark is London.'

'Then he hasn't been shipped to the Front.'

'Or he has, and sent this back with a soldier returning on leave.' Edward closed the drawer. 'You wanted to see me?'

Cedric set the papers he was holding on to Edward's desk. 'I've been through the rough draft of your new will and the instructions for transferring ownership of Llan House and the property next door.'

'And?' Edwards looked enquiringly at him.

'It's not straightforward, Edward, but then it never is for a man in your situation.'

'It's perfectly simple; all I want to do is cut my wife from my will and leave the bulk of my estate to Rhian Jones.'

'Who is your mistress,' Cedric said pointedly.

'Our relationship does not have to be detailed in my will.'

'But you can bet your last farthing it will be by the Pandy rumour machine. Have you thought of the scandal this will cause should your wife contest this document, which any reputable solicitor will advise her to do after your death?' Cedric tapped the papers. 'And it's not just your wife. You may want to give your son and daughter Llan House and the furniture now, but they won't get a penny piece under the terms of this new will.'

'Because they each have their own trust fund and are wealthier than me.'

Cedric made a note on the top sheet of paper. 'It might be as well to mention that in the will. Also, this business of signing the house next door over to Rhian now—'

'Cedric, I have known you all your professional life and my acquaintance with the law is on a par with yours. I know there is no difficulty other than the possibility of Mabel contesting this will, so please, tell me, what is your problem?'

'Can I be frank?'

'I'd prefer it to all this procrastinating over what may or may not happen,' Edward snapped irritably.

'Your mistress is a ripe little piece and I can understand why you are besotted with her. Where do you think I buy my cigars these days?' Cedric took two from his top pocket and tossed Edward one.

'First, I don't like you talking about Rhian that way and second I'm not besotted with her any more than a man should be with his legal wife. We lead a perfectly normal domestic life next door.'

'In sin.'

'Some may call it that.' Edward was finding it increasingly difficult to control his temper.

'She is thirty years younger than you.'

'So?' Edward challenged.

'Hasn't it occurred to you that she is with you only for what she can coax and wheedle out of you?'

'You don't know Rhian.'

'No? She was a maid, a nothing, a nobody, a skivvy without a penny piece to her name. Then she takes up with you and she finds herself in the lap of luxury. And before you say another word, I've seen the way she dresses and the jewellery she wears. And that's without your little jaunt to Brighton.'

'How do you know about that?'

'You can't sneeze without someone in Tonypandy finding out about it, Edward. You were seen.'

'By who?'

'Does it matter? The fact remains that you have bought this girl—'

'I resent your inference. I have given Rhian no more than I gave Amelia and a damn sight less than Mabel takes.' Edward's anger finally reached boiling point.

'All I'm saying is, take some time to think about what you're doing, before you sign over the house and shop to her. When word of this gets out, people are going to see you as an old fool and her as a golddigger. And that's without your new will.'

'I have the right to dispose of my assets any way I choose.'

'The way you have drawn this up, your wife doesn't even have the legal right to reside in Llan House during her lifetime.'

'Yes, she does.'

'At Julia and Gerald's discretion.'

'Which is perfectly fair. I want to sign the house over to them with vacant possession.'

'And Mabel?'

'I hope to get her out after Christmas.'

'You haven't succeeded in getting her out so far, so what makes you think you'll be successful in getting her out a week or so from now?'

'Her parents are visiting her at the moment. All the servants have left except for one young girl, so they had to bring their own housekeeper down with them. When they leave, Mabel will be on her own. She couldn't cope with a reduced staff; I can't see her coping with none.' Edward lit the cigar Cedric had given him.

'And if Julia and Gerald don't want to live in the house right away?'

'I'll shut it up and hand them the keys. I no longer want the responsibility of running the place or paying the bills that come with it. But I will continue to pay Mabel an allowance.'

'You give your children the house, Rhian next door and you're left with your share of this business, your stocks, bonds and cash and nothing else. Not even the legal right to live next door should Rhian throw you out.'

'She won't.'

'Are you sure about that?'

'Absolutely. That girl will do anything for me.'

'Anything?' Cedric leered suggestively.

'Anything,' Edward said harshly, his temper rising again at Cedric's tone.

'I'd give a hundred pounds for a couple of hours with her in your bedroom next door.'

Edward left his chair and hit Cedric soundly on the jaw. His partner's chair rocked and toppled over, leaving Cedric lying on his back with his legs in the air.

'For God's sake, Edward, you could have killed me.' Cedric clambered awkwardly to his feet and rubbed his head. 'She is a tart—'

'Rhian is my wife in all but name, Cedric. Go and draft my will and the transfer papers for next door and Llan House now, or I'll terminate our partnership before close of business.'

Chapter 19

RHIAN WRAPPED AN ounce of tobacco in a sheet of brown paper, folded the edges and tied it into a neat parcel. She smiled at the toothless old man standing in front of the counter.

'There you go, Mr Jenkins, one ounce of Skipper, navy cut. We'll see you next week.'

'You will. Ta, love.' He opened the door, setting the bell ringing as he left the shop.

'I think you have an admirer there, Miss Jones.' Mrs Ball carried a box of Taddy's Pigaroon cigarettes from the back storeroom and replenished the shelves. 'I can't believe how quick the stock goes down.'

'We shouldn't complain when it keeps us in work, Mrs Ball.' Rhian smiled again when the housekeeper from the vicarage walked in. 'Good morning, Mrs Davies, you've come to pick up your weekly order?'

Mrs Davies looked down her long nose at Rhian. 'That is why I'm here, Miss Jones.'

Rhian took her look of superiority to mean that the staff and family at the vicarage disapproved of her, but not enough to boycott the shop. Edward's decision to undercut his competitors in the town had paid dividends when it came to trade. He hadn't reduced the profits by much, but it had been amazing what a halfpenny and in some cases, a farthing reduction on a pack of cigarettes, ounce of tobacco or packet of cigars had accomplished in attracting custom.

'Four ounces of Hignetts smoking mixture, sixty Glory's Reward cigarettes and ten best Havana cigars.' Rhian lifted the parcel she'd already wrapped from the shelf.

'We'll expect your bill at the end of the month, Miss Jones.'

Rhian scribbled a note on the pad she kept beside the cash drawer but she waited until the housekeeper had left the shop before updating the ledger. Experience had taught her that customers disliked her detailing their purchases in front of them because it implied distrust. The door opened again and Edward's messenger boy ran in. He pushed an envelope across the counter.

'It's urgent, Miss Jones.'

Rhian opened the envelope and read the note it contained.

'You have to go?' Mrs Ball asked. Rhian usually received two or three 'urgent' messages during the week that necessitated her absence for half an hour and sometimes longer.

'I'm sorry, Mrs Ball. The lunchtime rush will start in ten minutes.'

'I'll manage,' the elderly widow said philosophically.

'Mr Ashton will be in this afternoon to look at pipes. Can you dust the cases for me, please?' Rhian asked diffidently. After years of service she found it difficult to give direct orders.

'I'll see to it right away, Miss Jones.'

Rhian left the counter and opened the door that connected to the staircase of the house. Without bothering to remove the white overall she wore to protect her clothes in the shop, she locked it behind her and ran up the stairs to the living room.

Edward was sitting, grim-faced, reading a letter in his easy chair, his feet propped on the fender in front of the fire.

'Is it from Gerald?' she asked, knowing how worried he had been about his son.

'Yes, but like last time, it's an ordinary not military letter, postmarked London so it can't be traced back to a regiment. All he says is that he's well. There's not even a hint as to whether he's in France or still in this country.' Edward folded it and pushed it back into its envelope.

'I am so sorry.'

'So am I.' Edward pulled her down on to his lap. 'I've tried just about everyone I know who has any influence, but they all say the same thing. More than a quarter of the volunteers in uniform are either overage or underage and it would be impossible to comb them all out of the services. I wrote to Gerald's school again this morning, but if any of the other boys have written home, I don't doubt they've sent the same kind of untraceable letter.'

He wrapped his arms around her and kissed her, hard on the mouth, bruising her lips against her teeth before unbuttoning her blouse and pulling her breasts free from her chemise and bust-shaper. There was no gentleness in his touch and she winced when he pinched her nipples. His lovemaking had become increasingly rough of late and she felt as though he were venting on her his rage and frustration with Mabel's obduracy, Gerald's absence and Julia's unsuitable marriage.

'Was the letter the only reason you wanted to see me?' Rhian tried to rise but he held her fast.

'I want to make love to you.'

'People are buying Christmas presents. The shop will be busy—'

'Mrs Ball can manage for half an hour,' he snapped. 'Go into the bedroom.'

Rhian knew there was no reasoning with Edward when he was in this mood. Mabel's rejections had scarred him and he needed to prove that he could have her any time he wanted to. But the more she acquiesced to his demands, the more possessive and insistent he had become. Sending her notes at odd hours during the day to tell her that he needed to see her upstairs in half an hour, an hour, two hours, and not to be one minute late. And sometimes when she did go to their rooms, she found another note, telling her to undress and wait for him in bed. He even left instructions as to what underwear and perfume he wanted her to wear.

She went into the bedroom and he stood by the door.

'Undress. I want to watch.'

She had remade and lit the fire in the bedroom that morning before going downstairs to work, but the air was chilly. 'It's cold.'

'I'll soon warm you.'

She took off her clothes one by one. Folding them neatly, she placed them on a chair before lying on the bed.

Edward stripped off his jacket and waistcoat, unbuckled his belt and unbuttoned his trousers, before climbing on to her. 'Don't move.'

'What?'

'I don't want you to move,' he snapped.

Rhian obediently remained passive. She closed her eyes and allowed him to use her body. She usually enjoyed their lovemaking, but whenever he assumed the dominant role, he gave no thought to her comfort or pleasure and not for the first time since they had shared a bed she felt exploited. The moment he climaxed he withdrew from her and looked at his watch.

'You have a client?' she asked.

'Not for half an hour, get into bed.' He stripped off and lay alongside her.

She crawled close to him and finally summoned the courage to ask, 'What is the matter?'

He almost told what had happened between him and Cedric, but sensing it would upset her, he held back. 'I just needed you. Do you need me?'

Need was their substitute word for love, the emotion neither of them truly felt for one another, and they both knew it. 'You know I do.'

'And you'll always come running when I send for you.'

'You don't want me to?' she asked warily.

Cedric had planted a seed of doubt and he wanted reassurance that she would stay with him even if he were poor, but instead he said, 'You were late for lunch yesterday and you didn't eat anything when you came up.'

'I told you, Bronwen and Meriel called in the shop and I went to the tea shop with them to say goodbye.'

'Do you wish that you were leaving Tonypandy with them?'

'No.' She entwined her fingers in the hair on his chest. 'Has something happened? Because if it has, Edward, I'd wish you'd tell me about it.'

'There's nothing to tell.'

'You said we'd always be honest with one another,' she reminded him.

'How long do you think this will last?' he said abruptly.

'This? You mean us?' When he didn't answer her, she murmured, 'I don't know.'

'You must have some plans for your future,' he persisted.

'Not beyond the present. I know what happened between us was sudden. If you regret taking me in and giving me the shop to run, please don't feel that you owe me anything. I'll go if you don't want me any more.'

Some devil in him wanted to try her further. 'To where?' he asked.

'Does it matter? I'd find a job and somewhere to live.'

'In Pembrey, with Mrs Williams, Bronwen and Meriel?'

'Probably. Mrs Williams invited me to stay at her cousin's boarding house and there's work nearby.' She looked up into his eyes, cool, blue and enigmatic. 'Do you want me to go?'

'No.' He swung his feet to the floor, picked up his clothes and padded in bare feet across the landing into the bathroom. She curled on her side under the bedclothes and stared at the wall.

Suddenly, he was pushing her away from him and she didn't know how to reach out to him.

'Some spring weather we're having, madam,' the cab driver shouted above the noise of his engine.

'You'd never think it was Easter in a few weeks,' Julia agreed. 'Stop, you can drop me here.'

'You sure, madam?' he asked dubiously. 'The snow's deep and it's coming down thick and fast.'

'I have an umbrella and I could do with the fresh air.' Julia had an urge to run through the snow and kick it, crunching the prints of her thick, rubber-soled boots into its smooth shining expanse. She wanted to twirl around, and catch flakes on her gloves so she could study their shapes just as she had done when she'd been a child and tossed snowballs at the trees . . .

'That will be ninepence, madam.'

Julia opened her handbag and extracted a shilling. 'Keep the change.'

The driver tipped his cap to her and drove off.

More than play time she also needed thinking time, she reflected soberly. Sali had introduced her to her solicitor, Mr Richards, and with his help she had just signed a contract to buy a half-completed, spacious and expensive villa on the outskirts of Pontypridd. Once the builder had confirmed that she was amenable to paying for extras, he had been happy to incorporate Geraint's demands into the specifications. But now, when she was committed to buying the place, she wasn't at all sure that she wanted to take possession and sit there in splendid isolation until peace brought Geraint's return.

When the war hadn't ended at Christmas, the newspapers began to print editorials predicting that the conflict would last for years, especially after the German and Allied troops dug themselves into opposing trenches in France. And the battlegrounds were covering an ever-widening front with troops being sent into the colonies in Africa, and German naval ships shelling towns off the north-east coast of Britain.

She wanted to do more for her country – and herself – than choose wallpaper patterns, arrange furniture and wait for the return of a husband whose only contact with her was a weekly duty letter. Brief notes that always ended with apologies for being unable to see her because the few days leave that he was able to take were not long enough for him to travel from France to Pontypridd and back. She often wondered what they would do if he did turn up. Rent the suite in the New Inn again, because he couldn't get on with Sali and Lloyd? Share stilted meals and conversations and sleep in separate bedrooms until it was time for his return?

She hadn't been happy in her father's house, but since she had left, her days had been just as empty, apart from the time she spent with Sali, Lloyd and their children. And despite their warm welcome and efforts to draw her into their family, she was conscious that she was an outsider, invited into their home because she was related. She only hoped the children would never resent her the way she and her brother had done her father's elderly and crotchety spinster aunts when they'd come to visit her family when she'd been a child.

Brushing the snow from the metal bars of the small pedestrian gate at the side of the towering main gates of Ynysangharad House, she compressed it into a snowball and flung it at a tree. It hit the centre of the trunk and she smiled in satisfaction before pushing the gate open and walking through. When she turned to close it, a uniformed soldier ran up only to stop a couple of yards away.

'Get back!'

'Pardon?' She had seen cleaner and more reputable-looking tramps. Several days of beard growth blackened his cheeks. His boots, trench coat and what little could be seen of the rest of his clothes was covered in snow, but it wasn't thick enough to obliterate the filth. And even from a distance he stank of male sweat, farmyard odours and other things she'd rather not think about.

'I mean it, get back,' he shouted.

She clutched her handbag with both hands and retreated.

He walked through the gate. 'I didn't mean to frighten you, but I'm lousy.'

She stared at him in confusion.

'I have lice,' he explained.

'Oh dear!' It was a ridiculous remark but she didn't know how else to respond to his declaration.

'I've come from France, and it's taken me two days to get here. I take it you're going to Ynysangharad House?'

'Yes.'

'So am I. That's if Mari will let me in. I'm Lloyd's brother, Joey.'

'Joey the one who . . .' She faltered when she realized he had been Rhian's fiancé.

'Enlisted,' he finished for her. 'If we don't get moving we'll become snowmen. It's brave of you not to be frightened of me. You're the first woman I've met since I left France who hasn't thrown up her hands in horror and run as fast she could in the opposite direction.'

'That's a bit harsh when you're fighting for us.'

'Thank you, but this war has shattered my illusions. I grew up on tales of the Knights of the Round Table. The book said everything about noble warriors, beautiful damsels, chivalry and heroic deeds, and nothing at all about living rough through a miserable freezing winter, coping with wet feet, equipment that chafes in delicate and unmentionable places, and being munched by lice. But then, it must have been a lot worse in King Arthur's time. I would hate to sit in a snow-filled or waterlogged trench in a suit of rusting armour.'

'I don't think the damsel would be too keen on dirtying her flowing white robe by embracing a rusty knight either.'

He burst out laughing. 'Perhaps we should get together and write an updated version of the Arthurian tales for nineteen fifteen. And that wasn't an invitation for you to get any closer. Please keep at least six feet away. Unlike fleas, lice don't jump, and they don't like the cold, which is why they graze under our clothes, but they move from one pasture to another at the slightest touch. I've spent hours wondering what they lived on before our army went to France.' He stepped smartly sideways when she slipped on the snow and veered towards him.

'You must be exhausted if it's taken you two days to get here?' she ventured, when he stopped to get his breath.

'I am, and I'm also starving, but most of all in need of delousing and a bath. I have no idea what Mari is going to say when she sees me. But I've a feeling it's not going to be welcome.'

'You're here for Easter?'

He laughed. 'No such luck. I only have six days leave and it will take me two days to get back, so I'll have to go the day after tomorrow.'

'You'll travel four days just to spend two days with Lloyd and Sali?' she asked in astonishment.

'I'd do it for two hours. I can't wait to see them.' He grinned and his teeth showed white against his dirty face. 'Do me a favour,' he asked as the house came into view, 'go ahead and warn Mari about my little friends. Tell her it might be better for me to deal with them in the outside washhouse than the upstairs bathroom. If they drop into the carpets it could take her months rather than hours to clean up after me.'

'I'm amazed they let you on a train.'

'We soldiers know our place, and generally it's in a guard's van.

By the way, who are you?' He smiled again. She looked into his eyes and, despite his soiled and encrusted state, felt as though she were the only woman in the world. Then she remembered Mrs Williams's reservations about Rhian's 'young man' who had a wandering eye.

'Julia – Julia Watkin Jones. I used to be Larch.'

'You married Sali's brother.' The smile dropped from his face.

'Yes.'

'My commiserations. Your husband is an idiot.'

'You do believe in speaking your mind, don't you?'

'Always, but after talking to you I can see that he had more luck than he deserved when it came to picking a wife.'

It was a flippant, throwaway remark, but Julia felt as though she had been paid the greatest compliment in the world. She walked into the house and went in search of Mari.

Rhian slipped on a pair of oven gloves, and lifted the two plates in the stove on to a tray. She carried it through to the living room where Edward was sitting at the table.

'Pork dinner with crackling and stuffing and it's the Hart's not mine.' She set one of the plates in front of him.

'It looks good. Who was the letter from this morning?'

'Sali.' She set her own plate on her cork tablemat and sat down.

He sprinkled salt on his meat and pepper on his cabbage. 'She's invited you to visit her again?'

'Yes, for Easter if I'm not doing anything.'

'I don't mind you visiting her, you know.'

'I know. But Sunday is the only day we both have free.'

'I am quite capable of looking after myself.'

'I enjoy our day together. I thought I'd wait to visit Sali until you make arrangements that can't include me.'

'Like visit Llan House, for instance?' he enquired frigidly.

She sipped the glass of sherry he had poured for her. Llan House had become a sensitive subject since Mabel's parents had arrived with their housekeeper and maid to spend Christmas with her. There was no sign of them leaving, although Edward had mentioned that he'd written to both Mabel and her father asking them to go.

'Not necessarily Llan House, Edward.' She struggled to keep her equanimity. 'Things being what they are, you can't visit your friends with me.'

'Why on earth should you think that I'd want to go anywhere without you, especially Llan House?' he burst out angrily.

'You mentioned Llan House, Edward, not me.'

'It was bad enough when Mabel refused to leave the house when I asked her to. But since her parents have dug themselves in there, the situation has become impossible.'

'I'm sorry.'

'There's no need to be. It's not your fault.'

'I hate seeing you upset.'

'If you want to spend Easter day with Sali, do so,' he said churlishly.

'Lloyd is driving up on Easter morning to pick up his father and his brother's family, Sali said there is room in the car for me if I want to go, but I can always buy chocolate eggs for the children and send them down instead.'

'Don't you want to give them to the children yourself?'

She did, but she murmured, 'Not particularly.'

'I could take you down to Ynysangharad House the Saturday before, after you close the shop.'

'You do know that Julia is living with Sali?' she ventured.

'No, I didn't.' He hadn't heard from Julia since her wedding to Geraint, but Cedric, to whom he was just about talking again after he had lashed out at him, had told him that she had been seen in Pontypridd.

'Sali wrote and told me that Julia is buying a house in Pontypridd. If you would like to see her—'

'I wouldn't,' Edward broke in sharply. 'Julia ignored my advice and if anyone should make amends and apologize, it should be her.'

'I'll take the train down.'

'No, I'll walk around the market. We . . . I used to enjoy looking at the stalls, especially before Easter and Christmas. It almost became a tradition.'

Rhian knew what kind of tradition. She was beginning to

recognize the change of tone in Edward's voice whenever he spoke of anything remotely connected to his first wife.

'Rhian?'

She looked expectantly at him.

'What would you like for Easter?'

'For us to be honest with one another.'

'I was thinking of jewellery.'

'I'd prefer honesty.'

'Really.'

'Really. I don't want anything else from you, Edward, and I mean it.'

He dropped his knife and fork. 'You're quite a woman. I'm lucky to have you and I know that I haven't been easy to live with lately but . . .'

She gave him a tentative smile when he hesitated. 'You've had a lot of problems. Between Gerald and Julia.'

'And Mabel and her parents.'

'Perhaps you should visit them, for appearance's sake?'

'I've told her the only Easter gift I want from her is for her to move out of the house, Tonypandy and my life. She can't get servants. Everyone's left except Mair, and if her parents hadn't brought their housekeeper with them she'd be doing her own cooking and cleaning.' He watched Rhian intently. 'I want to pay her off with an annuity and give the house to Julia and Gerald.'

'That is a good idea.'

'It is?' After Cedric's suggestion that Rhian was only out for what she could get, Edward had half expected her to show an interest in living there herself.

'It's a lovely house. Gerald may want to live in it after the war.'

'Yes, he might,' he agreed. 'You wouldn't want to live there?'

Rhian laughed. 'Me in a house that size? No, thank you.'

'I'm sure that after the war we'd find servants again to help you run it.'

Rhian shook her head. 'I'm happy here. I'd hate to run a house and I could never be a lady. I wouldn't know what to do with myself if I didn't work for a living.'

'You really would prefer to live in these rooms and manage the shop?' he asked incredulously.

'For the moment.'

'And afterwards?'

'I thought we agreed some time ago that we'd live one day at a time, Edward.'

'With the war and everything, you are probably right to adopt that attitude.' He picked up his knife and fork again, and resolved to meet with Cedric first thing in the morning. Despite his threats to dissolve their partnership if Cedric didn't carry out his bidding, he hadn't spoken to his junior partner about his will and the property transfers since the day he'd hit him. But this time, no matter what delaying tactics Cedric tried to employ, he'd see it done, and the sooner the better.

'A man is entitled to privacy when he's in the bath, Mari!' Joey grabbed his flannel and laid it across the top of his thighs when the housekeeper walked into the washhouse.

'You haven't got anything that I haven't seen before, Joey Evans.' Unabashed, she walked up to the old slipper bath and poured in a jug of boiling water before going to the old-fashioned, coal-fired wash boiler. She poked at his uniform with a pair of wooden tongs, dunking it beneath the water. 'There are an awful lot of drowned lice in here.'

'I wouldn't be too sure they're all drowned if I were you. From my experience the average louse has more lives than the proverbial cat.' He was sitting in his third change of water, which was a great deal cleaner than the first but still not clear. Leaving the flannel in a strategic position between his thighs, he ducked under the water and wet his hair.

'I suppose you have nits as well.' Leaving the washing, Mari inspected his head. 'And you have. Sit there, I'll get the nit comb.'

'I can get them out myself,' he said testily.

'Please yourself, but I warn you now, you're not setting foot in the main house until I've inspected every inch of you. I'm not risking Master Harry catching anything. The poor boy's only just got over the scarlet fever he picked up in that nasty school of his.

And the Good Lord only knows what those filthy little creatures of yours are carrying. Typhoid or worse, I wouldn't wonder.' She left and returned a few minutes later with the nit comb and a large brown glass bottle.

'What's that?' he shouted in alarm when she unscrewed the cap and tipped a stream of foul-smelling liquid into his bath.

'Carbolic lotion.'

'It stinks. No one will want to come near me.' Grabbing the flannel, he rose from the bath.

'That's the idea. It'll warn the ladies as well as lice.' Locking her fingers into his short hair, she pushed him forcibly back into the water.

'Mari—'

'You need a razor. Safety or cut-throat?'

'Cut-throat,' he retorted acidly.

'You must be tired. Shall I send the maids in to change the water a fourth time?'

'I'll do it myself,' he growled. 'You're enjoying this, aren't you?' He stepped out and wrapped a towel around his waist.

'It's a long time since I've made a man your age blush.' She looked him up and down. 'And all the way from his head to his curling toes.'

'Doesn't he clean up well?' Sali said to Julia when Joey joined them in the dining room for dinner. He'd slept for a couple of hours after his bath and, ignoring Bella and Harry's complaints about his smell, put them to bed and read them a story before coming downstairs.

'Apart from his cologne, and my trousers, shirt and sweater drowning him, he does,' Lloyd agreed.

'My, rather your, clothes may not be the best fit, but they are clean, dry and louse-free, and as for my cologne, all the best people will be getting bottles of carbolic lotion for Easter instead of eggs this year.' Joey picked up the glass of beer Lloyd had poured for him. 'Cheers, you have no idea how good it feels to be my own man again, without any little friends hiding in my underwear.'

'And since I set the maids to iron your clothes with particular attention to the seams, you should stay your own man when you go back.' Mari carried in the soup tureen.

'Only until I rejoin my platoon.' Joey made a wry face.

'I sent a message to the colliery to tell them I won't be in tomorrow morning, so if you want to go up to the farm I'll take you, Joey,' Lloyd offered. 'You two as well, if you'd like to come,' he said to Julia and Sali.

'You can't go without Harry, and if he goes, Bella will want to go as well,' Sali warned.

'He seems more grown up every time he comes home from that school of his.' Joey shook out his napkin and looked at the bowl of leek and potato soup Mari had set before him. 'When I gave him the present I brought for him, he asked to see my sword and gun.'

'I hope you left your rifle at your base.' Lloyd said.

'I did. I also told him that non-commissioned officers don't have swords only bayonets. Unfortunately I didn't have to explain how to use one. He described their use as "blood and guts sticking" and asked me how many Germans I had killed.'

'What did you tell him?' Sali asked anxiously.

'None as yet.'

Sali wanted to ask if that was true but lacked the courage. Freshly shaved and washed, Joey looked thinner, tougher, harder and years older than the young man who had enlisted only eight months before. There were new lines etched around his mouth and eyes and she didn't want to consider how he'd acquired them. 'Harry reads too much comic book propaganda,' she said anxiously.

'Non-commissioned officer?' Lloyd looked at Joey enquiringly. 'They've made you a lance corporal.'

'Sergeant, according to his uniform,' Mari broke in. 'It might be in a disgusting state but it has the right number of stripes.'

'Sergeant Evans?' Sali smiled. 'They'll be making you a lieutenant next.'

'Not if I have anything to do with it.' Joey sprinkled salt on his soup.

'Why?' Sali asked.

Joey could feel Sali and Julia's eyes on him and remembered that both of Sali's brothers were lieutenants. 'Because all officers are stuck-up nincompoops who can't think for themselves.'

Lloyd didn't comment until the meal was over and Sali and Julia had left for the drawing room. 'Have they offered you a commission?' He handed Joey a cigar and his lighter.

'Yes.'

'And you turned it down because lieutenants have short life-spans on the Western Front.'

Joey lit his cigar, puffed on it and returned Lloyd's lighter. 'Who have you been talking to?'

'Soldiers on leave.' Lloyd poured two brandies, picked up the bottle and carried it and the glasses down the table to where Joey was sitting. He took the empty chair next to his brother. 'What is it really like over there?'

'Do you remember those sermons the miserable old Jesuit who was in Tonypandy before Father Kelly used to preach when we were kids?'

'On hell and the torments the devil had lined up for sinners? I remember them,' Lloyd said shortly.

'I wish the Front was as good.'

'You have to be joking.'

'I wish I was. We're dug into trenches opposite the enemy, who are, incidentally, as bloody uncomfortable and miserable as us. If we're lucky and it's cold enough, the mud's frozen. If it's not, it's knee-deep, and if there's no frost at all, it's waist- or chest-deep, and cold and slimy. It gets into everything. Rations, clothes, what-ever you eat or drink is nine-tenths mud. Ten per cent of the time we're scared witless and it's so damn noisy from the shelling and bombing you can't hear yourself think. Any one of the brass can order us out to attack Fritz's machine-gun posts whenever they choose to, with nothing more than our rifles and bayonets, and then half of us die. If we're not shot to pieces, we're strung out and hung on barbed wire, or drown in shell holes. The other ninety per cent of the time we are freezing cold, tired, hungry and bored. There's no shelter to speak of and nothing to do except talk

337

to the person next to you and listen to him tell you about his home or talk about yours, and after ten minutes of that conversation all you want to do is desert except . . .'

'Except?' Lloyd prompted.

Joey took a mouthful of brandy. 'On my first morning in France, I was ordered to form part of a firing squad. I tried to argue my way out of it. An old sergeant who'd fought in the Boer War warned me that if I didn't obey orders it would be my turn next.' Joey topped up his brandy glass with an unsteady hand.

'What happened?' Lloyd asked softly.

'What do you think? We were marched into a courtyard. A young boy was tied to a post against a wall. He was dressed in civilian clothes, blindfolded and had a piece of white cloth pinned over his heart. We were told to fire at it and we did. Some of our rifles were loaded with ball, some with blanks. I could tell from the recoil that mine was a blank but that didn't make me feel any better. Afterwards one of the boy's mates went crazy. It turned out they were both sixteen-year-old volunteers.'

'What happened to his friend?'

'He was sent back home.' Joey finished the brandy in his glass and Lloyd handed him the bottle. 'I know what you're going to say.'

'I don't,' Lloyd said grimly.

'It is a capitalist war, it's not our fight and you'd be right except for one thing. I volunteered for all the wrong reasons but that doesn't alter the fact that now it's my fight too. I'm a sergeant; I'm responsible for the men under my command. Some are too old, some too young, I've a few cowards and a couple of out-and-out rogues who'd sell their grandmother for a tanner but the one thing they'd never do is let anyone else in the platoon down. And while I'm their sergeant, they're the reason I fight. Because I want to keep them alive as much as I want to stay alive.'

'And you have to go back there?'

'I signed up for the duration.'

'Can you look me in the eye and tell me that you're not sorry you signed your life away?'

'I am, and I'm not, for all the reasons that I've just said. And because the worst things of all, apart from the bloody awful waste of life, are the idiots who lead us.'

'And that includes your lieutenant?'

'He's a public school kid. Still wet behind the ears.' Joey fell silent for a moment, 'He's the fourth my platoon has had since we were posted to the front. As you said, the lieutenants have the shortest life span, first over the top, the first ones to stick their heads above the parapet, but don't tell Sali or Julia that. They'll only worry about Geraint and Gareth all the more.'

'Sali couldn't worry any more than she already does, and that goes for you as well as Gareth and Geraint. I'm not sure about Julia.'

'She married Geraint. She must be concerned about him.'

'Julia told Sali he only married her for her money.'

'Then why did she marry him if she knows that's his only reason for marrying her?' Joey asked in exasperation.

'Apparently she doesn't get on with her stepmother.'

'Edward Larch's wife,' Joey mused.

'We're all sorry about what happened to Rhian, Joey.'

'Have you seen her?' Joey asked eagerly. 'Is she happy?'

'I haven't seen her, but Sali writes to her. She's asked her to visit us at Easter. She invited her for Christmas, we got a parcel of toys for the children, and chocolates for us, but we didn't see her.'

'She's still with Edward Larch.' It wasn't really a question.

'The gossips have them living together. Whether that's true or not, I couldn't tell you, but they have rooms in the same building and she's managing a shop for him.'

'She is sleeping in his bed,' Joey said soberly. 'She told me she was before I left.'

'Joey—'

'There's nothing more to be said, Lloyd.'

The door opened, Sali looked in and saw the half-empty brandy bottle. 'Now I know why you didn't join us in the drawing room for coffee. Joey must be tired, Lloyd. Don't keep him up all night talking.'

'I won't. And I won't be far behind you.'

'Goodnight, Lloyd, Joey.' Julia walked across the hall behind Sali.

'Goodnight, Julia,' Joey called after her.

'I'll check the children.' Sali walked in, kissed Lloyd and went to Joey. 'You will take care of yourself. There are a lot of people who love you.'

'I know.' He kissed her. 'See you in the morning.'

'Sali's right, you look dead on your feet,' Lloyd said when Sali shut the door on them. 'You'd better go to bed.'

'After one more of these.' Joey held up the bottle.

'A small one,' Lloyd conceded. 'Want me to wake you in the morning?'

'Please. It may take a rocket after what I've been sleeping through since I reached France,' Joey replied.

Joey had a small brandy with Lloyd, and a slightly larger one after Lloyd went upstairs. He poured himself a third and woke, hours later. The fire had burned down low and the brandy was still untouched in his glass.

He picked up the glass, left the dining room and walked into the drawing room. Someone had opened the drapes ready for the morning, and the garden was bathed in the most amazing bluish-white, translucent light. Snow was still falling; enormous, cloud-shaped flakes like the illustrations in a child's picture book. He pulled a chair up to the French window and stared at the scene. He tried to imprint it on his mind, so he could dwell on it in detail, in a different and, he didn't doubt, harsher future. The room and his chair were luxurious after the privations of the trenches, the brandy burned his throat and warmed his stomach, and the magnificent view of falling snow that already blanketed the ground and skeletal tree branches was calm, quiet and peaceful after the madness of the Front.

Time lost all meaning as he sat watching and thinking how strange it was to go from mud, mayhem and slaughter to this still corner of the world. He poured himself another brandy from the drinks tray, unlocked the French door and stepped outside.

'Aren't you cold?'

Julia was behind him, wrapped in an embroidered burgundy robe.

'It's odd, but it's not cold out here. Come and see.' He offered her his hand. She took it and stood alongside him, her thin slippers sinking deep into the snow on the step.

'You're right, it's not cold.'

'You can't sleep either?' he asked.

'I bought a house today. I'm sure it's a bad decision. You?'

'I have such a short time it seems a waste to spend it sleeping; I can do that in the trenches. Even when snow falls there, it's nowhere near as beautiful, and the couple of falls we've had this month turned to black slush as soon as they hit the ground.'

'You're right, it is beautiful. But then I've always loved snow. One minute everything is withered, winter bleak, and suddenly it looks like a fairy has shaken out a pristine white eiderdown and covered all the ugliness. Sorry,' she apologized, realizing she was straying into the realms of childhood make-believe. 'I'm getting carried away.'

'I know what you mean.' He leaned against the doorway. 'I used to love the snow when I was a kid. I can remember waking Victor and Lloyd one morning at five to go sledging on the mountain. They wouldn't come with me, so I went by myself. What I like most about it is the purity. As you said, all the ugliness has been covered over.'

'I'd love to go for a walk.'

'Me too,' he smiled.

'It's three in the morning and neither of us is dressed for it.'

'Sali and Lloyd used to keep gumboots and coats in the cupboard off the hall.'

'They still do.'

'Then what are we waiting for?'

By the time she'd struggled into the boots and Sali's old raincoat, Joey was in the middle of the frozen rose garden. He held out his arms when she walked towards him. She slipped and fell into them.

'Listen.' He held his finger to his lips and she listened hard. 'Do you hear it?'

'What?' she whispered.

'Absolute silence.' And then he kissed her.

Chapter 20

JULIA FLOATED SLOWLY into awareness the next morning. From the first moment of consciousness, she knew that something wonderful had happened. That she was happier than she had ever been before and her entire life had changed for the better. She savoured the sensation until it was replaced with memories of the passion she had experienced in the small hours. Only then did she open her eyes. The curtains had been drawn, the room filled with the blinding reflected light of the snow and on the pillow next to her, in the impression where a head had lain, was an envelope. She sat up and opened it.

> *Dear Julia,*
>
> *I can't explain what happened between us last night. It would be easy for me to blame the brandy, the beauty of the snow-filled night, the moonlight, or the thought of going back to the Front and possible obliteration, but none of those things are responsible.*
>
> *Despite the brandy, I wasn't so drunk that I didn't know what I was doing; the snow, the moonlight and the night were beautiful, but I've lived through other equally beautiful nights without experiencing anything like the one we shared and despite the horrors of the Front, I'm egotistical enough to think I'll survive to see an end to this war.*
>
> *I told you that I dislike Geraint and I do, but I have long passed the stage of wanting to hurt him as he indirectly hurt me, and there is no reason for you to know any more of what lies between us. It is over and forgotten because we both have more pressing problems like staying alive to occupy our minds.*
>
> *Perhaps a desire to live every moment of life to the full would be*

closest to the truth of last night. Facing death does something to a man. It drives some insane, others to drink, a few into the arms of any woman who can be bought, but most of all it concentrates the mind. You were kind, intelligent and compassionate when I needed someone with all three qualities in abundance and to spare. And all I can say is thank you from my heart for a few hours that I will treasure for the rest of my life.

You don't need me to tell you that it can never be repeated. And not just because you are a married woman. It was one of those wonderful moments that will never bear scrutiny. Hopefully, you will transform Geraint into a man who deserves a woman like you, and I love Rhian. And even though she no longer wants me I will never love anyone the way I love her. Even if you were free I respect you too much to offer the poor dregs that are all I have left after loving her.

I will stay in Tonypandy with my brother Victor tonight, and leave for the Front from there so I won't see you again until my next leave – if then. I don't think Geraint is fit to wipe your shoes but I wish you every happiness with him, if that is what you want and if – the biggest 'if' of all – you do succeed in humanizing him. But then, after the way you made me feel last night, I believe you could do anything you set your mind to.

Thank you again for a wonderful memory. You are a very special woman.

Joey

Julia smiled as she slid down in the bed. The maid knocked and brought in a tray of tea.

'Is it still snowing, Gwen?'

'No, Mrs Watkin Jones, it stopped in the night. Shall I lay out your suit again for you today?'

'No, Gwen,' Julia's smile broadened. 'Mrs Evans said something about going to Tonypandy with her husband, brother-in-law, Harry and Bella. So I think I'll stay here and help Mrs Williams with the baby.'

'Yes, Mrs Watkin Jones. You want your blue housedress?'

'Please, Gwen. And as I have some letters to write, I won't bother with breakfast so tell the others not to wait for me.'

'Shall I bring up some toast for you?'

'Yes, please, just one slice.' After the maid left the room, Julia slipped out of bed and put on her robe. She opened the drawer in her desk and flicked through the selection of postcards she kept to write notes to friends and acquaintances. One was of a single red rose. She turned it over and wrote on the back:

Thank you for your letter and last night. You are so right in everything you said. I wish you health, wealth, happiness and a future full of love.
Julia

After addressing it to Joey, she took her teacup and stood in front of the window. Joey was standing to attention on the snow-covered lawn, acting as a target for Harry's snowballs. She waved to both of them. Harry lobbed a snowball and it fell short of her window, but she didn't see it.

She was too busy looking at Joey who was smiling back at her.

Cedric watched Edward draw an arrow and scribble a sentence in the margin of the document he was studying. 'Is there a problem?'

'A minor addition,' Edward replied. 'Llan House and the furniture—'

'Are to be transferred to your children immediately, not on your death, and that is exactly what that document states.'

'It doesn't make any provision for the furniture if they decide to sell the house.'

'They may want to sell that too.'

'If they do, all well and good. But it suddenly occurred to me that Julia and Gerald might want to divide the furniture between them. Most of it is mediocre and not worth a great deal but there are one or two good pieces. I'm not saying that could cause trouble, but I'd like a clause inserted to the effect that Julia has first choice, Gerald second and so forth.'

'And if they argue as children sometimes do?' Cedric asked.

'The choice has to be made in the presence of the executors.'

'Two representatives from this firm, and if they keep the house and furniture and their children decide to sell it, hopefully sixty years from now.'

'When I will be a hundred and ten?' Edward raised his eyebrows.

'And we'll both be retired with nothing better to do than while away our days in the gentlemen-only bar of the White Hart, testing and assessing their malt whiskies.' Cedric shifted to a more comfortable position in his chair.

'I'll look forward to it,' Edward commented dryly. 'In the meantime, to return to this document, at the first sign of an argument between Julia and Gerald, the executors will send the whole lot to auction, where the children can bid if they want to.'

'I'm sure it won't come to that.' Cedric rose to his feet. 'Is that the only change you want to make?'

'Yes.'

'I'm not sure that clause you inserted about Mabel inheriting nothing if she tries to contest the will, is legally sound.'

'Hopefully it will frighten her enough to back down. Because the income from five thousand pounds worth of investments is all that I'm prepared to give her and if she won't settle for that and be grateful, I'll come back to haunt her.' Edward handed the papers to Cedric.

'The haunting clause might make for interesting reading but, if you don't mind, I'll leave it out. I'll have Miss Arnold type these up.' Cedric held up the papers. 'Mr Rowan and his curate are calling in this afternoon to discuss the Thomas bequest. They can witness the papers.'

'Thank you, Cedric,' Edward said sincerely.

'I'm sorry for what I said about Rhian. I should never have—'

'I've accepted your apology.' Not wanting to discuss the matter, Edward cut Cedric short.

'And I'm grateful to you for allowing me to buy the practice in instalments.'

'It will give me a reasonable income to squander in my retirement,' Edward said lightly.

'But I still think you're mad to leave next door and the bulk of your estate to that slip of a girl.'

'That slip of a girl will be my wife, just as soon as I retire and divorce Mabel. Come,' Edward shouted at a knock at the door.

'Sorry to interrupt your meeting, Mr Larch.'

'I was just leaving.' Cedric showed Miss Arnold the papers. 'For immediate typing. I will leave them on your desk and I want them ready by two-thirty this afternoon when Mr Rowan arrives.'

'Yes, sir. Your daughter is here, Mr Larch, shall I send her in?' Miss Arnold asked.

Edward set his pen on his tray. 'I'm free for the next hour, aren't I?'

'Yes, Mr Larch.'

'In that case, see that we're not interrupted.'

'Shall I bring in tea, Mr Larch?'

'Only if my daughter wants a cup, Miss Arnold.' Edward leaned back in his chair and wondered if Rhian and Julia were in touch. It seemed too much of a coincidence that Rhian should mention Julia to him one evening and she should turn up in his office two days later.

'Hello, Father.' Julia walked in. She was as plain, and expensively and badly dressed as she had always been, but she was smiling. Very obviously happier than she had been the last time she had called on him before her elopement.

'Sit down, Julia.' Unsure why she'd called, he didn't return her smile. 'It seems a long time since I've seen you.'

'Eight months. And it's good of you to see me without an appointment.'

'I am your father,' he said heavily. 'How have you been?'

'As you see.'

'As I see, you look blooming and happy.'

'I wouldn't go quite that far,' she countered. 'How are you?'

Wondering how much, if anything, she knew about him and Rhian, he hesitated before answering her. 'Do you know that your brother is in the army?'

'Gerald has written to me, care of Llan House. Bronwen and later Mair forwarded the letters. That is one of the reasons I'm here. Gerald has never sent me a return address, to write back to him and now that Mair is leaving Llan House—'

'Mair is leaving?' he said in surprise.

'I'm sorry, I assumed you'd know. She is working her notice. She is starting in the vicarage on the first of next month.'

'That will please Mabel,' he said caustically

'Anyway, I would like to arrange for her successor to forward my mail to Ynysangharad House. I'm staying with Sali and Lloyd Evans.'

'So Rhian told me,' he said quietly.

'I saw Mrs Williams before she left Tonypandy. She told me about you and Rhian.'

'What exactly did she tell you?' he asked warily.

'That you are living together as man and wife.'

'And you've come here to tell me that you disapprove?'

'No, Father.' She smiled at the memory of what had happened the night before last. There was so much she hadn't understood. What passion could do to a man – and woman. How lovemaking could make a person feel special and as though nothing else in the world mattered. But then if she had known, would she have proposed to and married Geraint? And the most burning question of all. Would her husband ever make love to her? Because the one thing that she was certain of was the next time she saw him, she would ask him to do just that.

'Really?' He looked at her in amazement.

'What you and Rhian do is your own,' she only just stopped herself from blurting 'affair' and substituted, 'business.'

'That is gracious of you.' He looked her in the eye. 'Has marriage to Geraint Watkin Jones changed you that much?'

'Marriage to Geraint hasn't changed me at all.'

'I wish I could be as magnanimous as you, but I can't forget that you told me he only wanted to marry you for your money. However, that aside, you look well, in fact better than I've ever seen you before and if you are truly happy I am prepared to revise my opinion of your husband.'

'If I look good it's not down to Geraint.' She glanced down and straightened her skirt. 'But I have my independence and I am busy buying a house for us on the outskirts of Pontypridd. And shortly it will need furnishing, although I'm not sure when we'll be able to live in it. I haven't seen Geraint since he took a commission in August.'

'He is in France?' Edward asked in surprise.

'Yes, I know it's an amazing thing for someone as selfish as Geraint to do, but he couldn't wait to join the army.'

'Julia, I am sorry for everything I've done or rather haven't done since your mother died. I should have paid more attention to you.'

'I'm twenty-seven years old, Father, and well able to take care of myself. But what about you and my stepmother? She can hardly be pleased at the situation between you and Rhian.'

'She isn't, but I won't go back to her. Not for her sake, propriety, or even you, Julia.'

'I wouldn't dream of asking you to after living in the same house as the two of you.'

'I offered Mabel an annuity if she moves back to Carmarthen,' he revealed. 'If I succeed in getting her out, you could move back into Llan House more or less immediately. I want to give it to you and Gerald and I have made arrangements to sign it over to you.'

'No, Father, I won't return to Llan House. There is nothing left there for me now.'

'There is nothing left there for any of us.' His voice was tinged with sadness and regret.

'And I am sorry about you and my stepmother.'

'That was said with real feeling. Your own marriage not going so well?' he asked intuitively.

'With Geraint in the army we can hardly be said to have a marriage at all.'

'Children might make a difference,' he hinted.

'They might but I am not having a child.' She blushed when she realized that she couldn't be sure. 'Has Rhian told you that Sali has invited her to Ynysangharad House for Easter?'

'She did mention it.'

'When I told Sali that I was coming here, she suggested that I invite you to join us as well.'

'Won't that be extremely strange?'

'Not if you come in your capacity as my father instead of Rhian's lover.'

'Julia—'

'Think about it. You might enjoy the day.'

'I am sorry. I feel that I am to blame for forcing you from Llan House.'

'You didn't, and running off with Geraint was the best thing that I could have done, not because I'm married, but because I am independent. Buying a house teaches someone to make decisions and stand on their own two feet. And although I'm living with Sali and Lloyd now, it won't be for much longer.'

'Thank Mrs Evans for her invitation.'

'You'll think about accepting it?'

'No, but I'll discuss it with Rhian. The last thing I want is to create is any awkwardness between her and the Evans family. She is very fond of them.'

'You will be too if you get to know them. The children are delightful. Playing with them has made me remember all the wonderful things you and Mam did for Gerald and me when we were small.' Impulsively she went to his desk, leaned over it and kissed his cheek.

He grasped her hand. 'Perhaps you could ask Mrs Evans if it will be all right for Rhian and me to call in briefly without dining with them.'

'I will.'

'Tell her that if it is, she can telephone me here. And you'll come up again soon and we'll have lunch in the White Hart Hotel. My treat?'

'I would like that very much indeed.'

'Shall we say next Wednesday? Come here at twelve o'clock. I'll book us a table.'

'I'll be here.'

'We're all right?'

Julia gave him another kiss. 'We've always been all right, Father.'

Victor clucked his tongue at his horse to speed him up, then glanced at Joey who was sitting, lost in thought, alongside him on the seat of the cart. 'You'll look after yourself . . .'

'Don't you dare go all mushy on me, Victor,' Joey broke in tartly. 'It's bad enough having Sali, Megan and Betty crying all over me and our father and Lloyd getting all tight-lipped and paternalistic without you starting.'

'I suppose I could ask you to bring back the scalp of the next German you kill like Harry.'

'Bloodthirsty little beggar.' Joey shook his head fondly and laughed.

'And whose fault is that?' Victor asked, not entirely humorously. 'I've seen some of the Cowboy and Indian comics you've bought for him over the years.' He turned the corner and drove his cart into Dunraven Street. 'We're early, just as I warned you we would be. I can't understand why you wanted to set out a full hour before your train is due to leave, when it's only a half-hour journey from the farm to the station.'

'I thought I might call into the store and give Miss Robertson a kiss to tide her over until the peace treaties are signed.'

'Give her a kiss and she'll have a heart attack.'

'That's one way of getting her out of Gwilym James before the armistice brings me back.'

Victor slowed the cart as they drew alongside Gwilym James. But Joey wasn't looking at the store. His attention was fixed on the new tobacconist's shop across the street.

'You thinking of going in there?' Victor asked.

'Do you think I should?' Joey looked to his brother for advice.

'That depends on whether or not you need cigarettes.'

'She doesn't serve there?' Joey asked anxiously.

'She does.'

'And?'

'Whether or not you go in is entirely your own decision.' Victor looped the reins around his hand, jumped down and tied them to a post.

Joey didn't attempt to move. 'I think of her all the time, no matter who I talk to, who I see . . .'

'Or how many other girls you take out?'

Joey recalled what had happened with Julia, and fell silent. Taking his silence as an indication of indecisiveness, Victor said, 'There's gossip about her and another man.'

'You don't have to tell me, I know. She told me about it before I left Tonypandy.' Joey held on to the side of the cart and jumped down. He went to retrieve his kit bag.

'You can leave that there. I have to pick up a few things for Megan in Connie's. Do you have any messages for her – or Tonia?' Victor added deliberately.

'She's back working for her mother?' Joey asked in surprise.

'Connie keeps a tight rein on her these days.'

'Tell them I'm sorry to miss them, but if I have more time on my next leave, I'll make a point of calling in on them.'

'You mean it?'

'It's water under the bridge, Victor. You can tell Tonia that if you like and give her my address.'

'Really?'

'Remind her that all serving soldiers are short of cigarettes, dry socks and chocolate.'

'See you back here in ten minutes,' Victor suggested. 'That way you can decide whether you want to visit Miss Robertson or Rhian.'

'It's only five minutes to the station. We can say goodbye here, if you like,' Joey offered.

'What and miss the opportunity to find out which one you decided to call on? Besides I haven't finished lecturing you yet.'

After Victor walked away, Joey looked into Gwilym James. There was a boy on the door he didn't recognize and two new girls on the counter just inside the store. A tram rattled past at a reckless speed. He waited for the baker's cart behind it to turn around, then he crossed the road.

'I have to see Mr Larch and I have to see him now! It's urgent.' Mabel shouted down Miss Arnold's protests, pushed her aside and burst into Edward's office.

Edward rose when Mabel entered, muttered, 'Excuse me' to

the client in his visitor's chair and went to block Mabel at the door. 'This is a most inopportune moment.'

'A telegram came for you, I thought you'd want to read it right away.' She thrust it at him and he took the small yellow envelope from her.

There was a smile on her face, a triumphant, malevolent smile, and he felt as though the world had stopped turning for a few seconds. When it restarted, everything and everyone around him seemed to be moving in slow motion. It was then that he realized he hadn't seen Mabel smile since their wedding day.

Oblivious to his client's embarrassment and departure, he fumbled with the gummed flap on the envelope but his fingers had swollen into plump, flabby sausages that refused to obey his will. Afraid of tearing the message inside, he made his way back to his desk and picked up the sword letter-opener he had retrieved from his study on one of his trips to Llan House. When he finally succeeded in slitting the envelope open he understood why he'd had trouble opening it. The gum was damp. Slowly, carefully, he removed and unfolded the single sheet of paper it contained.

The black print on the thin white lines pasted on to the yellow sheet blurred into an indecipherable pattern. Words formed and danced, unrecognizable, before his eyes. He forced himself to concentrate.

Regret to inform you, Private Gerald Lark (found to be Larch) killed in action 20 March 1915.

'It's about Gerald, isn't it?'

He looked at Mabel then back at the envelope. It was sticky. She had opened, read and resealed it. She had known that Gerald was dead before she had come to his office. 'You're glad, aren't you?'

Her smile faltered. 'That is an appalling thing to say, Edward.'

'My son is dead and you are glad.'

'I know you are upset but—'

Edward stopped listening to her. He couldn't breathe. Shouldering her aside, he went to the door. He could hear her shouting after him but everything around him was wavering in grey shadow. He needed air. If he didn't have air he would black out.

Footsteps sounded in the passage behind him but he continued walking down the stairs, gasping in an attempt to draw breath into his bursting lungs.

Blood rushed through his veins. He could hear it roaring. Gerald – his Gerald Edward Julian Larch, his and Amelia's darling son. The small, perfect, white-gowned baby he had first seen in her arms. Blue eyes peering up at him from a minute scrunched face framed in feminine folds of lace, tiny perfect fingers complete with tiny perfect nails waving in the air. His son.

His darling son, Private Gerald Lark (found to be Larch) killed in action 20th March 1915.

Joey stood outside the tobacconist's and looked through the window. The bottom half was filled with narrow polished mahogany shelves that held an attractively arranged assortment of packets of tobacco, cigarettes, cigars, white meerschaum and polished wooden pipes, ornamental cigarette boxes, pipe cleaners, ashtrays and lighters. The top half was open to the shop, presumably so the assistants could reach down to the window and retrieve goods from the display.

He looked above the shelves and saw Rhian's head and shoulders. She was standing side on to the window behind the counter, talking to a customer. An elderly woman alongside her was wrapping a package in brown paper. Unable to look away, he continued to stare at her and as though she sensed him watching her, she turned and looked right at him.

They gazed at one another for what seemed like an eternity. He knew he should walk away but before he was able to make a move she disappeared from view. He turned, intending to walk back to Victor's cart. A door opened to the side of the shop and he heard her call his name.

'Joey.'

He whirled around. The snow on the pavements melted, the air grew warm and he was back in the summer before Tonia and misunderstandings had ended their engagement. But when he looked closer, she was different. Somehow taller, slimmer, dressed in more elegant clothes than she used to wear, her hair professionally tamed and dressed. She looked cool, beautiful and completely out of the reach of a common sergeant, who, for all of Mari's ministrations to his uniform, still felt decidedly grubby and scruffy.

'I didn't know you were home.'

Her voice was soft, low, musical, and he realized how much he had missed hearing it. He removed his cap. 'Only for two days. I'm catching a train in quarter of an hour.'

'For London?'

'France.'

'You're at the Front?'

He heard the concern in her voice and wondered what they would have talked about if they hadn't resorted to the commonplace. He longed to shout, 'I love you; I'll love you until my dying day. Marry me, now, here in the street.' But what he actually said was, 'You look well.'

'I am.' It was a struggle to keep control. It would have been the easiest thing in the world to pick up her skirts and run to him, throw her arms around him and cover his face with kisses . . .

'You work in the shop now?' It was an inane observation considering that he had just seen her with a customer, but it gave him an excuse to continue standing in the street absorbing her image.

'Yes. Joey . . .'

'Yes?' he burst out when she remained silent for a full three seconds.

'You've seen Sali and Lloyd and the children?'

'Yes.'

'How are they?'

'Fine. Sali told me that she's hoping to see you at Easter.'

'I'll try to see them.'

'Excuse me, miss, sergeant.' A large woman carrying a basket pushed her way between them.

'We're blocking the pavement,' she said superfluously.

'Yes,' he murmured.

'Goodbye, Joey.'

'Goodbye.'

She retreated to the doorway, as though she were afraid to remain close to him. But she didn't look away. 'You will take care of yourself?'

'I'll try, but it's not always easy when it rains bullets and bombs.'

'Of course, that was a stupid thing to say,' she apologized.

'You'll keep in touch with Sali?' he pressed, unable to bear the thought of not hearing any news about her at all.

'Of course.'

'Hello, Rhian, how are you?'

'Hello, Victor,' she greeted him enthusiastically when he joined them and raised his cap to her. 'I'm fine, how are Megan and the twins.'

'Fighting fit. We've all missed you, and Megan and the twins would love to see you any time you can spare an hour or two to visit the farm. Walking is no fun in this weather, so drop us a line and I'll pick you up in the cart,' he offered, giving Rhian no opportunity to refuse him.

'I'll visit very soon.'

'Is that a promise?'

'It is.'

'If you're going to catch your train, Joey, we'd better go,' Victor reminded.

'Yes.' Unwilling to tear himself away from Rhian, Joey made no effort to move.

'Goodbye again.'

'Goodbye.' He replaced his cap on his head.

Still gasping for air, Edward pushed his way through the crowd on the pavement outside his office door. He set his sights on the snow-covered mountain above and ahead of him. It would be cold up there, the wind would blow in his face and he would finally be able to breathe. Looking neither left nor right, he stepped off the pavement. A heavy blow felled him and the world went black but not silent. He heard a woman scream, a high-pitched wail that blocked out all other sounds. He didn't recognize the voice as Rhian's or see the tram that hit him.

Joey and Victor heard Rhian scream. They turned and ran, reaching Edward at the same time as the local constable, Gwyn Jenkins. Victor, who had administered first aid when he'd worked as a blacksmith in the pit, saw the blood flowing from Edward's cracked skull. He pulled out his handkerchief and tried to stem the flow although he knew it was hopeless.

'Let me go to him. I must go to him,' Rhian struggled free from a woman who tried to hold her back. She ran to the spot where Edward was lying and fell to her knees beside him. Joey gripped her shoulders.

'There's nothing you can do for him now, love,' he whispered, recognizing the sight of death that had become all too familiar to him in the trenches.

Gwyn Jenkins looked up and saw Connie in the doorway of her shop. 'We need a blanket,' he shouted.

She nodded and ran inside.

'I must hold him, Joey,' Rhian begged.

'Don't touch his head, Rhian, he mustn't be moved.' Victor glanced at Joey. They both knew it wasn't a warning for Edward's sake but Rhian's. From the amount of blood on the road, Joey guessed that the back of Edward's skull had been crushed.

Rhian reached out and gripped Edward's hand. Blood welled into his mouth and his head fell lifelessly sideways. Rhian sobbed just once, and Joey helped her to her feet. She clung to him, burying her head in his shoulder.

Connie came and handed Gwyn a grey blanket. Victor helped him to open it out and cover Edward's body. When they finished, Victor turned to his brother.

'You're going to miss your train.'

'I can't leave her.' Joey held Rhian fast.

Victor eased Rhian out of his arms. 'I'll take care of her, get your kit bag from the cart and run.' When Joey hesitated, he added, 'We've had enough death here for one day. It won't help her or you if you get yourself shot for desertion.'

Joey finally went to the cart, lifted out his kit bag and started to run down the street.

'Best get her inside before the undertaker arrives, Victor,' Gwyn Jenkins advised.

'Come on, love.' Victor lifted Rhian into his arms and carried her into the shop.

Red-eyed and tearful, Mrs Ball opened the door that connected to the hall and the rooms above. She threw the bolt across the shop door to secure it, and led the way up the stairs and into the bedroom. Victor followed and laid Rhian on the bed.

'You'll stay with her?' he asked.

Mrs Ball nodded.

'If you pack her things, I'll fetch my wife; we'll take her back to our farm.'

If Mrs Ball heard him she gave no sign of it.

'She needs to be with her friends.'

Mrs Ball nodded.

'I'm sorry.'

'He was good man and the best employer. I don't know what we're going to do without him,' she sobbed.

Feeling helpless in the face of her grief, Victor muttered, 'I'll be back with my wife as soon as I can.'

He returned to the street and looked down towards the railway station. There was no sign of Joey and he only hoped he had caught his train. The tram driver was talking to Gwyn Jenkins. The undertaker and his assistant were loading a makeshift rough pine coffin into a hearse but the stain remained a vivid crimson on the grey road.

A cold, clear voice rang out from the doorway of Edward's office behind them. 'Is my husband dead, Constable?'

Mabel Larch was watching them, Edward's partner Cedric standing, white-faced from shock, behind her.

Gwyn left the tram driver and went to them. 'Perhaps it might be best if we go upstairs, Mrs Larch.'

'I asked you a question, Constable. Is my husband dead?' Mabel shouted.

'We can't talk here. We should go somewhere private—'

'Is he dead?' she screamed hysterically.

Gwyn nodded. 'I am very sorry, Mrs Larch.'

'Then I want my husband's office, shop and the house he owned next door cleared of people and I want it cleared now!'

'Mrs Larch—'

'I am his widow, I have the right to inherit his estate, and I want these people out of my property now!'

'Mrs Larch, you're upset—'

'I know what I want, Constable. You are the representative of the law and I want these people evicted from my properties.'

'Mrs Larch, you are grief-stricken, there are procedures . . .' Cedric faltered when he recollected the new will and transfers he had drawn up for Edward that remained unsigned – and worthless.

'I want Edward's mistress and that old hag out of the building next door immediately.'

Before any of them could stop her, Mabel walked to the door of the house and started hammering on it.

Chapter 21

JULIA FLICKED THROUGH the papers Cedric handed her.

'Your father asked me to draw those up some time ago, but somehow I never got around to it,' he mumbled, embarrassed by the memory of the altercation between him and Edward that had delayed the settlement of Edward's affairs. 'He was going to sign them yesterday afternoon. I am truly sorry that I didn't get them ready sooner, because unsigned they are worthless.'

'What exactly is the legal position regarding my father's estate?' Julia made an effort to set aside her grief and concentrate on practical matters.

'The only will your father signed was made before your mother's death, and it was negated by his remarriage. So, in law, he died intestate. Mabel is entitled to a share of his estate, but so are you. You brother would have been, but because Gerald's death predates your father's, his estate will not benefit.'

'I forgot about Gerald's trust fund.' Julia looked to Cedric. 'Will it go to my father's estate? Will Mabel . . .'

'Your grandfather covered every eventuality when he set up your and your brother's trust funds. In the event of either of you dying before you reached your majority the fund was to go to the other. You were wealthy before Gerald's death. You are now doubly so, and your stepmother is not entitled to a penny of Gerald's money.'

'Does my stepmother know about the existence of this will and the transfer of property papers?' Julia held up the documents he had given her.

'No, he didn't tell her and I haven't seen her since . . .' He took a few seconds to compose himself. 'Since it happened two days ago. And there was no reasoning with her then.'

Julia shuffled the papers together and rose to her feet. 'Will you send your messenger boy to fetch a brake, please? I think that you and I should pay a call to Llan House.'

'There is nothing you can do, Julia. I only wish there was,' he said wretchedly.

'Just leave the talking to me, Cedric. And hope and pray that my stepmother is as ignorant of the law as she is about most things in life that don't interest her.'

Twenty minutes later Julia and Cedric stood side by side on the doorstep of Llan House. An elaborate crêpe-decorated mourning wreath, too large to be tasteful, had been tied to the rag-muffled door-knocker. It was odd to be standing on the doorstep of the house she had lived in for most of her life, and even odder to think that the only people she knew inside were the kitchen maid, Mair, and her stepmother.

Cedric rapped on the door with his knuckles. They listened to the muffled tones echoing dully into the hall. As he lifted his hand a second time, the door opened and an elderly woman in a white apron and cap opened it. She blocked the doorway, leaving them no choice but to remain on the step.

Presuming that the woman was Mabel's parents' housekeeper, Julia said, 'We wish to pay a condolence call on Mrs Larch.'

'Mrs Larch is not at home to any callers, ma'am.'

'I am Julia Watkin Jones, Larch as was, and this is my father's partner and solicitor, Mr Cedric Morgan. Would you please inform her that we are here to discuss my father's funeral arrangements?'

The housekeeper hesitated and Julia wondered if they'd be forced to shout into the hall to attract Mabel's attention but the woman closed the door in their faces. She glanced across at Cedric, before they had time to say anything to one another the door opened again and Mabel appeared. She was dressed in the deepest mourning and held a black handkerchief over her nose and mouth.

'My housekeeper said you wanted to see me.'

'We are here to discuss my father's funeral arrangements,' Julia said quietly. 'Please, may we come in?'

'No, you may not. Your elopement broke your father's heart. You are no longer welcome in this house.'

'I saw Father on the day of his death.'

'He didn't tell me,' Mabel snapped.

'There were a number of things that he didn't tell you.' Julia resisted the temptation to indulge in recriminations. 'Please, may I come in?' she repeated. 'We really do need to discuss his funeral arrangements.'

'I am your father's wife, his closest living relative, and I have already made all the necessary arrangements,' Mabel informed her coldly.

'Father would wish to be buried with my mother.'

'I have purchased a new plot in Trealow cemetery large enough for both of us and chosen a suitable double headstone. My name and date of birth will be put on it next to his name and dates.'

'Mabel,' for the first time Julia dared to use her stepmother's Christian name, 'you do know that Father died without leaving a valid will?'

'I am his wife. I inherit everything.' Mabel nervously fingered the black onyx mourning brooch at the throat of her black silk dress.

'Have you spoken to a solicitor?'

'I don't need to.' Her stepmother spoke too loudly and quickly.

Julia showed no sign of the small pleasure she felt at Mabel's omission but she sensed that she had hit a nerve. She turned to Cedric. 'Would you be kind enough to enlighten my stepmother as to the exact legal position when someone dies intestate?'

'A wife is not entitled to inherit her husband's entire estate. His children have the right to a share. Edward drew up a new will that he intended to sign on the day of his death. It would have left you with an annuity equal to the interest on five thousand pounds worth of stock and nothing else.'

'But I was his wife.' Mabel chanted the words as if they were a mantra.

'I could go to court and ask for the unsigned will to be implemented. I have taken advice, and have been told that I stand an excellent chance of winning the case.' Julia amazed herself by how coolly she lied. She knew as well as Cedric that there wasn't a judge in the country who would give a man's estate to his daughter, much less his mistress, on the basis of an unsigned will. But then she hoped that Mabel would assume that her father had left everything to her and Gerald, not his young mistress.

'I will fight you.'

'With what, Mabel?' she asked. 'Legal fees are high and you have no savings. You never did learn to live within the allowances my father made you.'

'Why have you really come here?' Mabel demanded.

'I want Father buried next to Mother and I want Father's legal firm to take over the funeral arrangements.'

'So you can make them?'

Julia didn't answer her. 'I also want to bring Rhian here to say goodbye to him.'

'His slut! His whore! That I will never agree to.'

'Then I will arrange for his body to lie in the church overnight before his funeral, so Rhian can say goodbye to him there. If you agree to those conditions I will ask my father's partner,' she indicated Cedric, 'to waive my rights to Father's estate and give it to you in its entirety.'

Mabel's eyes narrowed. 'This house, his bank accounts and the building in Dunraven Street and the shop . . .'

'Everything.' Julia was reluctant to hand over Rhian's home as well as her livelihood but there were other buildings for sale. And she was wealthy enough to look after Rhian financially. Emotionally was a more serious problem. The young girl had reacted badly to her father's death.

'I won't have that prostitute at Edward's funeral.'

'Rhian is not a prostitute,' Julia demurred. 'But if you insist, I will take her to his grave after the service. As the person closest to him, she has a right to pay her last respects.'

'Not in *my* house.'

'It's not yours yet, Mabel, but as I said, I will arrange for Rhian

363

to say goodbye to father away from here. Do you agree to my terms?' Julia looked her stepmother in the eye.

'I will have everything?'

'Everything that was my father's.'

'Then I agree.' Mabel slammed the door in Julia's face. Weak with relief after achieving what she had set out to with so little argument, Julia took the arm Cedric offered her.

'I don't know whether to congratulate you or not. You have succeeded in placating Mabel, and ensuring your father will have the funeral and final resting place he would have chosen for himself, but at the cost of disregarding his wishes in the disposal of his assets.'

'In the last two days I have lost my father and my brother,' Julia said flatly. 'And the one thing I have learned is that money is worthless.'

She stared at the garden. She had just given away every single thing that her father had worked for, but on the other hand, she had done what she felt was right. She walked down the short flight of steps. When Cedric handed her into the cab, she hesitated. She couldn't be absolutely certain, but she thought she heard the sound of a woman sobbing behind the front door.

Megan rolled out a sheet of pastry, glanced up from the table and saw Rhian watching the grandmother clock that Victor's father had given them after the birth of the twins. She brushed the excess flour from her hands and checked the *cawl* she was heating on the stove. 'They won't be long now, Rhian,' she reassured. 'Funerals rarely last longer than an hour and, given this weather, no one will want to linger in the cemetery.'

'You're probably right.' Rhian couldn't bear the thought of Edward's tall, slim body being lowered into the cold, hard ground, his coffin being covered by freezing earth . . . She shuddered, turned away from the clock and looked out of the windows. Both were steeped with snow that covered half of the glass and the light that shone through the upper panes was greyish purple. It was only just three o'clock, yet twilight was already falling.

Tom yelled in pain.

'Darling, don't cry.' Rhian went to the babies who were sitting on a rag rug behind a rail Victor had built across an alcove to the side of the range. His father joked that he was preparing his sons for a life behind bars but as soon as they had begun to crawl, Victor had made the pen to keep them away from the fire when Megan was baking.

'Not a year old yet, and already they're fighting,' Megan smiled fondly.

Rhian knelt in front of the rail, unwound Jack's fingers from Tom's hair, separated them and set their favourite box of wooden animals between them, but Jack wasn't so easily pacified. When she handed him a bear, he promptly threw it back at her.

Megan stirred the *cawl* and returned to her pastry. 'Funerals aren't important except to the people left behind.'

'I know,' Rhian agreed. 'And I'm grateful to you and Victor for taking me in. I don't know where I would have gone or what I would have done without you. And I feel so guilty for bringing my unhappiness into the house . . .'

'That's nonsense, we've loved having you and that goes double for the twins,' Megan said resolutely.

'No, darling.' Rhian tried to take the box that Jack was using to lash out at Tom, but he started grizzling and held on to it so tightly that she decided it was easier to move Tom out of striking distance. She bit her lip. 'It would have been so much easier if . . .'

Megan knew what Rhian was about to say: if she'd been allowed to attend Edward's funeral. But they both knew that Julia had achieved miracles in engineering a goodbye visit for Rhian in the church. Treating Rhian more like a sister and member of the family than Edward's mistress, Julia had kept her informed of all the funeral arrangements and promised to take Rhian down to see Edward's grave after the service when all the mourners had left.

Julia had turned up at the farm shortly after Megan and Victor had brought Rhian to their home on the day Edward had been killed. Fortunately, Mrs Ball had the foresight to pack all of Rhian's personal possessions, including the clothes, jewellery and bankbook Edward had given her, and smuggle them through the connecting door into Edward's office, entrusting them to Edward's partner. If she hadn't done so, there was no saying when they would have been able to retrieve Rhian's things, given Mabel Larch's hostility towards her husband's mistress.

The back door opened and Sali, Victor and Victor's father walked in, bringing a draught of freezing air and scattering snow over the flagstones in their wake.

'Is it as bad as it looks out there?' Megan asked.

'Worse. If this is spring, give me winter any day.' Victor pulled off his gloves and hat and unwound the muffler from around his face. 'Lloyd needed the shovel more than once to dig the wheels of the car out of the drifts.'

Sali took off her hat and shook the snow from her collar. She saw the anxious look on Rhian's face. 'It went well. Lloyd and Julia are waiting for you in the car. They thought this would be the best time for you to visit the grave. All the mourners have gone back to Llan House, and there aren't likely to be many visitors in the cemetery in this weather.'

'The service really went well?' Rhian sought confirmation from Victor when she went into the hall to fetch her coat.

'Mr Rowan read beautifully and the hymns were moving. I'm not sure how Julia managed it, but apparently they were all Mr Larch's favourites.' Victor held out her coat for her.

Rhian slipped her arms into the sleeves, pulled on her hat and gloves, and wound her scarf around her neck. 'You sure you don't mind us going now, after you've prepared a meal?' she asked Megan.

'*Cawl* is all the better for keeping,' Megan said. 'Go, the sooner you do, the sooner you'll be back.'

Rhian left the kitchen and opened the door to the cupboard off the back hall. She picked up the wreath she had made of ivy and spring flowers that Victor had bought for her. Holding it close to shield it from the wind and snow, she ran out into the yard to Lloyd's car. Lloyd had left the engine running. Julia, who was sitting in the back, opened the door and helped her on to the seat beside her.

'Thank you. Are you sure this is all right?' Rhian looked from Julia to Lloyd.

'There won't be anyone around in this weather to see you.' Lloyd put the car in gear and drove slowly out of the yard.

'You haven't put a card or a message on your wreath, Rhian?' Julia checked. 'Because if you have, the undertaker will collect it with the others and send it up to my stepmother.'

'I haven't.'

'I'm sorry that you have to sneak around like this. My father would be furious if he were here.' Julia gripped Rhian's hand.

'If my putting a wreath on his grave will cause trouble, I won't do it.'

'You have more right than any of us to say goodbye to him. After all, you were the one who was living with him. Besides, I doubt that my stepmother will go near Trealow cemetery again.'

'Surely she'll want to visit his grave?'

'Not even for propriety's sake,' Julia said caustically. 'She's already talking about returning to Carmarthenshire to live. The one thing my father wanted her to do more than anything else, and she finally gets around to talking about it after he's dead.'

Rhian looked down at her wreath. 'Even now, I find it impossible to believe I'll never see him again.'

'I know what you mean.' Julia would have found the ten days that had elapsed since her father's death unbearable if she hadn't had so many practical decisions to make. 'I spoke to the stonemason this morning. He said there won't be any problem putting a memorial to Gerald on my father's headstone. Will you help me with the wording?'

'I'm not sure I'll be much use.' Rhian knew that Julia was trying to be kind but she couldn't bear the thought of phrasing the last words by which Edward would be remembered. That privilege should fall to someone who loved him more than she had. 'I'm sorry, this must be so much worse for you than me. Losing your father and your brother, so soon after your mother.'

Julia looked grim. 'My dislike of my stepmother keeps me going. Did Father tell you that he was making a new will and outright gifts of Llan House and the house next door to his office?'

'He said something about giving Llan House to you and your brother.'

'He did intend for the house to go to Gerald and me. My stepmother was to have an annuity. The shop and the buildings in Dunraven Street, along with the residue of his estate were to go to you. Unfortunately he died before he signed the papers.'

'Possessions don't matter, only memories.' After the terrible day that Edward had died, Rhian wasn't sure if she was talking about Edward or Joey. She had good memories of both, but she had never loved Edward the way that she loved Joey. And for that she felt guilty. Almost as if she had stayed with Edward simply because of what he could give her, not material things, but sanctuary from her emotions and peace of mind.

'You don't mind that Father's wishes weren't carried out?' Julia sought approval for the arrangement she had made with Mabel.

'Yes, but only because he would have minded. The money's not important.'

'You are right. All the money in the world can't help Father, Mother or Gerald now.'

'It won't help Mrs Larch either.' Rhian rubbed a hole in the frost that covered the inside of the window and peered outside. 'Nothing and no one's ever been able to make her happy.'

'If you served her the world on a plate with two teaspoons of the best caviar on the side, she'd still be miserable,' Julia agreed.

Snow was still falling but the tracks Lloyd's car had made when they'd driven up to the farm weren't completely obliterated and he was careful to drive in them. When they reached the main road the traffic had churned the snow into a thick, dirty black watery slush and he was able to go faster.

He stopped the car outside the main gates of Trealow cemetery. The ground was white, the ledges on the massive Victorian tombstones ornamented with six-inch layers of frosting. He turned off the engine, left the driving seat and opened the back door. Julia slipped her hand beneath Rhian's elbow and helped her out of the car.

'Tread carefully,' Lloyd warned, 'there's ice beneath the snow.'

'We will.' Julia led Rhian up the path towards her parents' grave. She looked ahead and was thankful to see that the grave-diggers had finished their work. The mound was heaped high with floral tributes, some colourful, most a simple green and white.

'So many flowers.' Rhian wiped her eyes with her leather gloves, smearing cold, salt tears that stung over her face. 'They are beautiful.'

'Aren't they?' Sensitive to Rhian's feelings, Julia stopped at the foot of the grave and allowed her to pay her last respects alone.

Rhian walked slowly, looking down on the wreaths and reading the messages as she passed. A circle of red berries and white lilies bore a card inscribed '*To a colleague and friend who will be sorely missed, Cedric and Elizabeth.*' A cushion of hothouse pink rosebuds: '*Your loving and heartbroken daughter, Julia.*' A large plain wreath of greenery ornamented with white dahlias: '*From all your friends and neighbours in Dunraven Street*'.

Tears started in her eyes again, blurring the remaining cards. She lifted the simple wreath she'd made and laid it on the side, below an enormous six-foot cross of red roses. It was so ostentatious she guessed who it was from, and deliberately turned away from the card not wanting to see what Mabel had written.

She knelt beside the mound, felt the cold seep from the ground through her skirt, petticoats and stockings to her knees, and wept.

'Megan said that Rhian's had nightmares every night since she moved in with them,' Lloyd told Julia when she returned to the car and stood alongside him.

'She has taken my father's death hard.'

'It is good of you to comfort her.'

'I am not sure who is comforting whom, Lloyd,' Julia replied. 'I never thought I'd have to look at a grave that will bear my brother's as well as parents' names.'

'I know we can never take their place, but you have me, Sali – and Geraint,' he reminded her.

'Sali and you perhaps. I'm not too sure about my husband.'

'You and Rhian have a home with us whenever and as for as long as you want.' He allowed her comment about Geraint to pass.

'Thank you. Has Rhian told you that she wants to go to the boarding house that Mrs Williams is running and work in the munitions factory in Pembrey with the other girls from Llan House?'

'Yes, but it's so far away from everything she has ever known, I'm not sure it is a good idea.'

'I think it is, and I feel the sooner she leaves, the better. I'm going with her.'

'To work in munitions?' he asked in surprise.

'Why look so shocked, Lloyd?'

'You're the last person I expected to volunteer for factory work.'

'And why would that be?' She dared him to answer her honestly.

'If you want me to say because you're too posh, I'll say it.'

'According to the government, if we want to win this war, we all have to do our bit. And I could never really see myself sitting in that house outside Pontypridd, whiling away my time arranging flowers and doing ornamental embroidery until Geraint comes home. That's if he does.'

'Geraint's a survivor.'

'I don't expect him to die in battle,' she countered.

'You expect him to leave you?'

'We made a bargain when we married, my independence in exchange for an annuity for him.'

'The mercenary sod! I've never liked him, but—'

'We both got what we wanted, Lloyd. Isn't that what marriage is all about?'

'On a superficial level, maybe.' Remembering that he was talking to a lady, he brought his language and temper under control.

'We can't all be as lucky as you and Sali.'

'If you can't stand the work, or if either of should change your mind about working in the factory, you will return to Ynysangharad House?'

'Of course, and we'll visit whenever we get leave. A couple of months from now, you'll wish you'd never invited us.'

'I doubt it.' He walked around to the driver's door. 'Rhian's coming. I'll warm up the engine.'

Julia crossed the backyard of the boarding house behind the other girls and followed them into the washhouse. Although she had left the factory over an hour before, the tune of the last idiotic song that the girls had sung while they worked was still running through her head: *For you don't know Nellie like I do, said the naughty little bird on Nellie's hat.* She tried to put it out of her mind but *You are my honey, honeysuckle, I am the bee* popped in instead. She had been working in the factory for eight weeks. All the workers sang the full lengths of their shifts and their voices continued echoing in her mind through all the waking and sleeping hours that followed.

She closed the door behind her, checked all the girls were inside and latched it before going to her two pegs. The first thing she pulled off was the beret that completely covered her hair. Her hair, cut six inches shorter by Rhian, was wound into rubber bands that were painful to remove. But no one was allowed to wear anything metal that might cause a spark in the factory.

She untied the cloth belt from her thick, woollen, serge knee-length tunic, unfolded it and hung it on the hook where she kept her 'dirty' danger clothes. Her munitionette uniform was impregnated with the powder they used to fill the shell casings; it was also heavy, ugly and uncomfortable to wear. She unbuttoned the rubber buttons that held up her itchy trousers and dropped them. Pulling up a stool, she sat on it, unlaced her brown shoes and pulled them off, as well as the knitted men's socks that were two sizes too large for her.

'I could sleep for a week.' Quicker than Julia, Rhian slipped off the collarless flannel shirt they all wore beneath their tunics and peeled off her linen drawers and bust-shaper.

'We'll be able to next week when we're off.'

Rhian went to the bucket of warm water nearest to her clothes, threw in a flannel and began to wash herself. Within seconds the water was blood red.

Shivering and naked, Julia stood alongside and soaped her own flannel.

Meriel, who was behind them, looked into their buckets and shrieked in delight. 'Look,' she shouted to Bronwen and her sister Jinny, 'Miss Julia and Rhian's water is as red as ours now. Comes of being on shell filling,' she nodded knowledgably.

'Miss Julia is plain Julia,' Julia reminded. Her skin, fingernails and toenails had turned bright yellow. On the plus side so had her hair. But much as she'd hated her red hair, she had to admit blonde suited her even less.

'You could be a bloody Chinese, but not Rhian,' Meriel laughed. 'Her hair makes her look like a pixie.'

'Less of that language, you're not on the factory floor now,' Bronwen reprimanded.

'Sometimes I think you're in training to become a vicar's wife,' Meriel grumbled.

'Do you think our hair will stay this colour?' Rhian pulled a strand forward and examined it. Whereas Bronwen, Meriel and Jinny's brown and black hair had turned gold, and even Julia with her red hair had been transformed into a blonde, her fair hair had turned a ghastly shade of green.

'One of the men told me the colour takes a full year to work out of your system,' Meriel crowed.

'Would that be the foreman Dai Watson I saw you with round the back of the loading bay?' Jinny asked. 'You do know he's a married man only out for what he can get?'

'You shut your mouth or I'll push this into it.' Meriel brandished a bar of carbolic soap only to have Jinny snatch it out of her hand.

'Ladies, please!' Bronwen shouted.

Julia dried herself, went to the hook where she'd hung her evening clothes and pulled on her 'clean' drawers, bust-shaper and vest. She rolled on her stockings and because the temperature in the unheated washhouse was freezing, dressed as quickly as she could in thick flannel petticoats and a warm woollen skirt and sweater.

'Anyone going down the pub tonight?' Meriel asked.

'After a twelve-hour shift, I've barely energy enough left to eat supper and crawl into bed,' Rhian replied. Meriel asked the same question every night and although Bronwen and Jinny had accompanied her down the pub twice during the last week, she generally went alone.

'I have it on good authority that some of the local boys are home on leave,' Meriel added persuasively.

'I give you my share of them,' Bronwen offered magnanimously.

'You could waste your whole life waiting for Ianto to come home, when for all you know he could be lying dead in a field in France this very minute.'

'That's a vicious thing to say,' Jinny admonished. 'We all know that you're jealous because you don't have a fiancé.'

'I could have one if I wanted one. And if I did, I certainly wouldn't settle for a collier turned corporal.'

The washhouse door opened and Mrs Williams shouted, 'Supper's on the table. Come and get it while it's hot, girls.'

'What is it, Mrs Williams?' Julia asked.

'Rabbit stew, homemade bread and sponge cake, raspberry jam and custard.'

'I am ravenous.' Julia finished brushing her hair and followed Mrs Williams across the yard into the kitchen. After the cold of the washhouse and munitions sheds it was blissfully warm, clean and cosy. She sat on one of the bench seats at the table.

'You look peaky, Miss Julia.' Mrs Williams set a plate of stew in front of her.

'That's not to be wondered at considering how cold this spring has been and the way we have to work.'

'We all work as hard as one another.' Meriel sat on the bench alongside Julia and helped herself to bread.

'That's why I said the way *we* have to work.' Meriel could be aggressive and Julia tried to be diplomatic in her dealings with her. 'And, unlike the rest of you, I'm not used to hard work, as management has found out to their cost the last couple of weeks. Mr Grey even went so far as to call me worse than useless yesterday.' Julia had thought she was hungry but as soon as she looked down at her plate, her appetite disappeared.

'Mr Grey wears his slum upbringing on his sleeve as if it's

something to be proud of. He calls everyone with a posh accent useless.' Bronwen sat opposite Julia.

'And you're no more useless than the rest of us. The work was new to all of us when we started.' Rhian sprinkled salt on her stew and passed the shaker down the table.

'Any letters come today, Mrs Williams?' Bronwen asked.

'One for you from France.'

'Ooh, the collier corporal's written a love letter,' Meriel teased.

'One for Rhian, two for Miss Julia and none for you, Meriel. They're on the dresser.'

'I bet mine are from the solicitor.' Julia had been locked in a correspondence with Mabel through their respective solicitors since she had left Tonypandy. So far as she and Cedric could make out, Mabel had liquidated as many of Edward's assets as she could, cleaned out his bank account, put Llan House on the market and finally done what Edward had begged her to: returned to Carmarthen.

Well, you'd be wrong, Miss Julia,'

'Julia,' Meriel corrected.

'Old habits die hard.' Mrs Williams joined them at the table. 'One of the letters is from your husband – Julia.' Mrs Williams ladled stew out on plates and passed them down to the girls. 'You staying here for your week off next week, Rhian, Julia?'

'We haven't decided. Can we let you know tomorrow, Mrs Williams?' Rhian asked.

'You have until Saturday morning when I send the food order down to the shop.'

'Thank you.' Rhian ate her stew quickly. She had received a letter from Sali yesterday and Megan the day before and she hadn't answered either. She had a premonition as to who her letter might be from, but much as she wanted to find out for certain, she was prepared to wait. Because if she should be wrong, it would snap her last slim thread of hope.

When Rhian finished eating she carried her plates to the sink, picked up her letter and curled up on one of the wooden backed settles inside the enormous inglenook fireplace. It had become her and Julia's favourite place to sit, read and gossip in the evening because it was the warmest place in the house. She tore the single sheet of blue paper carefully along the perforated lines and opened it out on her knee.

> Dear Rhian,
>
> I asked Sali and Lloyd for your address. I hope you don't mind me writing to you. Please, don't feel that you have to answer this. Lloyd writes regularly and he told me how hard you have taken Mr Larch's death. I would like to offer you my sincere condolences. I know that you would never have remained with him if you hadn't loved and respected him.

Rhian suppressed a pang of conscience. Love – how could Joey think that she had loved Edward after what they had once been to one another?

> This is a hard letter for me to write, but if possible I would like us to remain friends. All soldiers like getting letters, they are a link with home and prove that we aren't entirely forgotten, but letters from you would mean so much more to me than that. When I looked into your eyes outside the shop that dreadful day in Tonypandy I felt as though nothing had changed between us
>
> Please whatever else you do, don't be kind. It would be better to leave things as they are if you feel nothing for me. My feelings haven't changed since the day I persuaded you to accept my mother's ring. And I won't pretend that I have spent every moment since then like a monk. There didn't seem any point when I thought you'd stay with Edward Larch.
>
> So can we be friends, Rhian? Would it be possible to salvage at least that much out of what we once were to one another? I do hope so.
>
> Dare I sign myself your, Joey?

'Bad news?' Julia asked Rhian when she sat on the settle opposite.

'Not exactly.' Rhian folded the letter into her pocket. 'You?'

'My solicitor said that the property market in Tonypandy is so slow because of the war that I could buy Llan House and all the contents for half its pre-war value.'

'Will you?'

'A few months ago I wouldn't have considered the idea, but now my stepmother has finally left I can't bear the thought of my family's things falling into the hands of strangers.' She gave Rhian a small self-conscious smile.

'Your husband is well?'

'Very by the sound of it.' Julia re-read his letter.

Dear Julia,

I enlisted in such a hurry we forgot to make arrangements to have the annuity you promised me paid into my bank account. The five hundred pounds you transferred after our wedding has almost gone and it is impossible to survive on my pay. In case you have forgotten I enclose the details of my account. Monthly money transfers of one hundred and seventy pounds will be acceptable (I have rounded up the figures for convenience sake), quarterly payments of five hundred pounds, or one lump sum of two thousand pounds annually would all be equally acceptable, provided the full two thousand pounds is paid immediately as I have tailor's, mess and other pressing bills to settle.

I am well, I trust you are too. My condolences on the death of your father and brother.

Please seek legal advice on claiming their estates.

Your husband, Geraint.

Mrs Williams handed Julia a cup as she sat alongside her on the settle.

'What's this?' Julia looked suspiciously at the contents.

'Beef tea, you need it to keep up your strength.'

'I'm fine.'

'I don't think so, and you can't carry on working in the factory, either. If you go in tomorrow, make sure it's only to hand in your notice.'

'I'm really fine . . .'

'You say that you're hungry but you can't keep any food down long enough for it to do you any good. You look pale, even when you've walked up the hill from the tram stop, and the other girls have roses blooming in their cheeks. And you've that far away look women get in their eyes. So when is the baby due?'

Rhian gasped in surprise, but when Julia looked at Mrs Williams she saw that further denial was pointless. She did a rapid calculation. 'Christmas, or thereabouts,'

Mrs Williams looked at the letter on her lap. 'Have you told your husband?'

'Not yet.'

'You should, it will give him that much more reason to be careful when there's bombs and bullets flying about. All men turn soft when they know they're about to become fathers.'

Julia thought of Lloyd and Victor's pride in their children, and realized with a start that her child would be their niece or nephew. 'You're right, Mrs Williams, I should tell him.' She wondered if the revelation would prompt Geraint to ask for a divorce or an increase of his allowance because he had an unfaithful wife. And she wondered if it was technically possible to be unfaithful to a husband she'd never made love to.

'It's a marvellous thing to happen so soon after your father and Gerald's death, Julia,' Rhian said. 'The baby won't make up for losing them, but at least you'll have a family again.'

'Yes, I will,' Julia glanced across at Rhian and realized she wasn't aware that she hadn't seen Geraint since last August either.

'You will tell them in that factory that you can't carry on working there. The Lord only knows what that yellow stuff is doing to your skin and hair, or what it will do a baby,' Mrs Williams left the settle. 'And drink that tea,' she ordered. 'That mite you're carrying needs it.'

'Why didn't you say anything about the baby?' Rhian asked when Mrs Williams left them.

'Because with everything that's been happening I've put it out of my mind.'

'But you are pleased?'

'Yes,' Julia smiled. 'Yes, I am.'

'I'll be an aunt – of sorts.'

'And a good one.' Julia hoped that Rhian would never find out who the father was. Because Joey had summed it up perfectly. It had been *one of those wonderful moments that will never bear scrutiny*. Yet it would result in the birth of a baby who would become the most important person in her life.

'You will tell them in work tomorrow?' Rhian pressed.

'Yes, but I won't leave here. I'll see if Mrs Williams will rent me a room.'

'You don't want to go back to Pontypridd?'

'Perhaps after the birth. I like it here near the sea, I enjoy your and' – she made a wry face when she looked at the other girls who were still sitting around the table – 'most of the other girls' company. And Mrs Williams will be here to help me when I need it.'

'She certainly will.' Mrs Williams passed both of them wrinkled red winter apples.

'And knowing that you've been listening, do you think that your cousin will rent me a room, Mrs Williams? I don't fancy staying in the dormitory with noisy girls getting up at an unearthly hour every morning.'

'I dare say we'll find one for you. The front bedroom is empty. It's large and it has a good view over the estuary. But you'll have to pay extra.'

'That goes without saying. I intend to be a very difficult boarder. I'll want a fire lit there every day until the weather gets warmer.'

'I'll warn the girl who does the heavy work.' Mrs Williams smiled. 'It will be nice to have one of you here during the day, you'll be company for me and it will be almost like the old days in Llan House.'

Rhian yawned and left the settle.

'You going to bed already?' Julia asked

'If you don't mind. I really am exhausted. See you all in the morning. Goodnight, everyone.' Rhian lit a candle from the lamp on the table, lifted the latch on the door and went into the hall. She climbed two flights of stairs to the loft that Mrs Williams had turned into a dormitory, placed the candle on a scarred pine chest next to her bed, and took a pen, bottle of ink and notepaper from her suitcase.

She sat on the bed, picked up a book to press on, smoothed out Joey's letter, and made a note of his rank and serial number before beginning to write.

Dear Joey,

Thank you for your condolences, although given my relationship to Edward, I'm not sure that I am entitled to receive them. Yes, I would like to write to you and see if we can be friends. You say you haven't lived like a monk. Given my situation with Edward you know I haven't lived like a nun so perhaps it would be better if we didn't dwell on the past but looked to the future. There are two boys in the factory who have been invalided out of the army; one has lost a leg, the other a foot. They told us about the dreadful conditions at the Front and after listening to them I don't know how you stand it. Hopefully it won't last much longer and you can all come home.

As you wrote to me here, Lloyd must have told you that I am working as a munitionette. The hours are long, the work hard and you'd run a mile if you could see me. All the people who work in the factory have turned yellow — skin, hair, everything — except the blondes like me. Our hair turns green.

The good thing is I am with the girls I worked with in Llan House, the maids you know: Bronwen, Meriel — who used to be Cook — and Mrs Williams, who keeps house for us. Edward's daughter Julia — I still find it odd not to call her Miss Julia — is also here. I don't think you met her, or perhaps just once at that Wild West Exhibition. She works alongside us and insists that we forget that she was once our mistress. She organizes surprises and treats like books, magazines and chocolates at the end of the week for us. She married Sali's brother, Geraint, just before the war, and he enlisted soon afterwards. She hardly ever mentions him and I have the impression that her marriage isn't happy. But there is one marvellous piece of news. She is having a baby and after losing her father, and brother at the front, it is wonderful to know that she will still have a family. She only told us about it tonight and I don't think she would have done so if Mrs Williams hadn't guessed. She hasn't even told Geraint. I don't know if you are in the same regiment or even see him but I would be grateful if you didn't mention it until she has had a chance to write to him.

Even before you wrote I thought of you often, Joey. I do so hope that we can still be friends. I will wait for you to answer this before writing back.

Rhian thought for a moment, then signed the letter

Your friend, Rhian

Chapter 22

MRS WILLIAMS WALKED into the attic dormitory carrying a candle. Shielding the flame from the draught that whistled through the door behind her, she went to the curtains that covered the dormer windows and pulled them wide. Rings rasped and grated over the metal rod and a clear, grey dawn light flooded in, dispelling the soft gloom. She blew out the candle and called out, 'Good morning, girls.'

'What's good about it?' Jinny turned face down in her narrow iron bedstead.

'It's six o'clock. Breakfast will be on the table in half an hour.' The housekeeper cheerfully ignored Jinny's moans.

'I don't know how you can be so bright in the morning, Mrs Williams, I don't want to move,' Bronwen murmured sleepily.

'You never do first thing in the morning.' Meriel flung back her bedclothes, sat up and stretched her plump arms above her head.

'All of you, in the kitchen in half an hour or you'll be late for work.' Mrs Williams took her candlestick and left.

Rhian waved a tentative hand outside her blankets. 'It's warmer than yesterday. Summer must have finally arrived.'

'It's not warmer, it's bloody freezing.' Meriel threw a robe over her sleeveless nightgown.

'Must you always swear, Meriel? It's so common,' Bronwen complained.

'Why must you always be so bloody prim, Miss Goody Two Shoes? Bags I the *ty bach* first.' Grabbing her towel, Meriel pushed her feet into her slippers and barged out of the door.

'I don't know why we always let Meriel go first and steal the 'lion's share of the hot water every morning.' Bronwen reached down, opened the chest alongside her bed and lifted out the American cloth toilet bag where she kept her soap, toothbrush and hairbrush.

'Because the rest of us will do anything for an extra five minutes between the sheets.' Jinny lifted her pillow and burrowed her head beneath it to block out the light.

'Lazybones.' Bronwen left her bed, lifted her robe from the hook next to her bed and headed for the door.

'That's me,' Jinny mumbled. 'Lazybones. And I swear now that when it's my next week off, I won't leave this bed for anything. Not to eat. Not to drink . . .'

'Not to go to the *ty bach?*' Rhian asked.

'Perhaps that,' Jinny conceded, 'but nothing else.'

'You all right?' Rhian peered anxiously at Julia who lay, still and pale, curled on her side under the blankets in the bed next to hers.

'I feel sick.'

'Stay there. I'll ask Mrs Williams to bring you up a cup of tea and I'll tell the supervisor that you're too ill to work.'

'The least I can do is see this week out. You know how short of workers we are.' Julia closed her eyes to stop the room from spinning round her.

'You really do look ghastly. I think Mrs Williams should send for the doctor.'

'For morning sickness?' Julia questioned. 'That would be silly.'

Bronwen returned and scooped her evening clothes from the chair where she'd left them the night before. 'I forgot these, and Mrs Williams will go doolally tap if I traipse dirt through the house tonight in my working clothes to fetch them.'

'Must you make so much noise?' Jinny complained irritably.

'It could be something more,' Rhian suggested in a low voice to Julia. 'Mrs Williams said last night that you look peaky.'

Julia opened one eye and closed it quickly again. 'Mrs Williams might be a Mrs but it is only a courtesy title afforded to house-keepers. Whatever she knows about having babies, she's heard second-hand.'

'And not just about having babies,' Jinny muttered in muffled tones from beneath her pillow. 'I doubt she's seen a man without his underpants on in her life.'

Rhian thought back to the conversation she'd had with the housekeeper about her 'moment' but said nothing.

'There's a lot more to life than seeing men naked, Jinny, and after what happened to you, I trust that you won't see another one without his trousers on until you have a wedding ring on your finger.' Believing that her sister's 'sin' reflected badly on her and the rest of her family, Bronwen had never entirely forgiven Jinny for giving birth to a bastard.

'I pity poor Ianto when he gets his next leave,' Jinny retorted. 'After months at the Front he's entitled to a bit of fun.'

'You can have fun with your clothes on. And Ianto and I happen to think that some things are best left until after the wedding,' Bronwen snapped back prudishly.

'Given the length of time you two have been engaged and the time this war is taking, you won't be getting married until you're both too old to do anything more than look at one another,' Jinny teased.

'You're disgusting.' Bronwen flounced out.

Jinny suddenly flung her pillow to the foot of her bed and looked at Julia. 'You've got morning sickness?'

'Yes.'

'You're having a baby?'

'The two generally go together.' Julia sat up slowly in the bed.

'Is it congratulations or commiserations?' Jinny demanded.

'When I'm not feeling like this, definitely congratulations.' Julia managed a weak smile.

'Your husband must be thrilled.'

Julia glanced at Rhian. 'You go on ahead. I'll be downstairs in five minutes. That way I get to miss the queue for the toilet.'

'You sure?' Rhian was reluctant to leave her.

'I'll be fine in a few minutes.'

Rhian slipped on her robe, gathered her evening clothes and ran down the stairs. She walked through the kitchen where Mrs Williams was frying slices of 'farmhouse' bacon, thick white layers of fat with two minuscule lines of pink running through them, and went outside.

The heads on the daffodils in the border by the back door had shrivelled and the tulips were already losing their petals. Another few days and they'd be finished too. But Meriel was right. The early morning air was still chilly. So much for the weather being warmer by the sea, she thought irritably. Despite Mrs Williams's efforts with the fires, it had been a lot colder in the boarding house through the tail end of winter than it had been in Llan House and Dunraven Street.

She went into the washhouse and hung her evening clothes on the peg next to her work clothes before waiting her turn for the *ty bach*. As Bronwen had predicted, when she came to fill her bucket, she found that Meriel had taken the lion's share of hot water – again.

'We ought to take it in turns to come down before Meriel and grab the hot water for ourselves. I hate washing in cold.' Bronwen dipped her fingers gingerly into her bucket and winced.

'We noticed,' Meriel commented when Bronwen gave her face the most cursory of splashes.

'It's your fault. I've never known anyone as greedy and selfish as you. Julia, you all right?' Bronwen asked in concern when she walked slowly through the door.

'Fine.' Julia gave a wan smile that belied her words. 'Do me a favour, Rhian. Tell Mrs Williams I don't want to put her to any trouble, but ask her if I can just have tea and toast this morning.'

'You ill?' Meriel wound her belt around her tunic and fastened it.

'Pregnant.' Julia decided there was absolutely no point in trying to keep it quiet now that Jinny knew.

'And I knew before you,' Jinny crowed, washing vigorously and deliberately splashing cold water over Meriel.

'You did that on purpose, Jinny.' Meriel dried her tunic with her towel.

'I did. What you going to do about it?' Jinny dared.

'Get you back any way I can later on today, so watch out.' Meriel threatened. 'That's lucky you getting out of the factory,

Julia,' she said enviously. 'If I could find a man to keep me, I'd get pregnant tomorrow. It would be worth having a baby to leave that stinking place.'

'There isn't a man daft enough to take you on,' Jinny taunted.

'That's what you think.'

'So, where you hiding him?' Bronwen asked.

'Wouldn't you like to know?' Meriel was first out of the washhouse and into the kitchen. When Bronwen, Rhian and Jinny joined her, she had already piled her plate high with fried bread, eggs and bacon.

'Leave some for the rest of us, won't you,' Jinny grumbled.

'First come first served, that's what I always say.' Meriel dropped four sugar lumps into her tea.

'We noticed,' Bronwen commented acidly.

'There's plenty for all,' Mrs Williams called from the stove, where she was frying more eggs.

'Just tea and toast for Julia, please, Mrs Williams.' Rhian helped herself to bacon and an egg.

'So, when's her ladyship going to break the news to management?' Meriel asked Rhian when she sat at the table.

'Don't you dare refer to Julia as her ladyship,' Rhian countered protectively.

'You have to admit she's slumming it,' Meriel said a little sheepishly when the others looked angrily at her. 'Well, come on, be honest, you wouldn't catch any of us working in the factory if we had her money.'

'That's the difference between Miss Julia and you, Meriel.' Mrs Williams topped up their cups with tea. 'She has a conscience and wants to do her bit to help win this war. All you can think about is how much money is in your pay packet at the end of the week, and the men you can meet down the pub in the night.'

'Good morning.' Julia pushed the plates of fried bread and bacon away from her chair when she sat at the table.

'And good morning to you. Here you are, Miss Julia . . . Julia,' Mrs Williams corrected herself. She left the stove and served her. 'Weak tea and toast. And don't forget to tell them in work that today will be your last.'

*

Rhian stopped at the top of the lane that led from the boarding house to the tram stop, and waited for Julia to catch up with her. Her two favourite times of day were mornings and evenings and she had never been able to work out whether she preferred watching the sun rise or set, especially over a stunningly beautiful landscape like the estuary in front of her.

A pale band of grey light hung low in the sky; below it the water shone still and gleaming like polished pewter. Gulls whirled above the mirror-like surface, screeching loudly as they dipped low in search of fish.

'You didn't have to wait for me, Rhian.' Julia drew alongside her.

'I was drinking in the view. I could never get tired of looking at the sea.'

'Neither could I after living in Tonypandy.'

'Besides, we've plenty of time to get to the tram.'

'We won't get a seat if we're late,' Julia warned.

'You will, because Meriel always manages to get one and I'll turf her out of it.' Rhian linked her arm into Julia's and they started to walk.

'I don't want anyone to fuss over me,' Julia protested.

'We're fussing over your baby, not you.'

'Same thing.'

'No, it's not. What do you want, a boy or girl?'

'I honestly don't know, I haven't had any time to think about it.' It was the truth. Until Mrs Williams had voiced her suspicions last night, Julia had pushed all thoughts of the coming child from her mind, never even considering it as a person in its own right.

'I thought it was traditional for men to want sons and women girls, until Sali had the girls. Lloyd seems actually to prefer them to boys. But then it's become something of a joke between them. Every time she gets pregnant, they argue about girls versus boys' names for nine months. But after living with them, you'd know that. And your husband might be different. He might want a boy.'

'He might,' Julia said.

'Did you ever talk about having a family?'

'Never.'

Julia's reply was so finite Rhian wondered again if her friend's marriage was a happy one. She rarely mentioned Geraint, and when she did it was usually in response to a direct question. Even their letters were weekly as opposed to the almost daily notes Bronwen received from her Ianto. 'You have so many things to think about and do. You'll soon be putting on weight and you'll have to make new clothes for yourself and the baby. I can help there, I love sewing. So does Mrs Williams and she's brilliant at embroidery. Baby clothes always look better for a bit of colour on them. And you'll have to choose names for both a boy and a girl.'

'That will be easy. If I have a boy I'll call him Edward Gerald after my father and brother, and if it's a girl, Amelia after my mother.'

'They are lovely names.'

Julia caught a wistful note in Rhian's voice. 'Would you like to have children?'

'Eventually,' Rhian replied guardedly, recalling how much Joey had been looking forward to becoming a father when they'd been engaged.

'I've never thought about it before, but you and my father could have had children.'

'He . . .' Rhian had never entirely overcome her embarrassment at talking about her private life with Edward with his daughter. 'He didn't want me to get pregnant while I ran the shop in Tonypandy because it would have led to gossip, so he used something.'

'Used something?' Julia repeated blankly.

'A French letter, men put it over themselves before they make love and it stops women getting pregnant.'

'Do all men know about them?' Julia asked, her curiosity roused.

'I don't know much about all men. I was engaged to Joey and then I was with your father.'

'I'm sorry; I didn't mean anything by that. But I've never even heard the term French letter before. I suppose it wasn't considered

387

a suitable topic of conversation in polite society. But come to think of it, it is surprising that I didn't hear about them in the suffrage society. Some of the married women used to talk about educating women so they could control the size of their families, but Miss Bedford always changed the subject before they could go into details.' Julia wondered why Joey hadn't used a French letter when he'd slept with her. Then she remembered that he'd just come from France and arrived 'lousy'. Perhaps he hadn't been expecting to find an accommodating woman on his leave, or possibly they were difficult to get hold of at the Front. Either way, when she thought of her baby, she was glad that he hadn't.

'I've heard more talk about the private side of married – and unmarried – life from Jinny and the girls in the factory in the last couple of months, than I heard in the four years I worked below stairs in Llan House,' Rhian divulged.

'I admit I was shocked by the way Jinny talks at first, and it's taken me some time to get used to Meriel's language, but I don't even notice her swearing half the time now.'

'Which goes to prove that it's possible to get used to almost anything.'

'Did you ever consider giving up working in the shop to start a family?' Julia knew that her question would embarrass Rhian but she couldn't resist asking it. Although she had been shocked when she had first heard that her father was living with Rhian, now that he was dead, she wanted to know whether or not he was happy during the last few months of his life.

'No, I . . . we . . . decided to take life one day at a time. Especially after the war broke out. Occasionally your father would talk about retiring in a few years and divorcing your stepmother so he could marry me. But he knew that his practice wouldn't survive the scandal if he divorced her while we both lived in Tonypandy. As it was, I'm sure that people must have talked about my living in the same house and working for him.'

'But you were happy?' Julia pressed.

'Yes, we were.' Nothing would have made Rhian say otherwise. She sensed that it was important for Julia to believe that her father had been happy after the misery of his marriage to Mabel. And when she compared the short time they had lived together to the life he had led just before in Llan House, they had been comparatively happy, despite the fact that they hadn't loved one another.

'And you would have married my father when he retired?'

'Like I said, we tended to live day by day and not plan too far into the future.' Rhian tried to think of something comforting she could say. 'You know your father. His tastes were simple, in food and in life.'

'Certainly in food, unlike my stepmother,' Julia agreed.

'He enjoyed plain cooking, sitting in front of the fire in the evening reading a book or the paper, smoking a cigar with a drink at his elbow.' Rhian blushed when she thought of the other things Edward had enjoyed that involved her. 'And we did have one particularly wonderful week in a hotel in Brighton. I'll remember it for the rest of my life.'

'I'm glad.' Julia gripped her hand.

'How about we ask Mrs Williams to get some layette patterns and white wool for us tonight, so we can start knitting for your baby?' Rhian suggested.

'How about we get a move on and catch the tram before we're given a black mark and have our pay docked for being late for work.' Julia couldn't think much further than the letter she had to write that night. Whichever way she phrased it, Geraint wasn't going to be pleased, so perhaps a *'Dear Geraint, congratulate me, I'm pregnant, Julia'* would not only be the simplest way to tell him, but the best. Blunt and informative, because the more she thought about it, the happier she was at the prospect of becoming a mother and having her father's first and very probably only grandchild.

'I have never seen anything so disgusting. This cloakroom is filthy. No woman – decent woman that is –' the tall, thin, middle-aged woman glared at the female workers gathered around her in the cloakroom – 'could possibly wash, change or do anything else in here.'

'You've been working in a National Factory?' Bronwen asked the newcomer, who was standing transfixed in the open doorway because she couldn't bring herself to walk inside.

'Yes, and it was a palace compared to this. How can you put up with it? There isn't even a tap and a plumbed-in sink. Don't tell me they expect us to wash in that?' She pointed to a scummy tin trough filled with blood-coloured water that bisected the room. 'I can smell the lavatories from here and there aren't even doors on the cubicles. Heaven only knows what germs or disease I'd pick up if I tried to use them.'

'There are always the sand dunes,' Meriel suggested.

'Are you serious?' The woman looked at her in disgust.

'There are fewer rats out there but you might come across the odd crab with sharp claws.'

Seeing that the woman wasn't sure whether to take Meriel seriously or not, Bronwen came to her rescue. 'We only use the lavatories when absolutely necessary and the trough's better than nothing, which is the only alternative.' She hung her coat on the hook nearest to the door.

'You go home without washing?' the woman asked in horror.

'I have my own bucket in my lodgings and the comfort of knowing that the dirt in it is all mine.' Jinny straightened her cap and headed for the factory floor. She opened the door and out wafted the roar of hundreds of voices singing, *My old man said follow the van and don't dillyy-dally on the way*.

'Are the conditions in the National Factories really so much better than these Controlled Establishments?' Julia asked.

'Yes, and if this is an example of a privately owned factory I never want to see another one. The changing rooms in the Nationals are cleaned at the end of every shift. We had games rooms and canteens with really good subsidized food. You can get good, hot, three-course meals in them for ninepence.'

'Well, don't go expecting to find anything like that here. The warmest things in our canteen are the rats' nests.' Bronwen picked up the sturdy wooden box Mrs Williams had filled with cake, sandwiches and bottles of water. She never let it out of her sight until after their lunch break.

'Rhian?' Their supervisor called to her from outside the door. 'Six new girls are waiting outside Mr Owen's cubicle and you're on initiation duty.'

'I'm on my way. You are going to see the manager now?' she said to Julia.

'Yes.' Fighting a fresh bout of nausea brought on by the latrine stench, Julia nodded.

Rhian joined the group of volunteers clustered around the cupboard-sized room the caretaker used to store his tools and brushes. There was something odd about them, and Rhian realized that after only a couple of months in the factory, she found their glowing pink-and-white complexions and glossy brown and black hair unusual. She unpinned the printed sheet of regulations from the door and faced them.

'Ladies, I am Rhian Jones, I'm going to give you a tour of the factory. I'll explain the rules and why it is so important that we all stick to them. Please stay as close to me as you can, and try not to get in the way of any of the workers, or stand too close to their machines.'

She braced herself for the noise and opened the door to the main factory floor. But whereas she was deafened by the singing and noise of the machinery she could see that a couple of the new girls actually found the level of noise painful.

'Stay close to me.' She strained her voice, trying to make herself heard, but no matter how loud she shouted she could barely make sense of what she was saying herself. And it was a struggle to make the talk interesting when it was chiefly comprised of warnings about carelessness, and why it was dangerous to bring anything metal that might cause a spark on to the shop floor.

When one of the new recruits started yawning, she was forced to stifle a yawn herself. She was halfway through reciting the catalogue of the accidents that could occur if care wasn't taken – acid burns, eye injuries – when they reached the sheds where shell casings were filled with high explosive.

Meriel and Jinny were lifting an eighteen-pound shell they'd just filled on to a packing cradle. Bronwen was standing outside being searched by a supervisor who had earned himself the nickname of 'Desert's Disease' because of the way his palms wandered whenever he searched the girls for contraband cigarettes, matches, metal hairpins and jewellery.

Rhian flashed Bronwen a sympathetic smile and encouraged the new recruits to stand in a circle around her in the hope that it would curb the supervisor.

'You can expect to be searched any time,' she warned. 'It is essential that we all have a safe working environment. Any questions?'

To her dismay, three hands shot up. It was quieter in the sheds than the main factory but the noise level was still considerable and by the time she finished talking, she was exhausted. She walked the girls to the supervisor who had been delegated to place them, returned the list of regulations to the cubicle and made her way back to the shed.

Bronwen was standing at their machine, waiting for her.

'Where's Julia?' Rhian mouthed.

'She's been put on light work.' Bronwen knelt in front of the machine. 'Let's make a start and see if we can catch up with Meriel and Jinny.'

At a quarter to one the whistle blew for the midday dinner break. Rhian helped Bronwen to lift the last shell they had filled on to its packing, climbed stiffly to her feet and rubbed her aching back.

'We're all going to be crippled when the war ends.' Bronwen fetched the wooden box she'd left in plain sight at the shed entrance.

Rhian squinted out into the sunlight. 'The weather looks good enough to eat outside.'

'You go to the toilets. I'll find us a good spot to eat, then I'll go before the afternoon shift starts,' Bronwen offered.

'Thanks.' Rhian made her way to the toilets, where three of the new recruits were screaming.

'Rats,' Meriel explained laconically, dipping her hands in the trough of filthy water.

'I'd sooner die than put my hands in that,' the woman who'd come from the National factory said.

'It's your choice. Some say a bit of explosive never did no one no harm. Me, I think different.' Meriel shook the excess water from her hands and wiped them on the back of her overalls rather than use one of the rags hanging on the metal bars beneath the makeshift sink. She looked around. 'Where's Bronwen?'

'Outside, waiting for us,' Rhian left the cubicle and went to the trough.

'Good, I'm starving.'

'You're always starving.' Jinny ran out ahead of them. 'First to reach Bronwen gets pick of the slices of cake.'

Bronwen had found a warm and sunny spot on a dune overlooking the factory sheds. She waved to Jinny, Meriel and Rhian when they emerged. Rhian waved back, pulled the cap from her head, shook out her hair and looked up at the sun.

'Funny how the small things you take for granted become so important when you spend most of your days working hard indoors,' Julia commented when she caught up with them. 'I never appreciated sunlight so much before.'

'You look better,' Rhian said in relief.

'I told you it was just morning sickness.'

'You finishing work for good today, Julia?' Bronwen prised the lid off the box and lifted out the individual paper bags of cheese sandwiches Mrs Williams had packed for them.

'Yes. And they've put me on light duties for the rest of the day.'

'That's a laugh in this place,' Jinny jeered. 'What the hell are light duties?'

'Small pellets.' Julia took her sandwiches, opened one to check inside and bit into it. 'I am absolutely starving.'

'That comes of not eating a proper breakfast,' Meriel lectured.

'I'd like to see you do that when you are pregnant.' Jinny took her bottle of water, unscrewed the top and drank half of it down in one noisy gulp.

'You know something.' Bronwen leaned back on her arms and stared up at the vast expanse of pale blue sky, scratched with wisps of clouds. 'When the sun's shining like this, and we've a whole hour free to eat our sandwiches and a comfortable house and a good supper to go back to, life's not half bad.'

'We've four and quarter hours of the afternoon shift to go and, even if the sun is shining when we're finished, it won't be as bloody warm as it is now,' Meriel complained.

'There you go, swearing again,' Bronwen reprimanded.

'Take my advice, give up Ianto and find yourself a vicar, you'll be great running the Mothers' Union and the temperance society,' Meriel snapped back.

'That's enough sniping, it's too nice a day to quarrel,' Julia interposed.

'I mean it, life's not bad,' Bronwen continued unabashed. 'We've money in our post office accounts and pockets—'

'And no vile mistress breathing down our neck.' Realizing what she'd said, Meriel glanced guiltily at Julia. 'No offence meant.'

'None taken.' Julia bit into her second sandwich. 'My step-mother was horrible to all of you but she was even worse to my father and me. She might not have made us work, but she had – has,' she corrected herself, 'an unerring talent for finding people's weak spots and tormenting them with their shortcomings.'

'I wonder what she's doing now,' Bronwen mused.

'I neither know nor care,' Julia dismissed.

'Jinny and I were talking earlier; if this weather holds, we might go to Barry Island for our next week off.'

'The way you two carry on, you'll kill each other,' Meriel warned, envious because she had a different week off to the sisters and couldn't join them.

'No, they wouldn't because although they fight like cat and dog they'll always stick up for one another. I bet you'll have a great time.' Julia lay back on the sand and shaded her eyes from the sun.

'Want my last sandwich, Julia?' Rhian offered.

'No, thanks.'

'If you don't eat it, I'll feed it to the gulls. I really have had enough.'

'If you're sure.' Julia took it while Bronwen rummaged in the box for the wedges of fruitcake Mrs Williams had packed for them. She distributed them together with the rest of the water bottles.

'Seriously,' Meriel said when the box was empty and Rhian had flung the last few crumbs for the birds, 'does anyone want to come to the pub tonight?'

Bronwen groaned. 'Don't you ever think of anything other than going to the pub to meet men, Meriel?'

'It doesn't look like it.' For once Jinny sided with her sister.

'Time to make a move.' Julia rose to her feet and brushed the sand from her uniform.

'It's all right for you, I wish it was my last day.' Jinny finished the water in her bottle.

'Last day here,' Meriel said. 'But not last of work. Not with a little one to look after soon.'

'I'm looking forward to it.'

Rhian collected the bottles and empty paper bags and pushed the lid on the box. 'I'll carry this back, Bronwen, if you want to go to the toilet.'

'Ta.' Bronwen ran off and Rhian heard the strains of *Ten Green Bottles* coming from the factory as the shift headed back to work.

The sheds and factory, so cold and draughty in winter, were uncomfortably hot that afternoon, and Rhian felt as though they had missed out on spring by going straight from a freezing cold winter to summer.

'No taking off your tunics,' a supervisor shouted when Meriel untied her belt.

'Old witch,' Meriel hissed, 'I'm roasting.'

'The uniform is for your protection.' The supervisor joined them in the shed and stood behind the girls, watching as they filled the shells. 'You two haven't done so well this morning,' she lectured Rhian and Bronwen. 'You're six shells behind these girls.' She pointed to Jinny and Meriel's stack.

'I was on initiation duty this morning,' Rhian explained.

The supervisor moved on.

Rhian helped Bronwen shift another shell on the packing cradle and they knelt down in front of the machine again.

The workers sang the last line of *Yellow Bird* and, inspired by the bird theme, moved on to *Only a Bird in a Gilded Cage* when there was an almighty bang, flash and the world turned crimson.

The first thing Rhian was conscious of was a silence so intense it seemed deafening. Then she was aware of pain. She felt as though she were swimming upwards towards the light. Her head hurt and her eyes were glued shut. She breathed in the acrid stench of burning rubber, wool and hair. She tried to move her hand to her eyes, to open them, but someone gripped her arm and held it fast. Her face was bathed with cool water and she was covered with something soft.

She felt that she should make an effort and force her eyelids open, but it was so much easier to slip back and allow someone else to look after her. Just for a little while . . .

Chapter 23

SALI AND LLOYD walked out of Swansea railway station, to see rows of people lining the pavements either side of High Street. Noticing a relatively clear spot lower down outside the Mackworth Hotel, Lloyd took Sali's arm and steered her towards it. All the shops were closed and their blinds were drawn, but the most noticeable thing was the silence; no one said a word, not even the children, and no traffic moved. It was almost as though they had stumbled into a cinema and were looking at a film that had frozen in the projector.

They stood and waited. Ten minutes later, an undertaker in full mourning dress and a black silk top hat, walked slowly out of the station yard ahead of a glass-sided hearse drawn by a pair of black-plumed black horses. The hearse was flanked by eight munitionettes, four to a side, dressed in full uniform and marching in slow step. A second undertaker followed them, walking in front of another hearse that was flanked by a similar complement of young women.

The coffins and the tops of the hearses were covered with wreaths and bouquets of bright spring flowers but it was still possible to make out the Union Jack flags that covered the caskets.

Lloyd slipped his arm protectively around Sali's shoulders as the first hearse drew alongside them. He had never felt prouder or sadder. Still bearing scars and burn marks, the first two munitionettes in the lines were Julia and Rhian.

'Mrs Williams warned us in her letter that neither of you would come back to Ynysangharad House with us.' Sali poured the tea they had ordered and passed cups down to Lloyd, Julia and Rhian.

'Not that her letter stopped Sali from hoping that you'd change your minds,' Lloyd said.

'We're both fine where we are,' Julia protested.

'I'll grant you that I look odd with my eyebrows, lashes and hair burned off, but it will soon grow back,' Rhian said philosophically.

'Your hair as well?' Sali asked in horror.

'Just the front bit that wasn't protected by this awful beret. Until it grows back I'll carry on pulling my hat down low.'

'You can't seriously want to go back to work in that factory after what happened to your friends?' Lloyd took a sandwich from the plate Sali offered around the table.

'The other girls have.' Rhian sipped her tea. 'Bronwen, who worked in Llan House with me and lives in the boarding house with us, was working right next to me but she was blown clear by the explosion. She had hardly a scratch on her but it was her sister, Virginia–Jinny, who was killed alongside our friend Meriel. Everyone expected Bronwen to pack her bags and go back to Tonypandy, but she was one of the first to go in the sheds and help with the clearing up the next day.'

'But it's so dangerous,' Sali protested.

'I think they know that, sweetheart,' Lloyd said flatly.

'It's bad enough to have to worry about my brothers and Lloyd's at the Front. But now you as well.' Sali bit her lip in an effort to hold back her tears.

Rhian gave a grim smile. 'It's far worse for the boys at the Front. We have accidents but these are the first deaths. However, as the vicar just said at the funeral, at times like this we all have to make sacrifices, women as well as men. And the soldiers need all the bullets, bombs and shells we can make if we're going to win this war.'

'Forgive my language, ladies,' Lloyd shook his head, 'but it's one hell of a price to pay for victory.'

'The doctor said I'll be fine to go back on Monday.' Rhian tried to sound more cheerful than she felt. The boarding house was empty without Meriel and Jinny and the bickering they engendered and she knew Bronwen and Julia were as devastated as her by their sudden and violent deaths. 'The worse of the burns on my face have already healed and there's only one left on my hand.'

'Julia, talk some sense into her,' Lloyd pleaded.

'Or do you intend going back to the factory as well, when your wounds have healed?' Sali studied the bandages on Julia's hands. They were so thick it was impossible to see the extent of the damage.

'Julia can't.' Rhian glanced from Sali to Julia. 'I'm sorry, you probably haven't told them yet.'

'No, I haven't.' Julia steeled herself. She had deliberately allowed Mrs Williams and Rhian to think that she had seen Geraint since his enlistment and he was the father of the child she was carrying, but there was no way that she could expect Sali and Lloyd to believe that, when they knew for certain that she hadn't seen him in over ten months.

'What news?' Sali asked.

Embarrassed, Julia glanced at Lloyd and looked away.

'If this is ladies' talk, I'll go and buy some cigarettes.' He left his seat.

Julia blushed, 'There's no need to go on my account, Lloyd.'

'I really do need cigarettes. I'll be back in ten minutes.'

'I'm having a baby,' Julia said when Lloyd walked away.

Sali looked at Julia's waistline. 'That is good news,' she began cautiously.

'Isn't it?' Rhian agreed enthusiastically.

'You must come to Ynysangharad House and stay with us so we can look after you. It will be wonderful for our children to have another cousin to play with. Does Geraint know?'

Julia looked Sali in the eye. 'I haven't had a chance to write to him yet with everything that's been happening in Pembrey. And it's early days. The baby isn't due until Christmas.'

Sali began to talk enthusiastically about layettes, nursery furniture and practical matters, but Julia saw that she understood why she hadn't written to Geraint. Simple arithmetic dictated that her baby had been conceived in March when she had been living with her and Lloyd in Ynysangharad House and Geraint had been miles away in France.

When Rhian went to talk to Bronwen, who came into the teashop with a crowd of munitionettes, Julia said, 'I will write to Geraint to tell him about the baby, Sali.'

'It might be as well before he hears the news from someone else,' Sali agreed.

'I'm sorry . . .'

'You have nothing to apologize to me for. I never could understand why someone as bright and intelligent as you married Geraint knowing that he didn't love you and was only after your money. Will you divorce him and marry the father?' Sali ventured, curiosity winning over tact.

'Geraint can divorce me if he likes, but there's no question of me marrying the baby's father,' Julia answered.

'He does know about the baby?'

'No, and there's no reason for him to.'

'You don't intend to tell him?' Sali asked in surprise.

'No. He has his own life and I don't want to complicate it. The baby won't be a problem; it will be a blessing. Marrying Geraint gave me my independence when I needed it. Now that I'm alone, I find it difficult to understand why I didn't have the courage to walk away from Llan House and set up my own household without marrying him, but hindsight is a wonderful thing. The one thing I don't regret is this . . . indiscretion.' She gave Sali a small self-conscious smile. 'It will give me someone to love and I need that desperately after losing my parents and brother. In fact, I'm happier looking forward to the birth than I have been for a long time.'

'But March . . . you spent that time with us, in Ynysangharad House,' Sali said uneasily.

Wary lest Sali guess the identity of her lover, Julia said, 'I wasn't there every day and I stayed in the White Hart in Tonypandy the week after my father died so I could be on hand to arrange his funeral.'

'I'm sorry, I didn't mean to pry. But I want you know that Lloyd, the children and I love you. You're a member of our family and welcome to stay with us any time. You will have the baby in Ynysangharad House?'

'Thank you for the offer, but I'd prefer to stay with Mrs Williams for the time being.'

'I doubt Geraint will come back to Pontypridd to stay with us ever again. And after you tell him about the baby I rather suspect that he won't want to see you again either.'

'We should never have married, but that's not why I won't stay with you in Ynysangharad House. I may not be a munitionette any more or be able to do any heavy work because of the baby, but I can help Mrs Williams and the girls around the boarding house in small ways. And after what's happened to Meriel and Jinny, I'd like to stay close to Bronwen and Rhian. I've become very fond of them.'

'I can understand that. And from the postcard Rhian sent us, Pembrey looks a lovely place.'

'It was prettier before the factory was built. But there are beauty spots close by and after living in Tonypandy for so many years it will be nice to spend the summer close to the sea. Could you do me one favour?'

'Gladly, if I can.'

'Give Mr Richards my address and ask him if he'd be kind enough to visit me. After what's happened to my family and now Jinny and Meriel, I've learned how tenuous life can be. I want to make a will and arrangements for my baby to be cared for should anything happen to me.'

'Childbirth isn't anywhere near as dangerous as it used to be,' Sali reassured.

'I'm not worried about the birth,' Julia said calmly.

'And you have already given up work?'

'Yes, but being pregnant has made me think more seriously about the future, and not just mine, the baby's. I want to make provision for its upbringing and appoint guardians for him or her, in the event that I am unable to care for it. Would you and Lloyd consider becoming godparents?'

'I'm sure I am speaking for Lloyd as well as myself when I say that it would be an honour,' Sali said sincerely. 'And we would take our responsibility towards the child very seriously.'

'I know you would, that is why I asked you. There is also someone else I want to ask.'

'Rhian?' Sali guessed.

'It has taken me this long to realize that since mother's death she has been my closest friend. The mistress and the maid situation came between us in Tonypandy. It's been so much easier here. You're lucky to have her for a friend.'

'I know.' Sali smiled when she saw Rhian and Lloyd walking back toward their table together. 'But then, she has also been very fortunate to have you as a friend.'

The summer was a long and hot one, and Rhian wasn't sure whether it was because she was becoming accustomed to working in the factory, or the work itself was getting easier, but the fact remained that she didn't find it the chore she had done when she had first started.

After Meriel and Jinny's deaths and funeral, a routine of sorts developed. She went into work with Bronwen every morning except on her week off, and returned to spend her evenings with Julia. They sat outside on a bench in the garden when the weather was warm enough, reading or playing cards with Mrs Williams, and after Julia bought a gramophone, listening to the records she ordered from Cardiff.

They all missed Jinny and Meriel, but as the casualty lists of those killed at the Front grew longer every day, and the newspaper print listing the names of the dead grew smaller, tragedy simply became an accepted part of life. Nobody could ignore or avoid the terrible deaths in their communities because there was scarcely a family in Wales that hadn't been touched by loss brought about by war.

They went to Pontypridd to stay with Sali a couple of times but when Julia's pregnancy became advanced enough to be noticeable, she preferred to stay in the comparative seclusion of the boarding house and Rhian remained with her.

Life wasn't as good as when she had been engaged to Joey, or even when she'd lived with Edward in Tonypandy, but it was tolerable, and she might have even been content, if Joey had replied to her letter. She knew that he was as well and safe as any soldier could be in France, because she asked after him in her letters to Sali and Megan and they passed snippets of news back.

When Sali told her that Joey had taken a commission as a second lieutenant, she broke her own rule about not writing to him until he had written to her, and sent him a congratulatory card. But she still heard nothing. And when summer faded and the cold autumn sea winds gusted up the estuary, blowing leaves from the trees and withering the last of the roses on the bushes Mrs Williams tended on the front lawn, she decided that he must have found another girl.

But even then it wasn't easy to put him out of her mind. There were too many memories for her to forget, and she didn't even want to try.

One dark November evening, Julia sat in the inglenook after supper, toasted her feet by the fire and re-read the letter she had received from Geraint that morning. It was only the second he'd sent to her since she had written to tell him that she was pregnant. And the first, sent in May just after he had received hers, had been so vitriolic she had burned it.

> *Dear Julia,*
>
> *I received your last letter and although I accept that our marriage was based on an unconventional agreement, I trust that you will understand that I cannot possibly remain married to you while you give birth to a bastard.*
>
> *Therefore if, as you say, it is impossible to arrange a divorce at such short notice I demand you contact a solicitor and at the very least arrange a formal separation. In the meantime I insist that you furnish him with full proof of your adultery, and urge him to arrange a divorce as speedily as possible. You can forward me the relevant papers to sign as soon as they become available.*
>
> *I trust that you will continue to pay the annuity of two thousand pounds into my account. I was not the one to break our bargain. Other than the papers that will need to be signed, this will be the last communication that you will receive from me.*
>
> *Geraint*

'A letter from your husband?' Rhian sat next to Julia on the bench seat. Like Mrs Williams, she had been concerned by how few letters Geraint had sent to Julia since she had become pregnant.

'Yes.' Julia thrust it into her pocket.

'Another month and you should have good news to tell him.' Rhian looked at Julia's swollen body. 'Mrs Williams said the doctor was pleased with you when he called today.'

'He was,' Julia glanced over at the table where Mrs Williams was playing cards with Bronwen and four new girls who had recently moved into the boarding house. She rubbed her aching back and rose stiffly and awkwardly from the bench seat. 'I know it's early, but I think I'll go to bed and read. Come in to say goodnight?'

'I will,' Rhian promised.

'Goodnight, everyone,' Julia called out, before lighting a candle and leaving the room.

She went into her comfortable bedroom on the first floor and moved, as restlessly as someone her size could, around the furniture. She opened the small wooden travelling desk she had bought and checked the letters she had written over the past few months and filed carefully away. Taking a clean sheet of paper, she folded them into it and wrote on the outside in her elegant sloping hand, *To be sent only in the event of my death.*

She felt silly and melodramatic afterwards. Sali's solicitor, Mr Richards, had assured her that all her affairs were in order. Her new will, drawn up by him, was simple, clear and couched in terms Geraint would be unable to challenge. She had left her entire estate, with the exception of a small, one-off bequest to Geraint of £5,000, to her child. And in the event of both her own and the child's death – she had found it unbearable to discuss the possibility of her baby's demise – she had arranged for her estate to go to Rhian.

The baby stirred within her, she smiled absently and patted her abdomen before sitting in the easy chair beside the fire, freshly stoked with small coal for the night.

'Come in,' she called at a knock at the door.

Rhian opened it.

'You going to bed this early?' Julia asked.

'It's almost nine o'clock and I was tired today. Probably just winter. I hate waking in the dark, and coming back here in the dark. You know how little daylight we see in the factory.' Rhian sat on the dressing-table stool. 'Are you really all right? You seem quiet tonight.'

'Battered and bruised by this one kicking me.' Julia patted her bump. 'But apart from that, just tired. I want it all to be over and to see him sleeping in there.' She nodded to the cot she had sent for from a catalogue. It stood in the corner, stocked high with nappies, sheets, linen and the layette Rhian and Mrs Williams had helped her sew and knit.

'Sali says the last few weeks before the birth are always the worst. But I am only repeating it, I have no idea if it is true,' Rhian said.

Julia lowered her voice. 'Geraint is divorcing me.'

'Why ever would he do that?' Rhian cried indignantly.

'Isn't it obvious?' Julia asked.

'Not to me.'

'He is not my baby's father.'

'Not . . . oh . . .' Rhian faltered, not knowing what to say or how to react. The thought that Julia had been unfaithful to her husband had never crossed her mind.

'Sali knows that her brother isn't the father, and as you've agreed to be the baby's godmother too, I thought you should know that your godchild will be, what's the expression?' She gave a wry smile. 'Born the wrong side of the blanket?'

'It's a horrible expression and what you've just told me makes no difference to the way I feel about you, or the way I'll feel about the baby,' Rhian said stoutly.

Julia wondered if Rhian would quite so certain of her feelings if she knew the identity of her baby's father. There had been several times during the past months when she had almost . . . but never quite found the courage to confide her secret.

Even if Rhian didn't feel anything for Joey now, the knowledge that he still loved her had stopped her from telling her about her short-lived affair. Because if Rhian and Joey did ever see one another again, she didn't want Rhian to tell him about the existence of a child he would undoubtedly feel responsible for, even though she wanted nothing from him.

'Will you marry the father after Geraint divorces you?' Rhian asked.

'No.'

'He doesn't want to marry you?'

'No, I don't want to marry him. He has given me what I wanted more than anything else in the world, a child. And I am wealthy enough not to have to worry about money. The only cloud on the horizon is Geraint. When he divorces me, and that is a "when" not an "if", I hope to persuade him not to announce to the world that my child is a bastard. It's certainly not the best way for someone to begin life.'

'No, it isn't.' Rhian hated herself for agreeing with Julia but she was a hopeless liar and she knew Julia would see right through her if she tried to be anything other than honest.

'Call in before you go to work in the morning?'

'At six o'clock?' Rhian asked in surprise.

'You always wake me going down the stairs anyway.'

'If you like. Sweet dreams.' Rhian kissed Julia goodnight, closed the door and left.

Julia had no idea why she felt so edgy, she only knew she did, and she wanted reassurance that Rhian was close by and would help her should she need it.

'Mrs Williams! Mrs Williams!' Rhian screamed down the stairs the next morning.

'Is the house on fire?' The housekeeper came puffing up the stairs, the wooden spatula she used to turn the bacon still in her hand.

'It's Julia.' Rhian ran to the bed where Julia lay, red-faced and cramped in pain.

Mrs Williams gripped Julia's hand. 'When did the pains start?'

'I think about half an hour ago.' Julia gasped between contractions.

'Why didn't you call me?' Mrs Williams demanded.

'Because the doctor warned me yesterday that I might go into false labour before the birth.'

'Even so, I think we should send for him. If it's false labour I doubt he'll mind coming out, and if it's the real thing, it will be as well to have him on hand.'

'But the baby isn't due for another month,' Rhian reminded.

'And probably won't put in an appearance until then, but it's better to be safe than sorry. Will you drop into his house on your way into work and ask him to call here, Rhian?'

'I will, Mrs Williams.' Rhian continued to look anxiously at Julia.

'Go downstairs. The sooner you wash, dress and eat breakfast, the sooner you'll be on your way.' Mrs Williams tried to sweep Rhian from the room, but she clung to Julia's hand.

'It's probably false labour.' Julia returned the pressure of Rhian's fingers. 'See you tonight?'

'I could stay here—'

'You'd be better employed making bullets for the boys to fire.'

'If you're sure,' Rhian said doubtfully.

'I'm sure, and if we're lucky, we'll have a new parcel of books to read tonight. I sent for them over a week ago. They should have arrived yesterday.'

'You'll be all right while I go downstairs and finish making the breakfasts?' Mrs Williams asked, after Rhian reluctantly left.

'Of course,' Julia retorted, feeling stronger because her pain had temporarily abated.

'I'll be back as soon as I've got the girls off to work.'

The pains started again before Mrs Williams reached the bottom of the stairs but Julia stifled her cries. Knowing how busy the housekeeper was in the mornings, she rose gingerly from her bed and inched her way towards the commode that she hadn't used since her morning sickness had stopped.

A horrendous pain tore through her and she stooped and gripped the arms of the chair. Gasping for breath, she looked down at her feet and saw that she was standing in a widening pool of bloody water.

'It may be early, Mrs Watkin Jones, but there's absolutely no reason why your baby shouldn't be perfect, just a tiny bit smaller than usual,' the doctor said briskly. He looked up when Mrs Williams bustled into the room.

Julia lifted her arms above her head and gripped the headboard as hard as she could while Mrs Williams set a pile of clean towels and a jug of hot water on the washstand. The housekeeper filled the basin and set a scrubbing brush and bar of soap beside it.

'Thank you, Mrs Williams.' The doctor began to scrub his hands. 'Now, we all know that babies, especially first babies, can take their time coming into the world, but something tells me this one isn't going to keep us waiting too long. So, what do you want, Mrs Watkin Jones, a boy or a girl?'

'I don't care,' Julia gasped, writhing on the bed when another pain took hold. She gritted her teeth to stop herself from crying out.

'There's only the doctor and me in the house, Miss Julia, so you scream as loud as you like.' Mrs Williams had to brush tears away from her eyes at the sight of the woman who had once been her young mistress in so much pain.

'I'll be all right,' Julia panted. She glanced at the clock on the bedside table. The second hand was moving around inexorably but slowly. It was ten o'clock and she had been awake at half past five. She felt weak, aching, battered and exhausted, and wasn't at all sure how much more pain she could take.

At three o'clock in the afternoon, Mrs Williams pulled the curtains against the twilight and lit the oil lamps. She had made the fire up twice during the course of the day and the room was hot. Julia was damp with perspiration and her face was red from the effort of pushing.

The doctor rolled up the sheet from the bottom of the bed and bent over her.

'Just one more push, Mrs Watkin Jones, and your baby will be here. I can see his head.'

Julia strained with all the strength she could muster. Seconds later she felt as though something was tearing away inside her. A moment later the doctor lifted a baby in his arms. He held it upside down, tapped it and the child screamed.

'An excellent pair of lungs, I think, Mrs Watkin Jones. Would you like to hold your son while I cut the cord?'

Mrs Williams bundled the baby into a towel before handing him to Julia. 'He's beautiful, Miss Julia. What are you going to call him?'

'Edward Gerald . . .' Julia smiled down at the miniature being in her arms. He was so small, so perfect. 'Larch,' she murmured. She touched one of the soft tiny black curls on his head. 'He looks just like his father.'

Mrs Williams took the baby and washed him while the doctor dealt with the afterbirth. Julia lay back on the pillows and watched her.

'I have never felt so happy.'

'Or so tired, I'll warrant.' Mrs Williams concealed her emotions beneath a veneer of briskness. 'As soon as the baby's tucked up beside you, I'll make us a nice cup of tea. With a drop of brandy in it?' She looked questioningly at the doctor.

'I wouldn't say no, Mrs Williams. I think we've all done a fine day's work here.'

He went downstairs to smoke his pipe. Mrs Williams changed Julia's bed. Helped to wash and change her and dress the baby in his first nappy and nightshirt. When Julia and the baby were clean and comfortable, the housekeeper took advantage of the doctor's return to carry the soiled linen and slop bucket downstairs.

She had only just put the kettle on when the doctor shouted. She ran back upstairs, the doctor had turned back the sheets on the bed and she stared in horror at the blood pooled on the draw sheet she had put over the bottom sheet to protect the mattress.

'Oh my God! Please God, no!' She couldn't have said with any certainty if she was praying or blaspheming. 'Not Miss Julia! Not after her brother and father! Miss Julia, you have the baby to think of! Miss Julia!'

Julia's grey face turned to her. 'The desk.' She lifted her hand, intending to point at her travelling desk, but it fell weakly back on to the bed. 'The desk . . . letters . . .'

'Please.' Mrs Williams grabbed the doctor. 'Do something!' she screamed. 'You have to do something!'

He stepped back, shaking his head. Mrs Williams lifted the baby from beside Julia and stood helplessly, watching while the last vestiges of life ebbed from his mother's eyes.

Mrs Williams was standing, oblivious to the cold, in the open kitchen doorway when Rhian, Bronwen and the other girls walked into the yard at the end of their day in the factory. Rhian took one look at the housekeeper's face and she knew. But she still refused to accept it.

'Julia.' Breaking the cardinal rule, which was to wash before going into the house, she pushed past the housekeeper and went into the kitchen.

'Is already in her coffin. The doctor did what he could for her, but it was hopeless. She haemorrhaged after the birth. There was nothing he could do to stop it.'

'Julia?' Rhian called out hysterically, not wanting to believe it.

A baby's thin wail answered her cry.

Mrs Williams reached out to her. 'It's a boy, a fine boy. She saw him and named him before he died. Edward Gerald . . . Larch. She said he looks just like his father.'

Rhian tore her beret from her head, ran to the inglenook and looked into the cradle. The baby's eyes were open and she saw something of Julia's expression in them.

'He's beautiful, isn't he?' Mrs Williams stood beside her. 'And as you agreed to be his godmother, you owe it to Miss Julia to look after him for her now.'

Chapter 24

'PACKAGE AND LETTERS for you, Lieutenant Evans.'

Joey took his post from the sergeant on mail duty, removed his cap and sank down on the low wall that fenced in the yard. He had been in the front line for two weeks, and he was in dire need of a bath, meal, drink and bed, in that order, but the rooms the billeting officer had requisitioned for officers were still being cleaned after the last occupants and he had opted to wait outside in the cold rather than inside the gloomy farmhouse that stank of sour milk and overripe camembert.

His letters were from his brothers. He read the back of the package and recognized the address as the boarding house Rhian was staying at, but there was no name and the writing was new to him. When he opened the package he found a large tin, a sealed envelope and two sheets of paper. He opened the tin and his mouth watered at the sight of a rich fruitcake. He picked up the first letter.

> Dear Joey,
>
> I don't know if you remember me, Lizzie Williams, I used to be the housekeeper at Llan House. Miss Julia died giving birth to a son yesterday afternoon. The last thing she did was point to her desk and I guessed that she wanted me to send the letters in it. After seeing one addressed to you and talking to my sister, Mari, who told me that Miss Julia's husband was divorcing her, I can guess why.
>
> I can only say what I've said to you so often, handsome is as handsome does, and in this case I hope you will prove more handsome in your dealings with the boy than you were with Rhian and Miss Julia.

The baby is beautiful and unfortunately for Miss Julia's poor husband, the image of you. Rhian is his godmother and she is going to take care of him. Miss Julia asked her and she agreed, I think she will make a good mother. Time will tell whether or not you make a good father.

Lizzie Williams.

The cake isn't for you but the other brave boys over there. I trust you will see that they get it.

Joey looked at the envelope. He didn't recognize the writing on that either, and the thought occurred to him that he and Julia had produced a son together and he didn't even recognize her hand. A second letter fell out, and he set it aside.

Dear Joey,

I'm sorry, it would have been wonderful if we could have cherished the memory of our night together and forgotten it until old age, when we could have used it to warm our memories, but it is not to be. If you are reading this then our baby has survived and I have not.

Please, do not mourn for me; it would be ridiculous because we didn't really know one another. I have left my estate to my baby, and an annuity and the use of my houses to Rhian so she can bring up the child.

I do not know if you would like to see your son or own him. When I wrote and told Geraint that I was having a child, he replied that he didn't want to see me again. I have left him a cash settlement in my will. I hope neither the child nor Rhian hears from him again. He was divorcing me, although that hardly matters now.

No one knows the child is yours, although I think that Mrs Williams may suspect, if she sends this letter on. But knowing Mrs Williams as well as I do, I am certain that she will keep our secret.

I enclose the letter you left on my pillow. It is the only evidence that we spent the night together. I could have destroyed it but I thought you might wonder whether I had or not. This way you can do with it what you will.

Thank you again for a beautiful memory.

Yours gratefully,

Julia

Joey picked up the letter that had fallen out on the grass and re-read it.

Dear Julia,

I can't explain what happened between us last night. It would be easy for me to blame the brandy, the beauty of the snow filled night, the moonlight, or the thought of going back to the front and possible obliteration, but none of those things are responsible. Despite the brandy, I wasn't so drunk that I didn't know what I was doing . . .

He opened his pocketbook and a card and a letter fell out: the card he had received from Julia after that night.

The letter was from Rhian telling him that Julia was pregnant; he had never found the courage to answer it. He picked up all the letters and carefully folded them into one envelope. Taking a sheet of paper from the notebook in his breast pocket, he wrote:

Dear Rhian,

Perhaps these will explain why I never answered your letter. All my love now and always,

Joey

He tied the envelope with a piece of string he found in his pocket, then went in search of a postage stamp – and his colonel.

'I feel dreadful leaving you here all alone with Edyth and Eddie while we go off to enjoy ourselves,' Sali apologized to Rhian after Mari had chased Bella into the hall where Harry was already impatiently holding her coat.

'Pantomimes are for older children.'

'Like me.' Lloyd stood holding the front door open.

'Daddy, you came home!'

'I promised I would, tiger.' Lloyd ruffled Harry's hair and caught Bella by the waist when she hurtled towards him.

'You are not to do a thing,' Sali cautioned Rhian. 'You have been up every night with that baby for the past two weeks and now he's finally sleeping, you should get some rest yourself.'

'Nothing?' Rhian asked innocently.

'Nothing,' Sali reiterated sternly.

'Not even put a few presents under the tree?' Rhian glanced slyly at Harry who had managed to excite Bella to the same pitch of Christmas anticipation as himself.

'Not a thing. Mari,' Sali turned to the housekeeper, 'after you have put Edyth down for her afternoon nap, you and Rhian are to sit in the drawing room and open a bottle of sherry.'

'And sing drunken ditties to the babies?' Mari questioned in amusement.

'If you like.'

'I've already promised the two new maids that I'll show them how to make Christmas biscuits.'

'Yummy,' shouted Harry who loved Mari's Christmas biscuits.

'We have all the food we need and more,' Lloyd commented.

'But the maids' families might like some biscuits,' Sali guessed. Unable to compete with the wages being paid in the munitions factories, they had lost Robert and three maids in the last two months. Mari was running the house with only their elderly cook, even more elderly butler and two thirteen-year-old girls. And although she and Rhian did what they could to help, and they had shut off half the rooms in the house, Lloyd was already talking about asking the trustees to sell the house or rent it out, so they could look for a smaller, more easily-run place.

'Enjoy yourselves.' Rhian ushered Bella to the door.

'You really will take it easy?' Sali asked.

'I found a copy of *Our Mutual Friend* in the library. It's the only one of Dickens's books that I haven't read and I will have a great time until Eddie's next feed is due.'

Lloyd helped Sali on with her new loose coat that did little to conceal her burgeoning figure. The new baby was expected in the spring and she and Lloyd had resumed their usual argument as to whether it would be a boy or a girl, but like everyone in the house, Rhian thought that Sali had resigned herself to having another girl.

She gave Harry a last wave, closed the door and returned to the drawing room where the baby was sleeping in his day cot.

She looked down on him, tucked the blanket over his tiny shoulders and dropped a kiss on the woollen bonnet Julia had knitted. She loved Eddie and not only for his mother and grandfather's sake. She remembered Edward's request that she call him Eddie and she used the name more than Edward because it was more suited to such a small bundle of humanity.

A few times she had even caught herself speaking about him as if he really were her son and she had felt guilty, and disloyal, although Lloyd and Sali kept telling her that the best tribute she could pay to Julia was to take care of her child as if he were her own.

She pulled the easy chair close enough to the cot for her to be able to look into it without moving, curled up and opened her book. She hadn't read more than a couple of pages when the doorbell rang. She went out into the hall, but Mr Jenkins had opened it. Joey was on the doorstep, in a pristine uniform.

He took off his cap. 'Hello, Mr Jenkins.' He looked past the butler to where Rhian was standing.

'Joey.' Mari came down the stairs. 'I'm glad to see you're cleaner than when you turned up here on your last leave. Do you have any little friends under that spotless tunic?'

'I managed to abandon them in France this time.'

'Good. I suppose you're hungry?' she enquired.

He heard the frost in her voice and knew that Julia had been wrong. Mari's sister hadn't entirely kept all her suspicions to herself. 'I can wait until mealtime.'

'I've just cleared lunch but I dare say I can find some bacon and bread if you fancy a sandwich.'

'That would be much appreciated, Mari, thank you.' He took off his greatcoat and cap and handed them to Mr Jenkins.

'I'll get the maid to bring it to you in the drawing room. Would you like tea, Rhian?'

'No, thank you, Mari.' Rhian stood back and allowed Joey to walk into the room ahead of her. 'Sali and Lloyd have just taken the children to the pantomime.'

'I saw them. Lloyd stopped the car at the gates. Sali wanted to come back but I told them I was tired.'

Rhian stood next to the cot. 'Would you like to see your son?'

'You got the letters I sent you?'

'Yes.'

Unable to meet her steady gaze, he looked down at the child. 'Can I pick him up?'

'You don't know much about babies.'

'Not at this age. Harry was two when Sali moved in with us, and I've only made fleeting visits to Bella, Jack, Tom and Edyth since.'

'The first thing you should know is that you never, never wake a sleeping baby, because you have no idea when you'll get your next five minutes peace.'

'He's beautiful.'

'He has your colouring, black curly hair, dark eyes and unfortunately a very strong pair of lungs. When he screams, he screams.'

He continued to look down at the baby. 'I rehearsed so many speeches on the journey here. Thought out what I was going to say to you a hundred times, but now I'm actually here I can't remember one of them.' He passed his hand in front of his eyes. 'I'm sorry, excuse me. If I'm going to eat, I have to wash my hands.'

Rhian sat in the chair, gazed into the cot and thought back to last Christmas when Edward had been alive, and they had spent the day together.

So much had happened in two short years: she had lost her first real home, her fiancé, her lover, her friends Jinny and Meriel – and Julia.

If she had learned anything, it was that life was transient and uncertain, and the slightest chance of love had to be seized and cherished because it was the most precious treasure anyone could give or be given.

Joey returned with a tray of sandwiches and tea that he set on the sofa table.

'It's Christmas – we could have sherry,' she suggested.

'Or brandy.' He went to the drinks tray and poured two brandies.

'How long are you home for?'

'Two weeks.'

She smiled. 'That's wonderful. Your father and brothers and the children will be so pleased.'

'And you?'

'And me,' she echoed, holding his steady gaze.

'It's embarkation leave.'

'But you're already at the Front.'

'There are other fronts besides France.'

'Do you know where you're going?' she asked apprehensively.

'Yes,' he said shortly.

'But you can't say.'

'I am not supposed to tell anyone, but bearing in mind that you could have me shot if you divulge my future whereabouts, I trust you to keep them secret. I'll be sailing for India.'

She smiled in relief. 'Then you'll be out of the war.'

'Not quite.' He didn't have the heart to tell her that he had 'bought' his leave by taking a commission in a regiment detailed to relieve the siege at Kut al Amara in Iraq. A conflict that was proving to be more bloody and costly in terms of lives than even the Western Front. But he had wanted to see her so much; it had seemed a small price to pay when it had been offered to him. 'Rhian, about the baby . . .'

'Edward Gerald Larch. Julia named him after her father and brother. You might think his name is a permanent reminder of my indiscretion, just as the fact of his being here is a reminder of yours.'

'What can I say, except sorry?'

'When you made love to Julia, I was sleeping in Edward's bed.'

'I meant what I said in that letter I wrote to you. My feelings towards you have never changed.'

'Mine towards you have, but then I have done a lot of growing up this last year. There is one bit in that letter you wrote to Julia that I have to know if you meant.'

'*Perhaps a desire to live every moment of life to the full would be closest to the truth of last night,*' he quoted from memory.

'No. "I love Rhian. And even though she no longer wants me I will never love anyone the way I love her." '

'You know that is true.'

'Yes.' She looked him in the eye. 'I do now. And I have discovered that the people we love have to be taken the way they are. The mistakes that were made were more mine than yours. I tried to take refuge from my feelings for you and my fear of being hurt by you, by running to Edward.'

'I'd ask you to marry me, but I'm going halfway round the world and I have no idea when or even if I'll come back. I——'

She placed her finger over his lips. 'Let's just take this next hour and day and week and fortnight.'

'And afterwards?'

She kissed him. 'For us, this is the afterwards, Joey. The present and the future rolled into one because I refuse to think any further. And we'll make it last for ever and ever.'